SACRIFICE

THE HEBRAICA TRILOGY
BOOK ONE

CHRISTINE JORDAN

First published in 2023 by Bloodhound Books.

Print ISBN: 978-1-5040-8290-7

ALSO BY CHRISTINE JORDAN

WRITING AS CJ CLAXTON

MisPer

I dedicate this book to Richard Curtis, my former New York literary agent, who believed in me, my writing, and this book.

"It is not against flesh and blood, but against principalities, against powers, against the rulers of the darkness of this world, against spiritual wickedness in high places."

Ephesians 6:12

GLOUCESTER

Harold's long, thin shadow, cast by a low pale sun, stretched out before him on the river path. A fear so primal pinned him to the spot as he watched three men on horseback bear down on him at speed. The sound of their hooves slamming into the hard ground seemed to echo the thud of Harold's heart.

After the special mass this morning for the start of Lent, the monks of Llanthony Secunda Priory had retired to their cells to begin fasting and to contemplate their transgressions. As Harold's worst transgression was to steal the odd apple or crust of bread from the kitchen, he saw no reason to do penance. In all of Harold's nine years, he had never ventured beyond the stone perimeter walls of the priory alone. Prior Clement kept him close by his side, a protective and watchful eye on his every move, but Prior Clement was not well and had retired with the other monks, leaving Harold to his own devices. So Harold had decided that today was his best chance to explore the outside world. The monks often talked about a place called the Cockayne, a fish weir close by on the River Severn, so he had set

1

off in that direction thinking it might be a good place to start his adventure.

Harold walked through the monk's orchard, the bare branches of the apple trees spreading out like scuttling spider's legs above him. The ground was carpeted with the pale-yellow flowers of wild primroses and the occasional flash of vibrant purple croci. As he weaved in and out of the spidery branches, his feet sank into the spongy, feathered moss beneath his flimsy leather sandals and the crack of fallen twigs could be heard in the stillness.

Beyond the orchard, a thickly wooded forest led down to the riverbank. Once there, he made his way along a worn path until it opened out onto a clearing. It was then he heard the hooves of galloping horses thudding into the cold, frosted earth. The noise grew louder, echoing in and out of the tree trunks. He turned and saw three men riding hard towards him. They were almost upon him when the lead horseman gave a harsh tug on the reins, his horse reared up and stopped short of where Harold stood.

'You, boy,' he growled.

Harold did not like the sound of his voice. It was deep and full of menace. He wondered what he could possibly have done to make this man angry. Perhaps he had wandered onto his land. Harold's stomach knotted, telling him something was wrong. He looked into the steely black eyes of the horseman and began to regret leaving the priory without the permission of Prior Clement.

'Y-yes, s-sire,' Harold stuttered, his heart thudding in his chest.

'Your name, boy?'

'Harold, sire.'

'Harold what?'

'Just Harold, sire.'

'What do you mean "just Harold"? Surely your parents gave you a name?'

The horsemen dismounted and came at him. Harold found himself surrounded. He took a step backwards but the man behind gave him a shove, making him stumble.

'I asked you a question, boy.'

'I never knew my parents,' Harold answered, looking around in bewilderment. 'I was taken in by the monks at the priory as a baby. They just call me Harold.'

The men grinned at him, one of them lolling his tongue, like a wolf apprising his prey. Something in their expression unsettled Harold. His palms grew clammy, and a nervous tic thrummed in his right eye. Their manner told him all was not well, but he was at a loss to know why.

'Do the monks know where you are?'

Harold didn't answer. Something told him he should not let them know he had wandered off alone. He wished with all his childish heart he was back in the inviolate sanctuary of Llanthony Secunda Priory. One of the men grabbed hold of him by the hood of his cloak and shook him so violently, his feet left the ground.

'He asked you a question, boy.'

Harold tried to break the horseman's grip, but he was no match for the man's strong and powerful hands.

'I think he'll do for our purposes, don't you?' the leader announced to the others.

They laughed, a hungry laugh.

'He's perfect,' one of them replied.

With that, the lead horseman withdrew a wooden cudgel from his saddle and with good aim landed a forceful blow to the side of Harold's head.

Harold heard his skull crack before he lost consciousness and fell to the ground.

CHAPTER

ONE

Z ev sat opposite the most bewitching woman he had
ever known. Her name was Arlette, and she was the
niece of Moses le Riche, the wealthiest Jew in
Gloucester. She had arrived from the French city of Rouen a few
months ago after her parents had been murdered by an anti-
Jewish mob. Being an only child with no other close relatives in
France her uncle Moses had taken her in. They had become
friends, but Zev wanted them to be more than that.

He stared at her across the synagogue, watching every
movement of her face. Her eyes were the colour of lapis lazuli,
her fair hair, covered by a translucent veil, fell in tight curls
around her face. She looked regal, haughty, like an ancient
princess. Her features were perfectly symmetrical. Small nose,
full lips, huge eyes. She was perfect. As she listened to the
reading of the ancient scroll from the Book of Esther, which told
the story of Haman, the persecutor and enemy of the Jews, her
expression changed. Whenever Haman's traitorous name was
mentioned, she would boo, hiss, and stomp her feet along with
everyone else to drown out the sound of his name. In her
delicate hand, she held a *ra'ashan*, a wooden rattle, which she

shook with vigour each time his name was spoken. Her face, previously unreadable, became animated. She became playful, joyful, vivid, arresting. Zev could not take his eyes off her.

The inner walls of the synagogue were painted with images of horses and birds, and in the middle stood the *bimah*, a raised wooden platform that faced east. This was where Rabbi Solomon stood, wearing a crisp white tunic. His prayer shawl looked new with its silk tassels, all hanging in a straight line, not twisted with wear. Rabbi Solomon was a wise old man with a long grey beard and a soft, intelligent voice. Every year he read from the scroll with such gusto no one would guess he had read those same passages countless times.

The sacred scrolls of the synagogue were housed in the ark. The ark doors were covered by a curtain decorated by Azriel's wife, Slema. She had chosen a motif showing the twelve tribes of Israel set against crowns, representing the crown of the Torah and biblical passages in Hebrew. The doors were carved by Zev's father, Rubin. He had used a stylised representation of the Ten Commandments.

Zev half listened as the rabbi told the ancient story of how Queen Esther, the wife of the Persian King, and Mordecai the Jew saved the Jewish people from annihilation. Zev wished Rabbi Solomon would get on with the story for today he would be allowed to drink alcohol and get merry. His father who was the *shochet*, the community's kosher butcher, had told him it was written that a person is obligated to become inebriated on Purim until he doesn't know the difference between 'cursed is Haman and blessed is Mordecai'.

Every year, Zev asked his father if he was old enough and every year his father said 'no' but this year he had said 'yes'. The thought of his first drink was making him agitated. He wanted the reading to be over and the drinking to commence. The Seudat Purim, the celebratory meal of the festival would begin soon in the open courtyard behind the synagogue. There would be *hamantashen*, sweet triangular pastries baked in the communal oven, filled with poppy seeds or honey or maybe even, his favourite, quince paste. They represented Haman's ears and recall how his ears were his downfall when he listened to those who said he should use his position to bring about the destruction of the Jews.

The usual solemnity of synagogue services had been abandoned in honour of today's feast, rattles clacked, and children stomped their feet. It was chaotic and fun, yet Zev was pleased when he realised Rabbi Solomon was nearing the end.

'And the Jews undertook to do as they had begun, and as Mordecai had written unto them; Because Haman...'

At the sound of Haman's name, the noise of the rattles and the shouting almost drowned out the rest of the rabbi's words. At last, the reading was over. Everyone began filing out of the synagogue and into the courtyard. Zev stood with his best friend Baruch. Baruch was the son of Rabbi Solomon. They had been friends since attending the Jewish school. Their bond was sealed when they were caught carving graffiti into the thick stone wall of the underground school behind one of the pilasters. Even though Baruch had been carving a sacred text from the Book of Kings, 'Let this house be sublime', his father had admonished him. Zev, realising the seriousness of this for Baruch because he was the rabbi's son, confessed to the desecration and took the punishment for his friend.

In the courtyard, an effigy of Haman leant against the wall. It had been made by the younger children and would be burned later that evening. The smell of baked sweet pastries, mixed with spicy lentil stews wafted toward Zev, reminding him he had not eaten since the day before yesterday, having observed the traditional Fast of Esther. His stomach made a loud, involuntary rumbling sound. Baruch gave him a mock look of disapproval. Zev placed his hand on his stomach as if to silence it. Baruch's expression suddenly changed from disapproval to one of wistfulness. Zev followed the direction of his gaze. His friend was staring at Arlette who was walking across the courtyard. At the sight of her, Zev's stomach flipped followed by an uneasy feeling at the thought his friend might also have designs on Arlette. She was wearing a full-length tunic of pale blue silk with wide trumpet-like sleeves, which allowed a glimpse of her slim and tiny wrists. On her dainty feet, she wore pointed silk shoes. Zev was still staring at her when he felt a sharp dig in the side from his mother, Damete.

'You're gawping again, boy,' she said.

'Sorry, *Ima*,' Zev replied, turning his head away from the vision of Arlette.

'Why you bother with that girl I don't know when you have a perfectly good match in Chera.'

His mother was referring to Chera, the daughter of Azriel. Zev liked her. She was a pleasant girl but a little plain. Zev's mother had always assumed they would marry. Zev had other ideas.

'Your idea of a good match, *Ima*, is not mine.'

'Your mother knows best. No good will come of your infatuation.'

'Don't say that. You don't know that. What have you got against Arlette?'

His mother huffed loudly, and crossing her arms said, 'Go and get some food and mind you don't drink too much. Your father knows nothing, don't listen to him.'

Zev left the group and found his father by the wooden cask of wine, supplied by Moses as a Purim gift. It was fine kosher wine from France.

'Zev, my son. You want some of this?'

Zev watched as his father poured the red liquid from the

barrel tap into a pewter cup. His father's hands were shaking. Zev studied his face as he handed him the cup. His cheeks were covered in thin red veins like threadworms. He looked a lot older than his years, much older than his mother. The tip of his finger on his left hand was missing, a butchery accident. His mother told him his father was drunk at the time.

'There you are.' Rubin handed him the cup and raised his own. '*Chag Purim sameach*,' he said to his son, wishing him a joyous Purim.

Zev put the cup to his lips, tipped his head back and took a long glug of the wine.

'Whoa, you are not meant to drink it like milk.'

Zev's dark eyes widened, and he tried not to cough. He cleared his throat and brushed his dark, unruly hair from his forehead. '*Chag Purim sameach, Aba*,' he said, his voice deep and throaty from the wine.

'What do you think of your first drink then?'

'I'm not sure. It tastes bitter.'

'You'll get used to that.'

Zev took another gulp. The wine gave him a warm sensation inside, and his head felt a little clouded. He scoured the courtyard for Arlette and spotted her standing by her Aunt Douce.

'You should forget that girl. It won't work,' his father said.

Emboldened by the wine he asked his father why.

'Because that aunt of hers won't let you marry her.'

'Why do you say that? Douce is always nice to me.'

'What's not to like?' his father replied. 'But if she knew you had designs on her niece, that might change.'

'But why would you say that?'

'Look, I'm only the butcher in this community. Do you think she'd want her niece to marry a butcher's boy?'

'I don't see what's wrong with a butcher's boy,' Zev answered, walking away from his father.

In truth, he knew what his father meant. He wasn't good enough for Arlette. This had crossed his mind, but he thought there might be a way he could win her heart and then it wouldn't matter that he was only the butcher's boy. The wine was having quite an effect on his mood. He had eaten very little and was now ravenous. The food was laid out on a trestle table, with mountains of sweet pastries and bowls of lentil salad with rice. It was time he ate something. He helped himself to a bowl of salad and then a few cheese filled Haman's ears. He was stuffing a poppy filled pastry in his mouth when he heard a familiar voice.

'Hello, Zev. Are you enjoying yourself?'

He turned, his mouth full of pastry. 'Mmnn,' he nodded, unable to speak.

'Oh, you make me laugh,' Arlette said.

Zev swallowed his food with a choking gulp and wiped the crumbs from his lips. 'Do I?'

'Always. You're always making me laugh. You know you do.'

'Is that a good thing?'

'*Mais certainement!*' she said, a smile in her voice. 'I'll see you later. I must go and help my Aunt Douce. She has her hands full with the new baby.'

Not only was she gorgeous to look at, Zev thought, but she was a delight to listen to. Her French accent made her sound mysterious and exotic. He watched as she walked away, her back held straight, her long hair cascading over her angular shoulders. Zev returned to his friends.

'Do you really think you have a chance with Arlette?' Seth asked.

'Why wouldn't I?'

'I don't know. She doesn't seem too interested in you.'

'What makes you say that?'

'Don't you know Seth is an expert on women,' said Baruch, laughing and giving Seth a friendly push.

'I spend more time around women. I have a sister, don't forget. And here she is.'

Chera joined them. She wore a plain cream tunic underneath a long mantle of forest green wool tied at the shoulder. Her mousy hair was scraped back off her face exposing her high forehead, her hair hidden under a matching green cap, drawing the colour from her face.

'Hello, how is everyone?'

Although she addressed her question to all of them, she focused her beaming smile on Zev.

Zev answered, 'I'm fine, Chera. I don't know about these two.' He gave Seth and Baruch a friendly push.

'I see your father has finally let you drink this Purim,' she said, nodding at the cup of wine in his hand. 'What's it like?'

'Tastes a little bitter, but I'm enjoying the feeling it's giving me.'

'What feeling?'

'It's like floating on a cloud,' Zev said.

'Be careful you don't drink too much. You might fall off that cloud.'

Zev laughed along with the others.

'I have to go now. I'll see you later.'

Again, Chera addressed her farewell to Zev. When she was out of earshot Seth spoke.

'My sister's sweet on you, Zev.'

'Why do you say that?'

'It's the way she looks at you. We might as well not have been here.'

Azriel the *hazzan* or prayer leader, chosen because of his fine voice, started to sing. He was accompanied by Samuel the Elder playing his old kinnor, an ancient musical instrument, much like a harp that he had brought with him from Rouen. The strings had been replaced hundreds of times using the small intestines of dead sheep, courtesy of Rubin. Bellassez the widow joined in, her high soprano voice contrasting with that of Azriel's. Zev felt a profound sense of joy, of belonging to a loving, joyous community; a community brought together by faith, tradition, and ritual. He was on his third cup of wine and was beginning to feel quite merry. He wished he could sing. Perhaps then he could romance Arlette by singing to her. It wouldn't work though. When he sang, he sounded like one of his father's animals being slaughtered. That would surely put her off him for life.

His bravado fuelled by his swift intake of wine was intensifying. Perhaps tonight was the moment to declare his love. If he wasn't careful, she would be snapped up by another suitor. Maybe by Baruch. He took another glug of wine. Arlette came back into view. She was standing by the food table clearing away the leftovers. She was alone.

'Arlette,' he said, speaking louder than he had intended.

She jumped and turned to face him. 'Oh, Zev, it's you. You startled me for a moment. Are you all right?'

Zev was aware that he was swaying, something he hadn't experienced before. It was a pleasant feeling. 'I feel great,' he said.

'You look a little odd,' she replied, staring quizzically at him.

'N-no. I f-feel really good.'

They stood for a moment, an awkward silence between them. Why did she turn him into a stammering idiot? A tongue-tied fool? He wasn't like that with other women. With Chera, for example.

Finally he spoke. 'I was watching you in the synagogue...'

'Were you?'

'You seemed to enjoy shaking that rattle.'

'I did.'

Arlette was being short with him, and he wondered why. 'Am I annoying you, Arlette?'

'No. Why do you say such a thing? I'm busy that's all.'

Zev put down his cup of wine. 'Let me help you carry those,' he said, stumbling a little as he moved toward her.

'Are you sure you can manage?' she asked, giving him a curious look.

'Of course, I can manage. Why wouldn't I?'

'I don't know. You look a little unsteady.'

'Nonsense. Here, give me those.' Zev stretched out his hands to take the platters from Arlette. He grazed against her warm flesh. The sensation made him quiver. He had to tell her how he felt. 'Arlette, do you know how I feel about you?'

They were standing inches apart, both holding on to the platters, staring at each other. Whether she saw the hunger in his eyes or something else Zev wasn't sure, but she turned away, pulling on the platters to release them from his grip. But Zev was not letting go. Finally, those three little words he'd practised saying to Arlette in his mind but never dared to say to her face found their own voice. 'I love you.'

Arlette flashed him a look of horror. It was not what Zev had imagined would happen when he played out this scene in his fanciful imagination. He waited for her to say it back. She didn't. Could it be she didn't share his feelings?

'I don't know what to say, Zev. I really like you. I really do.'

'That's a start,' Zev said, half grinning.

'You're funny, you make me laugh. But...'

'But?'

'I thought we were good friends.'

'We are.'

'Yes, but I think you want more than that. I just don't feel that way about you. You are more like an *ax* to me.'

'A brother? Is that the only way you think of me?'

'I love you like a brother, Zev.'

'Perhaps you could learn to love me like a husband... in time? I have some money put aside from my uncle. I've been saving it for when I marry. We could...'

'Please, Zev. People are looking at us.'

Zev could not care less that people might be looking at them. His whole future would be determined by this moment. 'Is it because I'm only a butcher's boy? I might not know a lot, but I have other qualities. I could...'

'Please, Zev, don't do this. It's nothing to do with that.'

'Then what is it?'

'My uncle has other plans for me.'

'What other plans?' Zev let go of the platters. The courage he was feeling left him. Deflated and feeling a little unwell but still determined, he continued, 'Perhaps I chose the wrong time to ask. Think about it. Sleep on it. *Sheol!* You might feel different in the morning.'

He was babbling like a fool and cussing, using words he would normally say in front of his male friends.

'My uncle wants me to marry Deudonne, Aaron of Lincoln's son. I'm to meet him on Saturday.'

Arlette stood clutching the platters tightly to her. Her look was one of pity, not passion. Her words were like stones pitched at his heart. He couldn't speak. His dreams shattered, the life he saw himself sharing with Arlette crushed to dust and fluttering to nothing in the gentle breeze. Zev would not give up.

'But you haven't met him yet. What if you don't like him? What if he has the face of a pig?'

Arlette laughed. 'I'm hoping he doesn't have a face like a

pig. But even if he does, I don't have much of a choice. Moses has been good to me, but I can't expect him to keep me for the rest of my life.'

'Then marry me?'

Arlette squirmed in her silken shoes and let out a frustrated sigh. 'It has been decided. I cannot go against my uncle's wishes. This would be a good match for the family.'

'And for you?'

Arlette said nothing. Zev stared at her, hoping she would give him a sign, something to hold on to. Some hope.

'I really must go now,' Arlette said.

Zev could do nothing but stare at her as she walked away from him. He had tried his best, more than his best. He had practically begged her.

The celebrations lasted long into the night as did Zev's drinking. His thoughts plunged into a dark and sorrowful place. He told no one of his conversation with Arlette, preferring to behave like nothing had happened. But inside his heart was breaking into tiny pieces, spurned by the woman he loved most in all the world. There seemed no point to his life now. He might as well get inebriated, as his father had counselled he should, on Purim.

CHAPTER

TWO

B rito lounged on a wooden bench by the window of the Lich Inn, a tankard of weak ale in his lap. He stared out idly at the ragtag of people walking past on their way to the abbey. The rain had been falling steadily all morning and the path leading to the abbey was muddy and rutted. There was an endless procession of miserable, ugly faces with bedraggled hair, mud-spattered clothing and mud-soaked boots. It was a depressing sight. Brito missed France and wished he was back in the company of his drinking comrades, heading toward another skirmish, lying in the arms of a lithesome French wench. Instead, he was here in this dreary little city on the orders of the king.

The landlord of the inn was busy setting up fresh barrels of beer. He was a rotund man who clearly liked a drink from the enormous proboscis jutting out in the middle of his face where his nose ought to be. It resembled a flowered cabbage, marbled with purple veins. A comely, young serving wench with shapely ankles was sweeping the floor and laying fresh rushes. She was humming a jolly tune as she swept past Brito. It annoyed him. Brito growled at the wench.

'Do you have to be so jolly this early in the morning?'

She stopped sweeping and looked up at him with a fetching smile. Her smile froze at the sight of his stony countenance, and she hurried away from him as if she were being followed by a swarm of bees.

The landlord approached. 'Can I get you anything else, sir?'

'Another one of these and some breakfast.'

Brito thrust his empty tankard at the landlord.

'Certainly, sir.'

The landlord disappeared into a room at the back of the building. As he walked away, he whistled the same irritating ditty.

'Confound them both,' Brito muttered through clenched teeth.

He turned back to watch the passers-by. His eyes were bloodshot from lack of sleep, having spent the weekend drinking heavily and only venturing out at night to go whoring at the local brothel. His puffy upper lids made his eyes appear narrow and hawk-like. His thick black hair reached to his shoulders in a tangled mess. His black eyes stared out coldly. He had once been a good-looking man, but the battle scars on his face and the deep lines around his eyes together with a hardened expression told of a life of hardship and violence.

The only good thing about being in England, he reflected, was he could visit his parents. Their circumstances were much reduced since their unfortunate dealings with the Jew, Jurnet of Norwich. He had called in their debt and taken their manor house and the land that went with it. They now lived in a cottage in the centre of Thetford in the county of Norfolk.

His mother had aged considerably since his last visit. She wore a cheap cotton tunic with an apron over it. When he had asked her why, she looked embarrassed. His father explained that they had cause to let the maid go and so his mother was now doing all the cooking and cleaning. When Brito heard this his anger exploded, but his mother had calmed him down and told him she rather liked cooking. Still, he swore vengeance on the Jew Jurnet. It was because of him that Brito had to leave home. He had learnt to survive by carving out a name for himself on the battlefield, eventually coming to the attention of King Henry for being a loyal knight who could be relied upon to carry out the more disagreeable tasks the king commanded. Since then, Brito had made it his business to be indispensable to the king by developing specific skills at dealing with the king's problems. In short Brito was a thug.

Last year an Irishman called Dairmait MacMurchada arrived at the king's siege fort at Fougères in France to ask for the king's help. He had lost his lands in Ireland at the hands of his enemies. Brito had no sympathy for him and took an immediate dislike to Dairmait. When the king asked his opinion, Brito advised against helping the Irishman, but the king sought to reward him for his help in the Welsh campaign of 1165 and issued him with letters patent. This gave Dairmait permission to find men willing to aid him. As a precaution the king sent Brito to spy on Dairmait.

Brito spent the first few months in Bristol after arriving in England. Dairmait was staying at the home of Robert fitz Harding and spent most of his time reading out the letters patent publicly in the streets of Bristol trying to drum up support for his campaign. His efforts were unsuccessful. But when Brito learned from gossiping servants in the local tavern that Richard de Clare, the Earl of Striguil known as Strongbow, was involved, he duly sent a dispatch to the king and received a concerned response.

Brito, you must at all costs prevent Dairmait MacMurchada and Richard de Clare from entering Ireland. In 1155, Pope Adrian the

Fourth issued the Laudabiliter, the papal bull, which gave me the right to assume control over Ireland and to reform the Irish church. It specifically said:

'Laudably and profitably does your magnificence contemplate extending your glorious name on earth, to enlarge the boundaries of the Church and to expound the truth of the Christian faith to ignorant and barbarous peoples.

'The Irish are savages in need of a firm, correcting hand. I am bound by my faith to be that correcting hand. I therefore command you, as your king, to do all in your power to prevent this invasion.'

Brito read and reread the command.

All in my power. At all costs.

The king had given him *carte blanche* to do anything he wanted. Brito gazed out of the window; his lip curled forming a snarl. A feeling of great power engulfed him. He crossed his arms and rested his pike-toed boots on a stool, exposing his cross-banded stockings from beneath his dark green woollen tunic and puffed out his chest. Then he remembered he was hungry and barked out an order to the inn keeper to bring him his breakfast. Brito knew of Richard de Clare. He was the titular head of the somewhat shadowy earldom of Pembroke and his fortunes had been at a low ebb for some time. Dairmait must have offered him something tantalising to make him take up with an Irish savage.

From that moment on, his interest in the affairs of Dairmait and Richard de Clare intensified. He made the acquaintance of a young girl who was one of fitz Harding's servants. He began by flattering her, occasionally giving her small gifts. He was always respectful towards her, drawing her slowly into his confidence. He may have given her the impression his intentions were more serious for when he told her he was leaving Bristol she broke down. Still she had served her purpose. She had agreed to listen to her master's conversations and report back to him. She had done her job well and when, at the end of January, she told him Dairmait and the Earl were to travel to Gloucester to seek a Jew by the name of le Riche, Brito knew the only reason would be to secure funds for his campaign in Ireland. He knew he must travel to Gloucester to ensure no monies would be forthcoming from this Jew they called le Riche. The very name sickened him. Moses the Rich. No doubt he was cut from the same cloth as the Jew, Jurnet of Norwich. Jews were the only people allowed to practise usury, the lending of money at interest. As a result, English Jews had built up a vast amount of wealth. This angered Brito beyond reason. He swung his feet off the stool and sat up. His anger would be unleashed on the innkeeper if he didn't bring him his food soon. He began to chew on his fingernails whilst he waited, and his thoughts turned back to his parents. His future and theirs depended upon his success. The king had intimated he would give back the land and property his parents had lost to that thieving greedy Jew. He would love to see the light return to his mother's eyes, to see her restored to her rightful place.

The key to his success was to cut off Dairmait's access to money. Raising an army was a costly business and if Dairmait did not have easy access to an endless supply of cash, he would never be able to invade Ireland and regain his lands. He had already implemented the first part of his plan. The second part was yet to be put in place. But that opportunity was falling into his path by chance. The Lich Inn offered suitable rooms for Brito's needs. It was a stone's throw from the local whorehouse and full of an assortment of dubious characters who after a few ales developed loose tongues. There was talk that le Riche's wife was spending obscene sums of money with local traders and yesterday he discovered the reason why. In a few days' time the city would be full of Jews to celebrate the birth of le Riche's son. Brito could not believe his luck. It was the right time to strike.

But first he needed to pay a visit to this Jew, le Riche.

CHAPTER

THREE

M oses le Riche's house was a stone fortress, constructed with security in mind. The design was much like the houses his forefathers built in Rouen based on Romanesque architecture with the distinctive decorative cabling work on the rounded arches above his doors and window openings. It was the grandest of all the houses in the Jewry, the area in Gloucester where the Jewish community lived. With so much money and goods on the premises, a solid stone house was a wise investment in his line of work as wooden houses frequently burnt down. At the rear of his house, he had built a synagogue, a *mikveh*, or sacred bath for ritual washing, a butchery and a communal oven around a large open courtyard. It was the centre of the community's social and religious life and Moses was its leading member.

Moses sat in the chill of his vaulted cellar working at his oak desk. Towards the end of the month, he would have to pay his taxes to the sheriff, and he needed to make sure his accounts were in order. Before him lay a mound of silver coins, a neatly arranged line of tally sticks made of hazel wood and a thick pile of *shetarot*. These were his clients' written credit agreements.

From a small, decorative brass chest he kept on his desk, he removed his personal seal, which he used as his signature to attest to all his financial records. It bore a lion rampant with his name in Hebrew around the edge. He scratched his wiry black beard, his head full of mathematical calculations, then reached across and picked up one of the coins. On one side was the face of the current king, Henry the Second, wearing a crown *fleurée* on his head and holding a sceptre topped with a cross *patée*. Moses flipped the coin to look at the reverse. In an inner beaded circle, the moneyer had stamped the familiar cross potent with smaller cross *patées* in each angle and on the centre of that was a very small saltire. The workmanship was of inferior quality as were most of the coins struck of late. A lack of pride in one's work saddened Moses. To him it represented a general decline of standards. He made a mental note to debate this with Radulf, the king's moneyer, when they next met on Hocktide, the date ascribed for the collection of the debt Radulf owed him. Moses enjoyed debating with Radulf or anyone else for that matter on subjects that interested him, such as the making of coins, religion, languages, philosophy.

Moses had always been fascinated by coins ever since his father took him to the mint in Rouen as a boy. He remembered the coiner holding the die in place and could still hear the mighty thud as he raised his hammer and took aim to dispense a heavy blow to the flan, which would produce the finished coin. That seemed such a long time ago. His father had since retired and he himself was married now. His wife, Douce, had given birth to their second son a few days ago and was busy in the kitchen preparing for his son's *brit milah*, the circumcision ceremony, which was tomorrow. Moses marvelled at his wife's energy. She never seemed to sit still. Making lists, cleaning the house, cooking. It was all too much for him. At least down here in his cellar he could escape the worst of it, concentrate on balancing his books whilst setting aside a considerable amount of money to give to her so she could pay the numerous merchants for the mountains of food and wine she had bought for the feast.

'She'll be my financial ruin if she carries on spending all my money,' he said to himself as he counted out more coins.

The past few years had been a busy time for Moses. Working as Aaron of Lincoln's agent, he administered and collected vast sums of money on his behalf, taking his agreed commission. Within the space of a few years he had become the wealthiest Jew in Gloucester. It meant he paid higher taxes to the king than his fellow Jews, but he saw that almost as a badge of honour, a public reflection of his wealth. The king taxed the Jewish community more heavily than their Christian counterparts when he needed money for his crusades or his family's marriages, but what annoyed Moses more was that he had the audacity to call the tax a *donum* or donation even though the tax was compulsory. When the king needed money for his Toulouse campaign in 1159, his father Samuel paid almost five marks in that donum.

Still, he reflected, as he counted the coins and dropped them into his money bag, the best part of being rich was spoiling his family, especially his wife.

Moses planned to visit Prior Clement of Llanthony Secunda Priory later that day. The priory was carrying out extensive building work requiring substantial funds and they had come to him for the loan. Moses liked Clement so had offered him a very good rate of interest at two pennies in the pound, per week. Working out at an annual interest rate of twenty-two per cent, it was still a sound business deal. If for any reason the priory were not able to pay back the loan, Moses would receive the extensive lands the priory owned and hence the rents from those lands as they had been pledged as collateral. Either way, Moses could not lose money on the deal.

He walked over to the niche in the stone wall where he stored his wooden tally sticks. Sifting through them, he picked out the tally stick for the priory's loan. Several thick notches were cut into the wood and by each notch Moses had written the amounts already paid in ink. He placed this in a metal chest which he took from a locked cabinet, then put on his heavy winter cloak and pointed felt hat and made his way up the cellar steps. Douce was nowhere to be seen, so he slipped out of the house and headed in the direction of the priory with the chest tucked under his arm.

It was some months since he had seen Prior Clement. Previously a religious cell from Wales the monks had found the climate in Gloucester hospitable and stayed on, building a substantial priory on the outskirts of the city. When Moses arrived at Llanthony Secunda, he found Prior Clement in poor spirits. This saddened him. Clement was a man of great intellect and wisdom. They would often debate aspects of modern life and occasionally discuss each other's religion to gain mutual understanding. For a Christian prior, Moses found him to be very open-minded and easy to talk to. But today was not a day for conversation or healthy debate. The cause of his sadness was the disappearance of Harold, a young novice monk whom Clement was particularly fond of. It seemed the boy had wandered off some weeks ago and had not been seen since.

'I'm sorry to hear that, Clement. Harold was such a happy boy and a blessing to you. You must miss him.'

Clement shook his head, a look of bewilderment darkening his sad face. 'It's very unlike him. He rarely left my side.'

'He can't have gone far, a boy of that age,' Moses said, trying to reassure his friend. 'Where have you looked?'

'Everywhere I can think of. It's like he's vanished.'

'I'll have a word with the sheriff. Maybe he knows something or can help. Perhaps he can organise a search party. I'm sure we'll find him soon.'

'I'd like to believe that,' Clement said, his face grey with worry.

'It won't help to dwell on it. I'm sure he'll come back,' Moses said, patting Clement's shoulder.

'I'm not so sure but thank you for your kind offer, Moses.'

'Harold was like family to you and family is everything. I'll see what I can do.'

Moses finished counting the coins Clement had handed over, and marked the agreement accordingly, placing them back in the chest and locking it.

'I'm sorry to leave so soon but I must go. It's getting late and the streets are not safe after dark.'

Clement nodded his head in understanding. They left Clement's study room and walked across the cloisters. Building work was well under way on a new grain store and the monks were overseeing the work of the builders and stonemasons. The priory was being funded in part directly by Moses but also by their benefactress, Margaret de Bohun, a wealthy widow and Clement's niece. She was also the mother of Humphrey, the king's Lord High Constable and very influential.

'What about Margaret?' Moses asked.

Prior Clement pulled up short and threw an enquiring glance at Moses. 'What about Margaret?' he said in an accusatory tone.

'I only meant that she knows people. Maybe she could help to find Harold. Maybe offer money for his safe return?'

'Oh. I see what you mean. Yes, I'm sure she'd want to help find him, but I'd rather you didn't mention this to Margaret just yet if you see her.'

Moses thought Clement was acting a little strangely, but he

put it down to the man's sorrow at missing Harold and noted Clement's request. When they reached the West Gate of the priory, Clement stepped out with him, taking the opportunity to scour the length of the muddy track in both directions, still hopeful for any sign of the boy. Moses tried to imagine how he would feel if it was one of his sons.

'When I find him, I'll give him a good talking to and bring him back here myself.'

'I'd appreciate that,' said Clement, shaking Moses' hand.

He left Clement at the gate and continued his journey. The sky was ash grey and a cold dampness seeped into his clothes as he made his way along Severin Street, his boots sinking into the mud. By the time he reached the South Gate an icy mizzle was falling. Moses looked up at the crenellated turrets of St Kyneburgh's chapel, then ducked inside the porch to pull the hood of his cloak over his hat. He was there but a moment when a stranger approached him and to Moses' surprise, addressed him.

'Is your name Moses le Riche?' the stranger said, his wet black hair streaked across his gnarled face.

The stranger was dressed in knightly garb and spoke with a Norman French accent. Moses was alarmed by his tone and sensing danger clasped his casket tighter to his chest.

'I am he. Who wants to know?'

'I'm here on king's business, that's all you need to know. Listen to me and listen well. An Irishman called Dairmait is going to call on you on the recommendation of a man named Robert fitz Harding of Bristol...'

'Fitz Harding the moneylender?' Moses said.

The stranger flashed a dark look at Moses.

'Don't interrupt. When he calls, he'll want to borrow money...' He paused. The stranger's black eyes fixed on Moses.

His tone was threatening, his words uttered between clenched teeth. 'Don't under any circumstances lend him money.'

'Why not?' asked Moses.

'Do you want to be the cause of the king's displeasure?'

'Not at all.'

'Just listen to me then and do what I say. You have been warned,' said the stranger and before Moses could say more, he was gone.

Grateful that the stranger was not there to rob him, Moses hurried back home, drawing his heavy cloak around him, turning every now and then to make sure the stranger was not following him. Once inside the thick stone walls of his home, Moses locked the door behind him. The house was warm and cooking smells wafted from the kitchen. He could hear faint laughter and the chatter of women. He went downstairs to his cellar where he unlocked his money chest and began counting the coins. Once he counted out his commission, he put this in a second pile. The king's tax money he placed in a third pile. He took three small leather pouches from the niche and emptied the separate piles of pennies into each one, tying them tight and putting them in the chest before locking it again. He then replaced the money chest in the large wooden cabinet, locking the door securely.

All this was done in quick, urgent moves. When he finished, he realised his heart was beating fast. He sat down at his desk and placed his hand on his chest and took a deep breath. The stranger mentioned Robert fitz Harding. Why would he be recommending me? Fitz Harding was a hard-nosed businessman and the only Christian moneylender he knew of. Why turn down the king's business when it usually meant plenty of profit for the lender? Moses was both puzzled and unnerved. There was no point worrying about it. The Irishman, if he existed, might never turn up. He resolved to put all thoughts of the stranger and the Irishman out of his head and enjoy the celebrations to come.

His thoughts turned to his good fortune, his loving wife, his thriving sons, his increasing wealth, his large house, his friends. All this was about to improve tenfold if plans for his niece came to fruition. Arlette was of marrying age. He hoped to secure a match with Aaron's son, Deudonne. The match would be financially and socially advantageous. Hopefully, despite the *brit* falling on Shabbat, the Jewish Sabbath, Aaron and his son as well as many of his friends from all over England and France would join him for the celebration.

Gradually his heartbeat slowed, and his breathing returned to normal. On balance, he decided, there was much to be thankful for. Moses reached behind him and took his *siddur*, his prayer book from its niche in the stone wall. It was not often he prayed but a sudden urge to give thanks came upon him. His encounter with the stranger had unnerved him. Perhaps it was foolish superstition. Still...

Holding the book in his hands, he whispered to himself. 'Blessed are You, Who bestows good things upon the unworthy, and has bestowed upon me every goodness.'

It was inexplicable, but he felt an instant easing of his mind.

FOUR

Dairmait MacMurchada was a desperate man. His enemies Tiernan O'Rourke, ruler of the Kingdom of Brenny, and the tyrant Rory O'Connor, the king of Connaught, had attacked him, overthrown him and driven him out of Dublin, forcing him to flee his beloved Ireland. For as long as he could remember, as King of Leinster, he had been at war with his enemies. With each victory he expanded his kingdom and his notoriety. He was feared throughout Ireland as a man who would think nothing of ransacking villages, stealing their cattle and leaving those still left alive to starve. He had lost count of the number of hostages taken, how many he had blinded or beheaded. So how had he found himself in this position? Without a kingdom and banished from his own country. He shook his head in disbelief. Treachery had led him here. Treachery and betrayal.

He left Dublin for Bristol on a Danish trading vessel hoping to stay with the only man he knew in England, his trading partner Robert fitz Harding. The two men shipped slaves between Dublin and Bristol, a lucrative business which had made Robert a very rich man. His plan was to seek an audience with the king and ask for his help in regaining his lands. Arriving in Bristol, his friend informed him that the king was in France and so he had made the long and exhausting journey to France where, after much fruitless wandering, discovered the elusive monarch in Aquitaine. After a brief audience, the king issued him with letters patent giving him permission to seek men willing to help him regain his lands.

On his return to Bristol, fitz Harding suggested he meet with Richard de Clare, the Earl of Striguil. He was known as Strongbow for his prowess with a long bow on the battlefield. Once a wealthy knight, he had fallen out of favour with the king. Their meeting was favourable, ending in the offer to Richard of his daughter Aoife's hand in marriage and the title King of Leinster, his kingdom in Ireland, on his death. Richard offered to use his connections to raise an army of English knights. Now all he needed was the money to feed and equip these men. He was now in Gloucester with his daughter and her suitor Richard. He had to admit they made a handsome couple though it pained him to think his daughter was marrying into English nobility.

After being shown to his room in the Portcullis Inn, he went downstairs to have a drink. The atmosphere was congenial. A fire roared and the smell of cooking wafted in from the kitchen. Dairmait's thoughts drifted to his enemies O'Rourke and that bastard O'Connor. He shuddered to think what was happening in Ireland in his absence. It was fifteen years since Dairmait carried off O'Rourke's wife *Derbforgaill* in the dead of night but still the man bore a grudge against him. Dairmait's unfettered anger welled up at the thought of those traitorous scum ruling over his subjects. He cursed loudly in his native tongue, slamming down his tankard of cider, his voice hoarse and booming coming from a man used to issuing commands on the battlefield. The room fell silent, all eyes on Dairmait. He glared back, muttering an Irish curse under his breath.

It was some time before Aoife joined her father. He was slumped at the table, his head resting on his hand.

'What's the matter?' said Aoife in her lyrical, Celtic intonation.

Aoife stood before her father. She wore a simple loose tunic of cream linen underneath a heavily embroidered red and gold cloak fastened at the neck by an impressive gold clasp fashioned in the shape of a Celtic cross. Her vivid green eyes looked out from underneath a mass of burnished red hair. She resembled a wild and exotic animal. Richard appeared next to her, wearing a sturdy pair of boots and dressed in a loose-fitting tunic of finely woven red cloth with his personal heraldic design emblazoned on the front.

'He hasn't been himself since he lost his kingdom,' Aoife said, flashing a mischievous smile at Richard and sitting down on the bench opposite her father.

'Neither would you be if you'd lost your lands to those traitorous scum,' her father barked back at her.

Aoife enjoyed teasing her father. She knew how far to take it without him losing his temper and giving her a slap. She watched as her father attacked the meal placed before him. His face was deeply lined and speckled with dark freckles which matched his chestnut-coloured eyes. He ate with the ferocity of a wild animal, tearing apart the carcass of a roast chicken and hacking at the meat with his yellowing teeth. Grease dripped from his matted, unkempt beard. He wiped his battle-worn face with the back of his hand, dragging strands of his tatted hair from his mouth. Dairmait picked up his tankard of cider.

'*Slàinte*,' he said.

'Cheers,' Richard replied, clanking his tankard against Dairmait's.

Dairmait drained the last drop and pushed it away from him.

'Feeling better now?' Aoife asked.

Dairmait grunted at her and ordered another.

Since being introduced to Richard at Robert fitz Harding's house and liking what she saw, she was trying to act less like a battle warrior and more like a lady in front of him. Many men had tried to secure her hand in marriage, but she had rejected them all. There was something about Richard that attracted her. He was older than her by seventeen years but that did not concern her. His voice was soft, unlike her father's, and he was cultured and well-mannered, gentler somehow than the Irish men she was used to.

'Once we find out where this Jew le Riche lives, I'll pay him a visit,' Dairmait growled.

'Wouldn't it be better if Richard went with you?'

Dairmait scowled at his daughter. 'Why?'

'I just thought...'

'You're not here to think. This is my business, and I will deal with it.'

Richard interjected. 'I think what Aoife is trying to say is...'

'I know what she's saying. I know my daughter better than you.'

Dairmait glowered at Richard, his crumpled face grey with exhaustion.

'Why don't we both accompany you?' Aoife suggested, giving Richard a concerned look.

'No. I need to handle this myself.'

'I think you are tired, Father. Why don't you retire early?'

Dairmait gave his daughter a suspicious look. Aoife knew what her father was thinking, and he was right. She wanted to spend some time alone with her suitor, something she had not managed to do so far. That sanctimonious wife of fitz Harding's Eva or Domina Eva as she liked to be called was always hanging around when they were in Bristol. They shared a similar name, but they could not be more different. The woman talked of taking the veil. Imagine that? Being celibate. *Not for me*, thought Aoife. She liked the touch of a man too much. There had been one or two men in her life that she had allowed to go further than kissing, but she was still a virgin. Whenever she looked at Richard, she wanted him to touch her. His grey eyes and full lips were inviting. She often thought about his lips on her body. She wished her father would go to his room.

'I'm very tired,' he said at last. 'I think I'll go to my bed. Are you coming?'

'I haven't finished my food. I'll be up as soon as I finish.'

Dairmait shook his head. 'Mind you do.'

Aoife watched as her father pulled himself up from his chair and walked slowly to the bottom of the stairs. He had aged since his journey to France and had developed a stoop. As soon as he disappeared, Aoife turned her attention to Richard. She shrugged off her cloak and adjusted her neckline, revealing the top part of her firm breasts. She shifted along the wooden bench to sit closer to him.

'Do you think that is wise?' Richard asked her.

'I don't think it unwise,' she said, leaning into him.

'What will your father say?'

Aoife flashed her green eyes at him and swept her thick, russet-coloured hair from her face. Her expression was that of a mischievous imp. 'Nothing. He's gone to bed.'

'But...'

'I can handle him,' she said, placing her hand on Richard's muscular thigh.

Richard reached across and placed his hand around her neck, pulling her toward him. Aoife moaned and moved her hand to his inner thigh. She kissed his full lips. They were soft. He responded. She felt him harden. She pulled back from him and looked into his soft grey eyes.

'You know as a Celtic princess I can choose whomever I marry?'

'I didn't know that. I'm flattered,' he said.

'You may address me as *banphrionsa choróin*. That means Crown Princess,' Aoife said, holding out her hand and lifting her chin in an exaggerated fashion.

Richard took her hand and kissed it, repeating the phrase as best he could in his stumbling Norman accent. Aoife let out a hearty laugh and placing her hands on his ruddy freckled cheeks, planted a kiss on his lips. Richard drew her to him.

'I'm glad you chose me,' he whispered into her ear.

'This is a respectable establishment,' the landlord said, lifting Dairmait's empty tankard from the table. 'If you want to behave like that there's a whorehouse around the corner.'

Richard went for his sword. Aoife restrained him.

'Don't. Remember why we are here. Father would not be pleased if you drew unwanted attention to us.'

Richard released his grip on the hilt of his sword and apologised to the landlord. He stood up.

'Don't go,' Aoife said, grabbing his wrist and tugging on it.

'I'll see you in the morning,' Richard said in a firm voice. 'Goodnight, Aoife.'

Aoife stood. She pressed her body against his. There was hunger in her eyes. She kissed him on the lips.

'Goodnight, Richard,' she said.

Then she turned to the landlord, pulled a face at him, and walked away.

The landlord tutted and cleared their table.

'She's a handful that one,' he said to Richard.

Richard smiled, his eyes twinkling with mischief.

'I know.'

FIVE

The kitchen in the le Riche household was in utter chaos. Douce stood in front of a metal tripod by the kitchen fire balancing a large pan in which she was searing chunks of beef in home-made *schmaltz,* made from rendered chicken fat. She was making *cholent,* a slow-cooked stew of beef traditionally served on Shabbat.

Arlette was at the kitchen table, peeling and chopping the last of the onions to add to the stew and to make the crust-covered meat dish they would serve at the celebratory meal. The two women worked well together. Douce looked upon Arlette as her own daughter.

Helping in the kitchen was the widow Bellassez and young Judea, the wife of Josce. Bellassez lost her husband Assel some years ago but not before he had given her four children whom she now looked after on her own. Her children were all under the age of ten and so, out of necessity, Bellassez had taken over her husband's moneylending business, but her real skill was as the community's physician. She had delivered countless babies and nursed the sick back to health. Bellassez and Douce had known each other since their arrival in Gloucester and grown close. Douce called her Bella. The name meant 'beautiful enough' in French, and it was true, she was a beautiful woman.

Bellassez was preparing whole chickens freshly slaughtered by Rubin that morning. She was plucking them before smearing them with the fat to be roasted in the communal oven. Judea was on her hands and knees picking up several pewter platters she had knocked to the floor. Luckily, thought Douce, they were empty. Judea had a reputation for being clumsy. Not a day would go by when she wasn't showing scars or burns from accidents she had sustained, in either her own kitchen or someone else's. The wives tolerated her, partly due to her age but also because she was such a kind and amenable young woman. Judea was the youngest of the wives. At fifteen she married Josce, a handsome young man, who was keen to make his fortune by delving into the business of moneylending. So far, his efforts had produced meagre results and to compound matters the marriage had produced no children. Douce often wondered how many moneylenders a place could sustain, but as long as her husband continued to prosper it didn't hold her thoughts for long.

Douce was busy browning the meat when she saw her husband hurrying towards her. He was holding a leather money pouch and she hoped it was for her. She had ordered so many things for the *brit* and hadn't paid for them yet. Bellassez was holding a platter of chickens and heading towards the door to take them to the communal oven when, out of curiosity, she stopped to listen to the exchange between them. Moses approached his wife and gave her a kiss on the cheek.

'Here. I've brought you this.'

He held out the money bag and jangled the coins inside. Douce went to take the bag from him, then remembered her hands were covered in grease.

'I can't take that just now,' she said. 'Leave it over there by my wedding ring?'

Moses shrugged. '*D'accord*,' he said in French, dropping the bag next to her elaborate wedding ring, then he shouted, '*Shalom*,' over his shoulder, wishing her goodbye in Hebrew, before leaving the kitchen.

'*Merci, mon chéri*,' Douce shouted after him.

Moses was fluent in Hebrew, French and English. He could write in both Hebrew and Latin, all prerequisites for a successful career in moneylending. Douce was so proud of him at times she could cry. He was also very generous with his money, often giving her more than she needed.

'You're a lucky woman, Douce,' Bellassez said, after he had gone. 'That husband of yours never leaves you wanting.'

Douce held a wooden spoon in her hand. Her face was red from exhaustion and beads of sweat were visible across her bony cheeks from the heat of the fire. Her dark hair was tied back and covered with a house cap, but straggly wisps had escaped, and these were stuck to her damp skin. She laughed for Bellassez was renowned for her double entendres and Douce knew she wasn't just referring to the money. She imagined that's the way you became when you were widowed. Being denied something made you want it more.

Bellassez turned to Arlette. 'And that butcher's boy, he seemed a little keen on Arlette at the Purim celebrations, didn't you think, Douce?'

'We're just friends,' Arlette snapped, her cheeks reddening.

'It didn't look that way to me.'

'Stop it, Bella, you're embarrassing Arlette. They are nothing more than friends. There's nothing going on between them and stop trying to make out there is. Besides, Arlette can do better than a butcher's boy.'

Douce liked Zev, he was pleasant enough but not marriage material in her opinion.

'There's nothing wrong with being a butcher's son. Money isn't everything, Douce.'

'I just meant...'

'I know what you meant,' Bella said and left the kitchen carrying the chickens. Judea followed behind carrying the platters she would now have to re-wash under the outside tap in the courtyard.

'That Bella, she's such a mischief-maker. Take no notice of her,' Douce said to Arlette.

'You haven't told her about Deudonne?'

'I haven't told anyone. I don't want to tempt providence.'

Douce touched the gold *kamea*, the amulet she wore around her neck to protect her from harm. It was engraved with divine words in Hebrew from the Kabbalah.

'Do you really think that works?'

'I'm sure it does. Anyway, it makes me feel better when I touch it.'

She touched the amulet once more for good luck. Douce had welcomed Arlette into her home and in a few short months they had become like mother and daughter. Arlette was a sweet girl, orphaned at a young age and in such a terrible way. Douce felt protective of her and wanted only the best.

'What do you think could go wrong?' Arlette said. 'Do you think he won't like me?'

'He'd be a fool not to like you.'

'But what else could go wrong?'

'Nothing. Don't pay any attention to me.'

Arlette wiped away the onion tears that were rolling down her pink cheeks and continued chopping. Bellassez returned with the empty platter upon which she piled more fresh chickens whilst Judea ladled honey into a bowl of mashed quince to make a milky pudding. The smells of sweet and savoury permeated the bustling kitchen. With the help of her friends, the meal would indeed be one with sacred status. One which would make her husband proud of her.

Douce glanced across at Arlette. The tears from the onions were still rolling down her cheeks but still she looked angelic. She was so naïve about the world, about what it meant to be an *isha*, a wife. They hadn't had that conversation yet – about what to expect on her wedding night. Whenever she thought of Arlette with Deudonne she could not visualise them together. She was unsure what this could mean. The uncertainty troubled her and yet Moses seemed determined to match them together. Perhaps he was thinking of his business rather than his niece's welfare. Typical of a man. Douce had met Deudonne a number of times when he accompanied his father on business trips. He seemed a pleasant enough boy, yet she was troubled by the match. She wondered whether she should mention her concerns to Moses. Arlette wouldn't understand and might take it the wrong way. Most people did. She took her inability to see them together as a sign, but she told herself she was being overprotective, superstitious, foolish even. Nevertheless, she decided to reserve judgement until the *brit* when Arlette would meet the young man in question. Until then it was better for all concerned that she didn't mention it to anyone.

CHAPTER
SIX

The men opened the heavy door to a dark, foul-smelling cellar and descended the narrow stone steps to where the boy Harold lay, his hands and feet securely tied with rope. As soon as he heard the men's footsteps, he started to wriggle. He had lost a considerable amount of weight in the weeks of his confinement, despite daily visits from his captors to feed him with bread and water. His chestnut-coloured hair was matted with dried blood from the blow to the side of his head and no attempt had been made to clean or bandage the wound. His body and clothes were grubby from rolling around on the cellar floor.

They had muffled his cries with a teasel, a wooden gag covered with cloth, which they had put between his jaw, fastening it at the back of his neck with a leather cord. One of the men loosened the gag. Harold, as weak as he was, cried out. His cries were not loud enough to be heard beyond the thick stone walls of the cellar, but they could not risk being discovered. The man retightened his gag and gave him a severe kick in the side, which winded Harold. This was followed by a blow to his face from the hammer he held in his hand. There was a crack of bone as his jaw broke and his front teeth snapped out of their sockets. Blood gushed from the wound and soaked the cloth that covered his mouth. Meanwhile, the other men gathered together the implements they would need. Harold's bruised, and bloodied body was stripped of all but his girdle. They nailed his hands and feet to a simple wooden cross, oblivious to the sound of crushing bone and Harold's muffled screams as the rusty nails were hammered into his limbs. Next, they wedged a crown of hawthorns upon his head and two more bundles beneath his armpits.

Harold was much weaker now, nearer to death. A metal pot containing dripping was bubbling over a makeshift fire. Just as a cook would prepare a joint of meat to roast, the fat was poured over him. Harold's body immediately tensed, and he cried out as the hot fat burnt his soft skin. His eyes opened wide, and he looked heavenwards. A look of momentary bliss came upon his young, innocent face but the ecstasy did not last long. He slumped back onto the cross; the light in his eyes clouded over. He would feel no more pain.

The men picked up the wooden cross with Harold's body still fastened to it and carried it over to the fire. They held it over the flames, turning it like a spit roast, until the flesh blackened on his back, sides and buttocks. The cellar filled with choking smoke and the smell of burning flesh. When they were finished, they dumped the scorched wooden cross onto the grubby floor. Harold's neck snapped and twisted to one side as the cross juddered to the ground. The men looked on for a moment admiring their handiwork before removing the gag from Harold's twisted mouth. Their final act of torture was to pour molten wax into his pale blue eyes, inside his ears and over his face.

Choking from the fumes, the men put out the fire and left the cellar by the stone steps, leaving Harold's charred body still nailed to the wooden cross.

CHAPTER
SEVEN

D ouce came into the dining hall holding a basket containing two loaves. Draped over her arm was a clean napkin of white cotton. She set the basket in the centre of the trestle table, covering it with the napkin. Next, she placed a ewer of water and some clean cloths on a side table. As it was a chilly evening, Moses had lit the *foudron*, a small stove he had imported from France. A healthy glow came from it. The table was covered with a cloth made from flax and place settings for four were laid out using her finest platters of silver with wine goblets made from pewter.

Two Shabbat candles, still unlit, were at one end of the table where Douce would sit. Wall candles flickered against the singed stone wall creating shadowy images across the hall. The floor had been swept with a besom that afternoon, and fresh rushes of barley were strewn across it. The baby was in his crib, wide awake and gurgling to himself. Douce always felt reassured when she heard him making sounds. Her eldest son Samuel had developed yellow skin after his *brit* and was ill for weeks afterwards. He had never fully recovered. A nagging worry that her precious *bechor*, her firstborn, might have suffered permanent damage never left her. He was a lot slower than other boys his age. He was the last to talk, the last to walk. Because of that she was probably guilty of being an overprotective mother.

When the rest of the family joined her, they had changed into their Shabbat clothes. Moses wore a full-length tunic of cream linen, tied at the shoulder by a decorative metal clasp. His father, Old Samuel, made less of an effort and wore his old Shabbat tunic, frayed at the edges but clean. Douce and Arlette both wore simple linen mantles which covered their ankles, and on their heads, they wore a soft linen cap to cover their hair.

Douce lit a wax taper to light the first candle. To remember. Then she lit the second. To observe. She waved her hands over the candles as if she were gathering the light to her face. Then she covered her eyes before reciting the blessing in Hebrew.

'Blessed are you, Adonai, Who has sanctified us with His commandments and commanded us to light the lights of Shabbat. Amein.'

She uncovered her eyes and completed the ritual, reciting the *kiddush*, a special prayer for Shabbat. 'And there was evening and there was morning,' it began.

The family listened to her words spoken in Hebrew. Even little Samuel tried hard not to fidget or look up, but he couldn't help tilting his head and squeezing one eye shut, the other half open in his childish belief he couldn't be seen. Douce finished with the words, 'Blessed are You, who sanctifies Shabbat. Amein.'

Once everyone was seated, she removed the cloth from the basket containing the golden-brown loaves, ripped one apart and passed the pieces around. Samuel the Younger snatched the bread from his mother and took a bite.

'Nu, nu. No snatching, Samuel. You know that is wrong,' she chided him, breaking the silence.

They gave each other the customary greeting of wishing peace on Shabbat.

'*Shabbat shalom.*'

Douce served little Samuel a bowl of steaming chicken soup. She added cold water to it before feeding him.

'I went to see Prior Clement today,' Moses said.

'How is he?' his father asked.

'Not so good. One of his young novices has disappeared.'

'Disappeared? How can someone just disappear?' Douce asked.

'I don't know but he has.'

'How old was he?'

'Barely nine years.'

'And how long has he been missing?' asked Douce.

'A few weeks. Clement has been looking everywhere for him.'

'And he hasn't come back?' Douce said, concern creasing her face.

'Not yet.'

'How awful for Clement. Is there anything you can do to help him, Moses?'

'I said I'd speak to the sheriff.'

'Please do. I don't know what I'd do if one of my children went missing,' she said, wiping the dribbles of soup from little Samuel's chin and looking over her shoulder at the baby in the crib.

Their conversation was accompanied by the spattering of wax candles, the hissing of green wood from within the stove and the occasional gurgling of the baby in his crib.

'*Ima, Ima,*' little Samuel babbled, speaking in his baby language and pointing at his mother.

Little Samuel was two years old. Moses adored him but like Douce worried he could not say more than a few words such as

'*Ima*'; mother, and '*Aba*'; father. Being their firstborn he was greatly indulged. His father, Old Samuel, was the worst offender.

'Are you tired, *chérie?*' Moses asked Douce.

'A little,' she answered, sitting up and taking a sip of her tisane. It contained a mixture of Abraham's balm, motherwort, the leaves of the wild blackberry and groats. It was given to nursing women as a restorative.

'You've been doing a lot considering you only gave birth a week ago.'

'It's impossible to rest. There's so much to do.'

'Don't you think she's looking a little pale, *Aba?*'

Samuel the Elder looked across at Douce and scratching his silvery beard commented, 'You do look pale, Douce. It's a good thing it's Shabbat so you can rest.'

Moses noticed his wife was not looking as bright as she normally did and had already lost some of her pregnancy weight. She was a slight woman as it was and needed to keep up her strength for the children.

'Why don't you rest before our guests arrive?' he said.

Their friends from Oxford, Jacob, his wife and their four children were staying over which meant more work for Douce.

'I feel fine. You shouldn't fuss,' she said, smiling.

'I've been helping her as much as I can, *Dod*,' Arlette added, not wanting her uncle to think she wasn't doing her fair share of the household chores.

'Why don't you let me employ a servant to help you, Douce?'

'You know how I feel about that. Let's say no more and enjoy our breakfast.'

'Mirabelle has a servant...'

Moses was teasing her. They were talking about their neighbour and wife of Elias de Glocestre who lived opposite. He was also a moneylender but not as successful as Moses. Moses had little respect for Elias. He was a quiet man who tried his best to please his wife, but Mirabelle dominated him, not in size but by the sheer force of her personality. She bullied him and everyone knew it. They employed a poor Christian servant who slept in the attic room. She bullied her too.

A thought crossed his mind. Why not send the Irishman to Elias? That was one way of solving his dilemma. The thought eased Moses' troubled mind. He felt the tightness in his chest release and his appetite return. Taking a deep breath, he tore at the loaf of bread and dipped it into his soup.

Douce said, 'I don't care what Mirabelle has or doesn't have. You know my feelings about that woman.'

Moses flashed a smile at his niece. She smiled back at him, raising an eyebrow. A pair of co-conspirators.

'What?' enquired Douce, frowning at them.

'Nothing, *chérie*.'

The baby who had been peaceful in his crib cried out.

'I hope he's well-behaved at the *brit*. If not, "you know who" will have something to say.'

Douce had unwittingly turned the conversation back to Mirabelle. The pair did not get on. Moses suspected Mirabelle's dissatisfaction with her husband's ability to create wealth was at the heart of Mirabelle's antagonism towards his wife. She could be caustic at the best of times, but it seemed Douce was on the receiving end of her vicious tongue much more so than the other wives. Moses could only conclude it was jealousy. Would it be so wrong to send the Irishman her way?

'Ignore her. She only says things to cause trouble. You shouldn't let her get to you.'

'Uncle is right, it's not as if her children are the best behaved,' said Arlette in support.

'I don't normally let her get to me, but I don't feel strong enough just now to take her nasty comments.'

'Let's hope she's on her best behaviour,' said Moses finishing his soup.

Samuel the Elder grunted. 'That woman never behaves well. I don't know how Elias stands her,' he said, picking up his dog-eared prayer book and opening it to a page he had marked.

There was a lull in the conversation.

'Are you excited about tomorrow, Arlette?' Moses asked.

'I am excited,' Arlette said, brightening. 'This will be my first big get together in Gloucester and I'm looking forward to meeting all your friends, Uncle.'

'Of course, Aaron of Lincoln and his son Deudonne will be there,' Moses said, a glint in his eye.

'What are they like?'

'Aaron is quite a solemn character, but he has a good head for business. He's built himself a substantial empire all over England.'

'With your help,' Douce added.

'And his son?' Arlette asked.

'I don't know much about him.'

'How old is he?'

'I'm not exactly sure. Older than you, I would think.'

'And what does he look like?'

'Much like his father I'd say.'

'Well that's not much help,' Douce said, laughing, then turning to Arlette added, 'He has a pleasant face, Arlette.'

Arlette took a small piece of bread and placed it delicately into her mouth.

'What if he doesn't like me?'

'What's not to like,' Moses said.

'Uncle,' Arlette exclaimed, wrinkling her nose in feigned embarrassment.

'Well you asked,' Moses replied.

'You're worse than the women, Moses, when it comes to matchmaking,' Douce said.

'What if I don't like him,' Arlette asked, her conversation with Zev playing on her mind.

'Nothing will happen without your consent, Arlette,' Douce said. 'We will not force you into this arrangement against your will.'

'But I'm sure you'll like him and he you,' Moses added.

Samuel the Elder joined in. 'I thought you liked that butcher's boy, Zev.'

Arlette scowled. 'Zev and I are just good friends. That's all.'

'Didn't look like that the other night,' Samuel the Elder continued.

'I don't know what you mean,' Arlette replied in a haughty tone.

'He was following you around like a lost sheep.'

'He was drunk,' Arlette said, a tone of disgust in her voice.

'Stop teasing her, Samuel. You can see you're embarrassing her,' Douce said.

Old Samuel went back to his prayer book.

Douce said, 'You should get an early night, Arlette, so you look your best tomorrow. It's going to be a big day for you.' She turned to Moses. 'And you better get ready for tonight. Josce will be expecting you at his house.'

It was the custom for the chosen godfather to hold a banquet the night before the *brit milah* where guests sang religious songs and much rejoicing took place. Moses was looking forward to it.

Thud. Thud. Thud.

'Who can that be? At this hour?' said Douce.

'And on Shabbat,' said Old Samuel, in a grumbling tone.

No one moved. All eyes were on Moses expecting him to rise and answer the door. Moses did not move.

'Aren't you going to see who's at the door, Moses?' Douce asked.

'It's no one,' he replied.

Thud. Thud. Thud.

Again, the same insistent knocking.

'Well, whoever it is, they're not going until we answer the door,' said Douce, standing up. 'I'll answer it then.'

'No,' shouted Moses.

Again, everyone looked at Moses, shocked at his raised tone of voice. His son Samuel began to grizzle.

'It's all right, *chérie*, I'll go. You stay here and settle little Samuel.'

Moses walked slowly to the door. The words of the stranger were ringing in his ears.

Thud. Thud. Thud.

His heartbeat quickened as he unbolted the heavy wooden door and saw a ferocious-looking man of mature years with a mass of untidy auburn curls and greying beard standing before him.

'Are you the Jew Moses? Moses le Riche?' the man asked, his voice rough and gravelly.

Moses recognised his accent. This must be the Irishman the stranger had warned him about.

'What is it you want with me at this hour?'

'Robert fitz Harding of Bristol recommended you. I'm here on king's business.'

When Moses heard the king's name, he was confused. Hadn't the stranger told him the king would be displeased? He had learned to be very careful whenever the king was involved in business transactions. It was rarely straightforward.

'What business of the king's do you have with me?'

'Do you always conduct business on the threshold? Aren't you going to invite me in to discuss this matter?'

Dairmait's tone rankled Moses. 'You are aware I am Jewish?'

Dairmait did not answer but glared at Moses.

'Then you should know I do not conduct business on the Jewish Sabbath.'

He went to close the door. Dairmait's boot blocked his move.

'Then I'll call again in the morning,' he said, adding with unashamed sarcasm, 'when it's no longer your Jewish Sabbath.'

'I'm afraid it will still be *my* Sabbath tomorrow morning so I wouldn't bother. Besides, I have a family gathering tomorrow. Come back on Sunday if you must.'

'Then that would be *my* Sabbath.'

The two men glared at each other, the verbal sparring coming to an end. Moses' heart was beating as fast as the clatter of a Purim rattle.

Dairmait removed his boot from the door. 'I'll return on Monday,' he said, and disappeared into the shadows of Jewry Street. Moses closed the door and secured it with bolts. With any luck, he thought, the Irishman would not return. But even as he thought it, he knew it was wishful thinking. He had only managed to put off the inevitable.

CHAPTER
EIGHT

Harold's blackened body was prised from the cross by the man sent to collect him. Handling Harold like a butchered piece of meat, he took hold of his tattered girdle and wrapped it around Harold's feet, then wrapped his tortured body in sackcloth. Hoisting him over his shoulder, he made his way up the stone steps and out into the cold chill of the early morning. His horse gave him a welcome nicker, its breath escaping in threads of white steam from its nostrils. He patted the horse's mane to calm him, then tossed Harold's body over the saddle of his tethered horse and secured it with rope.

It was still dark but already the sound of birds chattering in the trees could be heard in the stillness. He led the horse along the empty streets of Gloucester. The horse's hooves were covered in layers of soft cloth to deaden the noise and avoid unwanted attention. By the time the lone horseman arrived at the riverside, a slice of dawn light was visible on the eastern horizon. It would not be long before the elver men arrived with their nets to prepare for the morning's catch. He must hurry. It was important the body be found today.

A bone-coloured mist crept over the surface of the water. A

solitary white heron padded through the mud on the opposite bank. Certain that he was alone, the man removed the sackcloth and threw Harold's body face down onto the muddy surface of the riverbank. It fell into the yielding mud with a splosh. He pushed it with his boot just enough to be covered by the water but not be washed away by the tide. The muddy ochre-coloured water lapped over Harold's naked body, gently buffeting it and soaking the girdle that remained wrapped around his feet.

Keen to leave before he was spotted, the man strode back to his horse. He unwrapped the cloths from its hooves, stuffing them in his saddle bag, then put his boot into the stirrup and hauled himself up. With a soft entreaty to his obedient steed, he galloped into the darkness of the wood.

CHAPTER
NINE

The sound of men's chatter carried across the fields and out over the river. They each held boat-shaped elver nets, a bucket and a sack in which to carry home their catch. They would normally fish for elvers at night on the spring tides, but this morning's tide was an ebb tide which meant the water was flowing out towards Bristol, the second-best time to elver.

'This makes more sense than spending all night fishing,' said John, the older of the men.

'Yes, and you can have a few more ales down the tavern?' said his friend Simon.

'Not too many or you'd never get up in time,' John replied.

'A good night's sleep and a bit of the old "you know what" before breakfast is what I like,' said Ralph the youngest of the friends and newly married.

The men laughed.

'You're lucky. All I got was a dig in the ribs when I tried it on this morning,' Simon said.

'I wouldn't stand for that,' said Ralph.

'Have you 'sin his wife?'

They fell about laughing, slapping each other on the back in a show of bonhomie. As the men approached the river, eager to catch the annual delicacy of elvers, they saw something ahead of them, lying at the river's edge.

'What 'ave we 'ere?' said John. 'A porpoise?'

His son Edmund ran ahead towards the fleshy lump. Young Edmund, a boy not much older than Harold, was the first to see that the porpoise was really a small boy, naked but for his girdle. He saw the wounds on the body and realised the boy was dead. Edmund had never seen a corpse before. His hands went to his stomach, he doubled over and ran to the edge of the water where he emptied the remains of his meagre breakfast into the river.

'This 'ere's no porpoise. We got a dead boy. Look at the state of 'im. No wonder Edmund spewed his guts up.'

''Ere. Someone. Pass me my cloth. Let's give the poor mite some dignity.'

When elvering John carried with him an oilcloth to sit on or to put over his head when it rained. The ribaldry of earlier was no more, extinguished by the grisly sight of Harold's body. For a few moments the men stood in stunned silence.

'This 'ere's no accident,' said John. 'Look at those marks on 'im?'

'And that gash on his head. Someone's done that to 'im. Ain't no way he could o' got that from falling in the river.'

'What should we do?' asked Simon.

John said, unfurling the oil cloth and covering Harold's body, 'We need to fetch Abbot Hameline. He'll know what to do. Edmund, go and fetch 'im. Tell 'im a boy has been murdered. He'll come then.'

It was some time before Abbot Hameline arrived. With him was Brother Carbonel, the Sacrist at the abbey. Their stride was purposeful as they approached. Edmund followed behind, like a toddler trying to keep up.

Having lost their appetite for elvering, the men had spent their time guarding the corpse. Not because anyone would run off with it but as a reverential vigil. Abbot Hameline raised the corner of the cloth and let out a gasp. Momentarily, he looked away, then swallowed hard and pulled back the covering further to take a closer look. The boy had a bluish, black mark on the side of his head and his hair was matted with dried blood, indicating he had not been fully immersed in the water. Abbot Hameline noticed the way his hands were clenched, and from the type of injuries on his body, it appeared he had been tortured. Brother Carbonel knelt by his side. Abbot Hameline turned the body over.

'He appears to have burns to his sides, back and buttocks.'

'There are also wounds on his hands and feet,' added Brother Carbonel, getting to his feet and walking around the body.

'And look at this,' Abbot Hameline lifted the boy's arm. 'He has thorns under his armpits.'

The elver men standing around the corpse took off their hats and made the sign of the cross.

'And around his head. Look here,' said Brother Carbonel pointing to the remnants of a few blackthorns embedded in his forehead. 'Looks like he's been crucified, Father Abbot. Like our own Jesus Christ.'

CHAPTER
TEN

The small synagogue Moses built at the back of his house stood empty. For a moment, he stood and breathed in the tranquil air. Soon enough it would be packed with friends from all corners of the land and beyond to join him for the *brit milah* of his son.

Although he had tried, he could not shake the sense of dread he had woken to. Visions of the stranger's soulless, black eyes and the harsh voice of the Irishman tormented him. He had to think of a way he could extricate himself from this business without making enemies of the king or either of these men. But who could he trust? The stranger's words or the vexatious Irishman's? He would have to tread carefully for he could not shrug off the feeling he was entering a spider's web of intrigue and deceit. He decided he would hear out the Irishman when, and if, he returned.

Moses' first job was to check whether the *ner tamid*, the eternal flame remained alight. The last thing he wanted was for the light to go out in the middle of the ceremony. He wasn't a particularly superstitious person, unlike his wife, but this must not happen on the day of his son's *brit*. Everyone would see it as a bad omen, and he didn't want his son to live under that dark cloud. Burning olive oil instead of candles helped keep the flame alight for longer. A flickering flame rose up from the bronze-coloured, spherical light holder, telling Moses the oil needed replenishing. A metal Star of David hung from it, reminding him of his eternal connection to Hashem. He grasped this and poured fresh oil into the vessel. The flame sputtered as it was given new life.

Although it was a bright morning, the small windows let in little light. There was much work to be done. He lit the rest of the candles which were made of beeswax as tallow candles were forbidden in the synagogue. Next, he set out the special chairs used for the ceremony, often referred to as thrones. One for the spirit of the prophet Elijah, known as the 'Angel of the Covenant', the other for the godfather. Moses had asked Rubin to carve them for his son Samuel's *brit* two years ago. Rubin was a skilled kosher butcher and there was nothing he couldn't do with a sharp knife. The word 'Elijah' was carved in Hebrew on one, and on the other, the word '*syndekos*', the Greek Byzantine word for godfather.

Moses placed a white linen cloth, embroidered by Douce, on each of the thrones. Her work was delicate and highly skilled and once again, Moses marvelled at the talents of his wife. By the thrones he placed a small table, upon which he set two metal vessels, one filled with sand and the other empty. He placed a pile of clean hand cloths next to the vessels and a small cup for the wine. When he finished, he sat for a while breathing in the smell of beeswax and enjoying the stillness until he became aware of sounds outside in the courtyard. His guests were already beginning to arrive. He must leave.

When he returned home, Moses stole a quiet moment to explain to his sleeping son how this was his most important day. He knew his son couldn't understand him, but it was part of a secret ritual he had adopted from his own father. Washed and robed in a sumptuous garment of soft linen, embroidered in silk by Douce, with an equally sumptuous hat on his small head in readiness for the ceremony, his son looked like a little *putto*, a cherub. Making sure no one was present, Moses whispered to him.

'Did you know, little one, that the ancients taught us what you are about to have done to you is proof of your acceptance of Adonai, it will enable you to enter the Promised Land, and it will prevent you from entering the fiery and wormy depths of hell. You will not remember any of it, but you will be changed forever. My son, I love you with all my heart.'

And then he kissed him on the forehead and left in case Douce caught him and told him he was a foolish man.

The baby, who up to this point had been referred to as 'the baby' was brought into the synagogue by Moses. He would be given his name at the *brit*. Held aloft on a sumptuous pillow of silk, he lay cushioned, his chubby legs kicking out into the air. The atmosphere in the synagogue was not one of sacred silence but one of joy, celebration and excitement.

Zev sat with his father on one side of the synagogue, his mother sat across from them behind Arlette who was next to Douce on the front pew. Zev was in a sullen mood after his awkward attempt at wooing Arlette. Perhaps his mother was right. She was beyond his reach. Nevertheless, he hung on to the hope that one day he would hold her in his arms. His heart ached at the sight of her. Dressed in a cream silk gown, embroidered at the neck and hem, she looked like a virginal bride on her wedding night. He could not take his eyes off her. It was not long, however, before he noticed Arlette's attention was elsewhere. She was staring straight through him. Zev swung round in the direction of her gaze. A young man, a little older than him, and dressed in very fine clothing was standing behind him. Next to him was an older statesman-like man. Zev nudged his father.

'Who's that over there? The two well-dressed men, standing at the back.'

Rubin twisted round to peer at the men. 'That's Aaron of Lincoln, the wealthiest Jew in England.'

'And the young man next to him?'

'That's his son.'

'Deudonne?' Zev asked.

'I think that's what they call him. Why are you so interested?'

Zev did not answer his father. He slumped back onto the seat dislodging the cushion he was sitting on. He didn't bother to retrieve it from the synagogue floor. So, this was his rival. The handsome, well-dressed son of the wealthiest Jew in England. No competition, he thought. He was joking, but his insides were churning like a butter maker and his very skin was turning green with jealousy.

The synagogue was packed as Moses walked towards the thrones with his head held high, as proud as any father could be on this day. As soon as the baby appeared, everyone stood to greet him.

Azriel stood by the godfather throne where young Josce was already seated and waiting for the baby to be brought to him.

'Blessed be he that cometh.'

Moses responded. 'In the name of Adonai.'

Moses approached Josce and lowered the baby, who was

still lying on the pillow, onto his godfather's lap. Josce gripped the pillow with the inexperience of someone who has not yet had children and as he did so, he adjusted the level of his knees so that the baby would not fall. Azriel began the part of the procedure known as the *milah* from where the ceremony took its Jewish name. He removed the baby's garments, exposing his chubby legs and his baby-sized penis. Azriel instructed Josce to hold his legs apart. Josce held the baby's legs in the same way he would hold a delicate piece of art. The baby wriggled.

'No, no. Much tighter than that. Like this.'

Azriel, experienced in the procedure, showed Josce the correct way. He then carried out the whole procedure with the skill and swiftness of a fine tailor grasping the prepuce between the thumb and index finger of his left hand, exerting sufficient traction to draw it from the glans and placed a *gomke*, a shield in position just before the glans. Then Moses handed him the *izmail*, the sharp knife he would use and with one deft sweep he excised the baby's foreskin. The baby let out a piercing shriek. Douce covered her ears. She had attended many *brits* in her time, but she could not bear to hear her own son scream. Next Azriel removed the baby's foreskin. It took several tugs before the tiny piece of flesh was free. The baby's screams continued. Moses glanced at Josce now and then to make sure he was not about to drop the baby on the floor.

'As he has entered into the covenant, so may he be introduced to the study of Torah, to the *chuppah*, and to good deeds,' said Azriel above the baby's cries.

The chuppah. The wedding canopy.

Arlette heard the words and glanced across at Deudonne. She felt her cheeks burn. Could she really be betrothed to the son of the wealthiest Jew in England? Her stomach fluttered at the thought of it. Nervous excitement coursed through her veins. She was finding it difficult to concentrate. She first set eyes on Deudonne when he walked into the synagogue with his father. They exuded wealth and power by the way they carried themselves and their clothing which, thought Arlette, must have cost a small fortune. She studied his features. He was tall, narrow-faced, fair-haired. There was a meanness about his thin lips, but Arlette immediately dismissed this observation. He would make an excellent husband. Douce was right, as always. He was a good match. Whereas Zev...

She turned away from Deudonne to look at Zev. Since his declaration of love Arlette felt awkward around him. Now he was staring at her with a look of accusation as if she had done something wrong. She gave him an insolent stare. What could be wrong about wanting the best for herself? If he was the good friend he said he was, then he should be glad she had secured a worthy match. Zev was jealous that was all. She decided the best approach was to avoid him. She wouldn't want Deudonne to see her talking to another man. Nothing should get in the way of what might turn out to be the most important day of her life. Her gaze returned to Deudonne. She was surprised to find he was smiling at her.

Azriel took a quick swig of wine and swished it around in his mouth before performing the *metzitzah*, the sucking of blood from the wound. After a few seconds he spat the wine mixed with the blood into the empty vessel on the table. He repeated this procedure several times. The baby's severed foreskin was placed in the vessel along with the blood and then Rabbi Solomon threw sand over it. Azriel went about dressing the wound. Crushed cumin seeds to ease the pain were first applied, then he wrapped the wound with clean cloths soaked in olive oil. Next it was time to name the baby.

'Creator of the universe. May it be Your will to regard and accept this *brit milah* as if I had brought this baby before Your glorious throne. And in Your abundant mercy, through Your holy angels, give a pure and holy heart to Abraham, the son of Moses, who was just now circumcised in honour of Your great Name. May his heart be wide open to comprehend Your holy Law, that he may learn and teach, keep and fulfil Your laws.'

The baby was no longer 'the baby' but now had a name. Abraham.

The congregation gathered around Abraham. Zev was oblivious to the sounds of Abraham's cries and the cheering, and the cooing, and the aahing of the guests. His thoughts and his gaze were focused on Arlette and how he was going to win her heart even though her smiling eyes remained fixed upon his love rival.

CHAPTER
ELEVEN

H arold lay for hours by the side of the river, covered only by the elver man's oilcloth. Abbot Hameline and Brother Carbonel had stayed with the body inviting the elver men to join them in prayer whilst Edmund was sent to fetch a bier on which to place the dead boy. As they were praying for Harold's soul, a stranger approached. A small troupe of people walked behind him. Abbot Hameline could not tell if they were with him or had followed him from the city. He took in the stranger's appearance; a man in his early forties with craggy, sun-worn features and dark, sunken eyes. His hair, black as pitch, hung to his shoulders in a straggly mess but his clothes and demeanour were those of a Norman knight. He spoke with a deep, authoritative voice.

'What's going on?' the stranger asked, interrupting their prayers.

Abbot Hameline, still kneeling, looked up at the stranger. He studied him with an enquiring look upon his face. 'We are praying for the soul of this dead boy.'

The stranger walked towards the body and lifted the

oilcloth, throwing it back to expose Harold's tortured, naked body. 'Looks more like a murdered boy than a dead boy.'

The stranger studied the corpse, turning the floppy cadaver once or twice, inspecting the injuries. 'Looks to me like this boy has been a victim of the Jews.' He surveyed the growing crowd, making sure he had their attention and that they had heard him.

'What do you mean?' asked Abbot Hameline, rising to his feet.

'Look at the wounds inflicted on this poor soul. He has all the signs of a ritual killing,' said the stranger, turning the body on its side and revealing a gaping wound. 'And look here.'

He pointed to the festering holes in Harold's feet and hands. Gasps and expressions of revulsion emitted from the growing multitude. Abbot Hameline and Brother Carbonel gave each other an anxious look. It was Brother Carbonel who had pointed out the similarity to the Lord's crucifixion. It had not taken long for news of the boy's death to reach the city. Many more people gathered around the body to satisfy their morbid curiosity. They were listening to the stranger's words with alarm.

'What makes you so sure the Jews are responsible for this?' enquired Abbot Hameline.

'I've seen this before.'

'Where?'

'In Norwich, more than twenty years ago.'

Abbot Hameline observed how those around him, good people he knew from church, seemed to be drawn to the stranger against their better nature.

'May I ask what happened there?'

'A twelve-year-old Christian boy called William was ritually slaughtered by the Jews of that city.'

'What made people think the Jews were responsible?' Abbot Hameline asked.

'He was murdered some days after Palm Sunday on the day of the Jew's Passover. It's well known that Jews kill Christian boys at Easter time to make a mockery of the passion of our Lord Jesus Christ, is it not?'

'I confess I have not heard of this before. You say it is in mockery of our Lord?' Abbot Hameline made the sign of the cross as he said this. Brother Carbonel did the same. A murmur of prayer rippled through the crowd.

'Indeed so,' said the stranger. As he said this, he raised his voice and addressed his words to the gathering crowd. 'And is it not also true that there is a large gathering of Jews in this city today? Here, no doubt, to enact this crime of wickedness.'

Shouts of 'aye' ripped through the crowd.

'This is indeed a serious accusation to make...' began Abbot Hameline.

The abbot had conducted business many times with Moses le Riche and found him to be a most congenial character. He could not believe that Moses or any of his fellow Jews could commit such a monstrous crime.

'If indeed it is true,' added Brother Carbonel.

'By the bones of the saints, what I say is God's own truth,' Brito bawled, his eyes widening in anger and taking on a demonic quality.

The small gathering had grown into a throng, pushing, and surging towards the front to gape at poor Harold's body. Abbot Hameline could hear people talking, their voices raised in fury, swayed by the convincing words of the stranger.

'He says the Jews done it.'

'The Jews have murdered the boy.'

'The Jews have murdered a Christian boy.'

The clamour of the ever-growing crowd infused with blind

hatred intensified. Abbot Hameline prayed for the arrival of the bier so that the body could be taken away. His prayers were answered when the young boy Edmund pushed through the crowd followed by two burly men. Abbot Hameline bent down to cover Harold's body, but the stranger stopped him.

'Wait,' he said. 'Does anyone know this boy?'

Abbot Hameline had not thought to ask. The boy's mother would want to know what had happened to her son.

'We ain't never 'sin 'im before, Father,' said John, looking from the stranger to the abbot.

'Whoever he is he deserves a Christian burial,' said the abbot. 'Come, Brother, help me lift his body.'

With great reverence Harold's body was lowered onto the bier, re-covered with the oilcloth, and held aloft by the two men who had come to help. Leading the procession was Abbot Hameline and Brother Carbonel. The stranger remained close by. An agitated rabble was now following the bier on its way back into the city. More people joined the slow procession as it made its way through the South Gate towards The Cross, turning left into West Gate Street. By the time they reached the precinct of the abbey, the rabble had become a multitude of angry, Jew-hating Christians.

Abbot Hameline led the procession into the nave of the abbey. The bier was carried aloft with the reverence of someone high-born and carefully set upon the altar. The nave quickly filled, the crowd pushing forward to encircle the body. Abbot Hameline thought it wise to say a prayer for the boy to calm the situation until he could decide what to do. Sheriff Pypard would need to be told. He would want to investigate this strange death and make efforts to find the boy's family before he could be laid to rest. He asked for the bells to be rung and for a shroud to be brought to cover the child's body. He turned to his angry congregation.

'Let us pray for the soul of this sinless boy,' he said, holding his hands up to silence his flock.

It had the desired effect. Those standing closest to the body hung their heads to pray. A ripple of silence spread across the nave.

'We beseech thee, oh merciful God, to take him unto thee, Grant him a perfect end, Thy holy presence, a blessed resurrection, a heavenly reward, and eternal life. Amen.'

'Amen,' they echoed back.

'You must leave us now so that we can prepare this boy's body for burial. We have much to do. You may return tomorrow for the funeral service.'

The crowd did not move. A few could be heard muttering insults about Jews and for a moment the abbot thought the strife might reignite. The stranger who appeared to have appointed himself the spokesman of the people stepped up to the altar and stood beside him.

'Let the abbot and his monks take care of the boy. We must show respect for this poor unfortunate soul.'

To Abbot Hameline's consternation, like a flock of obedient sheep, they obeyed the stranger's words and began filing out along the central aisle. The stranger made the sign of the cross before turning to leave.

'Just a moment...' Abbot Hameline said.

The stranger half turned.

'I didn't catch your name...'

The look on Brito's face was inscrutable. 'They call me Brito.'

Abbot Hameline would have liked to question him further, but Brito strode purposefully away and was lost amongst the crowd.

CHAPTER
TWELVE

E arlier, Moses had spread a curtain across his door to show there was an open invitation to his home and as a sign for his guests to join in the rejoicing. On the doorpost was nailed a decorative metal *mezuzah*, a symbol of protection to be found on every Jewish doorpost. He touched the sacred case with the tip of his fingers, kissed his fingertips then whispered, 'Hashem will protect your arrival.'

He made his way into the great hall where the s*eudat mitzvah*, the sacred meal of the *brit milah* was laid out on trestle tables borrowed from friends. When Moses surveyed the hall, he saw before him a bounteous feast. Douce and Arlette had carefully arranged platters of meat and bread and placed fresh flowers on each of the tables. The floor was strewn with fresh rushes mixed with aromatic herbs of rosemary, lavender, and dried rose petals. Beeswax candles flickered in their sconces giving off their evocative scent. On another table by the wall, Moses had set out several bottles of kosher wine sourced from kosher vineyards in France. He was more than satisfied, he was filled with joy.

His first task was to gather together a *minyan*, a quorum of ten adult men to complete his son's *brit*. This was always a challenging task as the community was so small. Today would be different though. He went in search of Aaron and his son Deudonne. He had spotted them in the synagogue but not yet had the chance to speak with them.

'Aaron, my good friend. *Shabbat shalom.* So good of you to come.'

'*Shabbat shalom.* It's my pleasure, Moses. I wouldn't miss your son's *brit*. How is business?'

Even though this was a celebration Aaron could not avoid talking business. Perhaps that's why he has done so well. Moses admired him greatly.

'Business continues to be good. I've done well these past few years thanks to our collaboration.'

'It's been a pleasure working with you,' Aaron said. Then, leaning in towards Moses, he added under his breath, 'A man needs someone he can trust.'

'So true, my friend, so true. I'm about to carry out the final part of my son's *brit*. I would be honoured if you and your son would make up the quorum.'

'With pleasure, my friend,' replied Aaron, smiling at Deudonne, and following Moses to the corner of the room where Abraham lay sleeping in his crib.

Rubin and Zev, Azriel and Seth, Rabbi Solomon and his son Baruch stood waiting for them along with Moses' father Samuel, Josce the godfather, his guest Jacob and finally Elias de Glocestre. Moses placed the sacred book on his son saying the words:

'May this one fulfil what is written in this...'

Abraham stirred in his crib. Moses took hold of his tiny hand and placed a pen between his grasping fingers, saying:

'...and may he grow up a ready scribe in the Law of the Lord.'

The men recited some scriptural verses and then it was over.

Baby Abraham had finally been admitted into the fold, his rite of passage fulfilled.

'Come, my friends. Let's have some wine and food and begin the rejoicing.'

Judea studied Mirabelle, who was sitting in the corner of the room with her husband, Elias. They spoke very little to each other. Elias was short and a little overweight, a man of few words. Their son Bonanfount, a year old, sat on Mirabelle's lap. She wore a cream-coloured veil of gossamer-fine fabric and around her long neck, a heavy gold necklace with matching earrings. She held her head erect as a queen would do, but she lacked the grace. Her nose was pinched with an ugly brown mole by the side of it, her demeanour haughty and unkind. She wore a mantle of blue linen which spooled across the floor, covering her feet and swamping her slight frame. She looked more like a royal queen than the wife of a Jewish moneylender. Judea could not help but think she had dressed in such a way to outdo the hostess Douce. Everyone knew Aaron of Lincoln would be attending Abraham's *brit* today and Judea had no doubt that Mirabelle was in her most lavish costume to attract his attention.

Mirabelle's daughter Belia, an energetic three-year-old, was running around the room with little Samuel, Douce's eldest son. Samuel was unsteady on his feet and though he tried his hardest, he could not keep up with his friend. Mirabelle watched her daughter as she teased Samuel, a smirk upon her face. She turned to Judea.

'Look at my daughter. See how well she runs and talks, she never stops talking,' she said.

Judea did not respond. Douce was her friend and her loyalty lay with her and little Samuel, not Mirabelle.

'She can say all kinds of words and is starting to put together whole sentences,' she continued.

Judea nodded to acknowledge the comment but still she would not be drawn.

'Not like that little *tembel*, Samuel,' she added.

'Mirabelle!' Judea exclaimed. 'How can you call such a sweet boy an idiot? He's just a little slow, that's all. He'll catch up, you'll see. Maybe one day he'll outdo Belia.'

Mirabelle snorted disdainfully. 'Even Bonanfount talks better than him. Moses may be the richest man in Gloucester, but I'll wager that son of his will never follow in his footsteps. He jumps at the slightest noise and grizzles far too much.'

Judea said nothing hoping to put an end to any more vicious comments from Mirabelle, but Mirabelle was determined to have the last word.

'And what do you know of children? You have none of your own.'

Judea knew this would happen. Mirabelle was maddening. She hardly had a good word to say about anyone. The adults could take her vicious tongue up to a point but to be mean to a little boy. She was wicked. Judea thought of her friend Douce who would do anything to avoid confrontation even if it meant putting up with Mirabelle's sour tongue, but to attack a defenceless child? Unforgivable. And this is what happened when you stood up to Mirabelle. She found something to counterattack you with. Judea had been married over a year and still no sign of a child. She hadn't given it much thought until Mirabelle's comment. Now she was wondering whether she should be pregnant by now.

'The fact that I have no children has nothing to do with it.

That was a mean thing to say, and you should be ashamed of yourself.'

'Why should she be ashamed?' Douce asked, appearing out of nowhere.

Judea said nothing. It was up to Mirabelle to get herself out of this.

'Judea is being oversensitive. It was nothing,' Mirabelle said, waving her arm in a dismissive gesture.

Judea wanted to shame Mirabelle by blurting out the truth, but she couldn't. It would hurt Douce far more than it would hurt Mirabelle.

Judea said, 'No really, it was nothing.' Then changing the subject said, 'Isn't this lovely and so many people came.'

Douce smiled back at her friend. Judea gave Mirabelle a sideways look. Bellassez joined them holding a cup of wine. Her face was flushed.

'The children are enjoying themselves. I just picked little Samuel off the floor...'

'Where?' said Douce, turning in a panic.

'He's perfectly all right.'

'Are you sure? Perhaps I should go and see.'

'He is perfectly well. Not a scratch. He's gone outside with the other children. They're playing *pelotte*.'

Pelotte was a ball game much like tennis that the children loved playing in the courtyard.

'Let me get you a cup of wine. It will help you relax. You look tired.'

Douce tried protesting but Bellassez was having none of it. She left to fetch the wine.

'You're not looking your best, Douce,' Mirabelle said.

'Don't listen to her,' Judea said. 'You look lovely.'

'Thank you, Judea, but Mirabelle's right. I've been feeling tired since the birth.'

'I've tried telling her to rest, but she won't listen to me,' said Arlette, who was close behind Douce.

'Who's not listening to you?'

It was Zev. Judea noticed Arlette frown when she saw him. Judea had heard the gossip. That something had passed between them at the Purim festival. The awkwardness that now descended on the group confirmed it as far as Judea was concerned.

'We were just saying how Douce does too much work and that she should rest,' Judea answered, sensing the awkwardness between Arlette and Zev.

'She doesn't listen to me either, Arlette.'

This time it was Moses. With him was Aaron and his son Deudonne. Judea had heard a lot about Aaron and his empire. She was finally going to meet the great man. She looked around for her husband Josce, so she could affect an introduction. It would be good for Josce's burgeoning business to meet him, but she could not see her husband anywhere.

'I thought I would find you here with the women, Zev,' Moses said, grinning.

Zev did not respond. Judea saw him staring at Arlette intently as though he was trying to catch her attention. Arlette was ignoring him. Her attention seemed to be upon Deudonne.

'You've met my wife, Douce.'

Aaron addressed Douce. 'A pleasure. Thank you for inviting me and my son.'

'You are more than welcome. In fact, it is I who am honoured. You've travelled a long way to be here.'

'I have business in Bristol to attend to. It made sense to combine the two. I've heard it said you shouldn't mix business with pleasure, but I have never lived by that rule.'

Mirabelle laughed. It sounded forced, designed to attract his attention. Aaron nevertheless smiled at her. Judea scowled at

Mirabelle. It was obvious she was trying to draw Aaron's attention away from Douce.

'And this is my niece, Arlette. My sister's daughter.'

Turning to Arlette, he said, 'I was saddened to hear about your parents, Arlette. But you're in safe hands. Moses is a good man.'

'Moses is like a father to me,' Arlette beamed. 'I'm very happy here.'

Her voice was soft but tinged with sadness.

Mirabelle, slighted at the lack of attention she was receiving, sat with her lips pursed and her arms crossed. She could not compete with the youth and beauty of Arlette. More people joined in the conversation.

Judea noticed that Deudonne was studying Arlette with some intensity. It gave her an idea. Deudonne seemed like a perfect match for Arlette. He was rich and had good prospects. He was also handsome but, she noted with pride, not as handsome as her husband. Maybe this was fate, *bashert*; destiny that he should come today with his father. Then she noticed Zev. He was glowering at Deudonne with the intensity of a dog guarding his food. The food, she imagined, was Arlette.

CHAPTER
THIRTEEN

Although this was his son's *brit milah*, Aaron could not avoid talking business with Moses.

'Something is brewing in Ireland,' Aaron began. 'I've just come from Bristol where a brute of a man called Dairmait is approaching anyone he can for money to raise an army to regain the lands he's lost. I'm told he's in league with Richard de Clare, the fellow they call Strongbow. Strongbow's a client of mine and his debt to me is considerable. He doesn't have the king's ear nor his blessing. My advice to you is, if he comes knocking at your door asking for a loan, refuse him. Give him any excuse. He has no assets and no prospect of obtaining any. You'll be out of pocket. Take my word.'

'I've already been warned about the Irishman. A stranger stopped me in the street and said the king would not look kindly on me if I lent him any money. Only yesterday the very man came to my door. And on Shabbat. I turned him away.'

Moses had not been strictly truthful. He had not turned the stranger away but told him to return. He already regretted his decision. He should have stood firm and told him to go elsewhere.

'As you know, Moses, the king is my best customer, but he can be a very difficult person to deal with. If the king is involved no good can come of this that's for sure.'

'Thank you for the warning, Aaron. Strongbow sounds like somebody I should avoid.'

They concluded their business and Moses re-joined his family. He noticed with some relief that his niece and Deudonne exchanged the kind of glances that might indicate a mutual interest. He wanted only the best for Arlette and in his opinion, there was no one better than the son of Aaron of Lincoln. Moses was keen to ask his friend whether Deudonne was looking for a wife or if he was already taken but it seemed indelicate. Their previous conversations concerned only business matters. They had never broached subjects of a personal nature. A union between Deudonne and Arlette would doubtless strengthen his business relationship with Aaron. He decided he must strike whilst the opportunity arose. He pulled his friend aside and spoke quietly to him.

'May I ask you a delicate question, my friend?'

'Of course, ask me anything, Moses.'

'Is your son looking for...' Moses paused, struggling to find the right words.

'Is my son looking for a wife?' Aaron said.

'Yes, that's exactly what I was trying to say but not making a very good job of it.'

'I've told him it's time to take a wife. Whenever I mention it, he just tells me he hasn't found the right person yet. Why do you ask?'

'Just that I noticed he was showing some interest in my niece Arlette. It's high time she took a husband, but she's shown no interest in anyone until today.'

'Until today? You think she may be interested in my son?'

'I think she might.'

'I'll speak to Deudonne. A match between our families would be good for them and good for business.'

Moses was excited about the prospect of marrying Arlette into such a prestigious family. His plan to bind the two families together was falling into place effortlessly. Moses went in search of wine to steady his nerves. Hardly had the cup touched his lips when Aaron returned, a beaming smile upon his face.

'It would seem my son is very interested in your niece and I'm happy to say he has my blessing in this matter. I'd be delighted to welcome Arlette into our family. She seems like a very nice girl.'

'This is excellent news. Shall we shake on it?'

'Why not,' Aaron said, offering his large hand to Moses.

The two men shook heartily.

Mirabelle watched from her seat wondering what business deal they were cooking up and why her husband wasn't involved. A snarl formed across her mean lips.

Douce was in the kitchen settling baby Abraham who had woken from his slumber when Judea walked in.

'Have you noticed the way Arlette is behaving in the company of Deudonne?'

'I can't say I have but to be honest, I've been busy with my guests and the children. Is something the matter?' Douce asked, shushing baby Abraham as he lay in his crib.

Douce was playing ignorant. She knew only too well the plan her husband had for Arlette, but had not shared that with anyone, not even her good friend Bella.

'I think she likes him and he her.'

'Really? I hadn't noticed but I'll look more closely now you've said.'

'I've seen that look pass between them.'

'What look?'

'You know, you know, that look. Wasn't it like that for you and Moses?'

'Oh,' said Douce, her eyes twinkling. 'I know that look. It does sound like she may have a liking for him.'

'I must say, Douce, you are taking this very calmly. Do you know something I don't?'

Douce did not want to seem scheming to her friend and so continued to act as if she had no idea marriage plans were afoot.

'No. I just haven't given it much thought today. It's been a busy time.'

'Don't you think you should speak to Arlette?'

'I will. Later when it's quiet.'

'But if you don't say something while they are here Arlette might miss out and I know she hasn't shown a speck of interest in any of the young men here in Gloucester. Let's face it, who is left when you take out the married ones.'

Judea pulled a face and Douce burst out laughing. Baby Abraham, sensing the mood, let out a gurgling sound. Douce leant down and rubbed his stomach.

'Will you watch him while I speak with Moses?'

'Of course. Come straight back. I want to know if we will be celebrating a wedding,' she said, lifting baby Abraham from the crib and speaking to him in baby tones. 'Don't we, Abraham? We want a wedding, yes we do.'

'We haven't got as far as betrothal yet. Betrothal before marriage. That's usually how it happens,' Douce said before leaving.

'I know you, Douce. If it is what Arlette wants, you'll make sure it happens.'

Douce went in search of Moses. She found him talking to his

father. She called out his name as she approached, her tone impatient.

'Are you all right, *chérie*?' he asked, his brow furrowed with concern.

'Yes. I'm fine. It's Arlette.'

'Is she all right?'

'Yes, everything's fine. I've been talking to Judea. She thinks Deudonne may be interested in Arlette, which bodes well for our plans to bring our families together.'

Douce waited for Moses' reaction. Moses smiled at his wife as he tucked a stray wisp of her hair behind her ear.

'*Chérie*, I could have told you that an hour ago.'

'What?' cried Douce. 'Why didn't you say?'

'I did.'

'No, you didn't,' Douce replied, reproaching him.

'Not to you. To Aaron.'

'You've spoken to Aaron already?' Douce asked, her eyes widening with every word.

'Yes. I thought we agreed that we would.'

'I know, but I wanted to be sure it's the right thing for Arlette. I wanted her to at least see him before we made any approaches. I just thought you could have at least spoken with me before you approached Aaron.'

'I don't understand. I thought you wanted me to speak to him?'

Douce wanted to tell Moses of her reservations for the match, but when she looked into his eyes and saw how pleased he was she thought perhaps she had been wrong and it was just superstitious foolishness on her part.

'You're right,' she said, pushing her feelings aside. 'Well, what did he say?'

'He said he would approve of such a marriage.'

'That sounds very businesslike.'

'All right. He said he would very much like his son to marry Arlette. *Serre de main*. We shook on it.'

'Oh. It's official then.'

'Well not quite. He must go back to Bristol to complete some business, but he said he'll call back here before going home to Lincoln to draw up the marriage contract. It's not official until the *ketubbah* has been signed. You should know that,' he said, touching her cheek in an affectionate gesture. 'You know, we men may take a long time to make a decision but once we do, we act upon it.'

Douce laughed. Moses was a terrible procrastinator when it came to personal matters but an entirely different beast when it came to business, and it seemed he was viewing this alliance with the acumen of a businessman.

'We must approach this union with calm. We're going to be merging our family with the wealthiest, most well-connected man in the land. Next to the king, of course.'

Douce was amazed at how much her husband could accomplish when he set his mind to it.

'I suppose you've spoken to Arlette already,' she said, a hint of petulance creeping into her voice.

'I thought I would leave that to you, *chérie*.'

'I don't know whether to scold you or congratulate you.'

'You can congratulate me later when it's all arranged,' Moses said.

Douce hurried back to Judea.

'You were right,' she said. 'Moses has already spoken with Aaron, and they have agreed to the betrothal.'

'Really,' squealed Judea. 'What does Arlette say?'

'She doesn't know yet. I'm going to be the one to give her the news. Will you look after Abraham for a few more minutes while I speak to her?'

'Can I come with you?'

'I'd rather speak to her alone if that's all right.'

Judea lowered her gaze in disappointment.

'I understand,' she said, her voice quiet. 'I'll mind the baby.'

Douce found Arlette in the kitchen, emptying the remains of food into a pail.

'Leave that, Arlette. We'll do it together later when everyone's gone. I have something I want to tell you,' Douce announced.

'Are you sure? I don't mind...'

'I'm sure. Let's go into the courtyard,' Douce suggested, taking Arlette's arm.

The women walked into the courtyard where the children were still playing pelotte. They sat down on a bench under trailing twines of bindweed. Douce heard it was called wedlock by some as the white flowers were often used in wedding bouquets because of the ease with which they could be twisted into a posy. She smiled as she thought how appropriate it was to be sitting under the spring shoots of such a plant. It was a good omen.

'You said you had something you wanted to tell me,' Arlette said.

'I do. But don't look so worried. It's good news.'

Douce stared into Arlette's lapis-coloured eyes.

'Do you like Deudonne?'

The colour rose to Arlette's cheeks. 'Is it that obvious?'

'Judea caught you stealing glances at him.'

'I've done nothing wrong.'

A mottled pink rash appeared at her neck. Douce took hold of Arlette's hand.

'Of course not. No one is saying you have. We're pleased for you. So much so, Moses has spoken to Deudonne's father.'

Arlette removed her hand. 'And said what?'

'Calm down, Arlette. You're going to be married.'

'Married,' Arlette exclaimed.

'Don't you want to get married?' Douce asked.

'Yes, of course I do.'

'And you like Deudonne?'

'Well, yes but...'

'And he likes you...'

'How do you know he does?'

'Judea has been watching you both and says Deudonne likes you.'

The mottled rash on Arlette's neck spread. She smiled, a coy smile. 'He is very handsome,' she confessed.

'And he comes from a very wealthy family. Aaron of Lincoln is the richest Jew in all of England, perhaps France too. Some say he's richer than the king.'

'Richer than the king,' Arlette repeated in dreamy tones.

'So, it's settled. You are betrothed.'

'How long before I am to marry?'

'That hasn't been decided yet. How do you feel? Are you happy?'

'I think so. It's all so sudden,' Arlette said, somewhat bewildered.

'My mother used to say, "when you meet a man you like, and he has good prospects, you need to grab him with both hands before another woman sets her sights on him,"' Douce said, hugging her niece-in-law. 'I've so enjoyed having you in my home, Arlette. You have been such a help to me and become like my own daughter.'

'You made me so welcome after what happened to my parents. I cannot begin to thank you and Moses...'

'It was our duty as well as our pleasure, Arlette. You are the daughter of Moses' sister. You are family and you always will be.'

'When I'm married will I have to move away – away from you and Moses?'

'I expect so. Deudonne will be expected to follow his father in the business, and he'll need to be in Lincoln and London to do that.'

Douce glanced up at the sky. It was approaching sundown. The bells of the abbey were ringing. It was a timely reminder that she was a Jew living in a Christian country. It was a mournful toll, the rhythm of death. *Mort.*

'Someone important must have died for the abbey bells to be ringing at this hour,' she said, standing. 'We better go back inside. It's almost the end of Shabbat. We'll need to clear the table.'

The two women walked back into the house arm in arm. Judea was waiting for them inside. As soon as she saw them, she ran towards Arlette.

'Well?'

'It's done,' said Douce.

Judea threw her arm around Arlette. 'I'm so happy for you. He is such a good catch. It's as I said. *Bashert.* Fate.'

The trestle tables had been cleared of food and replaced by a single cup of wine in readiness for *havdalah,* the ritual signifying the end of Shabbat. A small *b'samim* box containing the spices cloves, cinnamon and bay leaf and the special twisted candle used for *havdalah* to mark the end of Shabbat lay on the trestle.

Moses and his guests stood around the table. The day had

been a complete success with much rejoicing and plenty of excellent kosher food. As always Moses' wife Douce had made him proud. She had produced a banquet fit for the King of Israel and now, as Moses stood in front of family and friends, his heart felt as though it would burst with a mixture of emotion, love, friendship, pride, and gratitude. It was time to thank his guests. He swallowed hard to dispel the lump in the back of his throat.

'I would like to thank everyone for attending my son's *brit milah*. Your presence here has made today such a special one for me and my family. I hope you have all enjoyed the food and the company. I know I have. *Shabbat shalom*.'

Moses' guests returned the greeting.

He picked up the cup of wine and began reciting the first blessing of *havdalah*.

"*Blessed are you, Lord, our God, sovereign of the universe, Who creates the fruit of the vine.*"

He then opened the exquisitely decorated spice box and gave the second blessing.

It was now time to light the entwined, multi-wicked *havdalah* candle and recite the second blessing. After this, Moses held his hands up to the flame, curving his fingers, so he could see their shadow on his palms. The final blessing was said over wine.

Moses picked up the cup of wine and drank it, using the last few drops to extinguish the flame from the candle.

'*Havdalah* signifies the end of *S*habbat and, sadly for us it also signifies the end of today's celebration. I am blessed to have such good friends and a wonderful family. *Shabbat shalom*.'

As if on cue, baby Abraham let out a loud, cooing sound. A cheer went up and everyone burst out laughing.

'*Shabbat shalom*.'

Arlette decided to seek out Deudonne who was in the great hall, not to speak to him, she was too shy to do that, just to observe him. As she walked from the kitchen towards the entrance Zev appeared and blocked her way.

'Is it true?'

Arlette tried to squeeze past him to avoid answering his question, but he sidestepped her. She hadn't spoken to him since Purim, after his drunken declaration of love.

'Is it true?' he asked again.

'Yes, it's true,' she said.

There was no point in trying to make out she didn't know what he was talking about. Everyone knew. The hurt Zev was feeling at the news of her betrothal was etched upon his face. He said nothing but stared at her like a wounded animal. Arlette felt a pang of guilt as if she had betrayed their friendship. Maybe she should have sought him out and broken the news to him, but she was so wrapped up in her own happiness and excitement she had not given a thought to how Zev would be feeling. The guilt turned to embarrassment as she became aware of the eyes of others upon them. And then she panicked. What if Deudonne was watching them? Arlette pushed past him. This time Zev gave no resistance.

When she glanced back, he was nowhere to be seen.

Arlette continued into the great hall and spotting Deudonne she positioned herself in the room, so she could stand nearer to him. She wanted to hear his voice. You could tell a lot about a person from their voice. It seemed incredible that she could be marrying a man without having first heard how his voice sounded. She hoped to speak with him before the day was out. As the wedding had been agreed by both sides, it wouldn't be considered too forward. Hopefully, he was thinking the same and would seek her out. She inched nearer, straining to hear.

'What are you doing?'

Arlette jumped. 'Zev, what are you doing creeping up on me?'

Arlette composed herself. She did not want a scene in front of Deudonne.

'I wasn't creeping, but it looked very much like that's what you were doing.'

'Sshh, he'll hear you.'

Zev pulled a face like a street jester. 'Oh him. Your betrothed,' he said with exaggerated sarcasm.

'Have you been drinking again, Zev? You know it doesn't agree with you. Makes you act crazy. Like now.'

'I haven't been drinking. Just observing.'

'People are beginning to look. Just go away.'

'No, I want a better look at your intended.'

Zev moved toward Deudonne and his father, Aaron.

'Please don't do this. If you have feelings for me, you wouldn't do this. Please.' Her voice cracked with emotion.

Zev's expression quickly changed from one of cruel taunter to one of shamed persecutor. She could tell her distress troubled him. He rubbed at his temples and simply said, 'I'm sorry, Arlette. I don't know what I was thinking.'

He whipped around and pushed his way through the guests, leaving Arlette alone. Her plan to speak to Deudonne was thwarted and Zev had embarrassed her again. She shot a quick look at Deudonne. He seemed oblivious to her distress, deep in conversation with his father. Arlette slipped away.

Zev sat on the bench in the courtyard watching the children play, a cup of wine in his hand. His father often used the phrase 'have a drink to drown your sorrows'. He finally understood what he meant. He wanted to drink until he could numb the pain. His heart ached. He had lost the one thing that meant the world to him. Taken away by another man. One he could never hope to compete with. It was over. His dreams. His future. He took another drink of the robust red wine.

'I thought I might find you here,' a voice said.

It was Chera. She looked happy. He supposed everyone knew about Arlette's betrothal to Deudonne by now. Had she come to gloat at his misfortune? Chera sat down next to Zev.

'How are you feeling?'

'Not great,' Zev replied, looking down at the ground.

'I heard about Arlette. I know how much you like her.'

'Is it that obvious?'

'I think everyone knows, especially after Purim.'

'Oh that,' said Zev, kicking at the ground with the heel of his boot and remembering his ineptitude. He took another slug of his wine.

'That won't help,' Chera said, pointing at the cup.

'I don't really care right now.'

'I came to tell you...' She swung round on the bench, her knee touching his, and took his hand. 'I just wanted you to know I care about you.'

'I know,' said Zev, pulling his hand away, 'but that doesn't help right now.'

Zev kept his gaze to the ground and did not see the hurt in Chera's sad face. She stood up.

'Maybe you'll feel better in the morning.'

'I doubt it.'

Chera looked down at Zev but still he did not look up. As she walked away, she turned and said: 'You know, sometimes you can't see what's right in front of you.'

FOURTEEN

The disgruntled crowd left the abbey and followed Brito into the nearby Lich Inn. It was not long before he had an audience of angry but pliable revellers. He expertly whipped them into a frenzy of hatred against the Jews, their malevolence building with each tankard of ale. Those listening appeared to believe every word he said.

'How do you know so much about this then?' one of them asked Brito.

'I once knew a Jew who converted to Christianity. He told me it was written in the ancient writings that Jews could neither obtain their freedom, nor could they ever return to their fatherland without the shedding of human blood. Hence it was laid down every year Jews must sacrifice a Christian in scorn and contempt of Christ, so that they could avenge their sufferings on Him.'

A man at the bar emptied his tankard and slammed it down. 'Well, they done that all right, poor little bugger.'

Brito continued his lecture. 'It was said that because of Christ's death they were shut out from their own country and were in exile as slaves in a foreign land.'

'They're hardly bloody slaves, wandering around in their fancy clothes and living in their big stone fortresses. They think themselves royal,' said another reveller.

'Well they ain't governed by our laws. The laws of this country. They got their own bloody laws. No one can touch 'em.'

'So,' another slurred, 'you're saying every year the Jews kill a Christian?'

'Not in the same place, but in some part of the world a Christian boy will be killed every year. They're as crafty in their intent as they are ingenious in their tortures,' Brito told them, swigging his ale. 'Once they've killed the Christian boy, they use his blood in their Passover bread.'

'And what's this Passover you speak of?'

'It's some Jewish ritual to remind them of their exodus from Egypt.'

'Where's Egypt?' someone piped up.

'Nowhere near 'ere,' another said and the whole tavern erupted into raucous laughter.

'What's an exodus?' a young man, worse for wear, asked.

'Christ knows but it sounds bloody painful.'

The revellers roared with laughter again, this time beating their tankards on the tabletops with the rhythm of a warring army.

'You seem very knowledgeable about these matters. You sure you're not one of 'em?' said a man, nursing his tankard on his bloated stomach.

Brito had no need to counter this argument. His supporters did it for him, turning their anger on the dissenter.

'Shut your bloody mouth or we'll shut it for you.'

The man drank up and left.

'But what evidence is there of this in the scriptures?' asked another.

'Did not the Roman governor, Pontius Pilate, wash his hands and say, "I am innocent of this man's blood. It is your concern," and did not the crowd shout back, "his blood be on us and our children,"' Brito said.

'I did hear tell there are Jews from all over England in Gloucester today. Maybe what this fellow is saying is true.'

'Maybe they've come 'ere for the very purpose of sacrificing that young Christian boy.'

The crowd erupted into a drink-fuelled tirade against the assembly of Jews in their city.

'They've taken the blood of the boy for their Passover bread.'

'They're mocking Christ.'

'No Christian child is safe in the hands of these Jews.'

'Shouldn't we leave matters to the abbot and the sheriff?' another asked, a voice of reason amongst the hatemongers.

'What's the abbot gonna do? Tell 'em to be good and pray for forgiveness?'

'That won't work. It's as 'e says, they ain't bound by our laws.'

'That's the trouble. A law unto themselves.'

'There ain't a man 'ere who doesn't owe money to one of 'em.'

'Aye, including the abbot!'

'And the sheriff!'

The hatemongers let out a roar of laughter, a brief respite from the wrathful bile spewing from their drunken mouths. As the night wore on, more revellers joined the mob, and the insults and stories became more fantastical. Then the door of the tavern flew open, and a young boy ran in.

'Father says to tell you they're all still here. Down Jewry Street,' he yelled above the noise.

93

'Give that boy a drink,' someone shouted to the landlord. 'He deserves it.'

The boy was manhandled to the front of the bar. Brito lifted him onto the wooden counter and thrust a tankard of beer into the young boy's hand. He drank it down in one go before anyone could take it from him.

'Father says if you go down there now, you'll catch 'em all.'

'What are we waiting for?' one of them yelled.

A roar went up and the crazed rabble emptied out of the tavern into the moonless street. As they made their way towards the synagogue, lit only by the faint flicker of candlelight from within the houses that lined their way, more people joined the throng curious to see what all the commotion was about. Firebrands were lit, and bludgeoning sticks were rattled with gusto. By the time they reached the front of Moses' house there were a hundred or more men, women and children, a fearsome army out of control. Their voices grew louder, angrier, flayed through with violence. Once outside the impressive stone fortress, the mob stopped, and for a moment, seemed unsure what to do. Brito came forward to stoke the hiatus.

'Do we want justice for the murder of this Christian boy?'

'Aye,' the mob roared, surging onwards with renewed courage.

CHAPTER

FIFTEEN

Arlette occupied a bedroom on the first floor at the front of the house. She had retired early after the celebrations were over but could not sleep. The news of her betrothal to Deudonne was still flitting around in her excited mind. How had she started the day a single woman and ended it betrothed to a virtual stranger? She turned over on her side. Deudonne was handsome. She had spotted him almost immediately in the synagogue. He had delicate features for a man and his lips were a little too thin, but he was well-dressed and, she imagined, although she had only heard his voice from a distance, well-spoken. Like a king. Once she knew who he was she hadn't been able to take her eyes off him, but she made sure she looked away before he caught her watching him. Then when she saw him at the meal, she had the strangest feeling in her stomach, like a wake of butterflies fluttering around. How embarrassing. She worried that Deudonne or her uncle or anyone else had noticed her reaction, but they hadn't. Thank the Lord.

At first, she couldn't tell whether Deudonne liked her. He gave nothing away. But she kept catching him looking at her and she thought he must like her. She hadn't been able to stop herself from blushing and before the day was out, she was being questioned by Douce outside in the courtyard and with such suddenness found herself betrothed.

Her happiness was marred by Zev's behaviour. She had never seen that side of his character. To her he was always Zev the joker, Zev the fool, Zev the smiler. Today he was like a snarling dog towards Deudonne.

Erusin. Betrothal.

She whispered the word into her pillow as if by speaking it somehow it would become more real.

Fiancée.

It still seemed unreal. Every time she recalled his face or the sound of his voice, the butterflies returned to her stomach. Her body was weary, but her mind would not calm. She twisted onto her other side. Wrapping her arms around herself she imagined what it would be like to lay beside him and feel the warmth of his body next to hers.

Through her window she heard distant noises in the street. It sounded as if it was coming from The Cross. Arlette jumped out of bed and peered through the window opening. A crowd of people bearing firebrands and wielding sticks were making their way along Jewry Street. They stopped directly beneath her window. One of them looked up and spotted her. She stepped back from the opening and hid by the side of it, straining to hear what was being said. 'There's one of 'em,' she heard a man shout above the jeering crowd. Arlette's elation at her betrothal vanished. Memories of the French mob and the night her whole world changed returned. That night she had just finished eating the Passover meal with her mother and father. They were planning to visit family in the South of France. Arlette was feeling excited, happy about the forthcoming journey. Then the mob arrived, and she had never felt so fearful in all her life.

Visions of her mother and father's brutalised bodies lying in the street where they had been dragged flooded back. The horror of it chilling her blood. She was saved by a Christian neighbour who hid her in the basement of his house and cared for her until her uncle arrived to bring her to England where she thought she would be safe.

Her legs trembled involuntarily, and she had a sudden urge to relieve herself. She knew she should raise the alarm, but she could not move. The terror of that night in Rouen, as fresh as the night itself, rendered her inert and without speech.

CHAPTER
SIXTEEN

Prior Clement had spent most of the day in prayer. Since the disappearance of the novice Harold, he had become morose. The piercing wit for which he was known had deserted him and he was now living a pious but joyless life. On the day of Harold's disappearance, he waited till nightfall, certain his protégé would return. He even thought of the words he would say to him; words strong enough to reprimand him but not harsh enough to upset the boy. The arrival of Harold as a baby in the priory was testing for a man who had taken an oath of celibacy and would never marry and have children of his own. He never imagined he would be obliged to look after such a tiny ward. The first few months were the hardest. The boy cried incessantly. Missing his mother was the obvious cause but even though Harold was not his son, the cry pierced Clement's heart. By the time the boy was three years of age they were inseparable. The feelings he had for Harold were the closest he would ever experience to a father's love for his son. By the second day, Prior Clement finally admitted the boy's disappearance was more than a youthful misdemeanour and something had happened to him. As the weeks went by, he knew in his aching heart it was something bad.

The baby had been left in his care nine years ago with the strictest of instructions. No one must know. He had given his holy oath of silence. But if the boy were dead...

He agonised over whether he should inform the boy's mother of his disappearance. His mother was Margaret de Bohun, the wealthy and generous benefactress of the priory. She was also Prior Clement's niece. Her father was Milo of Gloucester, former Lord High Constable of England and Sheriff of Gloucestershire, founder of the priory and also Clement's brother. Clement suspected she used her position to visit the priory, so she could stay close to her son without anyone ever knowing of their connection. He had decided to warn her not to visit the priory to see her son with falsehoods about the spread of disease amongst the monks, hoping Harold would return before he had cause to tell her he was missing. Perhaps she suspected something was wrong or maybe it was just coincidence, but she had sent word she would arrive the very next day.

To keep his mind active and to counter the grief he felt at Harold's absence Prior Clement threw himself into his theological writings. He was working in the solitude of the scriptorium by candlelight on his latest manuscript, a commentary on the gospels titled the Series Collecta when the silence was shattered by Sub Prior Roger who flew into the room, flustered and out of breath.

'Forgive me, prior. They have found Harold.'

Prior Clement leapt from his stool, knocking over the ink pot as he did so. The dark liquid pooled across a roll of parchment. Clement snatched it away, shaking it to dispel the ink.

'Where is he? Take me to him now.'

His joy at hearing Harold had been found was short-lived. The look on Roger's face told him the news was not what he wanted to hear.

'What's wrong? What has happened to Harold?'

'He's dead, prior. They found his body by the river this morning.'

Prior Clement slumped back on his stool almost falling off until Sub Prior Roger steadied him. As long as Harold was missing, he held on to the hope that one day he would walk back into the priory, maybe as a young man, but the news of his death crushed this hope.

'How do you know it's Harold's body? Has he been identified?' he asked, a flicker of hope remaining.

'No, not exactly. But a boy's body has been found and no one has claimed him. I fear it is Harold.'

'But it could be the body of any boy. Where is it now?'

He used the term 'it' not wanting to acknowledge the body could be Harold.

'I'll take you to him now. He was found by some elver men, and they called for Abbot Hameline. He's in the abbey.'

Prior Clement had little to do with the abbey or Abbot Hameline for that matter. They were of different orders. His was an Augustinian order, the abbey, Benedictine. What they did share was the devotion to daily prayer and a Christian conscience. Prior Clement wasted no time. He went straight to his private lodgings where he found his thick woollen cloak, which he threw over his surplice to guard against the chilly night.

'Come with me, Brother Roger. It's important we identify the body before it's buried in the ground.'

The two monks left by West Gate House, Prior Clement striding ahead with purpose and the shorter-legged sub prior almost breaking into a run to keep up with him. When Prior

Clement entered the abbey some minutes later, the first thing he noticed was the atmosphere. Tall night candles were alight along the length of the nave and their flickering shadows danced upon the cream stone pillars. Many more candles burned upon the altar where spirals of incense smoke swirled upwards towards the ceiling. The dulcet tones of the monks' voices, singing a familiar dirge could be heard, but the monks themselves were nowhere to be seen. There was no sign of a body and Prior Clement worried for a moment they were too late, and the boy had already been consigned to the ground.

'Prior Clement,' a voice said. 'How can I help you?'

It was Abbot Hameline dressed in an alb of white linen tied at the waist by a silk corded cincture. He came from the direction of the monks' private chapel. Upon his vestment were the customary ornamental squares of gold cloth, five in all, signifying the five wounds of Christ. Prior Clement was immediately curious as to why the abbot should be wearing such a vestment when there was no liturgy to be observed.

'I've come to see the body of the boy. I fear he is one of us.'

Abbot Hameline's welcoming smile disappeared.

'Why do you say that, Prior Clement?'

'One of our novices went missing on Ash Wednesday and I have reason to believe this boy's body may be his. May I see him?' Prior Clement asked, stepping toward the entrance of the monks' chapel.

Abbot Hameline remained where he was, blocking the way.

'I doubt this could be one of your novices if he went missing so long ago. This boy has been dead only a day or so.'

'Still,' said Prior Clement, edging his way past the abbot. 'If I could be shown the body so I can satisfy myself it is not one of ours.'

'Has anyone claimed his body yet?' asked Sub Prior Roger.

'No one has come forward.'

'Then may we see him?'

Abbot Hameline relented. 'Very well,' he said, stepping aside to let them pass. 'We have prepared him for burial and are holding a vigil in our private chapel. You may view the boy there.'

The small private chapel was packed with monks. Brother Carbonel was swinging a small thurible of incense and reciting a prayer. A row of monks chanted a discordant dirge in whispered tones. On a raised altar of stone lay a small body covered by a linen shroud and surrounded by candles. Prior Clement approached in slow measured steps. He was acutely aware that the fragment of hope he had clung to these past weeks could be crushed by the mere lifting of this piece of cloth. He stood looking at the shape beneath the shroud, willing and praying to God it was not Harold. He lifted the shroud just enough to make out the face, then gasped and fell to his knees. The last vestige of hope gone forever.

'Oh God,' he murmured, his head bowed, his hands clasped in prayer.

'It is God who gives and, therefore, can take away.'

Sub Prior Roger came to his side and placed a reassuring hand on Prior Clement's shoulder. Prior Clement stiffened, then his body juddered with silent sobbing as he wept for the son God, in his wisdom, had taken from him. Clement gathered his composure, got to his feet and addressed the abbot.

'I'll come back tomorrow morning to translate his body to the priory for burial. I am thankful to you for taking such care of him until now.'

'This body will not be leaving the abbey.'

'That is insane. Why not? He's like a son to me.'

'His body is to be buried in the abbey, I'm sorry.'

Prior Clement had not foreseen any dispute as to who

would 'own' Harold's body. He assumed, on claiming the boy, he would be returned to him for burial at the priory.

'I don't understand why?' said Clement, his tone harsher now as his grief turned to anger.

'This boy was found with signs of ritual crucifixion upon his body. He has suffered the death of a martyr. I have sent word of this to the bishop, and he will agree with me that the boy must be given the funeral of a saint here in the abbey.'

Abbot Hameline pulled back the shroud exposing Harold's body so that Clement could take a closer look. Although Harold's body had been washed and prepared for burial, the signs of torture were still visible. The burns, the hollow eye sockets where wax was poured and the wounds to his head and sides, all resembling Christ's crucifixion. Prior Clement let out an anguished gasp.

'Who has committed this evil act?' he demanded.

'They're saying the Jews killed him in mockery of our Christ. When we carried his body here an angry mob gathered. I sent them away, but they'll return tomorrow to witness a burial befitting that of a saint. I warn you if it doesn't go ahead as planned, we'll have another riot on our hands.'

Prior Clement was in no mood to argue with the abbot. His thoughts returned to the boy's mother. Harold's death and the nature of it and the fact it would now be public knowledge had changed matters. She must be told. He couldn't take the chance she would find out about her son's horrific death before he had time to break the terrible news to her.

CHAPTER
SEVENTEEN

oses and Douce slept at the back of the house overlooking the courtyard where it was quiet and free from the noise of late-night revellers spilling out of the city's taverns. But tonight, Moses was sleeping in the loft room at the top of the house underneath the rafters. This was because his wife was considered *niddah*, unclean after the birth of their child, and according to Halakhic law they were not permitted to sleep in the same bed until she became clean again by immersing herself fully in the ritual bath. He had one more night alone.

Moses was restless. He missed sleeping with his wife. He liked nothing better than to wrap his arms around her, nuzzle his face into the back of her neck and fall asleep next to her lissom body. He lay on his back thinking of Douce sleeping below him and how proud he was of her and their children. The *brit* had been such a success. Not only had he fulfilled his son's covenant with Hashem, but he had also instigated a betrothal between his niece and his business partner's son. With any luck, he would have a good night's rest ready for the day's work ahead. The last two days had taken its toll on him. The Irishman still preyed on his mind but seemed less of a sceptre now he had resolved to pass him on to the unsuspecting Elias and that harridan of a wife. It was not long before the house was quiet, and everyone was asleep. Lying there, warm and drowsy, he drifted off to sleep.

The smell of smoke awoke him. At first, he thought it was coming from the fire he had lit earlier but as he lay half asleep the smell intensified. He sat up with a jolt and swung his legs over the side and leapt out of bed to investigate. He put a warm cloak over his shoulders and crept downstairs to Douce's bedroom. He lifted the cord of the metal latch. The metal made a rasping sound. Douce stirred.

'Go back to sleep, *chérie*,' he called to her.

She turned and pulled the bedcovers over her shoulder. Moses closed the door as quietly as he could and carried on downstairs. By the time he reached the bottom of the stairs, a strong smell of burning wood hit him. It was then he heard the voices. They were coming from the door at the front of the house. He listened intently. The voices were more distinct now, loud and angry. He noticed smoke swirling underneath the door. Someone had set fire to it. Moses ran back upstairs.

'Wake up, Douce,' he shouted. 'There are people outside and smoke is coming under the door. Quickly, get dressed and get Abraham.'

Douce shot out of bed and went straight to Abraham. She grabbed him from his crib and held him close.

'Where's the smoke coming from, Moses?' she asked, now fully awake and alert.

Baby Abraham started to cry, unhappy at being woken.

'From the door at the front of the house. Someone's trying to burn it down.'

'What are we going to do?' Douce shrieked.

Baby Abraham, sensing his mother's fear, howled at the top of his tiny lungs.

'Get some clothes on and wait here for me,' Moses said. 'I need to wake the others.'

Moses ran into the next room where his elderly father lay asleep next to his grandson, undisturbed by the unfurling drama.

'Father, wake up. Get dressed. Someone's set fire to the front door.'

Samuel raised his head from the bed. 'What's that you say?'

'I don't have time to explain. Get up and dress little Samuel. Go into my bedroom and wait. I'm going to wake our guests and fetch Arlette.'

Moses fled from the room and onto the landing. Before he reached his guests' room the door opened, and Jacob stood there in his nightclothes.

'What's going on, Moses? I can hear voices outside and there's a strong smell of smoke.'

'Get dressed. I think someone has set fire to the door.'

From inside the room came a scream. It was Jacob's wife. She came to the door wrapped in a blanket.

'We'll be murdered in our beds,' she wailed.

'Please, Hannah. Be quiet, you'll frighten the children.'

Jacob's four children appeared at the door, pushing each other to see what was happening. David and Ysaac who were five and eight, and Hanna and Sarra who were ten-year-old twins.

'They'll kill us all.'

'Be quiet, Hannah, do as Moses says,' Jacob shouted at his wife, herding them back into the bedroom as if they were errant sheep. Moses ran up the narrow stairs to Arlette's bedroom. He found her standing by the window.

'Arlette, you must get dressed. There are people downstairs who mean to harm us.'

Arlette did not reply. Her face was grey, and she had the look of cornered prey about her.

'What's the matter, Arlette?'

Arlette did not seem to recognise him. She stood with her back to the wall and didn't move.

'Arlette! What's the matter?' he shouted again.

Still Arlette did not speak or move. She stared past her uncle, her eyes cold and lifeless. Moses had no time to find out what was wrong with her.

'Here, let me help you with your clothes.'

Moses grabbed Arlette's clothes and thrust them at her, expecting her to take them, but they fell to the floor. Moses pulled her arm, but it was clamped firmly to her side. It was as if she had been turned to stone.

'Arlette,' he shouted yet again.

Still no response. Moses could not leave her there. Whatever she'd heard at the window that had caused her to fall into this catatonic state must have been terrifying. Moses felt his chest constrict with the onset of panic. He feared every Jew's nightmare was about to begin. He gathered her clothes, swept Arlette's stiff body into his arms and carried her downstairs to the bedroom where the others were waiting. The smoke from the door was rising to the upper floors, smarting his eyes.

'What's the matter with Arlette?' Douce cried when she saw her.

'I don't know. I found her like this by the window in her bedroom. She won't talk. I think she saw or heard something from the people outside. Here, Douce, look after her and get her dressed.'

Moses lowered Arlette onto the bed. She curled into a foetal position and buried her head into her chest. He left her there and dashed to the door.

'Where are you going?' Douce shouted after him.

'To see what's going on.'

Jacob followed his friend down the stairs. Solid, repetitive thuds sounding like a battering ram were coming from the other side of the door. They could see the bottom of it was badly scorched and with each thud, it shook on its hinges.

'They're breaking in,' Jacob said.

'How many do you think there are out there?'

They listened for a moment. It had been hard to tell how many people were outside his house when on the upper levels. The walls were at least three feet thick and made of solid stone but here by the door the voices could be heard more clearly.

'I'd say a lot. At least a score.'

There was a sharp splintering of wood and more hammering on the door. It wouldn't be long before they were through. Moses could hear the words 'Christ killers' and 'murderers'. The words put fear into his heart.

'We must get out of here.'

They ran back upstairs to fetch the others. Douce was rocking baby Abraham, who was bawling uncontrollably. He could sense the terror around him. His son Samuel was clinging to his grandfather's leg and Hannah was pacing around the room making enough noise for all of them.

'We need to get back downstairs and go through the door into the synagogue.'

It was unorthodox to have a door from the house directly into the synagogue. Moses built it as a shortcut. He never dreamed he would be using it to flee from an angry mob outside his house. The words 'Christ killer' and 'murderer' nagged at him. What could possibly have happened to warrant such accusations? Since arriving in Gloucester, relations with his

Christian neighbours were harmonious. He had made friends. Radulf the Moneyer was one such friend. They played board games together. Was he part of the mob outside his house? Moses couldn't make sense of the sudden rage aimed at him and his family. It must be some terrible misunderstanding but how was he going to speak to anyone calmly when they were burning his house down? He had to get his family to safety and then speak to the sheriff.

Moses led the way down the staircase. Halfway down the burning door fell in, and the angry mob spilled into the house and lunged towards them.

CHAPTER
EIGHTEEN

Prior Clement sent the Sub Prior back to Llanthony Priory. He made the excuse he had to discuss the finer details of Harold's funeral with the abbot. What he had to say to Margaret must be said in private. She had arrived in Gloucester earlier that day accompanied by her son, Humphrey de Bohun the Third. As usual, they were both staying at the castle.

Once the sub prior was out of sight, he scurried across the abbey precinct and across West Gate Street. As he hurried down the main thoroughfare, he thought he heard shouting but, in his haste, he ignored it and carried on into Castle Lane until he was standing in front of the imposing wooden fortress. Prior Clement had never visited the castle at night. When he reached the drawbridge, he was challenged by a soldier.

'I am Prior Clement in charge of Llanthony Secunda Priory. I'm here to see Countess de Bohun.'

'It's late and no visitors are allowed at this time of night.'

'I must see her. It's a matter of foremost importance. She will not be pleased if she hears you have not let me in. I promise you.'

The promise from a man of the cloth seemed to work. He was allowed to pass. His leather sandals made a plunking noise as he was escorted across the drawbridge. He was then led across the bailey to a small stone chapel. Prior Clement noticed the flicker of candlelight through a window opening. The soldier left him at the door. Clement went inside. The familiar smell of incense and tallow greeted him. Margaret was kneeling at the altar. She was silhouetted against the dark shadows, her white tunic and veil iridescent in the flickering candlelight.

Margaret de Bohun had not long been widowed. Her much older husband, Humphrey de Bohun the Second died three years earlier leaving her with five children, the eldest being her son Humphrey who at the age of twenty had inherited the position of Constable of England from his father. Margaret frequently complained to Prior Clement that her son had the power of a tyrant but the wisdom of a fool. He was still unmarried and had the odious reputation of possessing a vicious temper, particularly toward women. The prior regularly witnessed Margaret's anxiety, not just over her son Humphrey, but also her brothers. This was why she made so many oaths to make good on the unfulfilled eleemosynary promises of her family and to rescue their souls from the danger of hell. The prior suspected a good deal of her anxiety was directed at her own soul. Margaret was now in her forty-sixth year and well past her childbearing days. She had given birth to Harold in her late thirties whilst still married to her husband, but the child was not his. Her husband had met his maker knowing nothing of her infidelity. Startled by the intrusion, Margaret swung round. Prior Clement held up his hands in a reassuring gesture.

'Oh, it's you, Prior Clement. What brings you to the castle so late? Is everything all right?'

He was standing close to her now and could see the worry etched on her face in the candlelight. Her father Milo had been dead some twenty years, shot through the heart by an arrow meant for a deer whilst out hunting in the Forest of Dean. Margaret never fully recovered from her father's untimely death, which was why Clement suspected she had married a much older man.

'May I sit with you?'

She nodded, and he sat beside her.

'Has something happened to Harold? Why else would you come here at this time of night?'

Was it a mother's instinct, the prior wondered? Whatever it was, she had already guessed something was wrong and that made it a little easier for him to tell her his sad news. He took her hand in his.

'Margery,' he said, using the name he called her. 'Harold is dead.'

For a moment there was no reaction, no scream, no gasp, no tears.

'Harold is dead,' she repeated, her tone flat and emotionless.

'His body was found by the river. He's been murdered.'

'Murdered,' she repeated, her tone unchanged.

The prior told her all he knew of Harold's demise.

'He had been tortured,' he concluded, leaving out the grisly details.

'Someone has tortured my son...'

It was the first time Clement had heard Margaret refer to Harold as her son. The strain of the pretence was no more. Her son was dead. All that was left for her was to honour him by claiming him as her own. A single tear trickled down her cheek. She didn't bother to brush it away. She was still a beautiful woman. Her face was unlined except for a few wrinkles at the corner of her amber eyes.

'The monks have washed his body, wrapped him in a shroud to prepare him for burial. They're holding a vigil for him at the abbey. He's to be buried with all the reverence of a saint tomorrow morning.'

'A saint? Why the burial of a saint?'

'They are saying the Jews murdered him.'

'But why would they want to murder a young boy and why would that warrant a saint's burial?'

'The abbot has asked the bishop to sanction it in view of the nature of the death.'

'I don't want to hear any more. Take me to him.'

'I don't think that's wise.'

'Why not? He's my son.'

'People might ask questions. Your secret will no longer be safe.'

'I don't care about that now. I just want to see him.'

'There's nothing you can do for him. If you go tonight, you will only cast suspicion upon yourself. Take comfort he's getting the funeral of one so honoured, one befitting of an aristocratic birth.'

She shot a look of defiance at him. 'He *is* of aristocratic birth.'

It was the first time she had hinted at the progeny of Harold. Although a celibate himself he could understand why his niece may have strayed. After all, did not the Bible warn him that the flesh is indeed weak? He had long suspected who the father was, but he had never pressed her to reveal her secret.

'I must see him,' she said, wiping her tears away from beneath her veil. 'Take me to him.'

CHAPTER
NINETEEN

When the door collapsed, a mighty cheer rose from the invading mob. Moses froze on the stairs, his arms outstretched behind him in a futile gesture to push his family back and out of danger. Men with cudgels, sticks and firebrands rushed in. Moses looked into their zealous faces. Their eyes were wild, frightening, black with hatred. They grabbed him and pulled him down the stairs. From the screams behind him, he knew his family and friends were suffering the same fate. Bewildered and afraid, he tried to break free but there were too many of them. As he was dragged across his threshold, he noticed the sacred *mezuzah* lay on the ground, its metal case tarnished from the fire. It was a sign. Surely, he thought with sickening dread, they would all be killed this night.

The vicious mob dragged him into the street along with the rest of his family and his guests. When he saw his neighbours were also being dragged into the street, his fear intensified. Josce and Judea, Elias de Glocestre and Mirabelle with their children, the widow Bellassez and her young children, the rabbi and his wife and Baruch. Alongside them was Azriel and his wife Slema, Seth and Chera. Then came Rubin, Damete and Zev. All of them herded into a huddle like cattle, ready for slaughter.

Judea's piercing screams set Moses' teeth on edge. Then he heard the remonstrations of Mirabelle. Her voice was as shrill as a virago. She was calling her attackers names in Hebrew, using words Moses would never utter. Her words were silenced by a blow to the face from a man in knight's armour. The sound of his fist connecting with the soft flesh of her face turned Moses' stomach. Even though Mirabelle could be the most unscrupulous and irritating woman she did not deserve that. No woman did. Mirabelle's lip was bleeding, and her cheek bore an angry mark from the knight's fist. Moses could not help but think, what would happen to his own precious wife and his sons? Anything was possible on such a night as this when the air was filled with bitter malevolence.

Moses took stock of the unfolding situation. Douce was cradling baby Abraham. Samuel, his firstborn, such a simple soul, was clutching at the leg of his grandfather and burying his head in the folds of his tunic. Moses stopped struggling with his captors. He knew it was futile.

'Let my wife and children go. They've done nothing. Take me instead.'

His pleas were ignored. Like animals they were corralled into the middle of the street where the mob was building a bonfire. He had never been in a position where he could not protect those who were most dear to him. Arlette had become separated from Douce but luckily Moses managed to find her and keep her by his side. He tried to move closer to Douce, but she had been pushed to the middle of the huddle with Hannah, Abraham in her arms. Arlette stood next to him her eyes wide with terror, shivering. He put his arm around her shoulder in a protective gesture. She squirmed and shifted away from him.

Two fearsome men dressed in knight's garb appeared in

front of Moses. One of them was the stranger. To his horror Moses realised the focus of his attention was Arlette. With a sardonic smirk aimed at Moses the stranger grabbed hold of Arlette and yanked her towards him. Arlette did not resist. Moses clung onto her, but the brawny knight held on to Arlette with an iron grip, and he lost his hold.

'You should have listened to me,' the stranger said to Moses.

Moses was stunned by his words. 'Who are you?'

'I am Brito, a name you'll never forget.'

'Why are doing this?'

Brito ignored him, turning his vile attention back to Arlette.

'Leave her alone, she's done nothing. Take me instead,' Moses pleaded.

'You haven't got what I want,' he said to Moses, a lascivious glint in his dark eyes.

When Moses heard these words, an anger fuelled by terror stirred within him. He pushed past Brito and lunged at Arlette, but Brito was quick to react. With the back of his hand, the knight landed a brutal blow to the side of Moses' head. It caught him on the temple and Moses fell to the ground, dazed. As Moses lay on the ground Zev ran towards them.

'Leave her alone, you bastard,' he shouted.

Brito swung round to face Zev. 'What did you call me?'

Without waiting for Zev's answer, Brito struck him. Although young and strong-armed, Zev was no match for this maleficent knight. Zev's bottom lip burst open, and blood poured down his chin. Stunned, Zev staggered back. Brito rushed forward, landing another punch to the side of Zev's head. Zev's eyes rolled in their sockets, and he dropped to the ground. The well-aimed blow had knocked him out cold.

Moses could do no more than watch as Brito dragged Arlette by her hair towards the courtyard, her feet barely touching the ground. He could not bear to think what fate lay in store for her. Helpless and frustrated, he picked himself up off the floor, wondering if he and his family would live to see another day. Moses did not have a vindictive bone in his body but that night, as he stood in Jewry Street, he swore vengeance upon her attackers.

'May Hashem avenge her blood.'

CHAPTER TWENTY

Arlette was paralysed with fear. She could neither move her limbs nor speak. The man dragging her into the courtyard smelled of stale sweat. He threw her onto the rough ground in the same spot where the children had been playing ball games earlier, and not far from the bench she and Douce had sat on to discuss her betrothal. She curled up into a ball, like a hedgehog protecting itself.

'Hold her down. We'll do her before we kill her. Ever had a Jewess before?' Brito asked his accomplice knight, Reginald fitz Urse.

'No, but I bet they're much the same as any quean I've had up to now,' said Reginald.

'We'll soon see, won't we?'

Brito wrestled with the leather string holding up his breeches, his eagerness causing him to fumble. They fell to his ankles revealing his excited state, hard as a rod of iron. He took hold of it and made a lewd gesture before dropping to his knees and straddling Arlette. He grabbed her arms. His hands were rough against her soft skin. He managed to pin them above her head. This brought his face close to Arlette's. She tossed her head from side to side as Brito tried to kiss her. He ran his tongue over her cheek.

'Salty. Nice,' he whispered into her ear.

The muscles in Arlette's legs became rigid with fear. Brito could not prise them apart. Frustrated he slammed his fist into her stomach. Winded, it seemed to trigger a muscle spasm and her legs jerked open. Brito jammed his knees in between hers, pushing them further apart. At the same time, he ripped at her tunic exposing her pert breasts. Brito latched onto her brown nipple like a feral animal biting hard at one, then the other. He worked fast, making the most of her vulnerability, ramming his stiff cock like a weapon into Arlette's tender virginal opening and gasping with carnal greed. The weight of him pressed upon her body. She could hardly breathe.

He continued to thrust in and out like a rutting animal. His thick black hair, wet with sweat, hung over his face. Sweat beads dripped from the straggly ends onto Arlette's expressionless face. Arlette did not move, nor did she scream, nor did she close her eyes. She lay on the cold, hard ground, her body buffeting from the powerful and violent thrusting of her attacker, her stare fixed upon the dark heavens above.

'You... dirty... dirty... whore... of... a... Jew,' he gasped, each word in time with his rhythmic thrusting.

Arlette tried to trick her mind into believing she wasn't there, that this was not happening to her but with every thrust the pain intensified, her insides burning from the unwelcome intrusion.

It was over in minutes. One final gasp and he was done, coming inside her and baying like a hound. He quickly withdrew and stuffed his subsiding cock into his breeches, hitching them back up and giving his cock a rub as he did so.

'Your turn. I'll hold her for you,' he said, talking as if he were discussing something routine.

'Look at her. There's something wrong with her,' Reginald said, staring down at Arlette.

Arlette lay there. Her shift hitched up at the front around her hips, her bare legs wide, rough red marks on her inner thighs, her eyes glassy, unemotional.

'Nothing wrong with that little jezebel. Nice little cunny on her. Go on, have a go while you can. She'll be dead soon. No good to you dead – or would you prefer that?' Brito said, amused at his obscene suggestion.

'I'm not touching her. The devil is at work here. I'm having no part of it, I'm off.'

'Please yourself,' Brito said. He turned to Arlette. 'Cover yourself and get up.'

Arlette did not move. Brito kicked her.

'Get up and move or I'll drag you back out there naked.'

In a daze Arlette fumbled with the neck of her tunic covering her breasts as best she could and picked herself up off the ground, straightening her skirts. Brito grabbed hold of Arlette by the hair and dragged her out of the courtyard.

TWENTY-ONE

The mob were out of control, shouting out orders to fetch wood for the fire and beating anyone who tried to speak or step away from the corral they were herded into. Raiding parties entered houses and brought out fine wooden furniture, throwing it onto the ever-growing pyre. Moses was powerless to act as expensive pieces of furniture, many of them family heirlooms, were thrown on top, his own mother's finely carved chest amongst them. In the chaos he had reunited with Douce and the children. The baby was screaming, and little Samuel was standing by his grandfather sobbing. Moses picked up his son and tried to comfort him, putting a reassuring arm on his father's shoulder.

'Where is Arlette? Where have they taken her,' Douce repeatedly asked.

He couldn't tell her what he had witnessed. She would be devastated. So far, he had only suffered a blow to the head and the indignity of being treated like cattle. Looking at the rising mountain of wood, he knew the worst was yet to come.

One of the mob set light to the tower of furniture. A blast of light shot upwards illuminating the stone houses in the dark street. Smoke billowed high into the dark sky. The orange flames curled around the expensive pieces of furniture like parasitic ivy, flaring and snaking on to the next piece.

Rabbi Solomon chanted passages from the Torah. Those who could hear him above the shouts of the mob repeated them, some rocking back and forth, shokeling as if in a trance. Zev, still dazed by the blow to his head, was propped against his father and being fussed over by his mother.

Moses kept his eye on the alleyway to watch for the return of Arlette. The first to appear was Brito's accomplice, hurrying along as if he had seen a ghost. Next came Brito, dragging Arlette by the hair. Her tunic was ripped, and he feared the worst. A sin against Hashem's will, committed against his sister's child. A child he vowed to keep safe.

'B'ezrat Hashem,' said Moses, invoking the almighty's help.

Brito dragged her towards the bonfire, stopping short of the flames, and threw her ravaged body to the ground. Douce spotted her. She shouted out her name, but Arlette did not seem to hear.

With Brito back in charge of the mob, events moved swiftly. He ordered the victims to be rounded up in front of the fire. A fierce blaze now raged, the flames shooting up into the dark sky. Moses watched as the glow from the fire lit up the tower of the recently built Christian church of St Michael the Archangel on The Cross. To Moses it was a sign from the Christian God. One of approval. For millennia, since the destruction of the first and second temples the life of a Jew was precarious and often hazardous. Jews were persecuted by the Christians and for what reason? Because they were Jews. He had hoped he would never experience such persecution, but he was, after all, a Jew. It was inevitable.

Moses could feel the heat from the raging fire even though

he was some distance away. He could only imagine how hot it must be for those who stood beside it. His neighbours were forced to form an orderly line, Arlette at the front. She appeared to be oblivious to the fate that awaited her. Brito approached Arlette. Moses told Douce to look away. He held his son Samuel close to him and closed his eyes, reciting the words of Hashem as spoken by the prophet Isaiah at the destruction of the temple. Isaiah had taken comfort in the belief that a better day was coming and in the certainty that good would triumph over evil. Moses needed to believe this was so as his faith was being tested to its limit. Standing with his eyes tightly shut, he recited the prophet's words, hoping against all hope that there was a better day to come.

'Comfort my people.'

The repetitious rhythm of the words calmed him until he became aware of a commotion. He opened his eyes. Several men on horseback were driving their way through the vengeful throng, amongst them Sheriff Pypard and his son, Gilbert. Moses' spirits rose. Could his prayers have been answered so swiftly? He could hardly dare think it possible.

'What is the meaning of this?' the sheriff demanded.

The crowd looked around for their spokesman Brito. Brito stood at the edge of the fire, Arlette's hair in his grip, poised to push her onto the makeshift pyre. He let go of her at the sound of the sheriff's voice. She dropped to the ground like a stone.

'The Jews have murdered a Christian boy,' Brito said to the sheriff.

'And who are you?' asked Sheriff Pypard, looking down at Brito from his steed.

Brito ignored his question. 'We've come for justice.'

'I can see that, but this is not what I call justice,' the sheriff shouted, his booming voice carrying above the noise.

The remains of Moses' door crackled, and a spurt of flames

flew outwards and quickly spread upwards around the frame. The sound caused Sheriff Pypard to turn around.

'Put that fire out,' he shouted, pointing towards Moses' house. 'And bring more water to put this inferno out. If there's to be a burning, there's to be a trial first and I will be in charge, not a lawless mob. Release these people and go home to your families.'

'But we want justice,' a reveller bawled.

The mob became a single entity, no longer acting as independent beings. The cry went up.

'Justice. We want justice.'

'The boy has been put to death in mockery of Jesus Christ,' Brito informed the sheriff.

'Aye. Fixed to a cross in mockery of the Lord's Passion,' someone shouted.

The mob surged towards Sheriff Pypard. His horse reared, and its hooves came crashing down striking an approaching dissenter. The dissenter cried out and dropped to the ground. This seemed to bring the mob to their senses. But Sheriff Pypard was taking no chances. He drew his sword and ordered his men to do the same.

'If you don't go home now, there'll be bloodshed. My men are ready. I need only give the order.'

'Jew lover,' someone shouted.

The sheriff lashed out into the crowd with his sword. Not low enough to hit anyone but close enough for them to scatter. The sheriff's men drove their horses further into the dissenters, their swords at the ready. This had a sobering effect on the unruly mob. One by one they lost their bravado.

'Get off home with you,' Sheriff Pypard shouted, brandishing his sword. 'Or by the saints you'll regret it.'

Like pouring water onto a fire, the energy went out of the mob. Finally coming to their senses, they drifted off into the darkness of the night, leaving Moses, his family and the rest of the community outside their blackened and smouldering homes. Moses ran to Arlette. Within seconds Zev, who had regained consciousness, joined him, followed by Douce holding baby Abraham.

'Go with my father and Samuel,' Moses urged Douce. 'I'll take care of Arlette.'

Silently and with tears running down her cheeks Douce clasped Abraham to her chest and followed her father-in-law, who held on to little Samuel's hand, towards the smouldering door of her home.

Arlette lay curled into a tight ball by the fire. Moses brushed the hair from her face. There were superficial burns to her cheeks and her hair was singed. He called her name several times before she opened her eyes.

'*Baruch Hashem*,' breathed Moses thanking his God when a look of recognition greeted him.

Then she went limp in his arms and passed out.

'I'll take her inside,' Zev said.

He placed his strong arms underneath Arlette's limp body and lifted her effortlessly from the ground and carried her away.

'I'll see you inside,' Moses said.

Moses went over to speak to Sheriff Pypard. He was dismounting from his horse with great difficulty. No longer a young man, the years had taken their toll. He hefted his heavy frame and landed on the ground out of breath.

'Is there any truth in this accusation, Moses?' the sheriff asked.

'What accusation?'

'A boy has been found murdered today. They're saying you Jews are responsible.'

'We are responsible for a boy's murder?'

125

'That's what they're saying. That you used the boy's blood to bake your special bread. Is it true?'

'Not at all. I've been celebrating my son's birth today. It has been a day of celebration and joy, not one of murder and ill will.'

'Why would they make such an accusation?' the sheriff asked.

'I have no idea,' Moses said, bewildered.

Moses spotted Prior Clement approaching them. His head was hung low, and he was clutching on to the large gold cross around his neck.

'Do you know anything about this, Prior Clement?' Sheriff Pypard shouted across to Clement.

Prior Clement approached them and looked up at his friend Moses, his watery eyes glistening in the glow of the fire.

'The boy is Harold, Moses.'

It had been a night of sorrows not just for him but also for his good friend Clement.

'I am very sorry to hear this news, Clement,' Moses said.

'You knew the boy?' Sheriff Pypard asked Clement.

'He was a young novice at the priory under my care.'

'And where are his parents? They should be told.'

'He has no parents. He was an orphan. Brought to us as a baby to take care of.'

Prior Clement was struggling to keep his emotions under control. Moses could feel his loss.

'And you knew him?' Sheriff Pypard asked Moses.

'Not well but I knew him from my visits to the priory. He was never far away from Prior Clement.'

Sheriff Pypard scratched his head. 'I'm puzzled,' he said. 'How does an innocent young monk end up dead in such a gruesome way?'

'I've been asking that myself since I found out,' said Clement.

'Who has been making these accusations, sheriff?' Moses asked.

'A stranger by the name of Brito,' said Clement.

Moses looked around him, but Brito was nowhere to be seen.

'I give you my word, Sheriff Pypard, we are innocent of this crime. As Jews we are prohibited from partaking of blood...'

Rabbi Solomon stood close by and overhearing the conversation quoted a passage from Leviticus. 'Ye shall eat the blood of no manner of flesh: for the life of all flesh is the blood thereof: whosoever eateth it shall be cut off.'

Sheriff Pypard listened to Rabbi Solomon with the same respect he would afford a Christian man of the cloth.

'The ancient rabbis laid down that prayer should replace sacrifice. The idea that we have killed a young boy to use his blood in our Passover bread is just plain madness.' Moses sighed, shaking his head in disbelief. 'What folly.'

'I believe you, Moses,' said Clement. 'I know you would never have harmed Harold, nor any other boy for that matter.'

'Well that's as may be,' said Sheriff Pypard, 'but it's late and I'm sure you both have homes to go to.' The sheriff sighed heavily. 'You better get off the street although I suspect they've had enough devilment for tonight.'

'For tonight? What happens tomorrow?' said Clement.

'I don't know,' Sheriff Pypard replied.

'What do you mean? Surely, you're going to find out who did this to Harold?'

'I will make enquiries to determine how this boy met his death.'

Clement seemed satisfied with the sheriff's answer and thanked him.

'I don't understand why this has happened?' Moses said.

'We've lived in this community for many years in harmony and without incident.'

'Who can say why men do the things they do.'

With that Sheriff Pypard took the reins of his horse and with some difficulty mounted his steed. 'Go home,' he called back as he and his men galloped off, leaving the smouldering fire to burn itself out. Prior Clement remained.

'I'm sorry, Clement. I know you were fond of the boy.'

'I was. Very fond. He was like a son to me.'

'You don't believe these accusations do you, Clement? You know I could never hurt the boy.'

'I know that, Moses. Do you know who this stranger is or where he came from? He seems to be the one spreading this rumour about.'

'I don't know him, but he stopped me in the street the other day and warned me not to lend money to some Irishman.'

Clement's brows knitted. 'Do you think that has something to do with Harold?'

'I can't see how.'

'Neither can I, but it does seem odd that this stranger arrives in the city and warns you about lending money, and then accuses you all of murdering Harold by some strange religious ritual.'

The two men fell silent, both lost in puzzlement.

'Do you know the Irishman?'

'No. But he did come to my house asking for a loan and I turned him away.'

'Probably a wise move. I don't know about you, but I'd like to get to the bottom of this. There's definitely more to this than we know.'

'All I know is we've been drawn into something not of our making.'

'It's a bad business, Moses, I'll warrant that.'

Moses said, 'My family are everything to me and tonight I failed them.'

'You mustn't think like that, but I understand, Moses. I'll leave you to comfort them.'

Prior Clement placed a comforting hand on Moses' shoulder.

'Do you know what this stranger Brito did tonight?' Moses asked as the prior took his leave. Prior Clement shook his head. 'He defiled my niece.'

Prior Clement sighed and made the sign of the cross. 'That is deplorable. I'm very sorry to hear that, my friend. I wish I had arrived sooner. Maybe I could have done something.'

'I doubt it. He was like a depraved animal. No one could have stopped him.'

'A man like that could do worse...'

'There is nothing worse.'

'She could be dead...'

'She may wish she were,' Moses said.

'Let me know if there is anything I can do.'

'I will and if you need anything from me, I will do what I can to help.'

'Thank you, my friend,' said Clement.

Moses watched Clement's stooping figure walk towards The Cross and disappear around the corner.

Rabbi Solomon had started an impromptu service. He heard the rabbi's reassuring words reciting the *Birkhat HaGomel* blessing and went over to join him. The men's chanting voices could be heard above the sorrowful weeping and cries of despair from the women.

'He Who has bestowed upon you every goodness, may He continue to bestow upon you every goodness. Pause and think on that.'

Moses joined in, standing with his community, their faces

smudged with blackened ash. Together they recited the blessing as smoke and ashes floated around them in the crisp night air.

TWENTY-TWO

D ouce was doing her best to undress Arlette, but it was proving difficult. Her body was as rigid and unmovable as a cork stopper in an old wine cask. Her arms were wound tightly across her chest, her knees pulled up to her chin. The side of her face was red and inflamed, smudged with black soot. It would need treating with some salve to stop it from scarring.

Zev had kindly carried Arlette to her bedroom and respectfully left. Douce was trying to reassure her all would be well. She felt as if she were trying to convince herself, too, but it wasn't working. Despite gentle coaxing, Arlette would not look at or speak to Douce. She asked Arlette what had happened, but it only made her whimper and shake her head. When Douce finally managed to pull the tunic over Arlette's head, the truth stared at her. The garment was heavily stained with virginal blood. A lump formed at the back of her throat, and she wanted to cry.

'*Pauvre petite*,' she whispered, kissing her forehead.

Arlette recoiled. Douce was shocked by her reaction and withdrew. She had been through such a terrible ordeal Douce worried how she would recover from such a violation. Her marriage to Deudonne was now in jeopardy and may never take place. Although Arlette had not brought this shame upon herself, she would be viewed by the community as unclean and not worthy of a husband.

Arlette resumed her foetal position and was shivering. Douce pulled the covers over her, picked up the soiled tunic, whispered goodnight and left.

She crept past the bedroom where the children were sleeping with their grandfather. Moses was not in his bedroom and so she continued downstairs where she found him securing the door with some fresh planks of wood. Jacob, Hannah and their children were in the hall. They had packed their belongings and dressed for the journey back to Oxford. She tried to persuade them to stay but it was more out of politeness than anything else. She was not in the mood for entertaining, and she understood their concern. If she was in the same position she would want to return to the safety of her own home. Safety. She doubted she would ever feel safe again after the events of tonight.

After a short while, Moses joined her in the dining hall. He sat down at the table and rested his head on his folded arms. She wanted to touch his hair, but she could not. Contact of an intimate nature was forbidden whilst she was unclean. Unclean and bleeding. Her heart ached at the thought of not being able to touch her husband when he most needed comfort. She sighed. Moses jolted from his half slumber.

'Sorry, I didn't mean to wake you,' she said.

'I'm jumpy that's all,' he said.

Douce sat down opposite him.

'I'm very worried about Arlette. She hasn't said a word and she has a strange, distant look in her eyes.'

'It's not surprising given what she's been through.'

'What are we going to do, Moses?'

'I don't know,' he answered, staring down at the table, rubbing his thumb up and down the grain in the wood.

'Are we going to let him get away with it?'

'What can we do?' Moses said, still concentrating on the grain in the wood.

'I'm not sure, but I want him punished for what he's done to Arlette.'

'Hashem will see to that.'

'It's not enough,' Douce said through gritted teeth. 'You have to speak with the sheriff. Tell him what happened.'

Moses rubbed at his forehead with the heel of his palms and sat back in his chair.

'All right, *chérie*. I'll speak to him on Monday.'

'What are we going to say to Deudonne and his father?'

'I don't know,' he repeated.

'And what are people going to say when they find out?'

'I think I have a good idea,' he said bitterly.

'Why has this happened? What has any one of us done to deserve this?'

'We are Jews, Douce, it's the only excuse they need.'

'But we've lived here all these years without any trouble. We have Christian friends.'

'After tonight, I'm not so sure.'

'Well, we have not made enemies.'

'No, we have not.'

'And Arlette? Why has Hashem seen fit to punish her? What has she done to deserve being...' She stopped mid-sentence, not wanting to speak the word.

'I don't know, I don't have the answers, *chérie*. None of it makes sense.'

'Something must have happened to make them behave this way,' said Douce.

'I heard them at the door. They were calling us murderers and Christ killers.'

'Christ killers!'

The words sent a cold, sharp fear into her heart.

'We won't have heard the last of this,' Moses said.

Douce said nothing. The fire crackled in the stove, reminding her of the pyre outside and she shuddered.

'Who was that man, Moses?'

She did not have to say more. Moses knew who she was referring to.

'I don't know him.'

'I saw him speak to you. What did he say?'

'He said I should have listened to him.'

A cold shiver raced through her veins making her skin crawl. There was more to tonight's events than she realised, and her wonderful husband was somehow involved.

'You said you didn't know him. You must know him if he spoke to you.'

'I've met him before. Only briefly. I thought little of it until tonight.'

'Why would you have anything to do with someone like that?'

'In business, Douce, you meet lots of different people. I don't ask them what their moral views are before I lend them money. I'm only interested in whether they can pay me back,' he snapped at her.

Douce's lip quivered. She looked down at her hands, falling silent.

'I'm sorry, my love, I didn't mean to lose my temper with you. I just can't help feeling I have in some way been the cause of what happened to Arlette and maybe all of tonight has been my fault, but I don't know why.'

Douce could see the anguish in her husband's face. She reached out her hand to him.

'We can't,' he said, his eyes full of need.

'We can. This is an exceptional time. I'm sure Hashem will forgive us. You will have to visit the sacred bath, that's all. We need to comfort each other. Come.'

She offered him her hand and he took it. The warmth of it in hers made her feel calmer.

'You say you've met him before. When and where?'

'He stopped me in the street sometime before the *brit*. He said that if an Irishman called asking for a loan, it was in my best interest not to lend to him. He came to warn me of a potential bad business deal. That's it.'

'There must have been more. Think, Moses.'

'There isn't. I've been searching my mind.' Moses wrenched his hand from hers and kneaded his temples as if this action would give him the answers he was searching for. He suddenly looked up. 'He did say something else. He said he was on the king's business.'

'The king has a hand in this?'

'I told you. I don't know, and I didn't ask. When the king is involved it's best not to.'

Douce went quiet again, mulling over what her husband had said.

'Did the man he spoke of come to see you?' she asked, convinced there was something her husband had forgotten.

'The Irishman came some days later, on Shabbat.'

'So that's who was at the door.'

'He looked like a ruffian, so I thought the stranger was right and I told him I didn't do business on Shabbat. He wasn't best pleased.'

'What did he say?'

'He said he'd come back.'

'Do you think he will?'

'Probably.'

'What will you say to him when he comes?'

'I don't know. I'll think of something.'

'You're not going to lend him the money, are you?'

'Of course not,' Moses shouted.

Douce grabbed hold of his hands again and held on, giving them a reassuring squeeze.

'You have done nothing wrong, Moses.'

'So why do I feel like this?'

'You mustn't blame yourself for what has happened tonight.'

'But I do. And what's more I cannot work out what lending money to an Irishman has got to do with the murder of this young boy or how the stranger is involved. Or the king for that matter. None of it makes sense.'

Douce let out a sigh of frustration. 'You're right it doesn't make sense but it's not your fault. You must put that thought out of your mind. Hashem will be the one to judge. It is *He* who sees the truth.'

'You're right, of course.' He drew her hands towards his lips and kissed her fingers gently. 'I love you.'

'I love you too,' Douce replied, trying to raise a smile.

'I don't know what I would have done if anything had happened to you tonight.'

'Don't think such things. We are safe, and we have Hashem to thank for that. But what are we going to do about Arlette?'

Moses groaned as if the weight of the world's burdens were upon his shoulders. 'I can't even think about that now. I need a clear head.'

'We should speak with the rabbi...'

'Yes. He'll know what to do.'

'Do you think they'll come back tonight?' Douce asked as she raised her weary body from the chair.

'Maybe not tonight, but they're out for blood.'

'Will we have to leave Gloucester?'

'I hope not.'

'You're tired. We should go to bed.'

'Bed?' Moses said, his voice raised in surprise.

'Yes, bed. You are already unclean. We can cuddle. I need you beside me tonight. I don't want to be left alone.'

'I don't know if I can sleep.'

'You will. Come on. We can speak again in the morning.'

She kissed his cheek and tugged on his hand. With his shoulders hunched from tiredness and the burden he now bore, he let his wife take him to bed. They held each other tight until exhaustion defeated them both, falling asleep in each other's arms.

CHAPTER
TWENTY-THREE

The air in the abbey was thick with choking incense, the atmosphere empyrean. Brother Carbonel walked up and down the long aisle of the nave swinging an ornate thurible, plumes of pungent smoke rising in the air. Abbot Hameline lit the tall altar candle. Exquisitely carved in the Romanesque style and engraved with reminders of sin, it was a gift from a rich benefactor some fifty years ago. It was only used for austere occasions and today's service seemed most appropriate.

The monks chanted one of their funereal compositions, the sepulchral tones of their voices rising and falling, drifting across the packed nave. Abbot Hameline, dressed in a fresh alb, stood on the altar next to Harold's body. The tallow candles had been replaced with fresh candles throughout the night-long vigil for Harold. A shroud covered all but his head. Gold coins were covering his eye sockets, the blood had been washed from his skull and his silky, titian hair had been arranged to frame his saintly innocent face.

The congregation was made up of the mob from the night before, along with Prior Clement and the monks of Llanthony

Priory, the elver men who found him, several dignitaries and Margaret de Bohun. Her son, Humphrey, was not by her side and the stranger Brito was noticeably absent. The sheriff and his men were there to keep order. She stood at the front of the altar by the body of her son dressed in a tunic of white linen, a diaphanous veil covered her face. In her hand she held a string of rosary beads, a small gold cross and a posy of golden saxifrage and coltsfoot. Her gaze did not wander from the dead body of her son. After a few whispered prayers, she laid the posy of wildflowers on his chest and returned to her seat.

Abbot Hameline spent the morning preparing an appropriate sermon. News of the riot the night before had reached him. Whether the Jews were responsible for the boy's murder he could not say but being an astute abbot he saw an opportunity to exploit the situation to the church's benefit. Harold would be given a funeral befitting that of a martyred saint and be buried in the west chapel by Edward the Confessor's shrine. In time, he would erect a shrine to the martyred boy and request that the Pope formally recognise him as a saint, confirming God's holy works and giving the abbey a source of income from the many pilgrims who would flock to the shrine of the martyred boy. But that was for the future. Today he must concentrate on the service and hope that the angry mob from yesterday would behave. The monks' chanting ceased, plunging the abbey into a reverent silence apart from the occasional cough or whine from a small child. Abbot Hameline surveyed his flock, lengthening the silence for dramatic effect. It was time. He was ready.

'We gather here today as one body to pray for the saintly soul of this boy whose name is Harold. Amen.'

'Amen.'

'His death has not been in vain for may his soul rejoiceth blissfully in heaven among the bright hosts of the saints, and may his body, by the Omnipotence of the divine mercy, rest here in this house of God.'

Abbot Hameline paused again. It was important his flock understood the gravitas of his words. That Harold would be known forever as a martyred saint. He hoped this would go some way toward appeasing the mob.

'Here lies the glorious body of Harold, boy and martyr of Christ, dying the death of time in reproach of the Lord's death, but crowned with the blood of a glorious martyrdom. He has entered into the kingdom of glory on high to live for ever. Amen.'

Abbot Hameline took the vessel containing the holy water. He poured a few drops onto his hand and sprinkled it upon Harold's face and body.

'He is a glorious and blameless martyr for Christ,' said the abbot. 'We await, O Lord, the glorious display of miracles which your divine power will carry out through the merits of this blessed martyr Harold.'

A martyr.

My son is a Christian martyr, thought Margaret.

This thought went some way to assuage the sadness she felt at her son's murder. The nature of his death and the reasons for it still haunted her. Her clandestine visit to the abbey the night before had been risky, but she'd wanted to see him. Had to confirm his death with her very own eyes. On reflection, she regretted going. The monks had worked hard to present Harold's body in the best possible state, and she was grateful for their attentions, but she would rather have remembered him as a guileless, happy child. She had also heard of the accusations against the Jews. Moses le Riche was known to her.

Her husband and her son Humphrey transacted business with him. She found him a quiet, courteous and well-educated man. One who followed his faith with the respect it deserved and not the zealousness which was so often present amongst some of the Jews she encountered. He had successfully assimilated into the culture of his adopted country. She could not believe he would be at the heart of such an appalling crime.

Abbot Hameline was coming to the end of the service.

'Unto him be glory in the church by Christ Jesus throughout all ages, world without end. Amen.'

Without thinking how it might look, Margaret walked to Harold's side to kiss him goodbye. In front of all the mourners and dignitaries she bent down, kissed the cold flesh of her son's forehead and whispered the words, 'I have always loved you, my son.' She touched his cheek and laid a gold cross at his side. Then she turned and walked down the long aisle, a solitary figure.

TWENTY-FOUR

D airmait had been furious when he returned from Moses le Riche's house. His insistence on seeing the Jew on his own had backfired. He'd then spent most of Saturday and Sunday drinking cider and cussing at anyone who came close and was now nursing a hangover. He was in a ferociously bad mood. The atmosphere at the breakfast table was prickly yet Aoife was not about to let her father get away with his error, particularly after she had suggested they should all go.

'I told you, Father, it would have been better if Richard and I had gone with you.'

'It wouldn't have made any difference. He said he didn't do business on his blasted Sabbath. How was I to know it was on a Friday and continued till blasted Saturday? Why can't they follow our Sabbath when they're in our country?'

'This is not our country, Father, and he is a Jew. They have a different religion to ours.'

'Well, business is business and it shouldn't be affected by religion.'

'Try telling that to the Pope,' Richard said, attempting to lighten Dairmait's mood.

Dairmait's eyes flared. Aoife recognised that look. He had blinded men for saying less. If she was not careful her entire future could end here on the floor of this tavern with the blood of her intended.

'Did you tell him who you were and that you had the king's grace?' she asked.

'I told him I was there on king's business. As to anything else, we didn't get that far.'

'Then I think we should go and see him again today and take the letters patent with us. Show him how serious this is and that we have the backing of the king in this endeavour. Don't you agree, Richard?'

Richard nodded. 'I'm sure at the end of the day Monsieur le Riche is a businessman. When he realises how lucrative this transaction is, he'll be more accommodating.'

'You probably frightened him, Father,' Aoife said, giving her father a friendly dig in his side.

Dairmait's expression softened, but he was still sulking. Their conversation was interrupted by a group of men who were talking in loud voices at another table. Aoife's ears pricked up when she heard the word 'Jew'. Listening in on what they were saying, she realised something potentially much more damaging than her father's ham-fisted attempt to secure the money they desperately needed had taken place.

'There may be another problem...' she said.

'And what for mercy's sake would that be?' Dairmait asked.

'Can you not hear what they're saying?'

Aoife remembered her father was hard of hearing and probably could not hear the conversation. She stood up to join the men. Richard rose to accompany her.

'No, stay here,' she said to him.

When Aoife approached, the men stopped talking and gave her an unwelcome look. Aoife met their disapproval with a solicitous smile.

'Sorry to interrupt, but I heard you talking about the Jews of this city. Has something happened to them?'

'Don't you know? Everyone's talking about it.'

'No, we are recently arrived in the city and are just passing through. Do tell.'

Once Aoife flashed her twinkling eyes at the men, they were only too eager to tell her everything. As Aoife listened to the terrible events, her heart sunk. This could have catastrophic repercussions for her father's plans. She thanked the men and returned to the table.

'It appears while you were spending the weekend revelling and feeling sorry for yourself, a mob attacked the Jews and tried to kill them all.'

Dairmait slammed his fist on the table and cursed in his native tongue. 'Were they robbed?'

'It seems they were about to burn them all on a hurriedly lit fire when the sheriff came along and sent the mob home so no, I don't think they were robbed.'

'Thank Christ for that,' Dairmait said.

'You said this le Riche character wasn't very friendly. He might be even less friendly towards you when you go to see him. He told you to return, didn't he? Today?'

'Yes.'

'This time we should all go.'

'Should we say anything about what has happened?' Richard asked. 'Offer our condolences?'

'I think it best we don't mention it,' said Aoife.

'But what if he thinks we had anything to do with it?' said Richard.

'I think we'll know if he thinks that by his attitude towards us. My daughter is right. It's best we act unawares and pray to God he doesn't let such matters get in the way of business.'

TWENTY-FIVE

Moses rose late, his sleep fitful and full of nightmares. He woke frequently with a start, worrying about his family and fearful of the least sound. He was alone in bed. Douce, sensitive to Abraham's cries and little Samuel's needs, had already risen. He dressed and made his way down to the kitchen. The atmosphere was as solemn as a loved one's funeral. Douce sat at the table breastfeeding Abraham and his father sat next to little Samuel making a clumsy attempt to feed him watery frumenty. His mood slumped even further when he looked at their joyless faces.

'No Arlette?' he asked, noticing her absence.

His father ignored the question, preferring to concentrate on his grandson who was unduly fretful and out of sorts.

'She hasn't come down,' Douce told him.

'Have you been to see her? Is she all right?'

'I thought it best to leave her, given how she was last night. I'm sure she'll join us when she's ready.'

'Well, you know best, *chérie*.'

Moses sat next to his wife and reached for the basket of

bread. He tore off a piece and dipped it into a bowl of honey. A dish of hard-boiled eggs stood on the table. He took one and smashed it to break the shell. The noise frightened little Samuel and set him off. Grizzling, he pushed the spoon from his mouth. His grandfather got up to leave the table.

'I'll take him for a walk. Tire him out.'

Douce was putting down Abraham. She swung round and screamed, 'No.'

Her father-in-law looked at her aghast.

'Sorry, I didn't mean to shout. I'm just not sure it's safe out there.'

'They'll be fine,' Moses reassured her. 'Those people will be sleeping it off if I know their sort.'

'I'm not sure if I'll ever feel safe on the streets of Gloucester again.'

'You will, *chérie*. This will blow over, it always does. They need us too much to get rid of us. Who would they get their money from to build their churches and buy land for their grand manor houses? No, trust me, all will be well.'

When she was finally alone with Moses, Douce broached the subject of Arlette.

'Are you still agreed we seek the advice of Rabbi Solomon?'

'We have to and as soon as possible.'

'Let's go now, while Arlette is still asleep?'

Moses agreed. 'All right,' he said, popping a whole, peeled egg into his mouth.

The sound of hammering greeted them as they emerged into Jewry Street. The clean-up from the night before had begun. The fire, now a smouldering heap of grey ash and charred pieces of furniture, was a grim reminder of the fate they had escaped. They made their way past the dying embers and on towards Rabbi Solomon's house, baby Abraham cradled in the arms of Douce. When they arrived, Rubin was outside nailing together a new door. He stopped working when he saw them approach, nodded and went back to his work. Moses detected a degree of awkward embarrassment. He turned to look at his wife. She was looking at the floor, avoiding Rubin's gaze. Moses took her hand and gave it a squeeze. Poor Douce, he thought, such a sweet thing but far too concerned about what people thought. She had taken on the burden of Arlette's shame and it was visible in her demeanour. He too felt it and the presence of Rubin seemed to intensify the feeling. Perhaps it was because they had both looked down on Rubin and his son all these years. He saw now how shameful that was of him. The events of the previous night, although harrowing, was proving to be a humbling experience for Moses. Rabbi Solomon came to the door.

'We must speak to you, rabbi, on a matter of some urgency,' Moses said.

'Of course, I understand.' Solomon welcomed them into his house. 'Come in. My wife will make us something to drink.'

As he entered the house Moses touched the *mezuzah* and kissed his fingertips. Hashem would protect him. Rabbi Solomon led them to a room at the back of the house away from the noisy workmen.

'I know why you're here,' Rabbi Solomon said.

Floria, the rabbi's wife, entered the room. She was carrying a ewer of red wine which she set down on the table beside them. 'I normally reserve this for Shabbat but today is different,' she said. She poured a cup and handed it to Douce. 'How are you?' she asked her, placing her hand upon Douce's shoulder.

No one had asked Douce how she was. Normally she would give her usual response, but today she was anything but fine. Her eyes filled with tears.

'I'm not good at all, Floria,' she replied, her voice catching as she tried to hold back the tears.

Floria replied, 'It will not endure.'

'Thank you, Floria,' Douce said, 'that's very kind of you.'

This sisterly exchange took only moments and throughout it the men said nothing, the usual pleasantries of a social call absent. Floria left them alone, promising to come back to say her goodbyes. The room remained quiet a little longer, heavy with a presence of something unspoken. Rabbi Solomon broke the silence.

'I presume you're here about Arlette?'

'Yes, rabbi. We don't know what to do.'

'It's a bad business, a very bad business.'

'I don't know if you are aware, our precious Arlette became betrothed to Deudonne, Aaron of Lincoln's son, yesterday. After what has happened, we're not sure if the marriage can go ahead so we wanted to know what the Torah teaches us about this.'

Solomon scratched his long grey beard. He had studied the Torah for most of his life, could quote directly from it and had memorised key readings.

'We must look to the Book of Deuteronomy for the answer to this difficult matter. Deuteronomy is the key writing on this.' Solomon flicked through the pages, studying the text. 'It says that in the case of a man who violates a virgin who was betrothed, as was Arlette, the place of the offence is the crucial factor as to whether she was coerced or willingly consented...'

'Willingly consented? How can you talk of consent?' asked Douce, her voice rising with anger. 'You were there? You saw her dragged off by that pig of a gentile.'

Moses was shocked by Douce's outburst. He had never heard her use language like that before or raise her voice to a rabbi.

'Please, Douce, calm yourself. I'm only reciting what the Torah says. I understand Deuteronomy does not help us much in this situation. We must interpret the meaning.'

Moses listened; his brow deeply furrowed in concentration.

'If the offence took place in town, both should be stoned to death...'

Douce let out an angry cry at the mention of being stoned. 'Oh, for goodness' sake, how is any of this helpful?'

'However,' continued Solomon, raising his long bony finger to show he had not finished, 'if in the field the man finds the girl who is betrothed, and the man forces her and lies with her, then only the man who lies with her shall die.'

Douce relaxed a little and took a sip of wine. Baby Abraham lay in her lap, contented and asleep despite her agitation.

'None of this helps Arlette,' said Moses. 'The man in question is not known to us, he's a Christian so he's not subject to our laws and he has powerful friends. There's no way we could have him put to death. And even if we could, how does this help Arlette and her marriage to Deudonne?'

'Be patient, I'm coming to the part which deals with what we call "ones", that is specifically where a person is compelled to act against their will. In this case regarding the rape of a betrothed maiden.'

The word was out. Arlette had been raped. Douce felt the shame of it as if she was the one to have suffered the violation. But she also felt rage burning inside her. Men were incapable of understanding the trauma of being taken against your will. Rabbi Solomon looked up from the text he was studying and gazed at Douce, tutted in sympathy, then continued.

'It states that unto the damsel thou shalt do nothing. From this the sages have inferred that in all cases of "ones" the merciful Torah exempts.'

Douce looked up on hearing the word 'exempt'.

'Does this mean Arlette is free of sin?'

Solomon continued, finding the passage in the holy book. 'But you shall do nothing to the girl, there is no sin in the girl worthy of death, for just as a man rises against his neighbour and murders him, so is this the case. When he found her in the field, the betrothed girl cried out, but there was no one to save her...'

At those last words, Moses hung his head. 'I wasn't there to save her. I let her down, Solomon.'

Rabbi Solomon closed the book. 'There was nothing you could do.'

'Does this mean Arlette is free from sin and the marriage can go ahead?' asked Douce.

'I cannot speak for Deudonne. He may think differently. But as far as Arlette is concerned, she need not blame herself. She should feel no shame.'

'I doubt that Arlette will see it that way. She hasn't spoken since it happened,' said Moses, his face etched with worry.

Moses and Douce left Rabbi Solomon's home feeling no more reassured about Arlette's future. Rabbi Solomon was right. Despite what was written in the holy book it would be up to Deudonne. What man would want a sullied woman as his wife? Deudonne was handsome and wealthy. He could choose any number of girls to marry. His father was the wealthiest Jew in England, transacting business with kings, consorting with royals, earls and knights of the realm. He had a reputation to think of. Moses could see that. It wasn't a question of what the Torah said on such matters. It was ordinary people with their prejudices, their reputations and their small minds that would make a difference to Arlette's future. A black-hearted demon had made sure of that.

TWENTY-SIX

Arlette remained in her bedroom refusing to see anyone but her aunt. Since the incident, Douce had climbed the stairs to her room bringing her food and something to drink. Each time she took the opportunity to coax Arlette out of the miasma which had descended upon her. She told her what Rabbi Solomon had said – that she should feel no shame. None of it helped. Arlette always had a counterargument. It was as if she wanted to argue her way into a life of misery. Douce took the view that however dreadful things were, life must go on. Arlette could not spend the rest of her life in a self-imposed prison.

'I know you think this is the end of your world right now, Arlette, but you'll see. One day you'll be able to put this all behind you.'

'How can you say that?'

Douce sighed. She didn't know how to answer her niece. It was true. Her life seemed a charmed one compared to Arlette's. How could Hashem visit such destruction on such a young soul? She couldn't imagine how she would feel if the same fate had been visited upon her. It was bad enough Arlette witnessed her parents' murder, but this? It was the worst thing that could happen to a woman. It was a sin above all sins.

'I can't, you're right. I don't know how I would feel but...'

'Exactly. You don't know how it feels.'

'I just think...'

'It's not about what you think. What are people saying?'

Douce hoped Arlette wouldn't ask her this question. Small, close-knit communities could be a blessing but also a curse. If Arlette knew just some of the things people were saying she would never set foot outside the house again.

'Everyone has been asking after you.'

'Have you heard anything from Deudonne?'

They had heard no news of Aaron and his son since the *brit*. It was possible they knew nothing of Arlette's troubles. It posed a moral dilemma for Douce and Moses. Was it their duty to tell the betrothed his future wife had been defiled? Douce shuddered at the word. Defiled. She looked over at Arlette, her head propped up on a pillow. Even she was guilty of seeing Arlette differently. A light had gone out in her eyes. Her purity sullied.

'We haven't heard anything since they left for Bristol.'

'He will know, everyone knows. He will disown me. What man wants a bride who is no longer a *betulot*?'

'You don't know that for sure.' Douce was trying her best, but she knew in her heart that no man would want to marry a woman who was not a virgin. 'Pray to Hashem. He's always there and always listens. Turn to him truly and he will not forsake you.'

'Hashem may not forsake me, but it is not him who is judging me now. I'm finished, Douce. I will never be someone's wife, a woman of worth. I'll never have children. I'll be a spinster for the rest of my life. I am impure. I will be cast out.'

Arlette burst into tears and sobbed into her pillow. Douce

did not want to admit it but Arlette was right. She would be shunned. She would never be seen as an *eschet chayil*. A woman of worth. She was destined to be an *alta moid*. A spinster.

CHAPTER
TWENTY-SEVEN

Z ev had called on Arlette the day after the attack, but Douce had not let him see her. She told him Arlette was too ill to see anyone. When he enquired as to how she was, Douce's stock answer was, 'as well as can be expected'. What did that mean? What could be expected? How was someone to be after such a thing? He wanted to see her, decide for himself how well she was but it was not to be. Douce would not be moved.

It was a cold and dismal day and finishing work early, Zev called again to see Arlette. Douce stood at the door like a sentry denying him access. He heard those same words again.

As well as could be expected.

He wanted to push past her and force his way in, but he knew that would further alienate him in the eyes of the small but feisty Douce. Frustrated at not being allowed to see her, he went for a walk. The sun was a pale disc in a grey sky devoid of warmth. He walked towards Westgate Bridge, reflecting on the events of the last few days. His disappointment at hearing Arlette was betrothed was nothing compared to the anguish he felt at her being attacked. How does a woman recover from something like that?

He was standing on the bridge, watching the mist rise from the water and the trowmen work on their boats, when he sensed someone standing close by him. He turned to see Chera. She smiled at him. He hadn't spoken to her since that day in the courtyard when he was drunk. He realised to his shame how rude he had been to her when she had only been trying to help.

'Sorry, Chera.'

'Sorry for what?'

'My behaviour.'

'Oh that. I've forgiven you. You weren't yourself.'

'Still, that's no excuse.'

'I know how much you liked Arlette. It must have been a shock to find out she was betrothed to someone.' She leaned on the stone wall and stared down at the water, adding, 'I know how it feels to have your hopes dashed.'

They stood in silence, each lost in their own thoughts.

'What will you do now?' she asked.

'What do you mean?'

'Now that Arlette...'

'Now that Arlette what?' Zev turned and his gaze was hostile.

'I only meant now she's no longer available.'

Zev's mood sank further into desolation at the mention of Arlette no longer being available to him. An aching pain entered his chest.

'I don't know what to do. I feel wretched, Chera.'

'I can see it in your face.'

'Is it that obvious?'

'It is to me.'

'I feel lost.'

'Remember, Hashem can change everything in the blink of an eye,' she said, smiling up at him.

'You're right but it isn't always the right kind of change. Arlette deserves more in this life.'

'As long as there is life, there is hope.'

Zev was beginning to feel irritated by Chera. Her constant optimism and her insistence on spouting religious platitudes. Perhaps they worked for her, but it only made Zev feel more depressed. His lips were dry, and his throat constricted. He had lost Arlette forever and his life would never be the same. The ache in his chest returned, pressing down on him.

'*Oy, vavoy*, Chera...' Then he remembered his manners. He was at risk of behaving badly again. 'I'm sorry, Chera. I know you're trying to help but I'm beyond that.'

'I've only ever wanted to help, Zev. I always thought that you would see the impossibility of marrying Arlette and that we...' She stopped. 'I-I,' she stammered, then burst into tears and ran off.

Zev watched her go, making no attempt to stop her. Women, he thought, were unfathomable. Perhaps he should convert and become a monk, then he wouldn't have to deal with them.

CHAPTER
TWENTY-EIGHT

Since his discussion with Douce, Moses had agonised over what to do about Brito. The man had violated his niece, incited Gloucester's citizens to invade his home and that of his neighbours and destroyed property. He may also have had something to do with Harold's death. And so far, no action had been taken against him. He decided to visit the sheriff and demand that he arrest Brito. The sheriff would be at the docks, his son beside him, assiduously calculating the taxes to be paid as the ships' cargoes were offloaded.

Moses set off early hoping to avoid the crush of people descending on the meat market. He walked the length of West Gate Street, past The Cross and through the narrow part of the street where they were building a new church. It was here that he had to squeeze through the mill of people stopping to buy fresh meat at the butcher's market stalls. Huge sides of beef were hung from hooks, the heart and liver still in their cavities, steam rising from their warm entrails. The sickly-sweet smell of raw flesh pervaded the air, turning his stomach. He was pleased when at last he reached the toll bridge at the end of the street.

Ships from far and wide docked at the port of Bristol but

were too large to travel along the shallower more treacherous currents of the River Severn. So the goods were loaded onto smaller boats with shallow hulls and collapsible masts able to pass under low bridges piloted by men who were masters at sailing the unpredictable tides and bores of the Severn. They had become known as Gloucester trows. Several of them were being unloaded when Moses arrived. As predicted, the sheriff and his son were checking and itemising everything brought ashore. The sailors were a strange bunch of men. Sinewy and muscular, they lifted loads most men would struggle with.

'May I speak with you for a moment, sheriff?' Moses said.

Sheriff Pypard spoke to his son. 'You all right if I leave you for a few minutes?'

Gilbert held up his quill and indicated he would be fine. Moses and the sheriff walked over to a stack of wooden chests and sat down on them.

'I wanted to talk to you about the other night,' said Moses.

'What about it?'

'I came to see if you'd arrested anyone.'

'What for?'

Moses could feel his hackles rising. The sheriff appeared to be behaving with deliberate obtuseness. He knew the sheriff liked a quiet life, preferring to turn a blind eye to most goings on in the city. But to ignore a serious crime such as the murder of a young innocent boy and what he saw as the attempted murder of him and his neighbours was bordering on negligence. Sheriff Pypard could be stubborn. He would have to tread carefully with him.

'What do you know of the stranger Brito?' asked Moses.

'Not much except he's one of the king's men.'

'Don't you think it odd that he seems to be at the heart of everything?'

'What are you getting at, Moses?'

'He was there at the riot. He arrived in the city around the time the boy disappeared. Don't you think that's more of a coincidence?'

'No, I don't. I think it could be just that. A coincidence.'

'I think you should find out more about him.'

'I'm a busy man, Moses. Unless you have solid evidence against this Brito, I suggest you drop this.'

'The man incited the mob.'

'What proof do you have of that?'

Moses had no answer. He didn't have proof. Just a feeling in his gut that this stranger Brito was behind all of the recent events.

'If you have no proof then I can do nothing. I can't go around arresting the king's men on your say-so.'

Moses hesitated. It was hard for him to talk about what had happened to his niece. 'Did you know Brito violated my niece, Arlette.'

Sheriff Pypard shifted uncomfortably on the chest and gave Moses a sideways look. 'He raped her?'

'Yes.'

'Oh,' he said, clearing his throat. 'I was not aware of that.'

'I didn't mention it because…Well I didn't want everyone to know. For Arlette's sake.'

'So why are you here now?'

'I think he should pay for what he's done.'

Sheriff Pypard scratched at his trimmed beard. 'What do you want me to do?'

'Arrest him.'

'It's not that simple.'

'Why isn't it?'

'Do you have any witnesses? Did you see him rape her?'

Moses felt his skin creep at the image the sheriff's question brought to his mind. He shook his head.

'I didn't witness it, but I saw him drag her into the courtyard and when she came out later her tunic was ripped.'

'That doesn't prove anything.'

'It was obvious what had taken place.'

'He'll deny it.'

The sheriff was right. Brito would never confess to the crime.

'If it was one of our own who did this, we would deal with him ourselves in our own court.'

'I know you have your own court and that is how you deal with these matters in your community, but as you say Brito is not one of you.'

'Exactly. That's why I've come to you. You're the only person who can do something.'

The sheriff squirmed even more on the bench.

'You're putting me in a difficult situation, Moses. Brito is not just one of the king's men, he's a mercenary.'

'Surely the king would not protect a rapist?'

'The king has men who work for him. Mercenaries carrying out what you might call his unofficial business. If Brito has direct instructions from the king, then something is afoot that neither I nor you should get involved in. I would be signing my death warrant or at the very least the end of my career if I go against him and the king.'

Moses was backing the sheriff into a corner, but the sheriff wasn't budging.

'This is a very messy business, Moses. I can't do what you ask.'

'Then I'll have to do something.'

Moses stood up to leave.

'That would be very unwise.'

'My niece's life has been ruined by this man. He has brought shame on her and jeopardised her betrothal.'

'I wasn't aware Arlette was engaged.'

'To Aaron of Lincoln's son, Deudonne.'

'A good match.'

'I fear the wedding will never go ahead when he finds out what has happened to her.'

'Men can be very unforgiving in these circumstances. I'm sorry for your niece, but what you are asking me to do is impossible. You have no evidence, no witnesses. He will simply deny it and I will look like I'm going against the king if I pursue this. I'm sorry, Moses.'

'It seems he can accuse us of the murder of that boy... without any evidence.'

Sheriff Pypard nodded. 'You have a point, but like I said he's no ordinary king's servant.'

'It doesn't seem right that he's going to go through life unpunished.'

'Life is not fair.'

Moses shook his head in disbelief.

'Think about it, Moses. Do you want to put Arlette through the ordeal of a trial? Have her stand up in front of everyone and tell them what he did to her?'

Moses hadn't thought of that. Arlette was fragile, damaged. She would never survive such an ordeal unscathed. And Brito being the brute he was would never confess to his crime.

'I hate to admit it, but I think you may be right, sheriff. I wasn't thinking about my niece. She is suffering, and this would cause her more suffering. I couldn't do that to her.'

Sheriff Pypard relaxed his shoulders. Moses could see the relief in his lined face.

'What about the mob? You could round them up along with Brito. There must be something you can charge them with?'

Sheriff Pypard stiffened. 'I'll make enquiries.'

'Enquiries?' Moses said, challenging him.

A mighty crash and a shout of 'Watch out!' rang out. A wooden barrel of wine had fallen onto the quayside spilling its rich blood-coloured liquid onto the cornerstone edging of the quay, turning the mud grey water a murky orange.

'Damn and blast,' cursed Sheriff Pypard. 'I will have to sort this mess out. I'm sorry I can't help you.'

This was the sheriff's way of wriggling out of an uncomfortable situation. Enquiries. What would that consist of? Probably very little knowing the sheriff.

'I'll call again when you've completed your enquiries,' Moses shouted after him.

The sheriff raised his hand behind him as he walked away. Moses felt cheated. He sat a while longer. The tannic smell of the wine reached him.

What a waste of a good wine.

Then he thought of his niece and felt ashamed. The wine was unimportant. Her life was not. Perhaps he should make his own enquiries.

CHAPTER
TWENTY-NINE

Moses walked back to the house in a daze, unaware of the crowded streets. He went straight to his cellar hoping to avoid Douce. He couldn't face her. She had taken Arlette's rape badly and would be angry that nothing could be done about it. Maybe when she realised Arlette would suffer if a trial was to be held to prove Brito's guilt or otherwise, she would relent and find some other outlet for her rage. Since the invasion of his home, Moses had been burying himself in mathematical calculations of interest rates, commissions and anything else he could find to keep his thoughts from wandering to that terrible night. They had a solidity, a certainty. They made sense to him. He was a man of business not of battle and bloodshed. The entire unholy affair was anathema to him. It made him feel uneasy, slightly nauseous.

He was keenly aware his niece, under the protection of his guardianship, had been brutally raped and now faced a life much different from the one he had planned for her. Her intended marriage to Deudonne was unlikely to go ahead although he did not have the heart to confess this to Douce. He was hoping against hope that all would turn out well.

Today was Monday and the Irishman said he would call back. Moses still couldn't think clearly. He was struggling to make sense of it all. What did the Irishman have to do with the stranger and vice versa? And what did Brito have to do with the murder of the boy? And were the two events connected somehow? His brain hurt he had dwelled upon the problem for so long. Every sound he heard coming from the street or from people passing his door filled his heart with dread. His chest felt tight and when he breathed, he was barely able to take a full breath. He still didn't know what he was going to say to the Irishman to get rid of him. The thought of sending him to Elias seemed unfair, dishonourable.

Thud. Thud. Thud.

The unmistakeable sound of the Irishman's fist on his door. His stomach churned, and his legs shook.

Thud. Thud. Thud.

He was not going to go away.

Fearing Douce would answer the door, Moses jumped out of his seat and went to open it. The man who stood before him looked less than happy. Their previous exchange had not placed him in the best of moods. Dairmait glowered at Moses. But to his surprise, two others accompanied him. An attractive young woman with blazing red hair and a man in his forties. This must be Richard de Clare, the earl who Aaron warned him about. The one who reneged on his debts.

Moses was unsure whether to invite them in or leave them standing at the door. Normally, he would show visitors into the great hall but the thought of inviting this savage over his threshold did not appeal. He decided to step out and speak to them in the alleyway.

'Is this where you normally conduct business?' Dairmait asked, his tone clearly showing his indignance.

'No...' Moses said, trying to think of an excuse. He could see by the disgruntled look on Dairmait's face he was affronted. At the same time, he noticed Richard place a hand on Dairmait's arm. At least someone was going to keep this barbarian in check it seemed. 'My niece is unwell. I don't want to disturb her. We're fine here. Please follow me into the courtyard, it's not used at this time of day.'

To Moses' surprise, the young woman spoke. Her voice was quite deep with a Celtic lilt that Moses found appealing.

'Monsieur le Riche, let me introduce myself. I am Aoife, Dairmait's daughter. I'm sorry to hear your niece is unwell. I hope it will not be too long before she's well again.'

Moses was thrown off kilter by the exchange. He had prepared for a difficult confrontation. Perhaps the Irishman brought her as a peacemaker. He had anticipated a verbal lashing, but it seemed he would have to be more conciliatory in the presence of his daughter. He noticed the older man was very attentive towards her, giving her appreciative glances from time to time.

'I thank you for your kind words.' Moses steered them into the courtyard towards the bench. 'Please take a seat,' he said to Aoife.

'Thank you, but I am happy standing,' she said, giving Moses an engaging smile.

He found himself returning her smile. There was something quite arresting and unusual about her. They were a strange coterie, he thought. An unlikely pairing. This time the older man spoke.

'Let me introduce myself. My name is Richard de Clare. You may have heard of me by a different name. Strongbow. My good friend here,' he patted Dairmait on the shoulder, 'is Dairmait

MacMurchada, who until very recently was the King of Leinster.'

'Until recently?' Moses said.

'He has recently been deposed by his enemies over in Ireland.'

'I see,' said Moses.

'He has been issued with letters patent from the king.'

Richard pulled out a roll of parchment and handed it to Moses. Moses unfurled it and holding it open, read its contents.

'Henry, King of the English, Duke of the Normans and Aquitainians, and Count of the Angevins, to all his liegemen, English, Norman, Welsh and Scots, and to all the nations subject to his authority, greeting. Know by these letters that we have received Dairmait, Prince of the men of Leinster, into our grace and favour. Wherefore, whosoever, within our frontiers shall be willing to aid him as our vassal and liegemen in recovering his dominion, let him be assured of our favour and permission for it.'

'This is all very well, but what has this to do with me?' Moses said, handing back the parchment to Richard.

'My father has the king's permission to gather together an army of men to fight for his rightful lands in our homeland,' Aoife said.

'And as you know, raising an army is an expensive business,' Richard added. 'He's looking to borrow a substantial amount of money to enable him to do that, with the king's permission of course.'

'But why come to me?' Moses asked.

'Robert fitz Harding highly recommended you to us. The arrangement would be most beneficial to yourself.'

'Are you able to help?' Richard asked.

Moses felt his stomach lurch. He had to tread carefully. There was still the question of the stranger and his warning to him. He had already done enough damage to his family. He did not want to give him more cause. He looked across at the Irishman. His expression was unchanged. He took a deep breath and swallowed.

'Ordinarily I would be able to help you, but I'm afraid I'm rather overcommitted at present.'

'Why didn't you tell me this when I called the other day? You've wasted my bloody time,' Dairmait shouted.

'Father,' Aoife remonstrated. 'Hear the man out.'

'I was not aware of the circumstances. We didn't quite get that far in our discussion if you remember?'

Dairmait grunted.

'I had no idea you would require sufficient to raise an army. I have taken on several clients recently and I simply don't have the capacity to help you at this moment in time. I wish I could.'

'We come with the good grace of the king in our endeavours,' said Richard.

Richard paused as if mention of the king's name would change Moses' mind. Refusing business went against the grain for Moses. He knew he could make a tidy profit from this business transaction. Wars could rage on for years and soldiers needed feeding, equipping and clothing. But Brito's words echoed in his head. Douce would never forgive him.

'I'm sure you do, and ordinarily I would like nothing more than to assist you, but as I said I'm overcommitted at present.'

Dairmait stamped his boots like an angry young child. 'Let's be off,' he growled. 'I'm not wasting any more of my time. If the Jew is refusing to do business, let's go elsewhere.'

'My father can be impatient at times. Don't mind him,' Aoife said. 'I'm sure you would help us if you could. Perhaps you know of someone else who is less committed and may be able to help?'

She smiled at him again, her red hair glistening in the bright spring sunshine and her eyes drawing Moses in. Did he know anyone else? Of course, he did, but should he foist trouble onto a fellow Jew? Dairmait was staring hard at him. He looked diabolically possessed. The blood in Moses' veins throbbed making his body quiver. The niggardly face of Mirabelle shot into his mind. This might be the only way out of this perilous business.

'As a matter of fact, I think there is. Have you tried Elias de Glocestre? He lives opposite. He may well be able to help you.'

Aoife shot a conspiratorial look at her father. 'Thank you, sir. We will detain you no longer.'

Moses had an afterthought. Elias might send them away. He didn't have the guile of Mirabelle. Besides, he wanted to foist this difficult business onto her, not Elias. He shouted after them, 'His wife rules the roost in that household. You may be better off talking with her. Her name is Mirabelle.'

The three conspirators walked away. Moses watched them disappear down the alley and out of sight. As he opened the door to his home, he felt a mixture of relief and achievement. He had survived the encounter unscathed.

CHAPTER

THIRTY

B rito had spent the weekend stewing in the Lich Inn. In between whoring and drinking, he slept. Today was going to be different. He had work to do. But, as usual, he had slept late, and it was already lunchtime. Brito was angry that no arrests for the murder of the boy had been made. Furious his plan had been thwarted he resolved to visit the castle to discover what the sheriff's intentions were regarding the Jews. The Jews had got off lightly. Someone had to pay for the murder of the Christian boy. Did no one care that a Christian had been murdered? Was the boy's life worth less than that of a stinking Jew? Still, the evening had not been a total waste of time. The Jewess was an unexpected pleasure. Lustful memories of his conquest returned giving him a hardness of impressive proportions. The sheriff would have to wait. Besides, he could not leave looking like the Roman god Priapus.

When Brito later emerged into the bright sunshine, he felt sated and ready to argue his point with the sheriff. Something must be done to bring the killers of the boy to justice. He made his way to the castle, cutting through Foxes Lane and onto Bare

Lands. The castle stood on the banks of the River Severn, surrounded by a wooden palisade and protected by a deep fosse. Brito was challenged by the sheriff's men at the entrance to the bailey and only allowed to pass when he told them he was there to report a murder. The bailey was thick with dust. Preparations were under way to replace the wooden keep. Skilled stonemasons were busy hammering huge blocks of stone brought from Painswick in readiness for the building works.

Brito climbed the vertiginous steps to the wooden keep, strategically built on top of the man-made motte, where he found Sheriff Pypard and his son Gilbert. Humphrey de Bohun was with them. At the sight of Humphrey, Brito smiled with smug satisfaction. In terms of station, Humphrey outranked Sheriff Pypard. Brito thought that at last he may have a powerful ally in this Jew-loving city.

The men sat in front of a roaring fire in the great hall, each drinking a goblet of red wine. Sheriff Pypard was getting on in years. His beard had turned white and his waistline had expanded. Brito heard the sheriff let out an irritated groan as he approached and realised Sheriff Pypard no longer had the stomach for warfare. Perhaps he could appeal to the callow youthfulness of Humphrey de Bohun who in his position as Lord High Constable had already gained a reputation for the unashamed exploitation of other people's lands and riches to advance his own standing. He had the morals of a feral dog.

Humphrey was dressed in a fine wool tunic, dyed green with gold trim. Over this he wore a mantle of animal skin lined with the bluish-grey fur of the vair, a type of squirrel popular with the Normans. He looked every inch a royal earl.

On seeing Brito, the sheriff sat up and slammed his tankard down, speaking in dismissive tones to him. 'I'm a busy man. State your business and be off. I have work to do.'

'I've come to see what it is you propose to do about the boy's murder. Are you going to arrest them?'

'I take it you mean the Jews?'

'Who else would have murdered the boy in such a way as to mock our Christ? You said on the night of the riot that the mob should let the law deal with it but what have you done? Nothing. Meanwhile this boy's murderers are free to roam the streets.'

'I beg to differ. I made enquiries on the night in question.'

'Not very exhaustive or you would have made some arrests by now.'

There was a noise at the door. Brito turned to see a woman of noble birth, dressed in white funereal clothing, walking towards them. She held herself well, walking upright, with a long neck and upturned nose. Brito could see she had been quite a beauty in her youth and even now, with advancing years, she had appeal.

Humphrey said, 'Ah, Mother, come join us by the fire. We're discussing the Jewish problem.'

'I didn't realise we had a Jewish problem?'

Brito's admiration for Margaret turned to irritation. There would always be a Jewish problem as long as the Jews were allowed to live in England.

Sheriff Pypard addressed Margaret. 'Good afternoon, my lady. I trust you slept well?'

Margaret replied, 'As well as can be expected.'

There was a frostiness in her reply, though Brito thought he detected a sadness to her voice. 'My lady,' he addressed her, bowing.

'And you are?'

'My name is Brito. I'm here about the murder of the boy.'

Brito's words appeared to knock Margaret sideways. 'You have knowledge of the boy's murderer?'

Brito wondered why she was showing such interest in the murder of some insignificant boy.

Sheriff Pypard interrupted, 'He is of the impression the Jews killed that boy, Harold. The one they found by the river on Saturday.'

'Why would they do that?'

'He seems to think they did it in mockery of Christ. Because of the injuries he received.'

Margaret winced and placed a white cloth to her lips.

'Please sit down, Mother,' Humphrey said. 'She's not been herself of late.'

Sheriff Pypard gestured for Margaret to take his seat. 'Sit here. I didn't mean to distress you.'

Margaret sat in the sheriff's chair by the fire, scooping her gown away from the grey ashes covering the wooden floor. 'I know Moses le Riche. I've done business with him. He's a charming man...'

'For a Jew,' Brito muttered under his breath.

'I cannot imagine he would do such a thing.'

'Maybe you don't know Jews that well?'

'Do you know Moses?'

'No, but I know others like him. They're like leeches.'

'Why do you have such hatred towards the Jews? What have they done to you?' Margaret asked Brito.

Brito hesitated. Should he tell them how his family had been ruined by a greedy Jew in his hometown of Thetford? What harm would it do? It was better they knew what lengths these godless Jews would go to for a piece of gold.

'They bled my family dry until there was nothing left. It crushed my mother.'

'But surely that was imprudent of them – to lose everything?'

A red mist of rage flashed in front of Brito. How could she

deride his mother and father? She did not know the whole story or the circumstances. It took all his resolve to quell the anger he felt towards this woman of high birth who probably had never suffered a trace of financial hardship in her pampered life.

'I shall pray for them,' Margaret said.

'What good will that do?'

Margaret was short with him. 'I find comfort in prayer. You should try it.'

Brito smarted at the memory of finding out his parents were destitute, his own future uncertain. It was only because of their connections and his adeptness on the battlefield that he had forged himself a place by the king's side.

Humphrey de Bohun was unusually quiet. Had he turned into a Jew lover? Brito addressed him directly.

'What do you think, my lord?'

Humphrey took a sweet pastry from a metal platter and dipped it into his wine before answering Brito.

'The Jews have done me no personal harm. In fact, they have proved themselves to be useful on occasion.'

'A boy has been murdered. I'm here only to see that justice is prevailed upon.' Brito looked around the room for support. None came.

Gilbert Pypard spoke. 'You seem to know a lot about this business.'

'Only because I've witnessed it before. In Norwich. I know what these Jews are capable of.'

'Still, it seems a strange coincidence you were in Norwich at the same time as a young boy was murdered and here you are again – in Gloucester with the murder of another young boy,' said Gilbert.

'I don't like your insinuation. Who is on trial here?' Brito snarled.

'Perhaps we should be looking elsewhere to discover who

murdered this boy,' Margaret said, a steely gaze directed at Brito.

'Why are you so concerned about this boy?' Brito countered.

'My uncle is Prior Clement. He was very fond of the boy. I seek justice on his behalf.'

'We all want justice, don't we, Sheriff Pypard?' Humphrey said, a hint of sarcasm in his voice.

'What my son means is that justice should be seen to be done. Don't you agree, sheriff?'

'Yes, my lady, but there is no evidence, no witnesses to the murder,' Sheriff Pypard replied. 'All we know is the boy disappeared from the care of Prior Clement and his body was found weeks later by the river.'

'With signs of ritual crucifixion. A classic modus operandi of the Jews,' Brito added.

'I wouldn't know,' Gilbert Pypard said.

'I know a ritual murder when I see it. I've seen it before. The Jews were responsible back then.'

'I seem to remember that no Jew was ever punished for that crime,' Humphrey de Bohun cut in. 'In fact, no one was punished.'

'Do you want that to happen here?' Brito asked the sheriff.

Sheriff Pypard shook his head.

'I don't think the king would be impressed with the way you've handled this situation.'

'What has the king got to do with the murder of this boy?' Margaret asked, her forehead creasing with concern.

'I didn't say he had...'

'You do realise the Jews are under the special protection of the king, and it is my duty to protect them?' the sheriff added.

'Not if they have committed the crime of murder. I doubt the king would want you to give sanctuary to a gang of murderers. You will have another riot on your hands if you don't do something. The citizens are angry and seek only truth and justice,' said Brito.

'He has a point,' Humphrey said. 'Remember the Jew's charter drawn up by our king gives them liberties but excludes certain excesses as belong to crown and justice. I seem to remember there was a lengthy list of instances including homicide.'

'I do not think for one moment that the Jews are responsible, but I would like to see something done for the sake of m–' She cleared her throat realising she was about to expose herself as Harold's mother. 'My uncle's novice. At the very least, we ought to find out what happened to him.'

'Aren't you taking your role as a benefactress a little too far, Mother?'

'I merely seek justice as I'm sure everyone in this room does.'

The men nodded in agreement. Brito was amazed at how much power this woman had. Ordinarily, he would stamp out such interference from a woman, but she was proving to be an unexpected ally. He held his tongue.

'And you want me to round up the whole Jewish community and put them on trial?' Sheriff Pypard said.

'I didn't say that,' Margaret replied.

'Mother, there are no other suspects.'

'It would be in the interests of justice,' Brito added, sensing his plan was back on course.

'I think it would be a prudent move, sheriff,' Humphrey said. 'These Jews need to be reminded that they can't act with impunity. Even if they have their own laws and have the king's protection they are not above the law.'

Sheriff Pypard sighed heavily. He could not go against the king or the Lord High Constable.

'Very well, then. I'll send my men to arrest them.'

CHAPTER
THIRTY-ONE

Two days after their visit to the rabbi, there was a knock at the door. When Moses went to answer it, he found Aaron of Lincoln standing there. Alone.

'*Sholom alaichem.*'

'*Alaichem sholom,*' replied Aaron, removing his pointed hat.

'Come in, my friend. It's good to see you again,' Moses said.

'Is there somewhere we can talk in private?' Aaron said.

He could tell by the reticence in his voice this was not going to be a business meeting. He was friendly but there was an edge.

'Certainly,' Moses replied. 'Follow me to the cellar. It's where I conduct all of my business.'

'As do I,' Aaron said. 'The safest place in the house.'

Moses led the way down to the cool, vaulted cellar.

'Is this about Arlette?' he asked Aaron as soon as they sat down.

'Yes,' Aaron said.

'You know then?'

'We overheard someone relaying the awful events while we were in Bristol. Such a terrible thing to happen.'

'What have you come to say?'

'Moses, my friend, we've been business partners for some years now and I was happy, very happy to cement that relationship with the marriage of my son to your niece, but after what has happened...'

'What does Deudonne think? Does he still want to marry Arlette?'

'This is hard for me, Moses, but I'm afraid this has changed everything. I cannot let my son marry your niece. It would not be fair to him. I must withdraw from our arrangement. I know we shook on it, and I am more than happy to pay a fine. Name your price.'

Moses was not angry with his friend. In a way, he had been expecting this. It was inevitable.

'There's no need to talk of a fine. We are friends and shall remain so.'

'You do understand?'

'Of course I do,' Moses said, playing with the coin he kept on his desk. 'Obviously Arlette will be devastated.'

'How is she?'

Moses did not want to tell his friend the truth. He didn't know why but he just felt he owed it to Arlette.

'As well as can be expected,' he replied.

'I'm glad. A terrible business.'

'Talking of business, Aaron, I trust this will not affect our arrangement?'

'Business is business, Moses. We work well together. I see no reason for this to change.'

An awkward silence fell upon them.

'I must go. Deudonne is waiting for me. We're continuing on to Lincoln today.'

Moses sat for some time in the cellar after Aaron left, avoiding Douce. He could not face her. He knew she would be upset, and it was more than he could bear. He felt an unease, a feeling that life would never be the same. Everything was changing. His business relations, his family, his friends. All would be different. He was losing his grip on life. Usually he would turn to his faith, but he was angry at Hashem. Very angry. He heard light footsteps on the stairs. Douce was looking for him. It was time to tell her.

'*Chéri*,' she called out. 'Are you down there?'

Moses went to the bottom of the stairs to answer her.

'Yes. I'm coming now.'

When he reached the top of the steps and saw Douce's face he knew she knew. He did not have to say anything. 'How will Arlette take this news?' he asked.

Douce raised her eyebrows. 'Who can say?'

'Should we keep it from her as long as possible? Wait till she feels better?'

Douce shrugged. 'When will that be?'

Moses expected his wife to sob, to rail against the injustice, but it seemed she had given up. He couldn't decide which was worse. He took his wife's hand in his.

'Arlette is like a daughter to me. I love her like she was my own. I want to do all I can to help her get over this. Help me, Douce.'

Douce released her hand and drew him towards her. They hugged, Moses hiding his silent tears.

CHAPTER

THIRTY-TWO

The news that Arlette's betrothal to Deudonne was called off was greeted by Zev with immense excitement and a good deal of hope. He had not seen Arlette since that terrible night, but the memory of her frail body so light in his arms as he carried her into the house and upstairs to her bedroom was still burning inside him. He had stroked her hair and told her she was going to be all right. Her vacant stare had unnerved him and caused him sleepless nights. He had tried to see her, but each time he called at the house Douce told him she was not well enough to see anyone.

He lost no time capitalising on the news. But first he must summon all the confidence he could muster considering the complete mess he had made of his inept and embarrassing proposal to Arlette at Purim. Even after recent events, Zev thought she might still see him as inferior. After all, he didn't live in wealthy Jewry Street, the realm of the moneylenders, but instead a lane for tradesmen at the back of St Martin's chapel. His house was wooden, hers a stone fortress. None of this mattered, he told himself. Now was not the time to be negative. He fussed over his attire, changing finally into his best Shabbat clothes. He must look his best even though his mother was determined to talk him out of his foolish plan.

'She didn't want you when she was...' his mother began.

'When she was what, *Ima*?'

Damete could not finish the sentence she had begun, nor could she look her son in the eye. 'You're a fool, Zev. You wear your heart on your sleeve but that will get you nowhere. You should marry Chera,' she said, tousling his hair.

Zev pushed his mother's hand away and ran his hand through his mass of dark curls. 'Mother, don't do that to my hair.'

Damete shrugged. 'For a butcher's boy you think too much about your looks.'

'What does it matter whether I am a butcher's boy or a rabbi? I still want to look my best.'

'This is foolishness. Douce will never allow this. You'll only embarrass yourself again.'

'I love Arlette. I always have and now I have a chance to be with her.'

'What if she says no? Can you bear to be rejected again?'

'I know you're trying to protect me, *Ima*, but you don't understand.'

'And what about Chera? She won't hang around for long. I hear Baruch is interested in her.'

'Baruch can have her and with my blessing.'

Damete sighed with frustration and went to see who was knocking at the door. When she returned, she had a trace of smugness about her. Zev soon saw the cause of it. Chera was standing behind her.

'Chera, what are you doing here?' Zev said, trying to sound surprised but in his heart, he knew why.

'I came to see you.'

'Oh.'

'Can I have a word with Zev?' Chera asked Damete.

Damete looked affronted but excused herself from the room.

'My mother is probably still listening at the door,' Zev said, trying not to look at Chera.

'I hear Deudonne has called off his betrothal to Arlette.'

'Yes, I just heard. I'm going over there now.'

'Oh, are you?' Chera said, looking surprised. 'I'm too late then?'

'Too late for what?'

'Your mother said...'

Zev was bent down putting on his boots. He looked up at Chera. 'What did my mother say?' he asked, his voice cold and challenging.

'She said you felt differently about Arlette...'

'Why would I feel differently?'

Zev knew what she meant. That because of what had happened to her, Arlette was no longer worthy, somehow less of a person. Not worth marrying.

'It's just your mother gave me the impression there was hope for me now that Arlette...'

Zev interrupted her, 'Now that Arlette is what, Chera?'

Chera's face crumpled, her courage visibly slipping away.

'I'm sorry, I shouldn't have come. Your mother...'

'My mother? You should *never* listen to my mother. She meddles too much in other people's lives.'

Zev stood up and was shouting now, hoping his mother could hear his every word. Dabbing at the corner of her eye, Chera turned to go.

'I didn't mean to upset you, Chera. I'm not angry at you. It's my mother I'm angry with.'

Chera had her back to Zev. She stopped and without turning said, 'I hope you are very happy with Arlette. *Mazel tov.*'

Then she opened the door and flew past Damete, who was standing in the doorway.

'What have you said to Chera to upset her?'

'What have *you* said to her?' Zev asked, his tone accusatory.

'I am only trying to make you see sense. Chera is a–'

'A good match. Yes, you've said that before. You're always saying it, but it won't make the slightest difference. I am meant to be with Arlette. I've always known it. Hashem has declared it.'

'Now you're being ridiculous, Zev. You're a dreamer. You should be more practical like your father.'

'Like a butcher's son?'

'There's no shame in being a butcher. Your father provides.'

'I know. Father is a good provider, but I want more.'

'*Oy lanu!* I don't understand young people.'

Zev smiled at his mother. It was her way of backing down. He kissed her on the cheek. She shrugged him off feigning her displeasure.

'Wish me luck,' he said, winking at her.

Zev knew he had won the argument, but it didn't make him feel any better. He loved his mother. She was infuriating when she tried to interfere in his life. She was sulking now. He held her firmly by the shoulders and planted a solid kiss on her cheek. 'There, that's better,' he said, winking again.

Zev knew she couldn't be angry with him for long. Damete blushed, then smiled weakly.

'Go, my son, and may Hashem be with you.'

Dressed in his finest clothes, even though they would never match the sumptuousness of those worn by Moses' family, he set off. Zev was relieved when Moses opened the door. He might stand a chance with him rather than Douce.

'I've come to see Arlette.'

'Come in, Zev, come in.'

Moses showed Zev into the great hall. Douce was sat by the fire, embroidering a piece of silk. She looked up when they came into the room.

'Zev. How nice to see you, how are you?'

'I'm well, thank you.'

'Zev has come to see Arlette,' Moses said.

Douce dropped the needlework on her lap.

'Arlette is seeing no one at present, Zev. She's not well.'

'I can't leave until I speak with her,' Zev said, removing his felt cap and gripping it between both hands.

Moses spoke, 'I think you should tell Arlette Zev is here, *chérie.*'

Douce left the men in the hall and went upstairs to speak to Arlette. Zev had never been alone with Moses. When he had visited as a boy, Moses was either out or in his cellar.

'May I offer you a cup of wine, Zev?'

'Oh, no thank you. I had more than enough at the Purim celebration. I'm not sure I'll ever touch it again.'

'I heard you didn't know the difference between "cursed is Haman and blessed is Mordechai."'

Zev laughed. 'I have my father to thank for that. For so many years I was looking forward to it, but the reality was not as good as I'd imagined.'

'It rarely is. If you don't mind, I think I'll have a cup.'

Moses went over to the bottle of red wine he kept on a small table by the fire and poured it into a goblet. He took a drink. 'My father says, "everything in moderation."'

'Wise words, Moses.'

There was still no sign of Douce or Arlette and after their

brief but pleasant exchange the two lapsed into an uncomfortable silence. Zev eventually broke it.

'They're taking their time.'

'Arlette has not been feeling well since... I don't know if she'll see you.'

There was a commotion on the stairwell. Douce came into the room followed by Arlette. She was dressed in the plain cotton tunic she wore to do her household chores and her hair was plainly swept back. There were deep grey bags beneath her eyes and she had lost weight. To Zev she was a vision of light and loveliness. Her usual imperiousness was gone. A vulnerability had crept into her demeanour. They stared at each other for a few seconds, neither speaking. Then Douce cleared her throat, nodding at Moses who was drinking his wine.

'Will you help me in the kitchen, Moses?'

Moses gave her a quizzical look and remained where he was.

'Now please, Moses.'

'Of course, *ma chérie*.'

Arlette and Zev were finally alone.

'Arlette,' he said. 'You know how I feel about you?'

'Yes.'

'Will you marry me?'

Arlette was shocked at Zev's outburst. She took hold of the back of a nearby chair to steady herself. Zev pressed on.

'I know you don't love me.'

'But why would you want to marry me if you know I don't love you and after what has happened...'

'None of that matters to me, Arlette. Don't you understand?

I love you. I've always loved you. I tried to tell you at Purim, but I made a complete hatchet of it.'

Arlette noted his use of the word 'hatchet'. Was he trying to speak French or was it an unintentional butchery joke? Her usual reaction would have been to chide him for it, to tease him, to gently point out his shortfalls. This time it didn't matter. Her heart was melting towards this kind man who stood before her, pouring out his feelings. She was seeing him in a different light, looking at him with fresh eyes. He was strong, manly, protective. His dark eyes, deep pools of liquid black, stared back at her honest and true.

'You still love me and want to marry me after all that has happened.'

It was not a question, more of a statement of astonishment that someone would still want her after she had been so defiled. 'I do,' was the only reply Zev gave. She had to make sure he knew what he was taking on. He was naïve, ingenuous.

'You must know I am no longer a virgin, Zev, no longer clean. Don't you understand? Surely you cannot want to marry such a woman?'

'Didn't you hear what I said, Arlette? I don't care. None of that matters.'

Arlette pressed on. He probably hadn't thought of the one thing that could ruin it all. She must tell him. 'It's too early to tell but I may be having another man's child. I cannot bring that shame upon you.'

'But the child will be part of you, Arlette, and I will love it as my own. And besides,' he added, in his characteristically flippant manner, 'no one will know it's not mine. *Sheol!* If you marry me tomorrow, even I won't know.'

Arlette's heart felt like it could break in two. She didn't deserve such devotion from the man she had spurned. She remembered their conversation at Purim. He said he had 'other qualities'. He was right. She could see that now. He did. She felt an unexpected surge of love for him. For the butcher's boy. His kindness was too much to bear. She broke down. Zev put his arm around her and comforted her. She did not stiffen but allowed her body to relax into his.

'The time has come to stop crying, Arlette. We'll be happy together. Just you see. We'll have plenty of children and our children will have children and they will look after us in our old age.'

Arlette laughed through her tears. He could always make her laugh. For the first time since the rape, she felt a flickering of hope. Hope for a life lived without shame. Acceptance by the community through her liaison with Zev. She would be a good wife to him. She would make him happy.

'I will marry you, Zev.'

Zev pulled back from her and gazed into her eyes with a look of sheer wonderment.

'And I think I can learn to love you,' she added.

Zev beamed.

'What did I say,' he said, injecting levity into a wretched situation. 'I predicted it.'

Douce and Moses must have been half listening in the hallway for they came running in. Douce was crying with happiness. She threw her arms around the two of them and hugged them.

'*Mazel tov*,' she said, through tears of joy.

Moses crossed over to Zev and held out his hand. '*Mazel tov*.'

Zev took it, they shook hands and then Arlette saw Moses do something she had never seen her uncle do before. He opened his arms and hugged Zev.

CHAPTER
THIRTY-THREE

Mirabelle stood in the fore hall of her grand stone house barking out orders to her Christian maid Joan. Joan as usual stood with her head bowed, listening to Mirabelle list the litany of daily chores she was expected to carry out.

'And don't forget to sweep under the bed,' Mirabelle ordered.

Joan, frail and overworked, slunk away without comment. Mirabelle tutted under her breath as she watched the lazy girl climb the stairs.

She must not compel a Hebrew servant to do the work of a slave, but who said she could not compel a Christian servant to work like a slave? She didn't have to get her hands dirty, but best of all, in her eyes, it raised her status. No one else had a servant, especially that simpering little wife of Moses le Riche. Secretly, she could scratch her eyes out. The woman maddened her, showing off her wealth, flouncing around in her expensive clothing, indulging that spoilt niece of hers. They weren't so high and mighty now.

As she made her way back to the great hall, she heard a

knock at the door. Normally, she would expect Joan to answer but as she had just sent her to the top of the house, she would not hear her calling. The knocking came again. Insistent. Mirabelle found herself getting annoyed. Who would knock at her door in such a rude way? Did they have no patience? No manners? She opened it, her face set into a scowl. She was met with an equally ferocious glare from a man she had never seen before. He was accompanied by two others.

'What do you want?' she said, her tone rude and uninviting.

'We've come to discuss business,' Dairmait said, meeting her rudeness with defiance.

'My husband is not home.'

Aoife stepped forward. 'Actually, it's you we've come to see.'

Mirabelle studied the threesome. The girl looked regal, and the man with her, a Norman knight. As for the ferocious knave with them, she decided to ignore him. The presence of the Norman knight told her there may be lucrative business to be had. She smiled at the young girl and invited them into the great hall. It was furnished lavishly with trinkets from faraway lands. Wall hangings from the East and rugs from Persia. The room exuded ostentation.

'Please have a seat,' said Mirabelle, her thin lips squeezed into a smile. 'How can I help?'

Aoife explained to Mirabelle the circumstances that brought them to her door. Mirabelle listened attentively, nodding and smiling in the right places. The smell of a lucrative business deal left her salivating with expectation. More so because they had asked for her, not her spineless husband whose hesitancy and cautious approach to business matters meant she had to be satisfied with being second wealthiest in the community, not first.

'Who recommended me?' Mirabelle asked.

'Your neighbour, Moses le Riche.'

Mirabelle's expression turned thunderous at the mention of Moses, her main rival for supremacy. Her immediate thought was why had he not accepted the business.

'I'm surprised that Moses should not want this business for himself...'

'Sadly, he told us he is unable to assist as he is overcommitted,' Aoife explained.

Mirabelle was not convinced. Moses would never refer lucrative business to her or her husband. Something was not right. Why was life so unjust? Just as she was about to make the deal of her life, she suspected it could turn to ashes in front of her very eyes. No matter how lucrative this deal, she sensed there must be a reason for Moses not to have grasped it with both of his grubby hands. She must put them off until she knew more.

'I'll need to speak with my husband,' she said.

Dairmait's face turned red, and his eyes bulged. 'What is wrong with you damn people. I thought you liked to lend money. Isn't that how you can afford to live in such luxury?' Dairmait waved his arm around the room.

'I think you should leave,' said Mirabelle, jutting out her bony chin and crossing her arms. 'I find your behaviour insulting.'

Aoife sighed with exasperation. Her father was suited to being in battle and herding slaves across the Irish sea, not for business diplomacy.

'Please don't be offended by my father. He's angry at losing his kingship, not at you. Perhaps we can return when your husband is home and you've had chance to talk with him?'

Even though it pained her to refuse business of any sort, her hackles were raised and the prickling at the back of her neck was a sure sign that this was bad business. She remained silent, glaring at Dairmait.

'Or perhaps you can recommend someone else we can approach,' suggested Aoife, a whiff of desperation in her voice.

Mirabelle's quick-witted, scheming nature never failed her. She thought of a way to simultaneously extricate herself from this trio of fraudsters, if that's what they were, whilst still enjoying a cut of the spoils. She addressed Aoife.

'There may be a way of helping you. Let me speak with someone. Where can I send word?'

'We're staying at the Portcullis Inn.'

'Very well, I'll be in touch.'

CHAPTER
THIRTY-FOUR

Moses jumped at the sound of hammering at his door so early in the morning as did everyone else sitting around the breakfast table. It sounded like the Irishman's knock. Loud and impatient. Hadn't he told that savage to go elsewhere? Moses was in a good mood and didn't relish another encounter with the irksome Irishman. The happy news that Arlette was betrothed to Zev after all that had happened to her brightened his spirits and hers too. It had brought her out of her bedroom and here at the table where she was eating breakfast and feeding Samuel just like the old days. Moses was humming with joy whilst eating his breakfast, but at the sound of the hammering his joyous mood evaporated and irritation crept in.

Thud. Thud. Thud.

'All right, all right. *Oy lanu.*'

Moses opened the door braced for an argument with the irascible Irishman. Instead, he was confronted with Sheriff Pypard and a posse of his men.

'May I help you, sheriff?'

'I'm sorry, Moses, I've come to arrest you for the murder of the boy Harold.'

'You know I had nothing to do with that boy's murder.'

'It's out of my hands now. Take him, men.'

The sheriff's men surged forward and grabbed Moses by both arms, pulling him over the threshold. Moses was too shocked to resist and before he knew it, he was being dragged into Jewry Street. It was not long before he heard a shrill scream behind him. It was Douce and Arlette following him down the alley.

'It's a mistake, Douce,' Moses shouted over his shoulder. 'Don't fret. I'll be all right. Go back inside.'

The sheriff's men tied his hands with thick rope. Douce ran after him in an agitated state, Arlette close behind.

Douce cried, 'What's happening?'

Douce tried to reach him but was pushed back by the sheriff's men.

'Go back inside,' he said again. 'There's nothing you can do here.'

Then he heard Arlette wailing as she ran to Zev across the way who was also being tied up, but she too was pushed back by the sheriff's men. Then Moses saw Brito. He was staring at Arlette with lascivious intent. Zev had seen him too.

'Arlette,' Zev shouted. 'Go back inside the house.'

At the same time, Moses shouted to Douce. 'Take Arlette inside where it's safe. Hurry.'

Douce ran to Arlette and urged her to go inside. Arlette resisted at first but then allowed Douce to place a protective arm over her shoulder and lead her away.

It was market day and as Moses was led past the stalls people threw vegetables and scraps of meat at him, jeering and cussing. As he walked past one of the meat stalls, a butcher threw the contents of a metal pail at Moses. The rotten, gelatinous entrails hit him on the side of his face. Moses gagged at the smell and wanted to wipe the bloody slime away but the ropes around his wrists cut into his flesh and made it difficult. Ahead of him walked Bellassez. They were dragging her along so roughly she stumbled and fell to the ground. Moses rushed ahead to help her, but he was held back. A woman in the street spat on her, another called out insults. Moses had never felt so ill-prepared, helpless, impotent. Once more he raged against the injustices of his people.

Inside the bailey they were taken to a small wooden outbuilding and pushed inside, the heavy door slamming behind them. Moses heard the metal bolt grinding into place. It was dark inside with one narrow window from which came a single shaft of grey light. The floor was covered with fresh straw, no doubt in preparation for their arrival, thought Moses. He went over to Bellassez, the only woman amongst them, to comfort her.

'What will happen to my children, Moses?'

'Try not to worry. Douce will take them in and look after them. She won't leave them on their own.'

'They'll be so frightened. I've never been away from them.'

'We'll be out of here soon,' he said.

'With Hashem's help,' she added.

'Why do they think we have anything to do with this boy's murder?' asked Zev.

This started a barrage of questions and they were all talking at once. Moses raised his hands and gestured for them to be quiet.

'I don't have all the answers.'

'But you have a good relationship with the sheriff,' said Rubin. 'Can't you speak to him?'

'I'll ask but I'm not hopeful.'

'The sheriff is supposed to be our protector,' said Elias.

'I know,' said Moses, 'but someone else is behind this.'

'Who?' Josce asked.

'I think it may have something to do with that stranger.'

Everyone fell silent at the mention of the stranger. They all knew who he was. They had seen him drag Arlette into the alley. Moses knew what they were thinking.

'The one at the riot?' Elias asked.

'Who is he?'

'What has he got against us?'

'Where did he come from?'

'Why's he here?'

'I don't know. I know nothing about him.'

Moses tried his best to answer their questions and was relieved when eventually the questions ceased. They were frightened, angry and exhausted. Rabbi Solomon recited a psalm to comfort them.

'Hashem is my light and my salvation, whom shall I fear? Hashem is the strength of my life, whom shall I dread? For He will hide me in His tabernacle on a day of adversity.'

Moses reflected on the words of the rabbi. How had his day started so well but quickly turned into a day of adversity? Despite the calming words of the rabbi a storm of emotions raged within him, mixed with the bitterness of knowing he would never see his family again. It was not easy to escape so-called Christian justice.

Some hours later when the guard returned with bread and weak ale Moses asked if he could speak with the sheriff. The guard grunted and told him the sheriff was a busy man.

'I know the sheriff. All I ask is that you tell him I wish to speak with him,' Moses said.

'You can ask all you like. I've told you, he's a busy man.'

Once again, the heavy door slammed shut and they were

plunged into the darkness of their airless prison, and once again Moses was assaulted by a clamouring of demands.

'I need to get back to my wife.'

'I need to get back to my business.'

'I need to be with my children,' Bellassez said.

'We all need to get out of here,' said Moses, his voice raised in annoyance.

'What are you doing about it?' said Elias.

Everyone was staring at Moses with accusing eyes.

'What do you want me to do? I've asked to see the sheriff. I can do no more.'

Bellassez wiped a tear from her eye and sat down in the corner. The others dispersed, their heads hung low. A silence filled with despair descended. Moses sat down next to Zev.

'You know, Moses, I was the happiest man alive yesterday. Betrothed to your niece, the most beautiful woman in Gloucester. A happy future ahead of me. Now look at me.'

Moses said, 'I never got the chance to thank you, Zev.'

'Thank me for what?' said Zev, surprised.

'For loving Arlette.'

'No need to thank me.'

'All the same, you were there for her when others weren't.'

'I've always loved Arlette.'

Moses had never heard Zev speak of his emotions. He was usually playing the fool whenever he saw him. Perhaps it was the circumstances they found themselves in. It made you say things you might not ordinarily say. As if this might be your last chance to say them. In the past, Moses dismissed Zev as foolish and unworthy, but he could see there was much more to him. He was honourable, steadfast. A sense of shame crept over Moses for being elitist and shallow. The events of the last few days had revealed cracks in his character. He enjoyed the status his wealth gave him, his sumptuous lifestyle, his good fortune but perhaps he had grown complacent, proud, unworthy.

'You'll make a good husband for Arlette.'

'I just want to make her happy, Moses. Keep her safe.'

'I don't doubt that.'

'I'd do anything for Arlette. If I ever get the chance,' Zev said, kicking at the straw beneath his boots.

'I hope you do, Zev.'

'What are the odds of getting out of here?'

Moses lowered his voice. 'Very slim. But don't tell anyone I said that.'

After spending an uncomfortable night on the cold, hard floor Moses woke to the sound of the bolt grating in its metal shaft. The stench of human faeces filled his nostrils, and he was reminded of the indignity of their confinement. The door opened, and a guard strode in.

'Which one of you is Elias?'

'I am,' said Elias, struggling to his feet.

'Come with me.'

'Where to?'

The guard did not reply. Elias hurried after him and left without a word to the others. The door slammed shut and he was gone.

'Where do you think they're taking him?'

'No idea.'

'What if they're taking him to the tower?'

'The Tower of London? What? You mean to be executed?'

By now everyone was awake and joining in the speculation of where Elias had been taken.

'Are they going to take us one by one?'

'Didn't the sheriff say there would be a trial?'

Moses finally spoke, 'I think it more likely that Mirabelle has something to do with this.'

'What do you mean?' Josce asked.

'She's probably bribed the sheriff to let him go.'

'Can't we do that?'

'I doubt the sheriff will let us all go.'

'That Mirabelle,' said Bellassez. 'If she fell into a cesspit, she'd come out smelling of rosemary.'

CHAPTER

THIRTY-FIVE

The chapter house felt cold when Margaret walked in. She pulled her woollen cloak around her and sat down next to her uncle on the stone bench that surrounded the meeting room.

'How are you feeling, Margery?'

Margaret stiffened. She knew Clement was referring to the loss of her son and she didn't want to talk about it.

'I'm a little cold today.'

'I didn't mean that.'

'I know what you meant. How do you expect me to feel? I've lost my precious son.'

'I miss him too.'

Margaret placed her hand on his. 'I'm sorry. I know you were close and I'm glad my son had a father figure in his life.'

'About the father,' Clement began. 'Do you think you should tell him?'

'No,' she snapped.

'But surely he would want to know.'

'It won't make any difference and besides he's in France.'

Clement had often wondered who the father was but whenever he broached the subject with Margaret, she became tight-lipped and dismissive. It seemed even though Harold was dead she was still determined to keep it a secret. But this was another revelation that led him to believe he knew who the father was.

'The king is in France. Is he the father, Margaret?'

Margaret took out a square of cloth and held it to her nose, sniffing a few times but not crying. She had a faraway look as though she were remembering something. A tear spilled from her eye. She wiped it away. Clement detected a faint nod of her head.

'If you think it best,' said Clement.

'I've asked the sheriff to join us.'

'Do you think he will? He's always protesting he's a busy man.'

'He won't be too busy to see me.'

The wooden door to the chapter house opened and in walked the corpulent figure of the sheriff. He was alone.

'You know I'm a busy man, countess. What's this about?'

'It's about Moses and his fellow Jews.'

'What is there to discuss,' said the sheriff, who remained standing.

'Please. Sit down, Sheriff Pypard. Would you like me to fetch you some wine?' said Clement, rising from his seat.

'I'm fine, thank you. Let's get this business over with.'

Margaret spoke. 'You arrested Moses and several of his community...'

'You know that. You were there when it was decided upon.'

'Yes, I know, but I wasn't in favour of rounding up the Jews if you remember. That was my impulsive son. Since then I've been talking it over with Prior Clement. We are both of the opinion that Moses and his friends are innocent.'

'I don't doubt that.'

'We think,' said Clement, 'that this stranger Brito has something to do with it, but we don't know how or why.'

'He's certainly capable of such a thing.'

'Then why aren't you arresting him for Harold's murder rather than Moses?'

Sheriff Pypard raised his voice. 'Because as yet no one has produced any evidence against him. I can't go around arresting people for nothing.'

'But he can go around accusing innocent people.'

'This isn't helping,' said Margaret. 'We need to be united, not argue amongst ourselves.'

'I'm sorry, countess,' said Sheriff Pypard, coming to sit with them.

'I know you're in a difficult position. As sheriff you are charged with protecting the Jews.'

'I'm getting too old for all this. I just want a quiet life. It seems wherever I go these days someone is unhappy about something.'

'You have a thankless job,' said Margaret, playing to his weaknesses. 'What do you know about this man Brito?'

'Not a lot. He appeared on the day the boy was found. It seems he was at the centre of the mob uprising against Moses. I heard he was getting everyone drunk at the Lich Inn and inciting them to attack the Jews. Convinced them all that they were responsible for the poor boy's death and whipped them up into a frenzy. There's no telling what they would have done if I hadn't intervened.'

'I'm grateful for that, sheriff. Moses is my friend,' Clement said.

'But you don't believe that Moses is to blame for Harold's death?' Margaret asked.

'I think it unlikely. We've all known Moses since he and his family arrived in Gloucester. We've never had any trouble with him.'

'He's an honourable man. He knew and liked Harold,' said Clement.

'What else do you know about Brito?' asked Margaret.

'He says he's here on king's business but when you ask him precisely what that is, he avoids the question.'

'A slippery character,' said Clement.

'Moses came to see me the other day. It seems his niece was violated the night the mob got out of hand and Moses accused Brito.'

'This is terrible news. Why haven't you done anything about this?' said Margaret, visibly alarmed on hearing that a woman had been attacked in such a way.

'What can I do? Brito would deny it and Moses has no proof. No witnesses.'

'This Brito fellow sounds like a very dangerous man, sheriff,' Margaret commented.

Prior Clement said, 'He's a wicked and sinful man if he does have anything to do with Harold's death or the rape of Arlette.'

'We don't know that for sure,' said the sheriff.

'But we all know Moses is innocent...' Clement replied.

'We don't know that as an absolute certainty either,' the sheriff said, raising a straggly eyebrow at Clement.

'Can't you find a way to release Moses?'

'I can't do that.'

'Why not? You let Elias go...'

Margaret gave the sheriff a look of reproach.

'That was different.'

'I don't see how.'

Sheriff Pypard coughed into his hand and stood up.

'I can't let them all go. It would look bad, and it wouldn't get Brito off my back. He'd be back again demanding I rearrest them.'

'Then we must make sure Brito has no reason to make your life more difficult than it is.'

CHAPTER
THIRTY-SIX

I t was hard to say how long they had been imprisoned as each day was much the same as the last. Their conditions were deteriorating. The straw had not been refreshed and the stench of the makeshift latrine was beginning to turn Moses' stomach. He longed to see Douce and the children. They were always in his thoughts, and he prayed they were safe and well. Despite his constant requests to speak to the sheriff, he had been unable to. When, finally, the guard came to announce they were to be taken to the great hall for trial, Moses was consumed with trepidation.

Relieved to be out in the fresh air, he climbed the steep steps to the great hall in the keep. Halfway up, he stopped. He had developed a hacking cough whilst confined and the exertion of climbing left him breathless. Every bone in his body ached. The guard was an ignorant and taciturn individual who bawled at him to keep going, digging him in the back and forcing him upwards. Moses carried on, his cough worsening with every step.

By the time Moses arrived in the packed hall he was pale and exhausted. His first thought was to search for Douce in the crowd. He saw her almost immediately and his heart ached. Abraham was in her arms. Douce acknowledged him with a tentative wave. Arlette was close by, holding Young Samuel's hand. His father Samuel sat next to them, grey with age and worry.

Sheriff Pypard and his son sat on a raised dais at the front of the hall. With them was Humphrey de Bohun, the king's Lord High Constable. The prisoners were forced to stand in front of them. To their side sat six male jurors. Moses felt sick to his stomach when he saw Brito was one of them. For Moses, Brito's presence marked the end. Any hope he had of Sheriff Pypard seeing sense left him. He was now more convinced than ever that this stranger was at the heart of this heinous affair. But why? He still could not figure that out. He probably never would. Sheriff Pypard grasped the wooden gavel and brought it down heavily on the block and addressed the jury.

'This jury of presentment is to determine the guilt or otherwise of the prisoners who stand before you. The charge is murder and that together they did conspire to kill the boy known as Harold whose tortured body was found by the river.'

At the mention of the boy's murder the crowd hurled obscenities at the prisoners. Sheriff Pypard blasted his gavel until the crowd fell silent.

'Order or I'll clear the hall.'

A jury of presentment was the Christian version of justice, such as it was. Each juror would be called to give evidence. They would testify under oath as to the crime allegedly committed. Their testimony was often based on rumour or hearsay and rarely based on fact. Brito would give his own gloss on the facts and had probably already convinced the other jurors of their guilt. That the crowd were already hostile to them only added to the futility of his predicament. After all they were Jews. From that point on Moses lost all interest in the proceedings. His fate was sealed. He would never hold Douce in his arms again or feel her soft skin next to his. He would never see his sons grow up.

The jurors stood to give their testimony. Each one told how the boy was found with signs of ritual crucifixion and the only possible conclusion was the Jews had killed him to use his blood in their Passover bread. That the crime was committed so close to Easter was to add greater insult to Christians and be further proof of their guilt. Not one person had seen the murder being committed. It was all conjecture. Moses spent the entire time looking at the floor but lifted his head when he heard a woman's voice.

'I would like to say something.'

It was Margaret de Bohun. Sheriff Pypard nodded his assent.

'Someone has murdered this boy Harold and whoever they are they must be punished but not at the cost of innocent lives. I believe something much darker is at the heart of this. I don't believe for one moment these Jews are guilty of the crime they have been accused of. Abbot Hameline, you have done business with Moses. After the terrible fire in the chapel, you were able to rebuild it with the help of Moses le Riche's money. Prior Clement owes much to Moses le Riche. Without his money he would not have been able to expand the priory or build the much-needed grain store.'

Abbot Hameline and Prior Clement both nodded their heads vigorously and in unison.

'Prior Clement, I believe you wanted to speak?' asked Sheriff Pypard.

'Indeed,' said Prior Clement. 'I have known Moses le Riche for some years and have found him to be a most agreeable man of good character. We have discussed at length the differences between our two faiths, and I know for a fact his religion does not allow him to partake of blood. He and the other prisoners could not have committed this crime. I am prepared to swear on the Holy Bible to this.'

To Moses the speech seemed rehearsed. The word of a Christian man of the cloth was tantamount to the sacred word of their God. It gave him a flutter of hope.

Brito jerked out of his chair. He stood in front of Prior Clement and yelled at him, spitting in his face. 'They are guilty as charged.'

Humphrey de Bohun addressed the jury, his voice composed and measured. 'My mother is the Countess of Hereford and well-respected. And this revered prior is a man of God. Are you going to take his word against theirs?'

Enraged, Brito's face turned scarlet. 'What is the meaning of this?' he bellowed, looking around him for support and finding none.

Moses was more convinced than ever there had been nothing short of a coup against Brito. Sheriff Pypard joined the conspiracy. Picking up a frayed roll of parchment, he read out its contents:

'The king, Henry the Second, much like his grandfather before him Henry the First, drew up a charter of protection for the Jews.

'Be it also known that all Jews, wheresoever they are in the kingdom, are to be under the tutelage and lawful protection of the king, and no one of them can serve under any rich man without the king's leave; for the Jews and all their property belong to the king. As though it were the property of the king.'

The sheriff looked up from the page and raised his voice.

'And if any person shall lay hands on them or their money, the king is to demand restitution thereof, if he so pleases, as of his own.'

A murmured approval passed along those gathered in the great hall. The sheriff continued.

'I am a servant of the king as are you all and am bound by this charter. If the accused swear on the Pentateuch – as this charter asserts, they must – that they are innocent of all charges I am bound to take this as evidence of their innocence.'

Moses could not believe what he was hearing. They would be required to give an oath as to their innocence on their holy book, the Torah, and they would go free. A court official appeared from the back of the court. He was accompanied by Solomon the rabbi, who held in his hands the sacred Torah. He presented it to each of the accused and one by one they swore their innocence.

'Let them go,' said the sheriff.

There was uproar in the hall. People shouted out 'Jew lovers' and worse. Brito was incandescent with rage, pacing the floor. Sheriff Pypard blasted his gavel repeatedly. Once order was restored, Humphrey de Bohun cleared his throat in an exaggerated fashion.

'There is one other matter,' he said. 'As Lord High Constable I fine each of you ten marks in settlement of this case.'

So, there it was, thought Moses. A sham trial. A deal had been done behind closed doors and, as ever, money was involved. What did it matter that a boy had been murdered and the perpetrator was still at large? They were not interested in justice but only in lining their own chests with ill-gotten gains. Moses made a quick calculation. Nine prisoners each fined ten marks. He estimated this would be almost one hundred marks straight into the money bags of the sheriff and that immoral son of the countess.

The guards untied the rope around his wrists. Douce came running into his open arms. He buried his face into the crook of her neck and held her tight. She was warm and soft and smelled faintly of roses.

CHAPTER
THIRTY-SEVEN

Arlette had long imagined her wedding day. She would be the centre of attention, surrounded by hundreds of adoring family and friends from every corner of England and France. They would congratulate her and wish her well and she would be delirious with joy.

It was nothing like she imagined.

Normally, Zev would have seven years to save the money he needed to marry Arlette, but there was nothing normal about this wedding. He had insisted they marry immediately because he said his ordeal in prison had brought his priorities into sharp focus. It was unorthodox to marry so soon after the announcement of the betrothal, but all agreed that, in the circumstances, it was the right thing to do. Zev had also intimated to Arlette that he was mindful of the fact she could be pregnant. Although no one could be sure at this stage, he would be able to say he was the baby's father and protect Arlette's honour for which she was grateful.

At the end of the *tenaim*, a ceremony which officially marked them out as bride and groom, Douce and Damete wrapped a clay dish in a cloth, as was tradition, and together broke it over the table corner to signify the sealing of the union and to symbolise there would be penalties if the engagement were to be broken. To Arlette these were all empty gestures upholding a pretence rather than the symbolic acts of an ancient tradition. Within hours she would be married to Zev.

Rubin had put together a makeshift *chuppah*, the wedding canopy using sticks of birch. He had erected it inside the great hall rather than outside in the courtyard because the hurried wedding ceremony was to be a private affair. Only those required to make up a quorum had been invited. Douce had draped one of her embroidered tablecloths between the four poles. It looked peculiar, thought Arlette, when later she walked into the hall; Douce on one side and Damete, her future mother-in-law, on the other. Douce had given her one of her old dresses as there wasn't time to buy a new one. Luckily, they were almost the same size and it required very little alteration. The long flowing garment was made of a rich cream silk, tied at the shoulder by an ornate metal brooch encrusted with rubies and diamonds. It had belonged to Douce's mother. Douce had also given her a veil of translucent silk which Zev would place upon her head at the veiling ceremony and earlier in the day, Douce had fussed around Arlette, fashioning her hair into tight curls and dressing it with specially prepared oil of myrrh.

When she was ready, for the veiling ceremony Zev was brought into the fore hall, accompanied by his family. Douce passed him the veil. He took it and very gently placed it over Arlette's head, adjusting it to fit. Then he recited the ancient words from Genesis spoken to Rebecca at her marriage.

'Our sister, be thou the mother of thousands of ten thousands.'

Arlette blushed. Then Zev added his own words from Ezekiel, whispering them to her. 'I cover with silk the woman I love.'

Arlette gazed into his eyes. They were full of love for her. Her heart ached with emotion, and she stifled her tears. Then it was time for Zev to leave her and await her arrival in the great hall. It gave Arlette a moment to reflect on the suddenness of events. She had confessed to Douce her grave misgivings about her marriage to Zev but having spoken about them to Douce she knew she was doing the right thing. She would have a husband and a future. Nothing else mattered. She pushed away thoughts of her marriage to Deudonne and concentrated on Zev's devotion to her, his steadfastness.

Arlette walked into the great hall where Zev was waiting for her beneath the *chuppah*. Azriel stood close by singing a traditional wedding hymn. Candles flickered, and the room smelled of spring flowers. Arlette walked towards the canopy, her head lowered partly through shyness, but mostly from shame. It might have been her imagination, but she was convinced everyone was looking at her not with admiration but with disgust shown towards the unclean, the sullied one.

Zev was dressed in a linen shirt with a full-length mantle and an embroidered hat. Arlette thought he looked comical rather than dashing. A fleeting vision of Deudonne wearing a sumptuous wedding outfit came into her mind. She ached with regret for what might have been but quickly pushed the thought to the back of her mind.

Beside Zev were his two witnesses, Seth and Baruch, his best friends from childhood. Around the canopy were the members of this close community, people she had got to know since her arrival in Gloucester. Bellassez the bountiful matriarch, her children beside her, looked happy for Arlette. Damete her future mother-in-law looked indifferent. Chera looked sad. The worst came from Mirabelle. The derisive smirk on her face said it all. She was getting what she deserved. Arlette turned away afraid that if she gazed upon the face of Mirabelle an instant longer, she would turn to stone.

Zev's reassuring smile and kind eyes calmed her rising panic. Rabbi Solomon stood beneath the canopy. He welcomed them both and holding up a cup of wine recited the first blessing.

'As you share this cup of wine, you undertake to share all the future may bring. May you find life's joys doubly gladdened, its bitterness sweetened, and all things hallowed by true companionship and love.'

He passed the cup to Zev. While he took a sip, Zev's mother and Douce lifted the veil from Arlette's face so she too could share the wine. Solomon then recited the second blessing. As she sipped the wine, Arlette realised she was symbolising her commitment to sharing her life with Zev. Zev then took hold of Arlette's delicate hand and with great tenderness placed the wedding ring on her index finger.

'Behold, by this ring you are consecrated to me as my wife according to the laws of Moses and Israel.'

It was a plain ring of gold with no stone. It was all Zev could afford. As the wife of a butcher, she was unlikely ever to possess a ring as elaborate or expensive as Douce's. She pushed these unkind thoughts away. She should be grateful to Zev. He had saved her from a solitary life of spinsterhood.

The marriage settlement had been drawn up earlier that morning by Azriel, who was also the community's scribe. Moses, acting as Arlette's father, signed the agreement along with Rubin. After the ring had been placed on her finger the marriage contract was read aloud by Azriel followed by the reciting of the seven blessings. Arlette and Zev chose the readers. One by one, they read them out. First Seth, and then ten-year-old Muriel who was delighted to be chosen. Her voice was strong with no hint of nervousness as she read the penultimate blessing. Her mother Bellassez beamed with pride. The final blessing was read by Azriel in his mellifluous tones.

'Blessed art Thou who has created joy and gladness, bridegroom and bride, mirth and exultation, pleasure and delight, love, brotherhood, peace and fellowship...'

Having both taken another sip of wine Arlette passed the cup back to the rabbi. Solomon wrapped the cup in a cloth and gave it to Zev. Zev placed it on the floor and stamped on it, smashing the cup into small pieces. A resounding cheer filled the room.

'*Mazel tov.*'

After Zev smashed the cup, he took hold of Arlette's hand and led her back to the fore hall. It had been transformed into the *yichud* room, a place of seclusion where in ancient times the bride and groom would have consummated their marriage. Zev would have been called upon to hand the bloodied proof of virginity cloth to the witnesses waiting outside. Arlette was thankful this practice had fallen into disuse for her virginity cloth was the soiled tunic she wore on the night of her rape. A cold chill ran through her veins, and she shuddered. Zev put his arm around her shoulder and gave her a squeeze. Instantly she felt better.

Earlier, Douce had prepared a tureen of chicken soup along with some unleavened bread which now lay on the table before them. As was tradition neither of them had eaten that morning. They ate in silence, Arlette reflecting on the ceremony and how simple but emotional it had been. She thought about her parents and wished they could have been with her on her wedding day. Then she shuddered at the thought of them knowing why she was marrying Zev and not Deudonne.

'Are you feeling all right, Arlette?'

'I'm fine. I was thinking about my family, that's all.'

'I would like to have met them. I imagine your mother was very beautiful.'

Arlette smiled as her mother's face came into her mind's eye.

'She was beautiful and kind too. And my father was handsome.'

'I knew it. To have a daughter as lovely as you.'

Arlette blushed. She didn't feel beautiful. She felt sullied.

Zev put down his bowl. 'Arlette, you've made me the proudest man on earth today. I never believed this day would come.' He touched her cheek, his finger tracing the pale scar left by the fire. She winced. 'Sorry. Does that still hurt?'

'It's a little tender, that's all.'

He took hold of her hands. 'Before today I always felt like half a person, but now we are married I feel encircled by you, completed somehow. I can't explain it. From the first day I met you I dreamed of us together. You made me want to be a better person. To do something with my life. Not be known as the butcher's boy.' He laughed and let go of her. 'I'm babbling, I know. I do that when I'm nervous. You'll have to get used to that.'

'I don't mind that you're the butcher's boy,' she said, taking his hand again.

Any misgivings Arlette had about her marriage to Zev were swept away by this declaration of togetherness. She felt a deepening tenderness toward him. She could not say it was love. It was not the outpouring of emotion which seemed to come so easily to her new husband, yet she knew she must say something to the man who sat before her. He was opening his heart to her and so should she. She remembered an ancient pledge and in a stumbling fashion recited it to him.

'May you merit to have a long life, and to unite with me in love from now until eternity. May I merit to dwell with you forever.'

As soon as she said it, she felt foolish, but she needn't have. Zev leaned into her and kissed her on the mouth. It was her first real kiss. She was unsure how to respond. The feel of his lips on hers was not unpleasant but it seemed to lack passion. But what did she know?

'I love you, Arlette,' he whispered to her as he held her close.

Arlette hesitated, unsure of what to say. She forced out the words she knew he wanted to hear.

'*Je t'aime*,' she whispered.

After the meal, they joined their guests. Bellassez approached her.

'Arlette, what a beautiful *kallah* you make.' She kissed her on the cheek then turned to Zev. 'And who would have thought Zev would make such a handsome *chatan*.'

'You're right about Arlette. She makes a beautiful bride. *Sheol!*' he corrected himself, 'she makes a beautiful wife but me, a handsome groom? I don't think so.'

Bellassez was such a kind person, always making people feel at ease and not judging them. Arlette thanked her and gave her a hug. The singing and dancing, joy and laughter went on well into the night. It was infectious. Perhaps, thought Arlette, she might be able to forget the past and lead a happy, guilt-free life after all. Only a few days ago she would not have thought this possible. She searched for Zev's hand and gave it a squeeze. He squeezed it back.

One by one their guests came to wish them happiness. Chera was the last. Her hair was swept back from her face and covered by a cap. Her doe eyes focused on Zev. She gave Arlette a cursory glance. Arlette knew Chera liked Zev and that she had probably stolen the man Chera thought she would marry.

'*Mazel tov* to you both,' Chera said. The words were there but there was no sentiment behind them. 'I hope you'll be very happy.'

'Thank you, Chera. I'm sure we will be,' Arlette replied.

Zev leaned across and gave Chera a peck on the cheek and thanked her. Chera held on to Zev a little longer than was considered respectful. Arlette wanted to push her away, remind Chera that Zev was her husband, but she didn't. This was her wedding day, and she did not want more grief. She had had enough of that. Zev disentangled himself from her and she left.

'Why did you kiss her?'

'I didn't exactly kiss her. I gave her a friendly peck,' Zev replied, turning to Arlette. 'Why? Are you jealous?' he asked, grinning from ear to ear.

'Of course not,' Arlette sniffed back.

'Is this our first argument?' Zev said, still grinning. 'And on our wedding day?'

'Don't be silly.'

'You like me when I'm being silly.'

He bent to kiss her on the lips. Arlette shrunk from him.

'Not in public,' she said, wiping his snatched kiss from her lips.

~

Arlette spent the evening dancing with Zev and her uncle. Even Old Samuel danced with her although he was a little unsteady on his feet. By the end of the night her hair was unruly, and her cheeks flushed from the wine, but she didn't care. She was enjoying the celebrations. When Zev left her for only a moment to bring more wine Mirabelle approached her with the guile of a fox.

'Such a shame Deudonne did not go through with the marriage. Your prospects would have been so much better than they are now. Still, you have a husband and I suppose you should be grateful for that.'

No sooner had she said it she was gone, leaving Arlette in shock. Her words stung like a slap in the face. Zev returned, a drink in one hand and a pastry in the other.

'What's the matter, Arlette?'

Arlette sucked in air, putting her hand to her stomach to steady her nerves. There was no point in telling Zev what Mirabelle had said. It would cause an argument on what was supposed to be the happiest day of her life. She made light of it.

'Nothing, nothing's the matter. I'm just overtired. Perhaps I've danced too much.'

'You can never dance too much,' he said, putting down the wine and pastry and scooping her up to dance again.

Arlette accepted the invitation, keen to show Mirabelle she was not upset by her vituperative and uncalled-for remark, but she could taste the sour bile of regret and missed opportunities gnawing away at her insides.

CHAPTER

THIRTY-EIGHT

Arlette was in her room waiting for Zev to arrive. She had changed into her nightclothes. The warming effects of the wine had worn off and she was shivering in her thin cotton shift. She sat on a chair in the corner of the room chewing on her fingernails. This was her first night with Zev, her wedding night. Her only knowledge of intimacy was Brito's brutality. She hoped Zev would be tender. She tried to imagine the soft touch of his warm skin against her own and the delight of languorous kisses, but it was not long before her thoughts were full of the night Brito robbed her of her virginity.

She was still sore from the brutality of her violation and had initially bled from the internal damage she had suffered but once that had stopped, she had been checking for menstrual blood and still nothing. The thought of having sexual relations again filled her with dread but she was a married woman now and she must fulfil her marital obligations.

She had seen the hunger in Zev's eyes all day. It frightened her. Just the thought of having sex with him made her tense inside. To feel someone enter her again in the place that now gave her such pain. Her thoughts made her skin crawl and tears trickled down her cheeks, falling like soft rain into her lap. She made no effort to wipe them away.

The sound of footsteps outside on the landing made her jump. She hurriedly wiped the tears from her cheeks. The door opened, and Zev walked in. Arlette tensed even more.

He greeted her with a kiss on the cheek then sat on the mattress. Arlette remained on the small wooden chair in the corner of the room, her hands tightly clasped. Zev undressed in front of her and climbed into bed. He pulled back the covers, an invitation for her to join him. Arlette rose slowly, her limbs heavy as if she had black molasses running through her blood. She self-consciously wrapped her arms around herself as she walked towards her husband, climbed into bed next to him and lay down.

Zev propped himself up on his elbow and stared down at Arlette. She knew he had been waiting for this moment a long time. He brushed the hair from her face and bent to kiss her. His lips were soft, his kiss different to the kisses earlier in the day. There was a hunger in them. His hand moved slowly towards her breast. He caressed it. She felt her nipple harden beneath his touch. His hand moved downwards to the tender part between her legs. Arlette stiffened.

'What's the matter, Arlette?'

'I don't know, but I'm not sure I can do this.'

'But we're married now, and I love you,' he said, pressing himself against her. Arlette lay there unresponsive.

'I know you do, but it doesn't make any difference. I don't think I can go through with it.'

'Well just try,' Zev said, as he lifted her shift.

Breathing heavily, he moved his hand toward her inner thigh. A rising panic engulfed Arlette.

'Wait,' she said, gripping his hand.

'Wait for what?'

'I don't know,' Arlette said.

She was confused. This was supposed to be the happiest moment in her life, the consummation of her marriage, her wedding night. Her faith taught her there was nothing sinful in sex, that it was to be enjoyed and seen as a pleasure and part of the joy of marriage. So why was she feeling such dread?

'This is our wedding night, Arlette. This is the best part.'

Arlette could hardly breathe. Her heart was beating fast, and her chest felt tight. It might have been the best part for Zev, but it was becoming the worst part for her. She felt sick and clammy. Flashbacks of the rape surfaced as strong as though she were back in the courtyard. The smell of Brito's sour breath. His grunting. His savagery.

'I can't do it,' she cried out, sobbing.

Zev pulled away from her and sat on the edge of the bed, staring into space.

'I thought our wedding night would be different.'

Arlette lay there wiping the tears away.

'I'm sorry, Zev. I thought so too. I don't know what's the matter with me.'

Zev turned to face her.

'It's all right, Arlette. I love you and I'll do anything to make you happy.'

He climbed back into bed and reached out to her. Arlette turned over and faced her back to him, her heart pounding in her chest with fear.

THIRTY-NINE

I n the days that followed Zev and Arlette were distant with each other. Zev spent most of his time working in his father's butchery and when he wasn't there, he went with his best friend Baruch to Robinswood Hill to hunt for small game. On one occasion Zev and his friend climbed to the top of the hill making their way to an old tree trunk that had been hit by lightning to sit down on the moss-covered branch and have a bite to eat. The cathedral dominated the skyline of the city below. The River Severn meandered through the verdant countryside dotted with the raised masts of Gloucester trows. Beyond were the black Welsh mountains.

'You don't seem yourself lately. I thought you'd be the happiest man in the world now you're married to Arlette.'

Zev said nothing.

'Something's the matter, I can tell.'

Zev had told no one about his difficulties with Arlette. He wasn't sure if he should force the matter with her or be patient and hope Arlette would come around. Waking up beside her every morning and knowing he couldn't touch her was driving him to distraction. He didn't know what to do. One thing he did know. He couldn't keep it to himself much longer.

'Only on paper,' Zev said, hurling a crust of bread to the ground.

'What do you mean?'

Zev told his friend everything. Once he started, he could not stop. A river of words and emotions poured from his mouth. They just kept flowing. Baruch listened intently.

'You mean you haven't done it?'

'No and it's driving me insane. I don't know how much longer I can keep this up.'

Baruch snorted. 'Sorry, Zev, it's just your use of the phrase "keep it up". See, I knew something wasn't right. You can't even laugh at your own jokes.'

'It's not funny, Baruch. I don't know what to do. I'm out of my depth.'

'Have you tried talking to her?'

'We've barely spoken. She's distant, unapproachable. She's changed, Baruch, she's not the same girl.'

'Give it time. Arlette has gone through a lot. It must have been awful for her when she was...' Baruch hesitated.

'Raped,' said Zev.

'It must be difficult knowing she wasn't a virgin on your wedding night. I don't know if I could marry someone who wasn't.'

'I didn't plan it that way,' Zev said, picking up a stone and throwing it with great force at the tree opposite.

The stone hit the tree trunk, shattering the bark, sending shards flying. It disturbed some nesting pigeons above. They flew out of the tree, wings flapping, branches crackling and foliage fluttering to the forest floor. Baruch aimed his bow at them, but they flew off, leaving the men in silence once more.

'Maybe I was naïve to think we could just go on with our lives as normal. As if nothing had happened.'

'Be patient with her.'

'I'm trying, but it's a struggle. I've become very good at chopping logs. Douce said the other day she'd never seen so many logs in the wood pile.'

Baruch gave his friend a puzzled look. 'What's that got to do with anything?'

'When I try it on and Arlette pushes me away, I go out of the house in the middle of the night and chop wood. It relieves me.'

'Ah. I see what you mean. There. You must be feeling a bit better. You're back to making light of it.'

'There's nothing light about it.'

'Sorry, Zev. I was just trying to make you feel better.'

Zev snapped at his friend, 'Well you're not.' This time it was Zev's turn to apologise. 'I just want the Arlette I fell in love with. It feels like she isn't mine, that she belongs to that bastard who raped her.'

'That would bother me. Knowing someone had been there before me.'

'It does bother me. I thought it wouldn't.'

'What are you going to do about it?'

Zev walked over to a pile of fallen dead branches. He loosened one from the brittle tangle and threw it some distance.

'I want to kill him.'

FORTY

The third quarter session of the year fell on a Saturday, the day on which Sheriff Pypard was responsible for making sure debts were paid, outstanding lawsuits were settled, and all financial transactions were recorded. He sat in the great hall of the castle with his son Gilbert surrounded by his scribes and his guards. He had fulfilled these duties as sheriff every quarter for the past three years, though it seemed much longer than that to him. He loathed the task. Gilbert had an aptitude for the work, and he hoped he would take over from him when he died.

Sheriff Pypard signalled to the guards to open the heavy oak doors. He knew there would be a gaggle of disgruntled citizens, all vying for his attention. He took a gulp of weak ale and leaned back in his throne-like chair. An involuntary sigh escaped from his dry lips; his mouth downturned in resignation. He nodded to his son to indicate he was ready. Gilbert nodded back, then turned away and beckoned the first citizen of the day.

Old Ailwyn, the richest mercer in Gloucester approached the sheriff. He exported wool and imported luxurious fabrics such as samite, a rich and heavy silk fabric from the Orient. He sold it to the abbots for their vestments and also to the Jews who were fond of sumptuous clothing. Ailwyn was in dispute over the granting of the fief farm to the burgesses of Gloucester. He had previously lost his case and been fined one hundred marks by the Crown and here he was a year later complaining about the same thing. Sheriff Pypard let out another sigh. If he didn't shut up, he would fine him again, or worse, forfeit his chattels. Sheriff Pypard was barely listening as he harped on about forming a sworn association of some kind. Instead, he was far more interested in the noisy kerfuffle taking place at the rear of the hall.

'Where are the money-grabbing Jews today?' a voice said. 'Not here to fleece us as usual?'

'Oh for Christ's sake,' said Sheriff Pypard. 'Does that man never give up?'

He let out an even deeper sigh and raised his bulky frame from his chair. He turned to his son.

'Take care of this business with Ailwyn, will you?'

'Very well, Father.'

Sheriff Pypard made his way towards Brito. 'What's going on here?' he asked.

'I was just wondering where the Jews were today?'

'Today is Saturday, their Holy Day. They don't work on holy days.'

'Well, we all have to come here to make an account for ourselves. Why should they get special dispensation? Are they above the laws of this great land?'

It was a stupid question, one designed to raise tempers and cement prejudice. It was common knowledge that Jews were not bound by Christian laws. King Henry had given them special status and, as such, they were permitted to govern themselves.

Sheriff Pypard said, 'You know they are. By the grace of the king.' The group murmured their assent. The sheriff was not about to have mob rule in his castle. No one present would be foolish enough to move against the king. 'It's no different to our holy day. We Christians don't work on Sunday.'

'I don't see why they should get different treatment to us. It's our land.'

Sheriff Pypard was unsure how to answer this. For as long as he could remember if a quarter session fell on a Jewish holy day, they would send a representative, usually Radulf the Moneyer. He searched the room for him and spotted him in the far corner. He signalled to one of his men. 'Fetch Radulf to me.'

The man scuttled off, returning with Radulf.

'Radulf, are you here today as the Jew's representative?'

'I am. Is there a problem?'

Brito cursed under his breath and spat on the floor in the direction of Radulf. Radulf took a step back, clutching the hem of his sumptuous tunic to avoid contamination.

'No there isn't,' the sheriff replied, staring directly at Brito.

'Are you all Jew lovers in this city?' Brito bellowed. 'They murder a boy, a Christian boy, and you do nothing?'

'They've been completely exonerated of any involvement in the boy's death.' Sheriff Pypard scowled at Brito. 'I don't much like you, and I don't like the way you're trying to turn these good citizens against the Jews.'

Brito's face hardened, and he placed his hand on his sword sheath, instinct from years on the battlefield. 'I'm here on king's business,' he replied.

Prior Clement, who was there to pay the priory's debts, intervened at the mention of the king's name. 'What business of the king's?'

'Stay out of this,' Brito growled. 'This has nothing to do with you.'

Clement took a step forward. 'If it is about the murder of the boy Harold then it is very much my business.'

'What was he to you?' Brito asked, a snarl appearing on his lips.

'The boy was very dear to me and to his mother.'

'The boy has no mother. He was an orphan,' Brito said.

A flash of suspicion narrowed Prior Clement's eyes. 'What do you know of this boy?'

The snarl disappeared from Brito's face. 'Nothing. I know nothing,' he said, waving his hand at the prior in a dismissive gesture. Then he added, 'Except he was killed by the Jews.'

'Enough of this,' yelled Sheriff Pypard. 'This matter has been dealt with. I will hear no more of it.'

'I apologise,' said Clement. 'I'm merely trying to get at the truth. This man knows more than he is letting on. If he knows something about the boy's murder, then I want him to tell me.'

'I doubt we'll ever get to the truth of this, Prior Clement. I know you are grieving but it is time to put this business to rest for all our sake,' said the sheriff, directing his gaze at Brito.

'You doubt I'm telling the truth?' said Brito, grabbing for the cruciform hilt of his *estoc* and taking a challenging step forward.

Two battle-worn men standing behind Brito moved to his side. There was a clanking of armour as the sheriff's men surged forward to protect him. Out of the corner of his eye, Brito spotted Abbot Hameline of St Peter's abbey. Brito fixed his cold black eyes on the sheriff.

'If you won't do anything,' he said to the sheriff, 'I demand a trial by an ecclesiastical court. Abbot Hameline, I insist you settle this.'

'What do you want an ecclesiastical court for?' Sheriff Pypard asked.

'To put on trial the Jews responsible for the murder of the Christian boy.'

'You can demand all you like but you won't get what you're asking for. They're not Christians and therefore cannot be tried or held to account by an ecclesiastical court. Is that not so, Abbot Hameline?' the sheriff said, beckoning Abbot Hameline to him.

'It is indeed.'

Brito's eyes widened in disbelief. 'Are you all Jew lovers? Are you really going to let them get away with their detestable crimes?'

The crowd was silent. The alcohol-fuelled hatred which Brito had so skilfully exploited was not in evidence today. Sheriff Pypard knew the occupants of the hall. They were men of business, not journeymen or sailors looking for a fight. He could see the defeat in Brito's eyes. There was nowhere for him to go.

'I can see I'll have to deal with this matter myself. Come on, men.'

'I wouldn't be doing that if I were you,' the sheriff called after him.

Brito swung round, his hand still upon the hilt of his sword, his face reddened with rage.

'And why is that?' he challenged.

'The Jews in this city are under my protection. Touch them and you defy the king.'

Brito was in no mood to argue. He had done his best to turn this gutless lot against the Jews. The time was not for talking but for action.

'I am the king's justice,' he roared and stormed out of the hall.

CHAPTER
FORTY-ONE

B rito spent the rest of the day drinking in the Lich Inn. Furious with both the sheriff and the abbot and annoyed at his own futile attempt to discredit the Jews, he sank into a morbidly belligerent mood. The men in the hall were men of commerce, but they were fools. Many of them would be heavily in debt to their Jewish neighbours. If they would only listen to him, he could wipe out their entire indebtedness. It would not have taken much, one word from the abbot, a nod from the sheriff, but both had stood their ground.

He drank into the night and after several tankards of ale, he and his drunken companions stumbled out of the inn and into the pouring rain. It was a miserable night. The weather seemed to reflect Brito's mood. They prowled the streets of Gloucester looking for prey, but the streets were empty save for a few revellers making their way home. At St Mary in the Market church they came across a malnourished dog asleep in the porch. Brito gave it a kick. The dog yelped, sprang up and cowered in the corner.

'You're no sport, you loathsome hound,' Brito shouted at the petrified dog. 'I'm looking for someone to put up a fight.'

As if on cue Brito spotted a figure dressed in distinctive Jewish garb scurrying across East Gate Street towards the synagogue.

'He'll do.' He ran off in pursuit, shouting at the figure, 'Hey, you.'

With the deftness of a hawk, Brito pounced upon the figure before he could make off.

'Let me go,' said Baruch, struggling to free himself from Brito's grip.

Brito pushed Baruch towards his men. They jostled him back and forth, then pushed him back to Brito. Instead of catching him, he punched him in the stomach. Baruch doubled over, retched and fell to the ground. Brito followed with a kick to the boy's side.

A voice coming from further down the street called out, 'Hey, stop that.'

Brito paused for a second and saw a figure approaching holding an armful of logs.

'Don't I know you?' Brito asked, when the figure got closer. 'Aren't you the boy from the other night? Didn't I give you a beating then when you made a pathetic attempt to save that Jewish whore?'

Zev threw down the logs he was carrying and hurried toward Brito.

'Who are you?' Brito asked.

'My name is Zev. And that whore you refer to is now my wife.'

Brito roared with laughter. 'You married her even though I'd been there before you. Opened her up for you, I did. You ought to thank me for that.'

Zev muttered *mamzer* under his breath. It meant bastard in Hebrew.

'What did you say?' he asked, grabbing the neck of Zev's cloak and pressing his face menacingly close.

'I said go to hell.'

Before the words were out of his mouth Brito landed a punch to Zev's stomach and as Zev folded Brito brought down the full force of his clenched fists onto his back. Zev fell to the ground. Brito then drew back his boot and with immense force kicked Zev in the head. The dull thud of leather against bone echoed in the empty street. Zev's body went limp. He did not cry out. Brito became a man possessed, pulverising Zev with demonic intent. Finally, he leapt in the air and brought his full weight upon Zev's bloodied head. There was a squelching sound as blood, bone and leather connected.

'Come on,' said fitz Urse, pulling on Brito's sleeve. 'You've done enough. Let's get out of this lousy city. The sheriff's a Jew lover and he's likely to lock us up and try us for murder.'

Brito gave one last kick to Zev's prone and lifeless body. A pool of dark liquid seeped from his head and spread across the damp ground, his face an unrecognisable mash of blood and flesh.

'You're right. I've done all I can here.'

When Baruch recovered and saw his friend's body, he went straight to the synagogue and alerted his parents to the attack. Rabbi Solomon raced down the alley to alert Moses whilst Baruch and Damete carried on into the rain-soaked street to attend to Zev. They found him in a pool of blood, his body lifeless. On seeing Zev, Moses' first thought was how to break the news to Arlette that Zev was dead. They lifted his body as gently as they could and carried him inside.

Arlette came downstairs and into the great hall where Zev's

battered body lay covered in blood. She dropped to her knees by his side and flung herself across him. 'What have they done, what have they done to him?' she wailed.

Bellassez arrived with her medicine bag. She immediately took charge of the situation. She spoke softly to Arlette. 'Let me see to him.'

Douce took Arlette by the shoulders and led her to a seat by the fire.

Once Arlette was out of earshot, Moses whispered to Bellassez, 'Is he dead?'

Bellassez put her head to Zev's chest and listened. She whispered back. 'No, but he very nearly is.'

'Is there any hope?'

'There is always hope,' Bellassez replied, keeping her voice low so the others couldn't hear.

'You'll have to help me, Moses. I don't think Douce or Arlette are up to the task.'

'Anything. Just tell me what to do.'

'It's too dangerous to move him but we can make him more comfortable.'

'There's a spare mattress upstairs. I'll bring it down.'

Moses left to fetch the mattress. Bellassez asked Damete if she could fetch some warm water and some clean cloths. 'And a bowl of cold water. As cold as you can make it,' she shouted after her.

Bellassez worked methodically and quickly. First, she administered a dose of hemlock for the pain, then cleaned Zev's wounds. Zev had a deep gash across his cheek and despite her best efforts she could not stem the bleeding. It would need stitching. Zev's face was virtually unrecognisable, his features distorted by severe swelling. Both eyes were horribly swollen, barely open and his nose was clearly broken across the bridge. Bellassez suspected his eye socket and his jaw were also broken.

A trickle of blood seeped from his right ear. Baruch told her Brito had jumped on Zev's head. Zev was showing all the signs of a serious head injury. He was unconscious, and his breathing was shallow. She knew something of head injuries from the many medical texts she studied and feared he would not last the night. She took from her bag a tincture of arnica which she often used to prevent swelling and bruising but had never used in such a severe case. She applied it gently to Zev's injuries.

With the skill of an embroiderer, she sewed the gash on his cheek, then wrapped a piece of clean cloth around his head and under his chin to support his jaw. Lastly, she soaked a cloth in the cold water and placed it across his forehead and behind his head.

Damete joined the women in the corner whilst Rubin stood with Moses, ashen faced. Bellassez told them to move Zev onto the mattress.

'I can do no more for him. Only time will tell. Keep putting the cold compresses on him to keep him cool. And pray. I'll call back in the morning.'

She packed her bag and before leaving spoke to Arlette. 'Zev needs you now. Be strong.'

Arlette's tear-stained face gazed up at Bellassez and she nodded. Rubin and Damete thanked Bellassez for all she had done. Moses accompanied her to the door.

'Please be honest with me, Bellassez. Is he going to die?'

Bellassez put her hand on Moses' shoulder. 'I didn't want to say anything in front of Arlette. He's a very sick young man. I don't know if he'll last the night. He's in the hands of Hashem.'

Moses needed time to think. Using the private door to the synagogue he slipped out. In the peace and tranquillity, he contemplated recent events. The mob at his door, the rape of Arlette, his imprisonment and now the ferocious attack on Zev. If Zev were to die, he feared Arlette would not cope. She was fragile and needed his help. But how was he ever going to ensure that none of this would happen again? How could he protect his family and future generations? He had no answers. He could only think it all had something to do with the stranger and his words to him that night.

You should have listened to me.

What did they mean? They could mean only one thing. This stranger Brito must think he went against him and loaned the money to the Irishman. Why else would he say such a thing? If he had only known. With a heavy heart Moses realised he might have saved Arlette and Zev and all the others who had suffered at the hands of the stranger.

FORTY-TWO

Three days after the attack Zev lay lifeless on the mattress, his condition largely unchanged. Arlette sat with him, sometimes sleeping by his side. She would stare at his chest to make sure he was still breathing, talk to him, and hold his hand. Arlette had no idea if he could hear her or understand any of what she was saying but Bellassez said it was important she talk to him, so she did, but it was like talking to a corpse. She remembered a family she knew from Rouen. Their daughter had been run over by the wheels of a cart, crushing her head. She lay for days lifeless like Zev and when at last she came to, she could never speak properly nor walk nor eat without assistance. Arlette prayed that Zev would not suffer the same fate. She would rather he be dead. Bella had told her to be strong for Zev. She wasn't sure what she meant by that. She felt anything but strong.

Bellassez visited every day. She washed Zev and tended to his injuries. His parents and Baruch were regular visitors too and when they came, Arlette would go upstairs to rest. Weeks had passed since the rape, and she had not had a show of blood. Her breasts felt tender, and her stomach was a little swollen. It was no use denying it anymore. She was with child, and it was not Zev's. Their marriage remained unconsummated, each attempt at intimacy ending in disaster. They barely spoke. Ironic as now she was talking to him incessantly. Every day. But it was a one-sided conversation and would never be more than that. What had she done to deserve this? Any of this?

She had a child growing inside her, the product of a brutal rape by a beast of a man. Her pregnancy was a dark secret. Something shameful. Every time she thought of the child, she remembered the rape. She felt nothing but revulsion. The news she was having a baby should be a joyous occasion, but this wouldn't be. She would have to tell her husband that she was pregnant by another man. How would he react? And what if Zev died? How would she cope on her own with a bastard child and no husband? What if he recovered but was like the girl in Rouen?

Her situation could not be more wretched. Today it had been made more so by the announcement that Douce was pregnant. On hearing the news Arlette could not help but feel a tinge of jealousy. Douce was happily married with two children and pregnant with a third. Under normal circumstances she would have been unreservedly happy for her aunt and uncle. It was wicked to feel this way. What was she becoming? She resented Douce for being happy, almost wished Zev dead rather than be the way he was. Arlette could not account for it. Her emotions were all over the place. Unpredictable. She could not remember the last time she had been happy. It was as if the ground beneath her was shifting. Nothing felt solid anymore. Her world was intangible, she had no compass to guide her. She was lost.

CHAPTER
FORTY-THREE

Mirabelle sat in her ostentatious great hall with her husband Elias. They were eating dried figs and almonds washed down with red wine. Their children had been put to bed and their servant Joan was in her room in the attic.

'I wonder when your Irishman will return,' said Elias.

'I thought he would have been back by now,' replied Mirabelle, stuffing a fig into her mean mouth.

'Maybe he's found someone else to lend him the money.'

'I hope not. I think there is profit to be had if we handle this correctly.'

'Mirabelle, I wish you wouldn't scheme all the time. There are ways of making honest money.'

'If I was as honest as you want me to be you might still be in that gaol,' said Mirabelle, reaching for another fig.

'You took an enormous risk going to the sheriff. He might have locked you up and what would have happened to the children?'

'Don't you know, Elias. Money talks.'

'Money isn't everything, Mirabelle. You would do well to remember that.'

'Oh, you worry too much, Elias. I can handle the sheriff. As soon as he saw the shiny gold coins he was dribbling with greed.'

'All the same.'

'All the same I got you of that hellhole, didn't I?'

Mirabelle was beginning to realise her husband had no backbone. No stomach for the more unpleasant aspects of life. He was a weak man. He protested at her methods but never stopped her. He liked the lifestyle it afforded him, and he wasn't about to give that up. They would argue but, in the end, he would come around to her way of thinking. As long as he didn't have to get his hands dirty. In her opinion nothing was achieved by being pleasant. You had to be ruthless and cunning if you were to succeed.

'I just wish you would be more delicate...'

'There is nothing delicate about the world of money. It is drenched in mire and political intrigue, and you have to stay ahead of the game if you want more than your share of the spoils.'

'You make it sound sordid.'

'It is.'

Mirabelle recalled her secret meeting with the sheriff. She could see he was an old man who wanted nothing more than an easy life in his dotage. He was another weak man, corrupt and greedy with it and Mirabelle had exploited that. She smiled smugly as she popped another fig into her small mouth.

'How exactly did you secure my early release? It must have taken more than money to convince the sheriff to let me go?' Elias asked, shifting himself into a reclining position.

'The sheriff owed me favours. It was time to call upon one.'

'What sort of favours?'

Mirabelle huffed in annoyance. She liked to keep her shadier dealings a secret even to her husband. She had learnt that if you never told a soul the secret would remain a secret and never be used against you. People were weak. They had an innate need to confess, to unburden themselves.

Answering him in a deliberately vague way, she said. 'I keep my eyes and ears open. I know what goes on in this city.'

'Do you know anything about that boy's murder and who did it?'

Mirabelle didn't answer. She rubbed at the prominent mole on her face, then took a slow sip of her wine.

'You don't think Moses had anything to do with it, do you?' enquired Elias, sitting back up.

'Moses is a businessman. He's not capable of murder.'

'Then who?'

'It could have been anyone. Didn't they say he was found naked?'

'Yes, but what do you deduce from that?'

'There may have been a sexual intent...'

'You mean?' Elias slumped back in his chair; his plump face drawn of colour. He wiped his forehead. 'I hadn't thought of that.'

'There's very little going on in that head of yours. You'd be nothing without me.'

'You are right of course. As ever.'

The two sat in silence listening to the sounds of passers-by in the street. Mostly drunken Christians.

'Listen to them. They have the morals of a dog,' Mirabelle said.

'They're not all like that.'

Mirabelle rolled her eyes and snorted. 'You're so naïve at times, Elias.'

Elias took on a pained expression and sat back in his chair.

'I've been thinking of a way to deal with the problem of the Irishman,' Mirabelle said.

'What are you scheming now?'

'I'm loathe to refuse a business deal, especially one so lucrative but I am wary of this one. I keep coming back to Moses. Why would he send business to me? There must be more to it.'

'I think you're right of course,' said Elias. 'You have a nose for this sort of thing.'

'I think I've found a way for us to make lots of money but not be directly involved.'

'So, if anything should go wrong it won't be laid at our door?'

'Exactly.'

Elias raised his goblet to toast his wife.

'You're as crafty as a fox, Mirabelle.'

CHAPTER
FORTY-FOUR

Arlette sat on the stone bench in the antechamber of the *mikveh* where the women would undress and wash before entering the sacred chamber. On the eve of her marriage to Zev this was the room she used to supposedly cleanse herself spiritually and enter her marriage in a state of complete purity. But that had no longer been possible. She was no longer pure. She would never be pure.

At this time of night the room was dark, cool and silent apart from the comforting sound of trickling water. She sat for a while without removing her clothes staring ahead of her. Try as she might, she had not been able to stop her dark thoughts. Her life was wretched. Her life was over. A voice in her head, relentless in its insistence, had told her so.

Your life is over.

She had been trying to push this thought from her mind all day, but to no avail.

Your life is over.

Your life is over.

Arlette crossed to the pile of clean cloths Douce provided for the use of the women in the community. She picked up a cloth and pressed it to her face. It smelled faintly of lavender. She put it on the bench and removed her clothes, folding them to form a neat pile. Then she removed her gold earrings, the gold bangle she wore around her wrist and finally the simple wedding ring Zev had placed upon her finger. These she placed in a neat arrangement on top of her clothes.

Moses had designed the *mikveh* so that the fresh spring water, essential for any ritual bath, poured from a spout and then drained into a gulley on the floor and disappeared somewhere underground.

Arlette soaked the lavender cloth under the running water and began washing her body, starting with her arms. She scrubbed the flesh until it became red and tiny dark blood blisters began to form beneath the skin. She hated herself, hated being alive.

A few short months ago she was to marry into the wealthiest Jewish dynasty in England, but this had been cruelly snatched from her. Her only hope was to accept Zev's proposal of marriage, but her husband now lay dying at the hands of her rapist. To add insult to injury, she was now compelled to carry the child of the man who was responsible for destroying her entire future.

She was nothing but black inside, black and worthless. No one could ever love her. Deudonne never loved her. If he had, he would not have forsaken her. Zev did love her, but he had been taken from her. His useless body lying in the great hall, taunting her. Her only chance of a normal life was gone and there was nothing she could do about it.

'Your life is over,' the voice said again.

Rinsing the cloth, and without ringing it out, she sluiced in between her thighs. She checked the cloth for traces of blood. It was clean, unlike the child inside her. It was as sullied as she was. A baby born of the devil. She was dirty, unworthy, spiritually defiled. The only person who wanted her was Zev and he was as good as dead.

Arlette hung the cloth on a nail and went over to the bench where she had left a pouch of leather. She unfurled it to reveal a sharp knife. She studied it for a while, tracing her finger over its recently sharpened edge. It would do the job. Holding the knife in one hand she pulled on her hair with the other, hacking at her lustrous locks until all of it was lying on the floor. She was now ready to immerse herself in the bath.

Naked, she picked up the sack of rocks she had been gathering secretly. Just a few small rocks each day. It wasn't a fully conscious thought, something vague and unspoken in the back of her mind told her she may need them one day. She walked to the arched entrance over which the words '*mayim zochalim*', meaning flowing water, were carved into the stone lintel. Inside, the sacred chamber was much darker. She placed the heavy stones on the side of the bath. Next, she walked barefoot down the seven sandstone steps into the purifying water. It was ice cold, but she was beyond feeling. As high as her waist, it was a murky lagoon ready to consume her black worthless soul. She let her body sink under the water. The coldness took her breath away. Breathing hard, her heart racing from the shock, she recited the usual blessing through chattering teeth.

She hoped to feel differently after the immersion in the living waters. A lifting of the curse, a return to ritual cleanliness, but nothing had changed. The blackness remained. The insidious voice in her head returned.

Your life is over.

End it now. It is time. There is nothing more to live for.

The water beckoned.

I am ready.

In the darkness Arlette found the end of the rope she used to tie the bag of stones together and wrapped the other end around her delicate neck, securing it tightly. She closed her eyes and slid under the water. All she could hear was the muffled sound of the stones as they scraped to the edge before splashing into the water. Her neck jerked as the weight of the stones plunged her naked body to the bottom of the inky water.

Whelmed by the darkness melding with her sullied soul she stayed pinned beneath the surface. Her body struggled but her weary heart cared no more. She opened her mouth to let the blackness devour her.

FORTY-FIVE

S ince Zev's attack, Douce was increasingly worried about Arlette's state of mind. She rarely joined in a conversation, ate very little and a vacant, distant look as though she wasn't all together there was ever present. She spent most of her time kneeling by Zev's bed, squeezing droplets of weak ale into his mouth chattering incessantly to him. Zev was for the most part unresponsive. He lay upon his mattress, still in the great hall for they dare not move him. Bellassez came daily to administer concoctions of turmeric and ginger to reduce the swelling on his face. Rubin and Damete were also at Zev's side and Baruch visited often. Her husband Moses spent long hours out of the house or in his cellar and her son Samuel was becoming increasingly unwell. He spent most days in bed or on his grandfather's lap, barely able to walk or talk. Samuel the Elder doted on his grandson and attended to his every waking need. She hardly had time to think about the child growing inside her for worrying about Young Samuel. What was once a joyful and happy household was becoming a place of melancholic hell. For Douce there was no respite from the misery. Even her love of cooking had lost its appeal as no one had much of an appetite. What sort of a world was she bringing this child into?

Douce lay in bed wondering what was to become of them all. Why had Hashem seen fit to plague her with such sorrow? She spent a fitful night, drifting in and out of sleep until something woke her. Trying not to disturb Moses, she climbed out of bed and tiptoed up the stairs to Arlette's room. She listened at the door and hearing no sound carefully lifted the latch. The bed was empty. It had not been slept in. Douce ran out of the room and down the stairs past her bedroom door and into the great hall. Zev lay on his back on the mattress. Arlette was nowhere to be seen. A sixth sense, or Hashem's guidance, she couldn't be sure, made her go to the sacred bath and look for her there.

When she opened the door, she noticed Arlette's clothes folded into a neat pile on the bench. A dark patch on the floor caught her attention. It was Arlette's hair. In an instant she knew something terrible had happened. She ran to the chamber. In the darkness she could make out a shape in the water. Without thinking, she jumped in. Instinctively, she knew it was Arlette. She tried to drag her out but discovered a rope around her neck was anchoring her to the bottom. Douce remembered seeing a knife next to Arlette's shorn hair. She clambered out of the water, her clothes dripping, and grabbed the knife from where it lay and returned. Back in the water she hacked at the rope until it cut through. With enormous strength she did not know she possessed, she dragged Arlette's body out of the water and onto the side.

Arlette was icy cold. Douce turned her on her side, rubbing at Arlette's back and arms to warm her.

Arlette did not respond. Her body was still cold as ice. Douce grabbed dry towels from the antechamber and wrapped them around Arlette, then she went to get Bellassez.

Her clothes left a trail of dripping water as she made her way across Jewry Street. Bella would know what to do. Douce banged on her door until she opened it.

'What's happened? You look as white as a shroud and your clothes...'

'It's Arlette,' Douce began, 'I think she's dead.'

Bellassez was rarely shocked but on hearing Douce's news was temporarily rendered speechless and it took her a moment to reply.

'Has she been ill?'

'No, you don't understand, Bella. She's tried to kill herself in the *mikveh*. If we hurry, there may still be time to save her.'

Bellassez grabbed her medical bag and left the house, leaving the children asleep upstairs.

'I cannot believe she's done this. Why, Bella, why?'

'I don't know, sometimes it's hard to know what's in a person's mind.'

The women hurried back towards the ritual bath.

'You better change your clothes first, Douce. They're soaking wet.'

Douce looked down at her tunic as if she were seeing her clothes for the first time. 'Not now,' she said. 'Later.'

When Bellassez saw Arlette's body on the cold stone floor she let out an anguished cry.

Listening to her chest, Bellassez was relieved to hear the faint sound of shallow breathing, she touched Arlette's cheek to check her temperature. It was cold.

'Arlette,' she called, watching her face for any sign of a response.

Arlette's eyes flickered in the darkness. After a few minutes of frantic rubbing, she finally took a breath.

'*Baruch Hashem*, you're alive,' said Douce, thanking Hashem. 'Arlette, can you hear me?' said Douce.

Arlette's eyes fluttered open, momentarily.

'We need to move her quickly and get her warm. You'll have to wake Moses and ask him to help us.'

Douce was staring at Arlette. 'Why did she cut off all her hair? It seems an odd thing to do.'

'Perhaps it was an act of punishment. Maybe she blames herself for what happened,' Bellassez said, rising from the cold floor to fetch more dry cloths.

'Punishment. She is not the one to be punished.'

Bella sighed. 'I'm just trying to make sense of this, Douce.'

'Arlette is to not to blame for what happened to her. She is without sin.'

Bellassez put her arm around Douce. 'I know that.'

Douce returned to her sleeping husband. He stirred when she sat next to him on the bed.

'What is it, *chérie*?' Moses said looking sleepy. 'What's the matter?'

'It's Arlette,' Douce said. 'She's tried to take her own life.'

Moses sat bolt upright in bed. 'Where is she? Is she all right?'

He pulled the covers off and jumped out of bed.

'She's in the *mikveh*.'

'In the *mikveh*?' he said, his eyes hooded, questioning her.

'I found her in the water, a rope tied around her neck. Oh, Moses, she tried to drown herself.'

'Try not to get too upset, Douce. You have the baby to think about.'

'But how could she do that? Such a sinful act.'

'Never mind that now. Is she all right?'

'I think so. Bella is with her, but we need your help to bring her into the house.'

Moses threw his cloak around his shoulders, pulled on his boots and hurried to the bath. His eyes clouded with tears at the sight of Arlette. 'Oh,' he said, his voice full of anguish. 'Ma *pauvre petite.*'

'She needs to be by the fire, and we must get some warm broth into her. Help me lift her, Moses.'

Bellassez wrapped more towels around Arlette to protect her modesty before Moses carried her into the great hall and laid her next to the fire not far from Zev. Bella looked at the young married couple lying side by side, both looking close to death. She couldn't help making the comparison that Moses' great hall looked more like a mausoleum than a home.

Bellassez sent Moses to fetch some dry, warm blankets and told Douce to change out of her wet clothes. When Moses returned, she told him to stoke the fire while she wrapped Arlette in the warm blankets. With fresh logs on the fire, the room soon warmed up putting some colour back into Arlette's cheeks. Douce returned wearing dry clothes and holding a bowl of steaming broth.

'How are you feeling now, Arlette,' Bellassez asked in a soothing tone.

Arlette opened her eyes. She quickly closed them and turned her head away.

'Give her some broth,' Bellassez said, packing her bag away. 'She'll be fine. Put her to bed and I'll call back tomorrow.'

Once they settled Arlette in her bed and Bellassez left, Douce went downstairs to sit with Moses. She found him hunched over the fire looking weary, lost, like a small boy. They hardly noticed Zev lying on the floor beside them he had lain there so long.

'Poor Arlette. She came to me for protection, and I failed her,' Moses said.

Douce reached out to Moses and laid her hand on his arm. 'You haven't failed her. You're not responsible for what happened, and you weren't to know she would do something like this.'

'I should have known.'

'None of us could have foreseen this.'

'She must have felt so desperate to do what she did.'

'I don't understand why she would do that, why anyone would do that. It frightens me, Moses. I don't know how to behave around her.'

'I feel the same.'

'To take your own life is to sin against Hashem, but to do it in the sacred *mikveh*. Such shame she has brought upon this house,' Douce said, gnawing on her knuckles.

'It is I who should be ashamed. I should have spent more time at home. I've neglected my family when they needed me the most.'

Douce squeezed Moses' arm again. 'Don't reproach yourself. You're a good husband, a good father. You love Arlette like she was your own daughter.'

'All I know is I don't know what to say to her when I see her next. I feel so angry.'

Moses stared into the fire. He looked unsure of himself. A countenance Douce had never seen before.

'Life is precious, Moses. Only Hashem has the power to give or take it away.'

'Perhaps if we gave Arlette something to live for. If she thought Zev needed her. Would that help?'

'It might.'

CHAPTER
FORTY-SIX

When Arlette woke her first thought was regret at still being alive followed swiftly by the thought of having to face her family. The shame of it. She touched her neck and felt the tender weal where the rope had been. A heaviness in her heart weighted her to the bed. Then she thought of the child. Was it still alive inside her? She could not tell. She felt dead inside. Numb.

She wondered how long she had lain there and what people were saying about her. What would they say when they found out she was with child and had meant to take it with her? Arlette pushed her face into the pillow muffling her anguished cries. There was a quiet knock at the door. Arlette stiffened and held her breath. Another knock and then the door opened.

'Arlette...'

It was Douce. She couldn't face her, couldn't look her in the eye for shame. Douce sat down on the bed beside her and swept the hair from Arlette's cheek, uncovering the red mark across her neck. Douce winced at the memory of the rope. If she had arrived moments later, they would have lost her.

'That's better, I can see you now.'

Arlette did not respond. She was in no mood for conversation. She buried her head further into the pillow, screwing her eyes tightly shut, as if by doing so she could shut out the cruel world around her.

'I have good news, Arlette. Zev opened his eyes this morning. Hashem has answered our prayers.'

'Zev is alive?' Arlette said, twisting round to look at Douce.

'Yes, he opened his eyes briefly, then went back to sleep. Bellassez says it's a good sign.'

Arlette didn't know what to make of this news. For a moment when Douce said he was alive she imagined him walking, talking, making jokes like he used to, but he was far from that. He had opened his eyes. That was all. What did that mean?

'Come down and see him. I'm sure he's missed you.'

'How could he miss me? He wouldn't know if I was dead or alive.'

'I think you're wrong, Arlette. I've noticed when you speak to him, he stirs. I'm sure he knows when you're in the room. Come and sit with him. I'll make us a hot tisane and he might open his eyes again.'

Arlette was struggling to understand Douce's behaviour. She was acting as if nothing had happened. Perhaps this was how it was going to be. Denial of her sinful act. Yet another family secret.

'How long have I been asleep?'

'We let you sleep late. Now get dressed and come downstairs. Zev needs you more than ever.' Douce rose from the bed to leave. 'Everything will be all right, Arlette. You'll see.'

Arlette lay a while longer going over Douce's words. She found it hard to believe everything was going to be all right. Just like that. Nothing was ever going to be right again. She was not right. Zev was never going to be right. Douce was well intentioned but maddening. As if a tisane would make everything all right. Arlette wondered why Douce had not mentioned her attempt at taking her own life. Was she going to act as if it never happened? To Arlette this seemed to diminish her. She felt small and insignificant. Would the world have been such a different place without her? Had she been successful they would have missed her at first. But life would go on. They would get over her death.

Her thoughts tortured her. She must get out of bed, but she didn't want to. She thought of Zev lying downstairs alone. Could there be any truth in what Douce said? Did he know she existed? Did he need her?

It took all her energy to get out of bed and dress herself. Her body felt heavy like her insides had turned to wet sand, yet her head felt light, foggy, her thoughts dulled. It seemed to take a long time for her to walk downstairs, stepping gingerly, as if she were learning to walk again. When she reached the bottom, she stopped. The shame returned. Her uncle might be there and how would she face him? To her relief Douce appeared.

'Everyone is out. It's just us. Come, I've made the tisane. Zev is waiting for you.'

Douce offered Arlette her arm, which she was relieved to take as she felt a little weak and dizzy. She saw Zev lying on the mattress, his eyes closed. There was no change. No flickering of the eyelids. No recognition of her presence. Douce handed her the cup of peppermint tea she had made.

'I must check on little Samuel. He's still not well and I have work to do in the kitchen. I'll leave you two alone.'

Arlette sat on the rug beside Zev's sickbed. She scrutinised his face for any sign of life. A twitch. An exhalation. A groan. Anything.

'Zev,' she whispered. 'Can you hear me?'

She took his hand.

'Zev, if you can hear me squeeze my hand. I need to know you understand me.'

She waited. There was nothing.

Give me something to make me want to carry on with my miserable life.

She leaned closer.

'Zev, it's Arlette.'

She was about to give up when she felt his fingers twitch. Encouraged Arlette continued, 'Zev. Can you hear me?'

His fingers twitched again, and his eyelids flickered.

'You can hear me?' she cried.

Arlette kissed his hand and held it to her cheek.

FORTY-SEVEN

Dairmait had turned Robert fitz Harding's home in Bristol into an unofficial battle headquarters. His campaign to defeat his enemies and win back his lands had begun in earnest. He had secured funding from an ambitious young moneylender in Gloucester. For one so young Dairmait had wondered how he had amassed such a large fortune, but as long as the money was forthcoming, he didn't care where it came from. It had meant that Dairmait was now able to discuss the finer detail of his campaign. His newfound ally and soon to be son-in-law Richard de Clare was proving to be an invaluable asset. They were in the great hall discussing who might join them.

'I could call upon my nephew Hervey de Monte Marisco. He's always keen to engage in battle and other sports,' Richard said letting out a raucous laugh, remembering his nephew's lascivious habits. 'Robert fitz Stephen may well join us but he's a prisoner of that Welsh rebel, Rhys ap Gruffydh. A shame because he's a gifted soldier and there are many who would join him.'

'Is there any way we can secure his release?' asked Dairmait.

'You'd be a better man than me,' Richard quipped, taking a long draught of wine. 'But if you do, he'll likely be able to call upon the services of Maurice fitz Gerald, Raymond le Gros and others from the Nest clan. Robert de Barri and Miles de Cogan would join them.'

'Sounds like the key to forming this army is Robert fitz Stephen,' Dairmait said, pulling on his matted beard. 'Where is he being held?'

'I don't know for certain. He's been in captivity in Wales since the end of the Welsh campaign.'

'The last time I was in Wales was to fight for the king against the Welsh,' said Dairmait. 'That's probably why the king gave me the letters patent.'

'Then I don't hold out much for your chances.'

'Allegiances change. If he is as good as you say he is and he can summon up an army of men, then I will do what I can to have him released. Perhaps a deal can be brokered.'

'You won't find him the most agreeable of fellows,' Richard said.

'Neither am I. And I'm Irish not English. That may make a difference.'

'Sounds like you might get that army after all, Dairmait,' Robert fitz Harding chipped in.

Taller than Dairmait, Robert wore a long tunic of fine grey linen tied at the waist by a leather belt. His greying hair was wispy and thinning on top.

'Maybe so,' Dairmait responded.

'I'll speak with my nephew Hervey. He might know where they're keeping him.'

'I'd be grateful to you if you would. The sooner we find this fitz Stephen, the nearer I'll get to forming an army.'

'It might work if the price is right,' Richard said, sitting down at the table and helping himself to a goblet of wine.

'I've always found money tends to oil the most implacable of men.'

'How soon do you think you can have these men ready to invade Ireland?' Robert asked.

'If we can secure fitz Stephen's release and the others follow as Richard has predicted then as soon as the spring of next year.'

Dairmait detected a look of dejection from Robert. His wife Eva was not entirely happy with the arrangement. They had practically taken over her home.

'I will do all I can to make it sooner. I'm keen to get back to Ireland and my people.'

'I appreciate that, Dairmait.'

Their conversation was interrupted by Aoife. 'I thought I would find you here.' Aoife was dressed in a heavy woollen cloak and leather boots, her red hair flowing over her shoulders.

'Going somewhere?' her father asked.

'As a matter of fact, I am, Father. With Richard.'

Aoife took Richard's arm and squeezed it. She was a wilful child. Always had been, insisting she join her father on the battlefield. But since her engagement to Richard, he had noticed a change in her. She wore fine clothes, dressed her hair with fragrant pomade and she seemed to have a permanent impish grin on her face. Richard would have his work cut out marrying such a firebrand. Richard's nickname Strongbow had been earned for his exacting skill with a longbow in battle. It was hard to imagine him on the battlefield as when he was around Aoife he became like a small puppy dog in her presence.

'You cannot keep dragging Richard off whenever the mood takes you. We have an army to raise.'

'Your father's right, Aoife,' Richard said, trying to resist.

'Without me you wouldn't have an army or any money to pay for it. You would do well to remember that, Father.'

'You played no part,' her father replied with reproach.

'Excuse me but if it wasn't for my diplomacy your plans would be dead in the water.'

Dairmait grunted, picked up the nearest thing to him, an apple from a platter on the table and threw it at the unlit grate, dislodging Robert's hounds from their favourite spot by the fire.

'Damnable woman,' he shouted as Aoife left the hall on Richard's arm.

CHAPTER
FORTY-EIGHT

Arlette continued to spend every day by Zev's side, talking, reading to him and telling him every minute detail of her day. From time to time she would ask for confirmation that he understood, and he would squeeze her hand. She wasn't sure if it was her imagination or wishful thinking, but she felt sure his grip was growing stronger. The scar on his cheek was healing, the swelling had gone down and the bruises on his body were turning from angry purple to pale yellow. He looked so much better.

One day Arlette's efforts were rewarded when Zev opened his eyes and gave her a strange look.

'What have you done to your hair,' he said, his voice weak from lack of use.

Arlette didn't know whether to laugh or cry. It was just the sort of crazy remark Zev would make. It was like he had never left her.

'Hello,' she said, taking his hand. 'How are you feeling?'

'Like someone kicked me in the head.'

This time Arlette did laugh. She felt the tension of the past

few days lift as she realised he would not be like the girl in
Rouen. She had her old Zev back.

From that day on, Zev's health improved dramatically.
Arlette was curious to know how much he could remember. He
remembered telling Brito to go to hell but beyond that nothing.
There was no lasting damage to his faculties, but he was weak
and found it difficult to walk unaided and he tired easily. But
despite this his recovery was nothing short of a miracle.

It was early July, and she was almost four months pregnant.
Her breasts were full, and her stomach was starting to show.
She had managed to conceal her swollen belly from Moses and
Douce by wearing looser fitting tunics. Zev though was still
unaware of her condition. She longed to talk to him about it,
but the opportunity had not presented itself. The constant
comings and goings in the household made it difficult to talk
about anything of such an intimate nature.

After a few weeks, Zev was able to walk unaided. He would
sit in the courtyard soaking up the warm sunshine and
breathing in the fresh air. Arlette could see he was improving
and each day her spirits rose. Today, he was to join her in their
marital bedroom. Her stomach had been churning all day. He
was sure to notice she was pregnant. How do you tell your
husband you are carrying another man's child? How would he
react? On the day Zev proposed he reassured her if she were
pregnant, it wouldn't change anything. All would be well. But
the Zev lying in his sick bed was a very different man from the
Zev who proposed to her, and the child's father was his attacker
who had almost cost him his life.

Zev was already in bed when she retired. She was searingly
conscious that he would notice her swollen belly especially if he
made another attempt at consummating their marriage. She
must tell him. He had taken to reading Moses' prayer book in
the evening. Arlette was not sure whether it was to alleviate his

260

boredom or because of his good fortune in avoiding Hashem's calling. She hadn't thought of him as much of a reader before she married him let alone a student of the Torah. She changed into her nightclothes shielding her belly from Zev and climbed into the large bed next to him, pulling the covers up to her chin. He looked up from the holy book, smiled and closed it.

'Zev,' she said in a tentative voice. 'I have something to tell you...'

'What is it, my love?' he asked. 'You look troubled. Is everything all right?'

There was no other way to say it.

'I'm pregnant, Zev.'

She waited for his reaction, trembling inside. She turned to search his face for a sign. Zev's face was blank.

'Oh,' he said finally.

Arlette could feel the tears welling up. 'Are you upset?'

'Not upset...'

'I did tell you. The day you proposed to me.'

'I know. I thought maybe you wouldn't be. I just wasn't expecting...' he trailed off, lost deep in thought.

'I've been dreading telling you.'

'Why?'

'You've been so ill. Does this change everything?'

'Well, I suppose it does.'

By now the tears were streaming down her face. 'Don't you want to be married to me anymore now I'm carrying another man's child?'

'It's not that. It's just a shock. A lot to take in.' He drew her to him. 'I'm sorry, Arlette. I didn't mean to make you cry.'

Arlette sniffled as she wiped the tears away with the hem of her sleeve. 'I haven't told anyone.'

'Douce doesn't know?'

'Not yet.'

'I'm sorry you've had to carry this burden on your own. I haven't been here for you.'

'Hardly your fault. We know who is to blame.'

Arlette blanched at the verbal reference to their attacker and intuitively looked down at her hands. Zev tilted her chin, so she had to look at him. He wiped the tears from her cheeks.

'I don't want that man to ruin our lives. We don't need to mention his name anymore. He's our past, not our future.'

'All right,' she said. 'What are we going to say to Uncle Moses and Douce?'

'What do you mean?'

'About the baby. I can't hide it from them for much longer.'

'We'll just tell them you're pregnant and leave it at that.'

'What if Douce asks questions?'

'She won't. If I know Douce, she'll want to keep up appearances. Even if she doesn't believe us, she won't question it. Her reputation will be lost upon it. And Moses... well, Moses just wants you to be happy.'

'Are we going to be happy?' she asked.

'I hope so, Arlette. These past weeks have been hard for us both. We must get through this together.'

'Remember what you said on the day you proposed to me. That if I was pregnant, you'd love it like your own. Do you think you can still do that?'

Zev took his time to answer. 'I don't know,' he said.

They lay a while in silence side by side. Then Arlette said, 'If it's a boy, shall we call him Rubin after your father?'

Zev didn't answer straight away. It was tradition to call your firstborn son after the grandfather.

Eventually, he said, 'Maybe, we'll see.'

Zev turned on his side with his back to her and went to sleep.

CHAPTER
FORTY-NINE

T he news that Arlette was pregnant was greeted with joy by Moses and Douce. Old Samuel took the news more phlegmatically as was his reaction to most things in life at his great age. Rubin was overjoyed, but Damete seemed indifferent. Arlette sensed she was not altogether happy to have her as a daughter-in-law. Her indifference at the news Arlette was pregnant confirmed this. Some mothers were more protective of their sons than their daughters. Damete was such a woman. Arlette tried to like her for Zev's sake. If Damete knew the baby wasn't Zev's, she would be unhappier still. They had agreed to tell no one of the baby's real father. Thankfully the time between her rape and her wedding night was close enough for them to keep up the pretence and no one had asked any awkward questions.

Zev was not fully recovered from his ordeal and still tired easily. He was often asleep when she retired for the night. So far, it had been easy to avoid her wifely duties but as Zev grew stronger, she knew it would not be long before he would expect her to be his wife in every respect. Their wedding night had been an unmitigated disaster. Every time she thought about it, she cringed with embarrassment.

Tonight, when she entered the bedroom Zev was wide awake. She undressed and climbed into bed. Instead of turning his back on her he placed his hand on her stomach and pressed himself against her. She could tell he was aroused. She took a deep breath, trying her best to relax. He leaned over and kissed her.

'Do you think we should be doing this whilst I'm with child?'

'I don't see why not. It's not forbidden.'

He kissed her cheeks, her neck, between her breasts. His touch was tender. She couldn't deny him forever. His hand went down to her inner thigh. She felt her body tense.

'Relax, Arlette. I'll be gentle. I want you to enjoy this.'

Zev pressed on. His hands seeking out the fleshy part between her thighs. He was more persistent this time, his knee wedged in between her thighs. Panic set in again. She was back in the courtyard lying on the ground and it was Brito's knee pushing her legs apart.

'Please stop,' she said to Zev.

Zev appeared not to hear her. Arlette's heart was racing, her skin clammy and her panic quickly turned to a sense of terror.

'I can't do this,' she said, pushing his hand away.

'But you're my wife,' he said, his breathing erratic, infused with pent-up longing.

'I know, I know. I want to, but I can't.'

'You did it with him, why not with me?'

Arlette froze. Her terror turned to anger, and she tried with all her strength to push him away. He pinned her down.

'How could you say that?' she shouted in his face. 'He forced himself upon me and now you're doing the same.'

At that, Zev relaxed his hold on her and she managed to wriggle from beneath him and curl into a defensive ball.

'I can't bear this,' he said. 'I love you.'

He jumped out of bed and got dressed.

'Where are you going?'

'I can't stand to be in the same bed and not be allowed to touch you.'

Arlette lay in bed listening to Zev's hurried footsteps on the stairs. She heard the front door open and close, then silence.

She lay there for some time wondering what her life would have been like if she had never been raped. As she thought this, she twizzled the plain band of gold Zev had given her around her finger. She tore it off and threw it to the floor. Instantly she regretted doing it. She retrieved the ring and placed it back on her finger.

She reminded herself that Zev was a good man. Hadn't he saved her from a life of spinsterhood and shame? Why couldn't she let him touch her? Brito had taken more than her virginity. He had destroyed any chance of marital intimacy and without it she could not see how she and Zev could ever be happy.

She looked down at her swollen belly, a constant reminder of the source of her troubles. Maybe once this thing was out of her, she might feel differently towards Zev.

The last piece of *him* gone from her body.

Zev marched at speed along Jewry Street and out of the city through the East Gate. Once he was over the drawbridge he was in open countryside. The moon was full and the night warm. A perfect summer's eve. By the time he reached the river he was beginning to tire. Before the attack he could have run all the way without breaking into a sweat. How his life had changed. Exhausted, he sat down by the river's edge to rest. That bastard Brito had taken more from him than his health. He had taken away the one thing in his life he loved the most. Arlette.

How he had longed to marry her. Make her his own. How proud he had been on his wedding day and how full of anticipation on his wedding night to finally take her in his arms and fully know her.

Zev knew his frustration had got the better of him. What man wouldn't be frustrated? But tonight he realised he was ill-equipped to know how to show her his love and ashamed of the tactics he had used to try. His marriage was a disaster, and he didn't know how to fix it.

Something else was troubling him. The news that Arlette was pregnant had been a shock. He thought it wouldn't make any difference to how he felt about her, but it did. She was now a part of him, the stranger. The thought Brito had been there before him and left his seed sent him into a vortex of hatred and resentment. This, he realised with shame, was being directed toward Arlette.

He still hoped he could love the child she carried as his own, but now he wasn't so sure. He was cuckolded. The woman he married was having another man's child. It made the rape even more real. The worst of it was he still hadn't been intimate with her. But what Zev found even more unbearable was the child's father was the man who had very nearly sent him to an early grave. Maybe if that hadn't happened, he might have had half a chance of loving this child. Right now, he resented the unborn baby. He knew it was an irrational emotion. The child was innocent, but Brito was not. Zev was reminded of the Torah.

'The iniquity of parents upon children and children's children, upon the third and fourth generations.'

No innocent child should be punished for the sins of its father. Zev might feel differently once the child was born.

He kicked at the mounds of earth with his boot to get rid of his pent-up anger. He shouldn't be so mean to Arlette. It was not her fault. What he said to her was unforgivable. He would apologise to her in the morning.

CHAPTER
FIFTY

Arlette grew bigger, and Zev grew more frustrated. To cope with this, he spent a good deal of time away from the house working with his father in the butchery or hunting with Baruch. Although his marriage to Arlette was not what he imagined it would be, it wasn't all bad. He still loved her and hoped one day they would resolve their problems. After his apology he made a promise to Arlette that he would not force himself upon her and would wait until she was ready. As the months went by, he convinced himself that things would change once the child was born.

When Zev arrived home, after a morning out hunting with Baruch, the first thing he did was ask Douce where Arlette was.

'She's resting upstairs.'

A worried look passed over Zev's face. 'Is she all right? Has anything happened?'

'No. She's just resting. You fret too much about this baby,' Douce said.

'I can't help it, Douce.'

Although Douce understood why, she dismissed his fears. 'Having babies is the most natural thing in the world.'

'I'll go up and see how she is.'

'Don't be too long. The meal is nearly ready.'

'I won't.'

Zev found Arlette lying on her side, facing away from him. Despite all their difficulties, he still cared for her. He went to her side of the bed. Her eyes were closed, and she looked peaceful.

'How are you feeling?' he whispered, bending over to kiss her on the cheek.

She opened her eyes and looked at him. He sat down beside her and stroked her hair.

'I'm just tired,' she said, closing her eyes again.

'Are you coming down to eat?'

'I don't feel up to it. You go.'

'Are you sure you're all right,' he asked again.

'Don't fuss. I'm fine.'

'All right, if you're sure.'

Zev left her to rest and went downstairs. When he returned later that evening, she was fast asleep. He undressed and crept into bed beside her. In the middle of the night, he was woken by a sound. He lay for a moment, not quite awake, but when it came again the sound was unmistakeable. Arlette was in pain.

'What's happening? Is it time?'

Arlette let out a muted groan.

'How long have you been like this?' he asked.

'A while but I didn't want to wake you.'

'I'm going to fetch Douce,' he said, the sound of quickening panic in his voice.

Zev returned with Douce. She was in her nightclothes and carrying a candle. She set the metal candle holder on the small table next to the bed. Arlette was lying on her back, breathing heavily. Douce smoothed her hair from her face and felt her forehead. It was hot. Arlette moaned with the pain.

Arlette spoke. 'The bed is wet. I think I've had an accident.'

'That's not an accident, Arlette. Your waters have broken. You're going to have your baby.'

Zev felt helpless. Delivering a baby was not something he was equipped to do. Give him a sharp knife and the carcass of an animal and he would get to work on it, removing the forbidden fat from around the liver and stripping the nerves and other parts of the animal they were forbidden to eat. But deliver a baby?

'Should we be doing something?' he asked Douce.

'Nature will take its course.'

Daylight came and with it more pain. Arlette's contractions were more frequent now. Douce remained at her side all that day despite being close to giving birth herself. Around the room in every corner she hung silver and gold amulets to protect Arlette from the *Ayin Hara*, the Evil Eye and from Lilith, the dangerous demon of the night known to steal babies in the darkness. By nightfall, Arlette was weakening, consumed with pain and still no sign of the baby's arrival.

'I think we should fetch Bella,' Douce said.

'Why do we need Bella? Doesn't she attend the difficult births?'

'Not always. I just want her opinion.'

Zev was not convinced by Douce's assurances. He knew Bellassez was called out when births were difficult. He remembered some years ago when his neighbour's wife Esther died in childbirth. Bellassez had been in attendance on that occasion. Zev left to fetch her. When he returned the two women hugged but said very little. Douce sat beside Arlette, a wet cloth in her hand wiping Arlette's face, chest and arms to cool her down and give her some relief. Bellassez set down her leather medical bag, rolled up her sleeves and lifted Arlette's shift to expose her belly. The room fell silent as she pressed her ear to Arlette's distended stomach to listen for a heartbeat. Her brow creased in concentration as she felt for the baby's position.

'Is everything all right?' Zev asked. His temples were stippled with sweat beads.

'The baby's not in the right position.'

'What does that mean? What are you *not* telling me?'

Zev saw a look of silent knowing pass between the two women. Zev knew that look. They weren't telling him the whole truth. Bellassez took Zev aside.

'The baby's head should be low down, about here,' she put her hands together in a V-shape in between the top of her thighs to indicate the birth canal, 'with the feet above so the head comes out first. But the baby is lying across her like this.' She drew a line across her middle. 'Normally, it would have moved by now, before her waters broke.'

'So, what can be done. Can it be moved now?'

'Maybe.'

'Maybe? What are you saying, Bella? What happens if you can't?'

Bellassez gave Zev a direct look. 'Then we may lose Arlette and the baby.'

Zev stared at Bellassez in stunned silence, then turned away and went to his wife who was growing weaker with each painful contraction.

'You're going to be all right,' he said to her, squeezing her hand tightly.

'I'm frightened, Zev.'

'No need. I'm here and so are Bella and Douce.'

Arlette smiled weakly before her face contorted into another grimace of agony, and she let out a howl. Zev winced as her fingernails dug into the palm of his hand.

'I'm going to turn the baby,' Bellassez said.

Bellassez kneaded and pushed Arlette's stomach with her strong hands. Each time she pressed Arlette cried out.

'Please stop. I can't stand anymore.'

'I have to, Arlette. I'm sorry.'

Arlette was growing weaker. Again, the two women exchanged looks. It was the same silent knowing but this time Zev detected an added dimension. One of grave concern. His blood quickened.

'I can't lose her, Bella,' he said, burying his forehead into Arlette's limp hand which was still entwined with his. 'I can't lose her.'

Bellassez placed her hand on his shoulder. He was trembling.

'I'll do my best,' she said.

'Please, Bella, do better than that.'

Zev moved out of the way to let the two women attend to Arlette. In the dim light of dawn, he slipped out of the room and using the secret entrance to the synagogue, let himself in. He sat down in front of the *bimah* to pray. The eternal flame flickered overhead. Not much of a religious man before Brito's attack, reading Moses' Torah was giving him a greater understanding of his faith. His seemingly miraculous recovery must have been an intervention by Hashem. He had told no one, not even Arlette, of his strange experience when he nearly died. He remembered floating towards a bright light and experiencing a moment of knowing, an indescribable clarity of thought. It was as if he knew all the secrets of the universe in that one moment. Then a soft voice had said, 'It's not time,' and the light faded and the next thing he remembered was opening his eyes and seeing the angelic face of his wife.

The tears fell from his eyes. He wept uncontrollably. When he could cry no more, he wiped the tears from his face, took a deep breath and stood to leave. The calm quiet safety of the synagogue comforted him. A silent prayer to save Arlette's life passed between him and his maker before he left to hurry back to Arlette.

When he entered the room, he could sense a change. The tension so palpable earlier had diminished.

'We've managed to turn the baby...'

Zev rushed over to Arlette and kissed her. She looked tiny despite her huge belly.

'We're not out of danger yet.'

'But it's better than it was?'

'Oh yes, much better, but Arlette is going to need all her strength.'

Arlette finally gave birth to a baby boy. The first thing Zev noticed about the child was his hair. There was a lot of it and it was black and shiny as a raven's feathers. Bella wiped the blood and mucus from the child, wrapped him in dry cloths and placed him on Arlette's chest.

Arlette stared down at the child for some time without touching him, then she cried.

CHAPTER
FIFTY-ONE

As soon as the first signs of spring appeared, Dairmait set off to Wales to negotiate with the Welsh king Rhys ap Gruffydh for Robert fitz Stephen's release. He was key to raising the army of men Dairmait needed to succeed. Aoife insisted that she and Richard accompany him. Richard's nephew Hervey had heard he was being held prisoner at Dinewyr Castle in Deheubarth where they would also find Rhys ap Gruffydh. They gained passage on a ship sailing from Bristol to Caerleon and along the River Usk. After disembarking with their horses, they set off through the rugged countryside of Wales. When they arrived at Dinewyr they were told Rhys ap Gruffydh was not there.

'I thought your nephew said he was here?' Dairmait hollered.

'He said he had heard he might be here,' Richard replied, sighing.

'My father is tired,' said Aoife.

'Where might we find him?' Richard enquired of the guardsman.

'At Carreg Cennen.'

'How far is it?'

'Less than two leagues in that direction.'

The guard pointed in the direction from which they had come. Dairmait groaned.

'We must have passed it on our way here,' said Aoife.

'You can't miss it. It's the castle on the top of the cliff.'

Weary and frustrated, the band of travellers turned their horses around and made for Carreg Cennen. They were not disappointed when they saw the castle, high on a limestone precipice. Rhys ap Gruffydh was building a fortress of stone.

At the barbican, Dairmait announced he was the King of Leinster come to seek an audience with the Welsh king. They were directed over a drawbridge where a tall and impressive twin-towered gatehouse was under construction. The inner ward was square and fortified on every side by a thick stone wall. Dairmait realised his thoughts of freeing the prisoner by force, if his talks with the Welsh king failed, were dashed. He might have to heed the words of his daughter and try to be more diplomatic.

They were shown into the great hall of the completed tower. Rhys ap Gruffydh stood by an impressive stone fireplace. Flanking him were two large hunting hounds. Stood close by was a bishop and two others.

Richard whispered to Aoife, 'We're in luck. That's the bishop of St David's – David fitz Gerald. He's the half-brother of the prisoner Robert. He's also the brother-in-law of William de Barri and older brother to Maurice fitz Gilbert who is standing with him.'

Aoife beamed as she recognised these names from the list of men Richard had drawn up as potential leaders of her father's army.

'I wonder why they're here?' Aoife whispered back.

'We're about to find out,' said Richard.

Rhys was a tall, slim man. His eyes were large and framed by thick dark eyebrows. His nose was thin, and he had a long, crimped moustache and beard. He greeted Dairmait cordially and introduced his guests. The other man with them was a Norman knight called Richard fitz Godbert de Roche.

'We have come to negotiate the release of Robert fitz Stephen,' Dairmait said, wasting no time on polite preamble.

The bishop, dressed in a brown woollen dalmatic with a heavily embroidered stole around his neck, came forward.

'Why, we were just discussing the terms upon which Robert might be released.'

'What makes you think his release is negotiable,' Rhys said, eyeing Dairmait with curiosity and ignoring the bishop's words.

'Everything is negotiable,' Aoife said, flashing her winning smile at the Welsh king.

'The bishop has been pleading for months to free his half-brother. Why should I release him for you?'

Dairmait explained his plight, showed Rhys the king's letters patent and asked again for him to look favourably upon releasing Robert.

'Why would I help the King of England?' said Rhys, narrowing his eyes.

'The letters patent say,' Dairmait scanned the document to recite the correct words. '"let he who helps me be assured of the king's favour."'

'What favour would you want from the king?' Aoife asked, showing her skill in diplomatic negotiation.

'The first and most important favour would be the confirmation of my tenure of the lands I have conquered. Comprising Ceredigion, the cantreds of Bychan and Emlyn, and two smaller commotes near Carmarthen,' answered Rhys.

'We cannot guarantee the king will grant this, but we can make the necessary pleas on your behalf,' Richard said.

Rhys twirled his wiry beard between his fingers.

'He's been rotting in my dungeon all this time and all the bishop can offer is my redemption.'

'Your majesty,' the bishop began.

Rhys held up his hand to quiet him. 'As there is no guarantee the king will grant me any favours, I may be inclined to release my prisoner on a further stipulation.'

'If it is within my gift,' Dairmait said.

'Oh, I think it will be,' Rhys said, grinning. 'If you give me your word and sign papers to the effect that you give in fee to the two brothers David fitz Gerald, the bishop here, and his brother Maurice fitz Gilbert the city of Wexford with the two adjacent cantreds I will release fitz Stephen.'

The bishop and Maurice both looked surprised. Dairmait was aghast at the suggestion he should give up the town of Wexford to a pair of Welsh rebels. He had already given his daughter's hand in marriage and the title of the King of Leinster to a Norman knight. What more did these rapacious men want from him?

'Father,' Aoife said, seeing her father's temper was about to explode. 'I think you should think on this proposal.' She turned to Rhys ap Gruffydh. 'May we prevail upon your hospitality this evening. My father is tired after his long journey.'

'By all means,' Rhys said, summoning his servants to show them to their chambers.

Once settled, Aoife went in search of Richard. She had noticed he had been more reticent than usual towards the Welsh king and wondered why. She found him in the grounds of the castle looking out from the battlements across the wild Welsh countryside. The light was fading, and Aoife felt a sudden chill. She drew her cloak tight around her.

'You were very quiet today,' she said, standing next to him.

'Was I?'

'You don't normally allow my father to do all the talking.'

'Neither do you,' he said, smiling at her.

Aoife smiled back. 'We both know why,' she said, now laughing. 'He's more used to giving orders than asking favours.'

'It must be hard for your father to find himself in this situation.'

'It is. That's why he's in such a foul mood most of the time. I put up with him because he's my father, but it's hard to be around him when he's like that. Is that why you were so quiet earlier?'

'Not really. I'm getting used to him.'

'Why then?'

Aoife sensed Richard was keeping something from her.

'Why what?'

'Why were you so uncomfortable today in the presence of the Welsh king?'

Richard gazed out at the view avoiding Aoife's question, then he turned to face her.

'My father once owned Cardigan Castle. It was built by my grandfather Gilbert fitz Richard who handed it down to my father. Rhys' brothers led an attack on the castle and held it under siege. The castle survived thanks to the valorous efforts of my father's friend Robert fitz Martin. When my father died, I inherited the title Earl of Striguil but not the castle. My father had fallen out of favour with the king and the king has still not seen fit to restore me to my rightful place. Then I suffered further ignominy when the castle, which is my birthright, was captured two years ago by Rhys himself.'

'I see. No wonder you were not at ease. I had no knowledge of this. Is this why you are helping my father?'

'Partly. Your father has the king's favour. If I help him regain his lands, then the king may look favourably upon me.'

'And if he doesn't?'

'I'll have the title of the King of Leinster.'

'Is that why you accepted my hand in marriage?'

Richard hesitated. 'In the first instance... Then I met you.'

'And what happened then?'

'I fell in love.'

Richard drew her close and kissed her. Aoife pulled back from him.

'Did you really or are you just saying that?'

'I'm a middle-aged man, Aoife. You are a beautiful, if headstrong, young woman. I find you irresistible.'

He placed his hand in the curve of her back and pulled her toward him. Aoife did not resist. Richard kissed her. She felt his soft lips against hers and yielded to him, pressing her body against his and feeling his manhood harden. He moaned as she ran her hand along his chest to his groin. She enjoyed the effect her beauty had on men. It made her feel powerful. She could let this go on or stop it now. She was in control. But it was not to last. Her father's booming voice halted their fevered fumblings. Richard let go of her.

'You should go to him.'

'I think I better,' she said, walking away. 'Coming, Father,' she shouted, not wanting her father to discover them.

She found Dairmait standing in front of the tall gatehouse tower. He was talking to one of the stonemasons but stopped when he saw her.

'Let's take a stroll, Father, before it gets too dark,' she said, taking her father's arm and leading him to the other side of the bailey.

The evening had turned cold, and the light quickly faded, the night sky now filled with a myriad of twinkling stars. The earthy smell of Richard remained with her, and she wondered if her father knew what she had been up to. They stood on the edge of the battlement. Aoife leant over the edge and saw an endless pit of darkness.

'This place is impenetrable, Father.'

'I know,' Dairmait said, a trace of defeat in his tone.

'Were you thinking of taking fitz Stephen out of here by force?'

'The thought had crossed my mind.'

Aoife picked up a stone and threw it as far as she could, then listened to see how long it was before she heard it hit the bottom. It was several moments before she heard it crash against the rock face below. 'You'd never get him out. Not with these fortifications.'

'That I'm also aware of.'

Aoife put her arm through her father's and leant into him. The cold was beginning to chill her bones. 'Are you really going to give over Wexford to those Welsh savages?'

Dairmait sighed. 'Although it pains me, I don't think I have any choice. The campaign hinges on the release of fitz Stephen. Men will follow him. I have to give in.'

'Is there no other way?'

Dairmait shrugged. 'I wish there was.'

FIFTY-TWO

I f married life was difficult for Zev before Arlette gave birth, it became much worse once the baby arrived. For such a small thing it demanded a lot of attention and Zev soon realised he was jealous of the child. In those first few weeks the baby got to sleep with Arlette and suckle on her nipple. Their closeness excluded him. The house was in turmoil. Hours after the birth of Arlette's son, Douce gave birth to a baby girl. Zev found himself in a household with two small babies who didn't know the difference between night and day and would wake him at all hours. He considered on more than one occasion moving back to his parents' house. He joked with Baruch that he would stay there till the children grew up.

The newborns shared a birthday and so had a joint celebration. A *brit* for Baruch and a *simchat bat* for Henne, Moses' and Douce's daughter. Zev chose Baruch after his best friend as his son's name, not Rubin as everyone had expected. He had thought about calling him Rubin after his father but could not bring himself to do that. When he had sired a son of his own he would give him his father's name, and only then. He suspected people would wonder why the child had not been called after his father, but he was beyond caring. The child was foreign to him. He cried all the time and so far, Zev had not held him or comforted him. The sound of the child's cries grated on his nerves. When he could stand it no more, he left the house and sought sanctuary at his parents' house. In his naivety and out of love for Arlette he thought he might be able to love the child because it was part of her. The truth was he resented baby Baruch.

Zev spent the evening with his father at the Purim celebrations. He could not believe a year had passed since his ill-timed declaration of love to Arlette. So much had happened since that night. Back then she had been a vision of perfection and purity to him. They were both very different people now. Neither of them perfect.

Zev drank late into the night. The alcohol took away the tension and frustration he so often felt. When he finally climbed the stairs to bed, he was a little worse for wear. Arlette had retired earlier with the baby. Baruch was in his own crib in their bedroom and for once he was sleeping peacefully. He climbed into bed next to Arlette's warm body, putting his arms around her waist. His hands began to wander. There was no response from Arlette. He lifted her shift and pressed his manhood against her buttocks. Would she let him do it? He wanted nothing more.

'Zev what are you doing?' she said.

'What does it look like?'

'You know what Bella said.'

'But that was months ago.'

'I'm still sore,' she said, clamping her thighs together.

Arlette had stitches after giving birth. Bellassez had advised them to refrain from intimacy for at least four weeks to allow the stitches to heal.

Baby Baruch let out a thunderous cry. Zev's ardour vanished

in an instant. It was as if the child was in on this conspiracy. Arlette jumped out of bed to tend to him.

'Let him cry himself to sleep,' Zev said.

'I can't do that. He'll wake everyone.'

Zev had to agree. For a small baby the child had a cry nothing short of stentorian.

'Damn that child.'

'Don't say things like that. He's not well.'

'He's never well,' Zev grumbled.

He was beginning to realise how challenging married life could be. He had made a promise to Arlette before the birth that he wouldn't touch her until she was ready. The drink had made him nearly break that promise. He turned on his side and went to sleep.

The next morning Zev had a sore head. He needed some fresh air so rose early and went for a walk leaving Arlette asleep. With every step his head thudded. When he reached the wooded glade at the bottom of Robinswood Hill, he stopped and stretched. A grey mist covered the surface of the grassy glade, and the cold dew soaked his boots. He stood for a while taking deep breaths to ease the pounding in his head. From the other side of the clearing emerged a female figure. She carried with her a woven basket and every now and then bent down and tugged at the stem of a plant. Zev walked toward the figure and realised it was Chera. She was crouched on the ground when Zev approached, shooting to her feet when she heard his footsteps.

'It's only me,' he said, reassuring her. 'What are you doing out here at this time of the morning?'

'I often come here. I gather herbs for Bellassez and

mushrooms for breakfast. It's the best time to pick mushrooms. Didn't you know that?'

She wandered off towards a clump of plants and began picking its leaves. Zev followed her.

'What's this plant for?'

'This is bear leek. My mother makes soup with it. Here, smell.' She snapped the stem and put it under his nose. It had an oniony smell.

'Smells good. Can it cure headaches?'

'Have you been drinking again, Zev?'

Zev looked down at the ground. His drinking was getting out of control. He knew the reason why but couldn't tell anyone, especially not Chera.

'My father recommends eating raw eels,' Chera said.

Zev gagged at the mention of raw eels.

Chera laughed. 'I can tell you're not impressed by that suggestion.'

'No, it sounds disgusting. Isn't there something else I can take?'

Chera looked about her. 'You could try dog's mercury.'

'What's that?'

'Here's some.' She crossed to the shade beneath some ash trees and bent down, plucking a spear-shaped, toothed leaf from the ground. She crushed it between her fingers and held it to Zev's nose. He smelled it and heaved. Chera grinned at him.

'I think I'll put up with the headache.'

Zev rubbed at his temples to ease the throbbing inside his head. His eyes were dry and sore.

'You don't seem happy, Zev. What's the matter?'

'Nothing, I'm fine.'

'Is Arlette not making you happy?'

Zev was taken aback by her question. Did everyone know? Had Baruch broken his confidence?

'I would have made you happy,' she added, not waiting for his answer. She fixed her gaze at Zev. It was filled with longing. It triggered something primal inside him.

'Would you mind if I kissed you, Chera?'

Chera's eyes widened. 'Why would you want to do that?'

'I'm sorry. I must still be drunk from last night. I don't know what I'm saying.'

She took a step toward him and touched his cheek. Her fingers were cold against his burning skin.

'I don't mind if you kiss me,' she said. 'If you want to?'

Zev thought of Arlette pushing him away. Her stiff body rejecting his need for her. He drew Chera into an embrace. She dropped her basket and wrapped her arms around him, and he kissed her on the lips. It was tender at first, hesitant. He could feel her heart beating through her tunic. A primal need so intense overcame him. Not to ravish her but to feel the tender loving caress of a woman. Given so willingly. The kiss went on, becoming more passionate. Zev kissed her cheek, her neck, losing himself in her. She kissed him back. He swept her up and lay her on the soft dewy grass. She yielded to him letting out a small cry.

Zev was in turmoil. His base instincts were getting the better of him, just like the drink. He lay on his side, his leg draped over hers, her fingers raking through his hair. Her touch, the warmth of her body. It was intoxicating. He was aroused now and on the point of no return.

'I can't,' he said, getting to his knees. 'I can't do this to Arlette.'

'She wouldn't know,' Chera said, drawing him back towards her, her face twisted with the pain of rejection.

'I would know,' Zev said, wiping the perspiration from his forehead and resisting her pull.

CHAPTER
FIFTY-THREE

One summer's morning Moses woke to the sound of Douce sobbing. He found her on her knees rocking back and forth, their son Samuel cradled in her arms. Moses feared the worst. Knew it. His precious firstborn was dead. Samuel looked as if he were sleeping peacefully but when Moses touched him, he was cold.

'Blessed art Thou, Adonai...'

They knelt beside the body holding on to each other, Moses occasionally wiping the tears from his eyes. For months he had watched his son grow weaker by the day. Bellassez had done all she could to ease his suffering, but the outcome was inevitable.

'How much more sorrow can we endure, Moses?' she sobbed. 'Haven't we had enough? I feel as though my heart is going to break in two it hurts so much.'

'All that Hashem does, he does for the good.'

'How can taking my son be for the good?'

'I don't know, *ma chérie*. I only know Hashem does not give us more than we can endure.'

'I don't know how much more sorrow I can endure.'

'He's testing us. For what, I don't know.'

'Well, I have failed the test. I can't take any more.'

Moses sighed heavily, dried his tears on his night shirt and rose. 'I'll get the candles. You stay with him.'

Moses returned with a basket of beeswax candles and straw for the floor. Over his arm was the simple linen shroud to wrap little Samuel's body in preparation for the afterlife. He gave the shroud to Douce and put the basket down. Douce set about scattering the straw and lighting the candles to place around her son's body. Then Moses lifted Samuel's limp body and placed it on the floor, his arms beside his side.

'I'll fetch a bowl of water and some cloths,' he said, and disappeared again.

'May peace be upon you,' she said, looking down at her son's peaceful expression.

She had performed the ritual washing of the body many times, usually with Bella for they were both members of the holy society, the *chevra kaddisha*, a band of carefully chosen volunteers. Moses was also a member. She would normally perform this ritual on women, and the men would do the same for men, but this was her son and she wanted to spend the last precious moments with him alone.

Moses returned with the freshly drawn water. Samuel's little body was washed in reverential silence. Next, they dressed him in a plain white shroud, covering his entire body and then placed a sash around his waist, tying it in the form of the Hebrew letter *shin*, a name for Hashem.

When this was finished, Moses suggested that he be the *shomerim*, the one to guard Samuel's body for it could not be left alone until he was buried in the ground. This was out of respect and in the belief that the soul lingers a while after death. In this brief time of solitude before Douce's return Moses felt the presence of his son's soul. Memories of the times they had shared before he became so very ill surfaced. The way he would try and say his name, his tottery walk, his smile. It would not be long before the others would learn of Samuel's death and join them. They both needed this time of quietude before little Samuel's long journey to London began.

As a Jew, Moses was not allowed to bury his son in Gloucester. He would not be able to visit Samuel's graveside because the only place he was allowed to bury him was the *bet 'olam*, the Jewish cemetery at Cripplegate in London. It would be the longest, saddest and cruellest journey he would ever make.

Moses wept silent tears in the stillness of the room. Not just for his son but for all the sadness that had been rained upon them. Arlette's rape, Zev's beating, his unnecessary imprisonment. All of it unjust and all because he was a Jew.

The stillness was broken when Arlette came into the room, her face stained with tears. She hugged Moses and joined him in silent vigil. Then came Samuel's grandfather. When Moses saw his father's pained expression and depth of sadness, the tears flowed again. Arlette took her uncle's hand and squeezed it.

When the time came, Moses lifted Samuel's shrouded body and carried it out to the waiting horse and cart his father had arranged. Although it was barely first light Moses could tell it was going to be one of those long, glorious summer days with a cloudless blue sky. Samuel should be playing under that sun in the courtyard with his mother and brother and baby sister and all the other children, not wrapped in a shroud to be buried in a place that was foreign to him.

Moses placed Samuel on the back of the cart. It was going to be a very long journey and he was already beginning to feel nervous about it. He had little experience with horses and now wished he had asked for help. Douce could not bring the children on such a hazardous journey and his father was too old to travel. He would have to bear the burden alone.

He threw a protective cloth over Samuel's shroud and stowed the bag of food Douce had prepared for him behind his seat along with a wooden cudgel for protection. He hugged everyone, kissed Douce and the children and set off. Before he left the confines of the courtyard, he did what he normally did if he was going on a long journey and recited a prayer for safe passage.

'...May You rescue me from the hand of every foe, ambush along the way, and from all manner of punishments that assemble to come to earth.'

Jewry Street was quiet as he guided the horse toward The Cross, turning right to pass through the North Gate and on to the old Roman road out of Gloucester towards Cirencester, and finally on to London. The return journey would take four days. He had to get to London as quickly as possible. The warm weather meant that Samuel's body would putrefy much quicker and the smell might attract feral dogs. He also didn't want to be away from Douce and his family for too long.

As the day wore on, the heat intensified. He had no shade to shelter under and neither did Samuel. Moses fretted that the smell of his son's body might draw unwanted attention and he was still far away from the capital. By late evening, he had made good progress and was able to spend a few hours resting by the side of the road. He shared his weak ale and food with the horse before settling down to sleep next to Samuel's body on the back of the cart. He woke early, cold and stiff and carried on through the bleak plains of Wiltshire and on towards Silchester. On the second day, as he neared London, the sun came out more ferociously than the day before and the temperature rose quickly. The villages became towns until the countryside was no more. He was nearing the capital.

Weary and in need of some respite from the heat of the sun, he stopped at a roadside inn to order some food and water his horse. He had been gone but a few minutes when he returned to find a pack of feral dogs on the cart tearing at the cloth covering Samuel's body. Dogs did not respect the dead.

Before Moses could reach the cart one of them tore open the shroud and bit into Samuel's thin arm, tugging at it to pull it to the floor. A low growl and a show of sharp teeth was enough to stop Moses from getting any closer. Remembering the cudgel stowed in the cart he edged toward it and reached inside. He took a firm hold and with a swinging motion and a wild guttural sound, he charged at the snarling, snapping dogs. He walloped the dog nearest to him but instead of running away it turned on Moses barking at him. Moses took another swipe. This time the cudgel connected with the dog's jaw, sending it flying off the cart. The remaining dogs dragged Samuel's corpse part way off the cart. Moses slammed the cudgel down again and again. They yelped in agony and at last gave up and ran off. Moses chased after them shaking his cudgel in an agitated state hoping he had done enough to make them stay away. As he walked back to the cart, his heart thudding in his chest, he reflected on his reaction to the dogs. His rage was wild and feral. He had become for that moment like one of them. Perhaps grief did that to a person. Unhinged them.

Moses wiped the sweat from his brow and surveyed the scene. The shroud covering Samuel had been torn, his head and shoulders exposed to the roiling heat of the sun. His arm had a bite on it, the flesh grey and bloodless. Moses remembered the countless times he had held that warm and delicate hand. He threw the cudgel down, sank to the ground and this time raged at Hashem.

Afterwards, as he wrapped Samuel's body in the shredded shroud, he could not help but wonder why this was happening.

His faith had been sorely tested this past year. This final act of cruelty against Samuel was more than he could bear. He whispered a blessing before climbing back onto the wooden seat.

'May peace be upon him.'

With a sharp flick of the reins Moses encouraged the horse to move forward at a steady pace. The horse was tired and plodded along painfully slowly. It wasn't long before the feral dogs reappeared. They followed the cart at a distance, patiently waiting at each water stop for an opportunity to reclaim their meal. No matter how many times Moses shook his cudgel and roared at them, they remained in pursuit. Moses could not rest. He spent the last few hours of the journey cussing the horse and turning around to shout at the snarling dogs. When finally the impressive stone fortress of Cripplegate came into view after two days of travel with little rest, he sent up a prayer of thanks to God.

Douce sat in the darkness of her bedroom. The house was quiet. Everyone had retired for the night. Arlette had cooked the evening meal, and Zev had tried his best to lighten Douce's mood and take her mind off the death of her son and the perilous journey Moses had begun. She was grateful to both for their efforts, but nothing could lift her mood. Her son was dead. She would never look upon his guileless face again or hear his stumbling words or smile at his tottering walk.

Henne slept peacefully in her crib by the bedside whilst Abraham slept in his grandfather's bed. She leant over the crib to check if her daughter was still breathing. Henne lay on her back, a faint smile upon her cherubic face. Douce stared intently at the child's chest, her own chest tight as a knot, holding her breath, only releasing when she saw Henne's chest gently rise and fall.

In the few hours since little Samuel's death she had spent every waking moment worrying about her remaining children. Old Samuel had been sleeping in the same bed since his grandson was a baby but now, she worried he might turn over in his sleep and crush Abraham or that Henne would stop breathing in the night. Douce rubbed at her eyes as if she could rub away her thoughts. She looked up at the tenebrous shadows in the room. The same gloomy darkness had entered her soul. She was alone, bereft. She looked at the floor where her son Samuel had lain, wrapped in his burial shroud and wondered how far he had gone on his final journey. How was Moses coping? Was he safe? Why couldn't her son be buried in Gloucester where she could visit his grave? It was cruel of the king to make her bury her son in London. Wasn't it enough to have lost a loved one?

Henne stirred in her crib. Douce looked over anxiously again. The child was well, thriving even. It was insane to be so worried. She got under the covers. The bed was cold and empty. She ached with loneliness. She needed Moses by her side, not trundling the body of her dead son across the country. He should be home, comforting her in her grief.

Her thoughts turned to Arlette and for the first time ever she understood why her niece had wanted to take her own life. Sometimes it was just hard to stay living in this cruel world.

She thought of all the people she had cause to hate. The king for forcing all Jews to bury their dead in London. Mirabelle for all her vindictiveness towards her and her family. But most of all her hatred was directed towards the man they called Brito for raping Arlette. A clarity of thought, a moment of intense introspection. He had been the start of all their troubles. From the moment he arrived in Gloucester. Who was he? What did he want from them?

Eventually, a new feeling emerged. One of wrath.

She knew why he had raped Arlette. She was beautiful, innocent, desirable. An easy target for a man to satiate his unbridled animal needs. Her insides twisted at the thought of him. Vengeance. That was the one thing that would make any sense out of all that was happening. The one thing that would give her purpose.

'To me belongeth vengeance and recompense; their foot shall slide in due time: for the day of their calamity is at hand, and the things that shall come upon them make haste.'

FIFTY-FOUR

The dogs had stopped following Moses, chased off by angry merchants at Smooth Field meat market worried they would affect trade. He was now making his way along Red Cross Street where a tall Christian preaching cross stood. It reminded him of The Cross in Gloucester. The church of St Giles without Cripplegate stood at the end of the street just beyond the gated entrance to the cemetery. It seemed a strange co-existence, a Jewish cemetery next to a Christian church.

Moses guided his weary horse through the open gateway. The cemetery was a long rectangular plot of land bordered by a high stone wall, the wall a remnant of the Roman occupation. Its creamy stone was golden in the bright sunshine. It was hidden and tranquil, laid out with mature ash trees and pendulous willows. Mature bushes, fragrant with summer flowers, bordered the wall. At the entrance was a small stone building, the *bet tohorah*, the cleansing house where Moses could wash Samuel's body before his burial. Moses stopped the cart. It was already midday and the sun beat down on the back of his neck. He was not surprised to see a queue of carts already waiting, each carrying a loved one, this being the only Jewish cemetery in England where Jews were permitted to bury their dead. He realised he would have to leave little Samuel alone on the cart whilst he washed his hands at the sacred spring in the corner of the building to remove any impurity from death and go in search of the cemetery keeper.

He found Jacob de Coemitereo sitting at a table with his scribe. There was a line of people waiting to register the details of their loved one. Moses joined them. It was some time before he was able to complete the paperwork. He was advised to visit a reputable stonemason to make and deliver the headstone and to return within two hours when the service would be held.

Moses was not happy leaving his son alone, but he had no choice. He hurried to the nearest stonemason only to find he had to wait in another queue. When he returned to the cemetery, he climbed onto the back of the cart and fell asleep under the sun. He woke with a headache and the smell of rotting flesh in his nostrils. Moses made his way to the graveside where a small headstone lay. It bore Samuel's name in Hebrew lettering and the year of his death, 4928. In the centre, the stonemason had carved the Star of David. The rabbi and the prayer leader arrived along with eight other strangers. Strangers were brought along when there were not enough family mourners to make up a quorum. If no quorum could be gathered together, Moses would not be able to perform the emotional prayer of sanctification. The service was a simple one. Moses stood by the graveside looking into the freshly dug hole that was to be Samuel's last resting place. A vision of his son's smiling face came to him. He heard him call him father. *Aba.* One of the few words he had learnt to say properly in his short life. It was all too much for him. He wished Douce was by his side to comfort him, give him the support he so needed right now. He felt so alone and utterly bereft. He tore at his tunic, performing the ritual rending of the garment.

The prayer leader began by chanting psalms, his tremulous voice resounding across the tightly packed gravestones. A gentle breeze blew through the willows, making a calming swishing sound, bending their pendulous branches. It was as if they were bowing in respect to the memory of little Samuel. The rabbi read out the memorial prayer.

'...grant true rest upon the wings of the *Shechinah*, in the exalted spheres of the holy and pure, who shine as the resplendence of the firmament, to the soul of Samuel, son of Moses le Riche of Gloucester.'

Samuel's small body, ravaged by illness and beast, was lowered into the prepared grave. The gravediggers worked fast, covering his body with the freshly dug soil. Moses was aware of the dull thud of the clods hitting Samuel's corpse. When the burial was complete Moses raked the freshly dug earth into his hand and recited a prayer, speaking in the ancient language of Aramaic.

'He remembereth that we are dust...'

As he spoke, he cast the earth behind him three times. When he came to the last part, he took three steps back and bowed.

'He Who makes peace in His heights, may He make peace, upon us and upon all Israel.'

Then he left his son alone and returned to Gloucester.

CHAPTER
FIFTY-FIVE

Brito returned to France after his frenzied attack on Zev. After leaving him for dead, he had drunk more wine at the Lich Inn, then fallen into bed and was woken the next morning by his loyal knights. They had ridden to Portchester and took the boat to France where they landed in Caen. It was some time before he caught up with the king in Acquitaine. Since then, they had travelled northeast to the chateau of Montmirail.

King Henry had been eager to hear news of Dairmait and Richard de Clare. Brito could not admit failure. Neither could he lie to the king. He decided to omit certain facts and tell the king only half the truth – that he warned the Jew Moses le Riche not to lend money to either Dairmait on pain of death and that to ensure he got the message loud and clear he had engineered a mob riot to frighten him and any other Jew who might be tempted to do business with them. Henry was satisfied with this account and congratulated Brito on his efforts. Riding high on his putative success, Brito once again broached the subject of his parents' lands and again the king reassured him that it was in hand. The matter was concluded, and nothing more had been said.

Today the king was to meet with his French adversary King Louis VII of France, an awkward meeting for both kings for they had married the same woman, Aliénor d'Aquitaine. Brito was fascinated by her and admired her cunning. At fifteen she married Louis, but the marriage was annulled after fifteen years because she had not bore him a son. Within a mere eight weeks of the annulment, she married the Duke of Normandy, the present King Henry. That was seventeen years ago and so far, they had produced eight children, five of them sons. Their youngest son John was two years old.

Over the years Henry had agonised over the inheritance of his empire after his death. He had decided on a division that would see his son Young Henry receive England and Normandy, his other sons Richard the Duchy of Aquitaine, and Geoffrey would get Brittany. But he required the consent of Louis as King of France. There was an added complication for King Henry. His former loyal friend and trusted mentor Thomas Becket the Archbishop of Canterbury was present. It was a difficult meeting which saw his sons Richard and John paying homage to the King of France. Afterwards, Henry was in a foul mood. Brito was used to the king's temper. It was one thing they had in common.

'I don't trust the French and I don't trust that sanctimonious excuse for a king,' King Henry raged.

'But you have at least agreed to an alliance between his daughter Adèle and Richard. He has given you permission to take her to England and prepare her for marriage.'

'Richard is twelve and she is barely nine years old. That is not a proper marriage.'

Brito knew when the king was in such a mood there was no way to lift him out of it. It was going to be a long day, so Brito suggested they go hunting in the nearby forest. The king's mood improved, having speared a large and ferocious wild boar. Afterwards, as they were resting outside a hunting lodge one of the king's men rode towards them at speed. He jumped off his horse, approached the king and bowed.

'Your Highness.'

'What news do you bring from England?'

'Sire, the news is not good,' the courier said, out of breath.

A dark cloud descended upon the king's mood. Brito braced himself.

'Your English subjects Robert fitz Stephen and Hervey de Monte Marisco have invaded Ireland, Your Majesty. They landed at Bannow with Robert de Barri and Richard fitz Godbert de Roche with a force of one hundred and thirty knights, sixty men-at-arms and over three hundred Welsh archers.'

Henry flashed a murderous glance at Brito.

'Go on.'

'A few days later, Maurice de Prendergast along with Meiler fitz Henry and Miles fitz David landed nearby with ten more knights with thirty horses and sixty archers. They joined forces with Dairmait of Leinster who brought with him five hundred of his own kinsmen. From there they marched to the town of Wexford where it was laid to siege. The town surrendered on the second day. Dairmait has given the cantreds of Wexford to fitz Stephen as reward. He has successfully regained Leinster and has control of Waterford and Dublin, Your Majesty.'

'Is Richard de Clare with them?'

'He is not, Your Majesty, but is expected to join them.'

King Henry threw the goblet of wine he had been drinking to the ground and drew his sword aiming its point at Brito's neck.

'I charged you with preventing this from happening,' he

said, a spittle of froth appearing at the corner of his mouth, his prominent eyes bulging.

Brito felt the sharp point of the king's sword press against the tender skin of his neck. His heart thudded under his tunic. His response to the king was stilted.

'I was certain I had been successful, Your Majesty. I would not have returned to France had I thought otherwise.'

'It is obvious from his account that you were not successful. Not in the least. That Irish savage is taking over Ireland. He must be getting the funds from someone to launch such an audacious invasion. You were supposed to stop that,' the king yelled, pressing his sword further into Brito's neck.

'I'll return to Gloucester, Your Majesty, and find out who has gone against you. I will not fail you this time, I promise.'

The point of the king's sword was piercing Brito's flesh and pressing on his windpipe. He could barely speak. The king withdrew his sword, pointing it this time at his heart.

'I have enough troubles without having to deal with Ireland. You were set a simple task and you have failed.'

'You know how conniving these Jews can be. I won't be deceived next time, Your Majesty,' he said, rubbing at his neck, his voice hoarse.

'Make sure you're not this time,' he said, coldly, 'or this sword will piece that braggartly heart of yours.'

Brito slumped forward coughing when the king removed his sword.

'I am heartily sorry, Your Majesty. I promise on my mother's life, I will not fail you.'

'You better not. If Dairmait succeeds, he will colonise the whole of Ireland with English lords and I will lose my right to assume control over Ireland. And *you* will be the cause of it.'

The king replaced his sword in its sheath, mounted his horse and rode away, followed by his retinue of aides, leaving

Brito to recover from his wrath. Brito picked up his goblet of wine and drank it down in one.

'Bring me another,' he barked at the servant from the hunting lodge.

Another full goblet was brought immediately, the servant backing away from Brito as soon as he placed it before him.

The king was right. The Normans were incomparably superior to the Irish in terms of their military organisation. Even if the Irish mustered a huge army of men compared to the diminutive force already camped there, the fighting strength of the Norman invaders was altogether out of proportion to its numbers. The knights would be clad in armour from head to foot, carrying long lances and fighting on horseback. The Irish armed with only sword and axe would not be able to get within striking distance of their enemies. It was only a matter of time before Richard de Clare joined them and he was a formidable force to be reckoned with. His skill with a long bow would be decisive. They also possessed the very effective crossbow, which could pour a deadly hail of arrows into the Irish savage's ranks before the opposing battalions came to close quarters. Once defeated in battle the invaders were men skilled in the erection of strong fortifications and castles. Brito had seen them in action many times. It would not be long before the Irish were oppressed into submission by a force acting outside of the auspices of the King of England. Henry had every right to be angry.

Brito had failed his mission. He had failed the king. Worse, he had been made a fool of by a Jew. Why did he and his family suffer so at the hands of these Jews? They were at the bottom of all that was rotten in the world. He had underestimated them. He wouldn't make that mistake again.

Brito lost no time in returning to Gloucester. He was lucky to have left with his life. This time he had to be successful. Not only was the restoration of his parents' land and title in jeopardy but his life depended on it.

The king had been clear. Dairmait had to be stopped or the king might lose his rightful dominions in Ireland. Someone was obviously funding his campaign despite Brito's efforts to warn them, and Brito had to find out who. If he could cut off Dairmait's money supply, then that would be the end of it. It had to be a Jew. They were the only ones with the means to fund an army. And Brito was convinced it was Moses le Riche. He had been too lenient with him. He was a fool to believe the Jews would take notice of him.

When he did reach Gloucester a week later, he was none too pleased at being back in the drab little city. He enjoyed being in France with the king, amongst men who thought like him. Not a bunch of self-serving Jew lovers.

His first task was to call on Moses le Riche. The man should have listened to him. But first he thought he might rekindle his liaison with Molly, the accommodating whore in Three Cocks Lane.

FIFTY-SIX

rlette lay in bed next to Zev who was sleeping heavily as he did most mornings having taken to drinking wine most evenings. She still had no interest in sex. No interest in her life. Most days she could barely drag herself out of bed. She watched the shafts of late summer sunshine make flittering patterns on the wall opposite. Unusually, Baruch had slept through the night, but now he was wide awake and wanting her attention. She picked him up, dressed hurriedly and left while Zev slept on. After breakfast she went into the courtyard with Baruch. The sun was warm, and a light breeze blew. Arlette decided to take Baruch for a walk. He was an active child, never still. Maybe a long walk would keep him occupied and out of mischief. It was market day. She would take him there.

Baruch was growing up quickly, a stocky little boy with long raven-black hair, toddling around on unsteady legs. Arlette held on to his small hand as they made slow progress towards The Cross where the Christian church of St Michael the Archangel stood and where the many market stalls were laid out with meat, vegetables, bushels of corn, leather goods, ironmongery and her favourites – the cloth stalls. She would run her hands across the bolts of cloth that came from ships docked at the quays. Ships from exotic sounding foreign lands. Undyed cottons, soft silks, velvety damasks and linens. Baruch was not fond of holding her hand, he preferred to be free and would often wander off to look at something that interested him. A squashed blackberry or a sliver of onion peel. She had lost count of the times she had wrested a piece of rotting vegetable from his hand before he could put it in his mouth. He liked rummaging around underneath the stalls, crawling across the hard, dusty earth.

In the middle of West Gate Street, they passed the building works of St Mary in the Market. It was nearly finished, and the newly carved stone shone golden in the late summer sunshine. Not far from there, another church was being built, Holy Trinity. Arlette wondered how many more churches the Christians needed. She needed only one synagogue. The noise from the stonemasons mixed with the noise from the stallholders was deafening and Arlette was pleased when she reached the quieter part of the city near the abbey. The streets were particularly busy today and many of her acquaintances – she would no longer call them friends – were out shopping, taking advantage of the unseasonal weather. Arlette felt the sun on the back of her neck as she sauntered along holding Baruch's hand.

They walked as far as the abbey and on through the walled entrance. It was bustling as usual with worshippers, dignitaries and the abbey's tenants arriving to pay their rents. Arlette stopped to look up at the magnificent building. No other church in the city could compare, not even the newer buildings. She had to admire the skill and devotion of these Christians to build such edifices. It was not uncommon for Jews to visit the abbey, mainly for business. Her uncle Moses had frequent business dealings with Abbot Hameline who always seemed to be needing money for repairs or extensions. Arlette decided to go inside. The heat from the sun was making her feel light-headed. Her throat was dry from the stone dust and the abbey would be cool within its thick stone walls.

The space and sheer size of the building never failed to impress her. A small shrine had been erected to keep the relics of the murdered boy Harold who had been made a martyred saint by the Pope. There was talk of the boy having enacted miracles after his death. Of course, it was all nonsense to anyone of the Jewish faith, but the Christian pilgrims poured into the abbey to pray at the shrine and make a donation in the hope they would be cured of their ills. Her uncle said it was only there to make money for the church.

She pointed out the high, vaulted ceiling to Baruch, but he was only interested in the rushes that covered the stone-flagged floor. As she gazed at the ceiling, she felt dizzy and to steady herself she leant against the cool stone of the rounded Norman pillars. Baruch plonked himself down on the stone flags rolled onto his chubby knees and crawled towards the shrine. She let him go so far, then ran to retrieve him before he disappeared out of sight. As she did so, she heard a voice that struck fear and loathing into her very soul. For a moment she froze, not able to move or breathe. A passing Christian stood on baby Baruch's foot, and he let out the loudest of screams which echoed within the vast nave. Her first instinct was to reach for her son and quiet him down.

She grabbed hold of his hand to pull him off the floor. Baruch was having none of it. Wriggling and screaming at a piercing volume he was attracting everyone's attention.

Then she heard the ominous voice again. This time immediately behind her. It made her jump and she turned. It was him. Her abuser. She stared into his cold, black eyes. The colour drained from her cheeks. A scornful smile appeared upon his face.

'Well look who it is.'

Arlette turned away from him, looking to see where her son had gone. He had stopped his yowling and was crawling towards the altar.

'Leave me alone,' she managed to say, her heart thudding in her chest.

'You should be nicer to me. After all, we've shared something special.'

Arlette felt the bile rise in her throat. She did not want to be sick inside the abbey or to draw attention to herself. Her dearest desire was to flee. She ran after Baruch. Brito followed her, catching hold of her arm and drawing her back towards him.

'You've grown a little, a bit more up top,' he said, as he reached to squeeze her breast.

'Get off,' she shouted, pushing his arm away.

He was too quick and too strong for her, holding on to her with his powerful warrior grip. The feel of his flesh against hers made her skin crawl. Her throat burned with bile.

'I must go to my son,' she said, hoping he would release her.

The moment she said son she knew it was a mistake.

He glanced across at the fast crawling, chubby-legged child, a curious expression on his face.

'That's your son? How old is he?'

'He's not yours,' she spat.

Brito let go of her arm and followed the child, who was dodging in and out of legs. Arlette ran after him, reaching Baruch before he did. She grabbed her son and picked him up with some effort.

'He looks like me, he's got the same hair.'

He touched a lock of the boy's hair. Baruch who had been wriggling in her arms stared at Brito with childish curiosity.

'Don't touch him.'

'You've got more fire in your belly than when I last saw you.'

Brito spoke directly to the boy.

'What a handsome young man you are. Take after your father, no doubt.'

'Yes, and he has your foul temper and bad manners. Now let me pass.'

'So, he is mine?'

'Yes, he's yours but as long as I live, he will never know you're his father.'

'A boy ought to know who his real father is, don't you think?'

'He has a father and that's the only one he'll ever know or need,' she said.

She planted Baruch on the floor, unable to carry him anymore and took his hand.

'Not that idiot I left for dead.'

'He's not an idiot and he didn't die. He's my husband.'

'Shame. I could have had you all to myself.'

'You disgust me,' she said, pushing past him.

'Don't worry. I don't want a dirty little Jew for a son. You can keep him.' He followed behind her. 'I might want to have a go here again though,' and he thrust his hand between Arlette's thighs and grabbed at her private parts. She shrieked and heard him laughing behind her. Dragging poor little Baruch behind her, she tried to dodge the press of people but with little success. They blocked her way making her escape difficult.

Finally, Arlette reached the abbey porch. The heat of the sun hit her like a gust of warm air as she ran into the abbey grounds the sun blinding her vision. She stopped suddenly, feeling weak and dizzy. The sounds around her became muffled. Her world went black.

'Are you all right, dearie? You've had a funny turn.'

A craggy old woman was leaning over her prone body. Arlette raised her head.

'Where's my son?'

'It's all right, he's 'ere.'

She had hold of his hand. As ever, Baruch was trying to wriggle free of her grip.

'I only just managed to grab hold of the babber before you fell. Went down like a sack of corn, you did,' she said, keeping a tight hold of Baruch's hand.

Arlette tried to sit up but was gripped by a wave of nausea. Without warning, she retched and was sick on the ground.

'Ooh, you're definitely not well. Something you ate?' she asked.

'I'll be all right,' Arlette said, wiping a dribble of vomit from her lips. 'Give me my son back.'

Arlette reached out to Baruch.

'Please yourself. Only trying to help.'

The woman handed over Baruch.

'I'm sorry, that sounded harsh. I'm grateful for your kindness.'

'That's all right, dearie. I can see you're not well. Looks like you've had a fright or maybe you've seen a ghost.'

'Something like that,' Arlette said, taking hold of Baruch's hand and hoping he was going to behave himself. All she wanted to do was get home. It had been a bad idea to go into the abbey.

'Thank you,' she shouted back, remembering her manners.

'You take it easy now and look after that babber. Handsome little boy.'

Arlette walked as fast as her weak legs would take her, dragging Baruch behind her, who was resisting and grizzling, upset at being hauled around.

When she reached home, she went into the kitchen where

she knew she would find Douce. She needed to lie down, and she couldn't do that with Baruch around.

'Can you take Baruch for a while?' she asked Douce. 'I'm not feeling well and would like to lie down.'

'You look awful, Arlette. What's happened?'

'I had a funny turn whilst out. Probably just the heat.'

'Come on then, Baruch. Let your mother rest.'

Baruch tried to wriggle out of Douce's hands. Grizzling, he held out his arms to his mother, wanting her to take him.

'I hope he behaves for me. I'm feeling tired myself.'

Arlette could not get away fast enough. She ignored Douce and rushed out of the kitchen. She wanted to get away from everyone and everything. When finally she was alone in her room, she collapsed on the bed. The room was hot and airless. She couldn't get her breath. She would have to visit the *mikveh*. Like before, she had been soiled by his touch. It had not occurred to her that he would return to the city. As time passed, with no sign of Brito, she believed she would never see him again.

Her shameful secret about her son's real father was out. What evil mischief would come of him knowing? Did he really mean it when he said Baruch was a dirty Jew? She shuddered at the slur.

She hated that man. Wished he was dead.

When Zev arrived home Douce told him Arlette had gone upstairs to rest. He went to see her and found her lying on the bed, her face pale.

'What's the matter?' he asked, sitting next to her.

'I saw him,' she said, her voice trembling.

Zev clenched his fist. His expression shifted from one of

concern for Arlette to that of anger.

'Brito?' he said coldly.

Arlette nodded.

'Has he hurt you?'

'No.'

'What did he say?'

'Not much.'

'He must have said something.'

'He called Baruch a dirty Jew.'

Zev stood up and walked towards the door.

'Where are you going?'

'To sort this out.'

'What are you going to do?'

'I don't know.'

'Please don't do anything reckless. Look what happened last time. Brito will kill you.'

Zev swung round and gave Arlette a tortured look. 'I might as well be dead. I'm married to a woman who won't let me touch her. I'm father to a child who is someone else's son. The same man who nearly killed me. And the man who defiled my wife continues to taunt me and you want me to do *nothing* about it.'

He was shouting now, pacing the room. Arlette had never heard Zev talk like that. It was as if a veil had been lifted from her eyes. She had never considered how life must be for Zev. How selfish she had been. Only seeing things from her point of view. She had been living the victim. And who was winning? Brito. Whilst they suffered. All of them. Zev. Baruch. Her. She reached out for him and took his hand. His hand was warm, comforting. Suddenly, she saw him in a different light.

'I nearly lost you, Zev. I can't go through that again. Baruch would lose his father.'

'I'm not his father.'

'But you love Baruch, despite everything.'

Zev was silent.

'You do love him, don't you?'

'I find him difficult to love.'

'He is difficult to love.' She looked at Zev and he at her. It was a moment of honesty. Nakedness. 'He tests my patience at times, but I do love him, he's my son,' she said.

'I know. It's different for you, he's part of you. I've tried to love him, Arlette, but it's hard. When I look at him, I see that devil.'

They had never been this honest with each other since their wedding day. They had grown apart, becoming like strangers. Her heart softened toward him.

'I hoped we'd never see him again.'

Zev sunk down on the bed. 'Does he know Baruch is his?'

'He guessed it.'

Zev's brow knotted in frustration. 'We'll never be free of him.' He pulled his hand away and started pacing the room again. 'I can't just do nothing. I *have* to do something.'

'He's not worth it.'

'He can't be allowed to get away with all he's done.' He went towards the door and opened it.

'Nooo,' she shrieked. 'Don't leave me. I couldn't bear it if something happened to you.'

Zev swung round. 'You don't care about me, Arlette. Why would you be bothered if anything happened to me?'

'I do care. If anything happened to you, I couldn't go on living.'

'Don't say things like that.'

'It's true.' Arlette fell silent. A look of guilty shame coloured her pale cheeks. 'When you were ill, and I thought you were dead, I did something, something you'll hate me for.'

'I could never hate you, Arlette. Despite all that's happened, despite the arguments.'

'I tried to kill myself.'

'What! What did you do?'

Zev was visibly shocked.

'I tried to drown myself in the *mikveh*. Douce found me.'

'You never said. All this time.'

'I couldn't bring myself to tell you. No one knows except Douce, my uncle and Bella and now you.'

'I couldn't imagine a world without you in it. How could I have carried on without you? If I had woken that day and not seen your face. I would have wanted to kill myself. I can't live without you, Arlette. You mean everything to me.'

Zev took her in his arms and buried his face into the curve of her neck. Arlette held him close. He was sobbing. She had never seen or heard a man cry. Something touched her deep inside. They held on to each other in a tight embrace, neither wanting to let go, both now sobbing from a mixture of sadness and relief.

'We have to forget that man. He has come between us from the very start. I don't want him to do that ever again,' Arlette said.

Zev kissed her on the lips. Arlette responded. There was no roughness, no baying like a hound. It was full of love and mutual respect. She felt no pain and for once her body was completely relaxed and she let him make love to her. Afterwards Zev wrapped his arms around her.

'I love you so much, Arlette.'

'I do love you, Zev, I just didn't realise it.'

Arlette stroked his hair until her hand went limp. Completely relaxed she drifted into a reverie.

That night Baruch remained in his bed. He grizzled once or twice but Arlette ignored him, and for the first time in their marriage they lay in each other's arms until sleep took them.

CHAPTER
FIFTY-SEVEN

After the death of Young Samuel, Moses spent much of his time moping around the house or working in his cellar. The only time a light came into his eyes was when he watched Abraham playing in the courtyard. He would sit in the sunshine, his shoulders would relax and the deep furrows on his brow would recede for a while.

After a morning spent in his cellar, surrounded by credit agreements, he decided to join Arlette in the courtyard. The children were playing hide-and-seek with help from Arlette. Squeals of laughter and the sight of his daughter toddling around lightened his spirit. Henne and Baruch were inseparable, like twins. They were holding hands and, like small children do, believed that if they closed their eyes, no one could see them. He chuckled at their simplicity, then felt sadness as he remembered that his son Samuel used to do that. The sun warmed his stiff joints as he sat on the bench and watched the children. This near perfect moment was cut short when Brito appeared, striding toward them with a thunderous glare, his hand upon the hilt of his sword.

'Take the children inside, Arlette. Use the synagogue entrance.'

Arlette looked surprised at his outburst, then saw Brito. Moses was shocked to see her stare at him with defiance. Not a trace of fear.

'Quickly, Arlette,' he urged when he saw she was not going to leave.

'All right, Uncle,' she said, gathering the children together and disappearing through the synagogue door.

Moses looked up, shading his eyes from the sun. He thought he had seen the last of his tormentor. Hadn't he done enough to him and his family?

'What is it you want?' Moses demanded.

'I warned you not to lend to that Irish savage,' he said, drawing his sword and pointing it at Moses' heart. 'But you went against me and lent him the money.'

'I did not,' Moses said, his heart thudding.

'He got the money from somewhere.'

'Why do you say that?'

'Because he's raised an army against the king.'

'Against the king?' Moses was shocked by this revelation. Brito had said the king would be displeased but he had seen the letters patent giving his approval. Even so, he had not lent the Irishman money. 'But the Irishman showed me letters patent from the king giving him permission...'

'So, you did lend him the money?' Brito said, pressing his sword against Moses' thin cotton tunic and tearing a hole in it.

'No,' Moses cried out, feeling the cold steel against his flesh. 'I took your advice.'

Moses' heart was thudding like a blacksmith's anvil when it meets the full force of the hammer.

'Then who gave him the money if it wasn't you?' Brito

snarled, leaning forward for greater purchase, both hands on the hilt of his sword.

Moses felt the tip of the sword pierce his flesh. At the same time, he felt as though something, or someone was tying a tight band around his chest, crushing it until he could not breathe. His hands were clammy, and his legs would not stop trembling. Was this what it felt like just before death?

'Who gave him the money?' Brito shouted; his black eyes boring into Moses, who was struggling to breathe.

'Elias de Glocestre,' Moses managed to say, 'and his shrew of a wife.'

The pressure of the sword eased but remained pointed at his heart.

'And where would I find him and the shrew?'

Through desperate gasps for air, Moses told Brito where Elias lived. He had to tell him. Brito would have killed him if he hadn't.

'So, you did listen to me?' Brito said, his face twisting into a smarmy grin. He slotted his sword back in its sheath. 'I'll be back if I find you've been lying to me.'

Brito left. Moses put his hand on his chest. A spot of blood stained his tunic, and the cloth was torn. His heart was thudding so hard he could hear it pounding in his ears. The stranger was a dangerous man, an evil man, violent and terrifying. He would not have thought twice about running Moses through there in the courtyard. Would he ever be out of their lives? He wondered what Mirabelle would do when he confronted her? Wriggle out of it, like the slippery eel she was. Would Brito run her through or cart her off to the sheriff along with Elias and put them on trial for treason. What had he done? Nothing but save his own skin.

Once his breathing returned to normal Moses rose and went

back to the coolness and safety of his cellar and the certainty of his mathematical calculations.

A few hours later, Josce arrived at his door in an agitated state. Moses led him into the courtyard. The sun was still shining and the sky, an azure blue was cloudless.

'What's the matter, Josce?'

Josce rubbed at the back of his neck. His forehead was stippled with perspiration. 'Something's happened Moses and I don't know what to do.'

'Is it Judea? Is all well with the baby?'

At last, after years of marriage, Judea was pregnant. The baby was due any day.

'Yes, yes, they are fine.'

'What is it then? Sit down, my friend.'

Josce sat next to Moses, his gaze lowered to the floor. A nerve twitched in his cheek.

'I've been keeping a secret even from you, my friend, and it would have remained a secret had my hand not been forced.'

'What are you talking about?'

'Please don't tell the others.'

Moses had never seen Josce look so worried. 'We are friends. You are the godfather to my son. I think we can trust each other. You'd better tell me what's on your mind.'

'I am ruined, Moses.'

'What do you mean?'

'My business, everything.'

'Surely not. What's happened?'

'I've been summoned by the sheriff to attend the Michaelmas Court in October.'

'Whatever for?' Moses asked.

'I don't know. The king has ordered it.'

'Why would the king order that? What on earth have you done, Josce?'

Josce looked shamefaced. 'Some while back I brokered a very good deal with an Irishman.'

Moses' heart sank.

'Was his name Dairmait by any chance?'

'Yes, that's him. How did you know? Do you know him?'

'No, but he came knocking at my door and I sent him away.' Moses regretted with a heavy heart that he had sent the Irishman to Elias. He knew at the time it was probably a bad idea, knowing Mirabelle. 'Did Mirabelle send him to you?'

'Yes. How do you know so much about this?'

'It was me who sent the Irishman to her. I think you better tell me everything.'

A vein in Josce's temple pulsed. He rubbed at it. 'An Irishman called Dairmait came to see me. He had an English earl with him called Richard and a young woman with flaming red hair. They said Mirabelle had recommended me to them. I was flattered. I thought at the time Mirabelle was doing me a favour. You know how I struggle to find business.'

'Why would Mirabelle pass business on to you? She never does anyone a good turn. There must be more to it.'

Josce looked away again, a telltale sign that he wasn't telling Moses all there was to know. 'When those men approached me, they said they were on king's business and that if I lent them the money, I would be helping the king. They said the king would reward such loyalty. They hinted at future business. They asked to borrow a considerable sum of money. As you know, Moses, I'm not in your league and didn't have that amount of money at my disposal.'

Josce was a small-time moneylender usually local people, the occasional merchant. Moses and Aaron conducted most of the lucrative lending to royalty, churchmen and wealthy landowners.

'What possible business would the king have in Gloucester? He has his hands full fighting the French.'

'I didn't ask. I was thinking too much about the money, the profit I could make. I told them I needed time to get the money together. I said it would have to be at a very high interest. At least four pennies for every pound per week. I thought they might haggle with me; I couldn't believe it when they just accepted that rate without argument. I would have lent the money at the normal rate of interest, but I was just pushing it a little to see how far they would go. The Irishman was particularly eager to go ahead.'

Josce was naïve when it came to business. Moses would have sensed all was not kosher. His father always told him if something seemed too good to be true then it usually was. But Josce was an ambitious, foolhardy young man with a beautiful young wife and a child on the way, desperate to make his mark in the world. The moment they agreed such a high rate of interest Moses would have been alerted.

'They were keen to sign the agreement and be given the money there and then. I panicked. So, I went to see Mirabelle and Elias for a loan...'

'Why didn't you come to see me?'

'I don't know. Probably because I knew deep down something wasn't quite right, but I was dazzled by the prospect of finally making it.'

Moses frowned and shook his head. He ran his fingers through his beard and let out a sigh.

Josce continued, 'I thanked them for passing the business on to me and asked why they hadn't lent the money themselves. They said I deserved a helping hand, and it wasn't fair that you,' he gestured towards Moses, 'got all the best contracts in the area just because Aaron of Lincoln chose you as his agent.'

'I've always known Mirabelle was jealous of me.'

'I'm not jealous of you, Moses. I didn't agree with what they were saying. I just wanted to get my hands on the money. It would have changed our lives.'

'Did she charge you interest?'

Josce looked down at the ground and mumbled, 'Yes.'

Mirabelle was no ordinary Jew. She would sell her own grandmother if it meant making money. It didn't surprise Moses that she would charge interest even though it was against rabbinical law to loan money at interest to another Jew. But he was shocked his friend had agreed to such a thing. Moses found himself quoting the passage from Deuteronomy. 'Unto a foreigner thou mayest lend upon interest; but unto thy brother thou shalt not lend upon interest.'

'I wasn't thinking straight,' admitted Josce.

'I still don't understand what this has got to do with you being summoned to the Michaelmas Court by the king?'

'A few hours ago, that stranger they call Brito knocked at my door.'

Moses' mouth went dry. He had inadvertently sent the stranger into Josce's path.

'He asked if I had given money to the Irishman. At first, I told him it was none of his business. He said if I didn't tell him the truth, he'd kill me. I was petrified.'

'So, you told him you'd given Dairmait the money?'

'Yes. He drew his sword and I thought he was going to kill me, but something changed his mind. It was odd. He smiled as if he were smiling at his own joke. Then he said he would deal with me later. He left but not before he told me not to lend the Irishman any more money. I promised him on my unborn child's life I would not go against him or the king. Then the sheriff arrived and told me the king would summon me to attend the first sitting of the Michaelmas Court. When I asked him what was going to happen to me, he wouldn't say. You know as well as I do that if the king summons you to a quarter session it is not to congratulate you.'

'It might not be as bad as you think. The sheriff might have been bluffing or acting to appease Brito. He dislikes him as much as we do. If you were going to be sent to the tower, you'd have been carted off there by now. I wouldn't think too much about it until you know for sure. It might never happen.'

'But it will ruin me. My business will suffer, and I already owe Mirabelle a king's ransom.'

'It's better than losing your life,' Moses said, becoming short with his friend. 'Think of Judea and the baby.'

Josce hung his head in shame. 'You're right, Moses. I've been foolish. Very foolish. I should never have got mixed up in this.'

'Not where Mirabelle is concerned. She has the kindness of a hangman. You should have known she was up to something.'

Moses could not believe his friend's naivety, nor his unfettered greed. He was reminded of the writings in the Hebrew scriptures:

'One who loves money will never be satisfied with money.'

It saddened him that his friend had been morally corrupted by money. *Kesef*. When used as a force for good money could transform lives, it could also destroy. A man who has one hundred shillings wants two hundred. His father had taught him that lesson as a boy. Greed is futile. It is a goal with no end. And now Josce was paying the price.

'I know, you're right, Moses. I should have come to you first.'

'Go home to Judea and pray to Hashem for a good outcome at the Michaelmas Court.'

Josce shook Moses' hand.

'*Alaichem sholom.*'

Moses was beginning to understand what the stranger had to do with the Irishman and why the king might be implicated in all this. If the king did not want the Irishman to raise an army for whatever reason he would not want him to be in a position to fund it. Everyone knows Jews are the major moneylenders able to lend the sums of money required to wage war. Kings were constantly raiding the coffers of the Jews for their warring campaigns. Brito had been sent to warn us off and he would have been successful if it wasn't for Mirabelle.

'Damn that woman.'

FIFTY-EIGHT

A s soon as Prior Clement heard the king would be in attendance at the Michaelmas Court, he made the decision to seek an audience with him.

Clement had aged since Harold's death. Now an old man, his stooped figure trudged across the footbridge and for only the second time in his life, he entered the castle. It was packed full of men, war horses and provisions. The king never went anywhere without his army and his hordes of servants. There was barely room to walk through the gate. Clement was shown into the great hall in the central tower. He had sent word that his business with the king was highly personal and should only be discussed in private.

The king stood at a long oak table with his usual retinue of aides, poring over battle plans for his return to France and discussing tactics. Clement's stomach churned in trepidation. *What if the king insists I discuss my business with him in front of these men?* If he did, then Clement decided he would have to make something up and call the whole thing off. The king looked up when the prior was announced. He took a good, long look at him before dismissing his aides.

'*Laissez nous.* Leave us for a moment.'

They left without argument, leaving Clement in the great hall alone with the king. Clement suddenly felt very small. The king retired to a grand ornamental chair which resembled a throne, his bloated stomach bulging over the leather belt tied at his waist. He beckoned Clement to step forward.

'I'm curious,' he began, 'why would an Augustinian prior want a private audience with the king?'

The king stared at Clement with his piercing, cold eyes and waited for him to answer.

Clement opened his mouth to speak but only a croak came out. He coughed, apologised and started again. He had thought long and hard about his decision to speak to the king on this matter, questioning its prudence.

'Your Majesty, some time ago the people of this city accused the Jews of murdering a young Christian boy, you may remember.'

'I don't recall,' said the king, looking bored already, 'but it seems a common enough occurrence these days for a Christian to accuse a Jew of something. But what has this to do with me after all this time?'

'No one, not Christian, not Jew, was ever found guilty of the crime.'

'That is also not uncommon.'

Prior Clement could see the king was becoming impatient with him, yet he had prepared what to say and now he was here it all must be said. 'The boy in question suffered a monstrous death, one of unspeakable violence. His eyes were blinded with molten wax, his teeth were knocked out and his jaw broken, his body burned, and thorns attached to his head and armpits, and his hands and feet had been nailed to a cross. The boy was only nine years old and yet, to this day, no one was ever punished for this crime.'

'Yes, this is all terrible, but I still don't see what this has to do with me and why you needed to speak to me in private when what you are telling me is of public knowledge,' the king shouted, his temper flaring.

'The boy was your son.'

The king shot up out of his chair, his short fuse lit instantly by the insinuation that some common boy was his son.

'My son,' he growled under his breath, raising his hands and slamming them hard onto the arms of his chair. The noise was so sharp the door to the great hall flew open and the king's men came rushing in.

'*Sortez!* Get out!' the king yelled.

His men did not move. Their swords were unsheathed, and they looked ready to attack Prior Clement.

'*Mon dieu, vous imbéciles.* Leave us alone.'

The men looked startled at his request but did as they were told. Prior Clement had never seen such anger in a man. He took a few steps back, fearing what the king might do.

'If you were not a man of God, I would strike you down now,' he said.

'That the boy is your son is irrefutable, Your Majesty.'

'What madness is this you speak of? Am I not standing before a fool?'

'The boy was brought to me in the month of January in the year of our Lord, eleven hundred and fifty-eight...'

'So? More nonsense,' the king muttered, stepping away.

'...he was brought to me by the Countess of Hereford, Margaret de Bohun...'

At the mention of Margaret's name, the king swung round. The colour had drained from his florid complexion and his grey eyes softened. For a moment he said nothing. He seemed to be trying to recollect a time, a date, and memories.

'I thought you should know. If he was my son I would want to know.'

The king returned to his throne, slumping back into the seat, exhibiting all the signs of a man in shock. When he spoke, his voice was soft and tremulous.

'She said there was a son but that he had died at birth. I never questioned it. The affair was over by then and she had gone back to that doddery old husband of hers.'

'Margaret never told me who the father was until Harold – that was the boy's name – until after he was dead.' Prior Clement's voice faltered towards the end, his grief at losing the boy returning.

'Why was no one brought to trial for this?' the king asked, now keen to know more.

'At the time a stranger tried to convince Sheriff Pypard that the Jews were responsible for the crime, but Sheriff Pypard said there was not enough evidence against them.'

'When did you say this all took place?'

'In the month of March, in the year of our Lord eleven hundred and sixty-seven.'

The king scratched at the stubble of his chin. 'You mentioned a stranger. What stranger?'

'A man of immense terror. He was behind the accusation against the Jews.'

'What was his name?'

'A tall fellow with black hair. He called himself Brito.'

Prior Clement thought he saw a flicker of recognition from the king when he said the name Brito. The colour came back to the king's face. His prominent eyes widened, and a look of sheer madness came upon him, but Clement was not prepared for what happened next. The king put his head in his hands and shook it from side to side whilst muttering something. Prior Clement drew closer.

'How could I have known? How could I have known?' the king said.

Prior Clement spoke in a gentle, almost conciliatory tone. 'Is there something you wish to confess, Your Majesty?'

The king looked up at the sound of Prior Clement's voice, with a haunted expression as though he were looking at an apparition.

'I have blood on my hands.'

Prior Clement thought that a strange thing to say. As a warmongering king he would have plenty of blood on his hands. What had this got to do with Harold? He had to know.

'Did you order Harold's murder?'

The king was well known for his sudden temper. Prior Clement had heard that once, as a young man, he had gotten so angry he had frothed at the mouth. He feared such a bold question might have the same effect. His present mood was so wild and unpredictable, vacillating from unbridled anger to self-reproach, anything was possible. Clement held his breath, waiting for his answer.

'Does Margaret know the boy is dead?'

Prior Clement was struggling to cope with the king's quick changing moods. He couldn't tell whether the king was deftly avoiding his question or whether he had even heard it. He decided it would be prudent to answer. 'Yes. She attended the funeral.'

'Where was he buried?'

'He's buried in the abbey, Your Majesty. He has been made a saint.'

'That is no good to Margaret.'

'But it is of some comfort to her.'

'How is Margaret?' the king asked, his face marked with pain and the trace of poignant memories.

'She is well, Your Majesty. She is a widow now.'

Henry raised his eyebrows. 'A widow.'

'Yes, Your Majesty, the Earl of Pembroke died recently. Margaret has become a generous benefactor of the priory for which we are eternally grateful.'

The king grunted. He lapsed into another reverie. Thinking of past times. Prior Clement was determined to know what the king had meant earlier. He was stepping into dangerous territory, but it was probably the last chance he would have alone with him. He had to know if the king had somehow had a hand in the murder of Harold. He swallowed hard.

'What did you mean when you said, "you couldn't know"?'

The king was somewhere far away. Prior Clement repeated the question. The king still did not answer.

'Do you know the stranger Brito?'

The name Brito jolted the king back to the present. He narrowed his eyes and gave Clement a stern look. 'I sent Brito here...'

Prior Clement's heart began to race, not sure what he was about to hear. Not wanting to know the truth but still wanting the truth so desperately, as if the truth would somehow give him resolution of the grief he carried with him, like a shroud of gloom. The violent death of Harold had raised more questions for Clement than answers. Why would anyone want to kill a boy and in such a macabre way? If the Jews had not killed Harold, then who had and why? That question had haunted him these past years. He often woke in the night from a fitful sleep and the puzzle as to 'why' would snap into his waking thoughts. He could not be sure, but he thought he might be about to find out. The beginning of a confession of sorts.

'...I asked him to spy for me. I gave letters patent to Dairmait, the king of Ireland, giving him permission to find men to help him gain back his lands. I sent Brito to keep an eye on him and find out who was funding him. When he arrived back in France, Brito said nothing about the murder of a boy. I later found out that a foolish young Jew called Josce had lent Dairmait the money to raise an army against my interests. That's why I'm here to make an example of the Jew they call Josce. To put an end to Dairmait's plans. I swear I knew nothing of this murder, nor did I sanction it.'

'I have no proof that Brito killed Harold. I have only suspicions.'

'A man of God should trust his instincts.'

The shroud of gloom loosened its grip on Clement's soul. Harold had been killed by men serving the king in a scheme to discredit the Jews. This knowledge could never make up for the loss of his beloved Harold, but it had solved the mystery of his murder. It had been a puzzle that had plagued him for so long and haunted his dreams. It was obvious by the king's reaction to the news of Harold's death that his murder had not been sanctioned by him. Then he thought of Margaret. Should he tell her that the man who fathered her child had also been instrumental in his murder? No. He could not. It would destroy her. This was a secret he must take to his grave. No good would come of anyone knowing.

'What will you do?' Clement asked, worried he had inadvertently become responsible for the stranger Brito's death sentence.

The king's answer puzzled him.

'I never knew my son. What is done cannot be undone.'

CHAPTER
FIFTY-NINE

The courtroom was bristling with anticipation. Citizens from every walk of life were crammed into the great hall for news had travelled that the king was to be in attendance. Moses stood with his friend Radulf the Moneyer. They often met on quarter sessions and played a game of tabula – a popular board game handed down by the occupying Romans. Radulf was teaching Moses the rules but so far, he had failed to win a single game.

Josce stood close by, wringing his hands and occasionally wiping the perspiration from his forehead. He had lost weight. Moses felt sorry for him. Judea had given birth to a son and they had named him Mannasser after his grandfather. Moses had been the godfather at the *brit*, but the occasion had been marred by the threat overhanging Josce of a possible fine, internment or worse.

Sheriff Gilbert Pypard sat at the top table with his scribe. His father William had died soon after the last quarter sessions and Gilbert had been appointed his successor. He assiduously collected the king's taxes, making a far better job of it than his father had. Moses had little to do with him other than on quarter days.

'Silence! Your king is in attendance,' Sheriff Pypard shouted, slamming the gavel down on its wooden block.

King Henry appeared walking with a pronounced gait. He was a man of thirty or so years and looked somewhat dishevelled for a king. He was still handsome, despite his larger than normal head and bowed legs. His eyes were grey, narrow and piercing. His hair was close cropped and a tawny colour, and his face was mottled with a mask of freckles brought on by the sun whilst in France. He wore a long tunic of scarlet cloth dyed bright red with kermes and trimmed with gold thread. Over this was a heavy woollen cloak, trimmed with lynx fur and fixed by a crescent-shaped gold clasp, encrusted with precious stones. He wore a simple gold crown upon his head and delicate pointed boots on his feet. His stern expression and ominous presence changed the mood in the hall. To Moses' surprise, Dairmait, the earl and the pretty young woman who called at his home were following behind, the earl in contrite pose, Dairmait looking defiant as ever. Moses imagined Dairmait was livid at being summoned to court in Gloucester.

'Today is a special hearing of the Michaelmas Court in the presence of your king,' Sheriff Pypard said, his voice booming across the silenced crowd.

Moses looked over at Josce. He was as grey as ash and mopping his brow feverishly.

'He wishes to address the citizens of Gloucester.'

The king stepped forward. He scowled at his subjects standing before him. 'I am your King, Henricus the Second, and as your king I hereby command that no more money be given to the two men that stand here before you in furtherance of their campaign in Ireland. Dairmait MacMurchada and Richard de Clare, the Earl of Striguil.'

Dairmait's face was red with rage. Richard looked like a child who had lost his favourite toy while Aoife in comparison looked beautifully serene like a woman in love.

'Let it be known that against my prohibition funds have been made available to finance their campaign. I will not tolerate it. Call the Jew Josce forward.'

Sheriff Pypard called Josce to stand in front of the king.

'Your Majesty,' Josce said, bowing.

'Let it be entered into the record.' Henry motioned to the scribe who dipped his quill in the ink pot and started writing furiously on the parchment in front of him. 'That Josce, Jew of Gloucester, pay an amercement of one hundred shillings to the king for the monies he has lent to those...' he turned to face Dairmait and Richard and gave them a thunderous look, '...who against my prohibition went over to Ireland.'

Moses had been holding his breath. He let out a sigh of relief. Josce was to pay a fine of one hundred shillings. He would not be sent to the tower, nor be hung from the neck. The king had shown mercy. He had publicly shamed Josce and made certain Dairmait and Richard and everyone else knew his thoughts on the matter. There could be no doubts, no uncertainties. It had all been about power and land-grabbing in Ireland.

The king gave Josce a menacing look. 'You have been warned. I do not want to see you before me in this court or any other again. Do you understand?'

'Yes, Your Majesty,' Josce said.

With that the king left the court. Dairmait and his small retinue followed dutifully behind. The business of the quarter session carried on as normal and once Moses had paid his taxes to the sheriff, he left the hall. He wanted to congratulate Josce but could not find him. As he pushed through the remaining crowds, he spotted Brito at the back of the hall. Moses wondered why he was not at the king's side. Moses rushed past him, fearing he was inciting hatred against the Jews again. Besides, Douce would be awaiting his return for the start of Rosh Hashanah, the Jewish New Year.

The massive carved doors leading out of the great hall were open. Moses was just about to pass through them when a firm grip on his arm arrested his progress.

'How is my son doing?' Brito asked.

'I'm sorry, I don't know who your son is,' Moses said.

'Yes you do, that little brat of your niece's. He's mine. Didn't you know?'

Moses heard the words but could not believe them. The blood drained from his face. He felt himself go cold.

'No, you're wrong. Baruch is Zev's son.'

'Ask your niece, she knows.'

CHAPTER
SIXTY

All the way home, Moses could not get Brito's words out of his head.

How is my son?

The thought that the child he regarded as his grandson might be the progeny of that Satanic beast turned his stomach. The image of Arlette burned into his memory since that night came to him; her torn tunic, Brito dragging her out of the alleyway by her hair. Arlette must know the child is Brito's, but did Zev know? He had to speak to Douce. He found her in the kitchen washing apples.

'Leave that,' he said. 'I must speak to you.'

Douce followed Moses into the hall. 'What is it?' she said, wiping her hands on her apron. 'Is it Josce? Oh no, please, don't say they've sent him to the tower. What will happen to Judea?'

Moses raised his voice. 'No, this is not about Josce. He got off lightly with a fine of a hundred shillings.'

'A hundred shillings,' Douce repeated. '*Oy lanu!* How will he pay that back? He hardly makes enough to keep him and Judea.'

'It's better than losing his life.'

Douce nodded. 'Then what is it?'

'It's Arlette,' said Moses. 'Well, actually it's about Baruch.'

'But he's safe upstairs playing with the children and Arlette.'

Moses was getting more exasperated by Douce. 'Sit down and listen to me,' he said. 'I've just come from the court. Brito was there. He asked me how his son was.'

'Oh,' said Douce.

'What do you mean, "oh"?'

'Did he say Baruch is his?'

'Yes. Did you know?'

'No. I had my suspicions. But it all makes sense now. The arguments, the way Zev is with Baruch...'

'Do you think Zev knows?'

Douce nodded. 'I think he must know.'

Moses walked over to the bottle of wine he kept on the table and poured himself a cup.

'Would you like one?'

'No, thank you.'

'I know it's a little early, but I need one.' He sat back down, took a sip of wine and stared into the fire. 'Should we say something to Arlette? Should we tell her we know?'

'I don't think that's wise. If they wanted us to know they would have told us.'

'What are we going to do, Douce?'

'Nothing. What can we do? It's none of our business.'

'I suppose you're right.'

That night during the New Year celebrations, Moses could not take his eyes from Baruch. Every expression, his dark eyes, the way he teased Henne, all of it reminded him of Brito. Satan. The devil.

Moses and Douce retired early. Moses slept fitfully, the news of Baruch's paternity weighing heavily on his mind. He woke in the middle of the night to the sound of someone banging on the door. He bolted out of bed half asleep, thinking the banging was another angry mob outside his house baying for his blood. Brito was back in Gloucester. Had he incited a horde of Jew haters? Were they to be subjected once more to this terror in their own home? He pulled his cloak over his shift. Douce lay asleep. He let himself out and went downstairs and listened at the door. It was not a throng of haters, but the voice of a solitary person.

Hasatan.

Satan.

'I want to see my son. Let me in. I want to see my son.'

Bang. Bang. Bang.

Moses opened the door. 'Shut up or you'll wake everyone.'

'I don't care about that. I want to see my son.'

'He's not your son. Now go away. You're drunk. Go home and sleep it off.'

Moses tried to shut the door. Brito fell against it.

'What's going on?' Zev said, coming along the hallway.

'Go back to bed, Zev,' Moses replied. 'I can handle this.'

'Who is it?'

'No one. Go on back to bed.'

Zev emerged from the gloom. 'What's he doing here?' he said.

'Let me handle this, Zev. Go back to bed.'

Moses was only too aware of what happened the last time these two crossed paths.

'Ah, I see it is the cuckolded one. How's my son?' Brito sneered.

Zev flew at Brito and landed a punch to his face. Brito, worse for wear, staggered backwards and fell into the alleyway. As he lay on the ground feeling his jaw to check it was not broken, he roared with laughter.

335

'Not a bad punch for a cuckold,' Brito said, getting to his feet.

Zev went for him again. Moses tried to pull them apart but, in the mêlée, received a blow from one of them. He staggered away, blood gushing from a split lip.

'Stop this. Stop this now.'

It was Arlette, standing in the alleyway in her nightclothes.

'There you are. Where's my son? I want to see him.' Brito lunged at Arlette. She dodged him, and he fell to the ground again.

'You're drunk,' she said. 'You're not fit to be Baruch's father.'

'And that husband of yours is?'

'Yes, he is.'

Brito rolled onto his back, like a dying cockroach, cackling.

'He's nothing but a...' Brito used the French word for cuckoo, making a sound like the bird. '*Cucuault. Cucuault. Cucuault.*'

Zev kicked him as he lay on the ground. He would have kicked him again if it hadn't been for Moses who held him back. 'I'll kill you if you say that again,' Zev shouted, struggling to break free.

Arlette came forward and stood over Brito. 'I swear if you ever come here again, I'll kill you myself.' She turned to Zev and took hold of his arm. 'Come, husband, let's go back inside.'

Just then Douce appeared holding a *pot de chambre*. 'What's *he* doing here?' She stood defiantly over Brito, who was rolling around on the ground cackling, too drunk to pick himself up. She raised the chamber pot high and emptied its acrid smelling contents into his face.

'You bitch,' Brito said, spluttering.

'If she doesn't kill you, I will.'

Zev and Arlette went back to bed without speaking to Moses or Douce. It was obvious to Douce it would be a family secret never to be spoken of. Douce cleaned Moses' split lip and poured him a cup of apple brandy. Moses saw it off in one gulp.

'What are we going to do about him?' said Douce as she wiped away a smear of blood from Moses' chin.

'What can we do?'

'We must do something, or we'll never be rid of this beast. He taunts Arlette. He taunts Zev. Now he's calling at the house. He wants to see Baruch. It can't go on.'

'Well, the sheriff won't do anything. He's one of the king's men.'

'Then *we* must do something. You know we missed an opportunity just now.'

Moses had been holding a cloth to his lip, dabbing at the wound. He stopped dabbing and stared at Douce, open-mouthed, and tried to take in the enormity of what Douce seemed to be saying.

'What are you saying?'

'When he was lying on the ground drunk.'

'What are you saying?'

'It wouldn't have taken much to finish him off.'

Moses had never seen his wife like this before. Since the death of Samuel, she had been morose, but now her eyes were full of fire, glowing with murderous thoughts.

'This man has destroyed Arlette's life and continues to do so,' said Douce.

Douce's words brought back the image of Arlette coming from the alley, an image that would be burned forever into Moses' memory.

'What if he comes back and claims the child as his own? Takes him from Arlette. We can't let that happen,' Douce said. 'And what if he forces himself on her again? Or attacks Zev again? He nearly killed him. He'll never leave us alone. He'll destroy all our lives if we let him.'

'I need to be clear, Douce. What are you asking me to do?'

'I think you know,' she said, her voice measured, cold.

'Think about what you're saying. You're asking me to...' Moses lowered his voice, 'you're asking me to commit murder.'

CHAPTER
SIXTY-ONE

Douce and Arlette were in the kitchen preparing for the first meal of Chanukah, the festival of lights. Douce was skilfully twisting plaits of sour cream dough into crescent-shaped pastries and filling them with dried fruit, cinnamon and chopped walnuts.

'You make that look so easy, Douce,' Arlette said.

'It is easy. Look.' Douce wrenched a piece of the soft olive oil dough from the squidgy mound she had made earlier, rolled it into a strip, and deftly laced it together, stuffing it with the filling as she did so. She then moulded it into a crescent shape, placing the finished pastry with the others to be baked ready for that night's meal.

Arlette's attempt to copy Douce's effort looked somewhat less accomplished. 'See,' she said. 'Looks nothing like yours. Mine's more like a pile of worms.'

With uncharacteristic temper, Arlette scrunched up her effort and threw it down on the bench they were working at.

'You're tired, Arlette. Let me finish these.'

'Sorry, Douce. I don't know what's the matter with me lately. The slightest thing seems to upset me.'

'You've had very little sleep since Baruch was born. Go and lie down.'

'I do feel tired today. Are you sure?'

'I'm sure. You need to look after yourself. I'll watch Baruch. Off you go.'

'I feel bad though. You have enough to do.'

'I can manage. Baruch is asleep. Now go and lie down.'

Arlette gave her a weak smile, removed her floury apron and left the kitchen. Douce went to check on the children. Baruch, Abraham and Henne were in their beds, sleeping peacefully through their afternoon nap. She returned to the kitchen to continue preparing the food. First, she made batter for the *crespes*, a pancake fried in olive oil and filled with goat's cheese. Then she made a sweeter batter for the *beignets*, a doughnut eaten hot and dipped in honey traditionally served on Chanukah. There would also be Moses' favourite – slices of apple fried in olive oil. Alone in her kitchen, Douce reflected upon how the food she prepared was intimately bound up with the struggles of the Jewish people. Her family had struggles of their own, but they were coping and here she was celebrating an event from their shared history of struggle. Surely, she should take heart from that. That whatever was done to her and her kind, she would triumph just as the Maccabees had over the Greeks when they drove them out and reclaimed the Holy Temple in Jerusalem. She walked over to the amphora-shaped earthenware jar in which was stored the olive oil, so symbolic of that event. As she ladled the oil into a smaller jug, she wondered how one small cruse of olive oil could have lit the temple menorah for eight long days. It could only be a miracle and for that she would be forever grateful to Hashem. As she poured the unctuous, grassy green liquid she thought also of those ancient people and what they must have suffered. It was for them and all others that had suffered that she toiled in the kitchen to make sure her food met the lofty standards her family had come to expect of her.

~

The long, dark night had closed in, and a keen wind was blowing through the gaps in the wooden door. Arlette drew the heavy damask curtain across to keep out the draught and joined her family in the hall. Moses sat by a roaring fire, a cup of wine in his hand. He was staring into the flames as if looking for answers to a puzzling question, his brow furrowed in concentration. Douce was keeping a watchful eye on the children who were playing together in the corner.

Arlette was still unsure how she felt about her son. Sometimes she wished Bellassez wasn't such a good healer and they had both perished that day. Then he would say something, and his eyes would sparkle, and she would chide herself for having such feelings. She was sure she loved Baruch but then some days she had dark thoughts about him. Baruch rarely slept through the night and when he was awake, he wanted her constant attention and if he didn't get it, he cried for what seemed an eternity. Nothing seemed to pacify the child. Milk, *havitz*, frumenty, cuddles. Nothing worked. It was at those times, when she felt tired beyond weary, she wanted to harm him.

Since the difficult birth, Arlette had felt unwell. Ever since that night in the sacred bath morbid thoughts of her death had never left her. It was like a weakness within her, an infection that would not go away. She was tired all the time, barely venturing out of the house except to sit in the courtyard. She shunned all invitations to visit her friends. She struggled from one day to the next, Baruch a constant drain on her energy.

Arlette watched as Zev played with Abraham, a lively

three-year-old. It was clear Zev adored him. In contrast he merely tolerated Baruch. He showed no interest in the child. Every milestone Baruch had reached, his first smile, first tooth, first crawl was met with supreme indifference. It was true, he was a difficult child to love. Even she found it hard at times.

Zev was playing the traditional game of *sovinen*. It was a version he had invented to entertain Abraham. Abraham sat on Zev's knee, whilst Zev spun the *sovinen*, a small wooden spinning top. Each time the spinning top landed on a letter; he had made it correspond to something Abraham liked. The top landed on the Jewish letter *he*.

'You got a *he*, Abraham. You know what that means, don't you?'

Zev talked to Abraham as if the child were an adult. Arlette thought him foolish but maybe she was wrong to think this. Maybe Abraham could understand what was being said to him. She watched his expressions and saw that they changed depending on what Zev said to him. Abraham chuckled. Zev lifted him onto the end of his leg and bounced him up and down, holding on to his tiny hands. Abraham squealed with delight causing Moses to wake from his reverie. Moses smiled at his son and nodded off again.

'Let's see what you get next?' Zev spun the wooden top. It landed on the letter *gimel*. Baruch had toddled, unseen by Zev, to the table and made a grab for the spinning top. Zev snatched it from his hand. Baruch started to cry. 'That's not for you and you know it. Arlette, come and take Baruch. He's spoiling the game.'

Arlette went to her son, saddened at the thought of her unloved child. She took his hand and led him away. Baruch tried to break free from his mother's grip and not having the energy for another tantrum she let him go. He toddled back towards the game. Zev spun the top again. This time it landed on the letter '*shin*'.

'Ah, your favourite, Abe,' Zev said to the delighted Abraham.

Abraham's eyes widened in understanding, as if he knew what was coming. Zev lifted the child high above his head and flew him around like a bird. The child was wild with joy, a high-pitched squeal emanated from his tiny lungs and his chubby legs flailed around vigorously.

'Say *shin*,' Zev said. 'Ssshin,' he repeated, elongating the sound.

Abraham repeated the word to which Zev rewarded him with another lift much to the child's delight.

'That's enough of that. There are candles to be lit and food to be eaten. If you keep twirling him around you'll make him sick and he won't eat his food,' Douce said.

Zev set Abraham on the floor and picked up the spinning top and put it in his pocket. The festival candelabrum stood by the window opening. It was much like a menorah but with eight candleholders in a row with a ninth set a little above the others, there to light the other candles. It was only used for eight days and then stored away until the next year. The candelabrum represented the cruse of olive oil that had sustained a light for eight days – long enough for the Jews to ritually purify their temple. It stood unlit waiting for the first candle to be ignited. By the end of the eighth day every candle would be alight, and Chanukah would be over.

Moses woke up and raised himself from the chair with a sigh and walked over to where everyone had gathered. Traditionally Moses liked to give a little sermon, a reflection of what Chanukah meant to him.

'Chanukah teaches us we must never be afraid to stand up for what's right. Judah Maccabee and his band faced daunting odds, but this didn't stop them. With a prayer on their lips and faith in their hearts they entered the battle of their lives and won. When faced with our own battles we can do the same.'

'So true,' Old Samuel said, nodding his head sagely in agreement.

Abraham ran to his father repeating the sound 'sssshin'. Douce pulled him to one side to allow Moses to continue.

'The candlelight serves as a beacon for the darkening streets. No matter how dark it is outside, a candle of Hashem's goodness can transform the darkness itself into light.'

Moses took hold of the candelabrum and the burning cruse of olive oil and with great care he lit the first of the candles.

'*Chanukah sameach.*'

Moses and Douce sat by the fire drinking wine. Arlette and Zev had retired early.

'Have you noticed how those two seem a lot happier?' said Douce.

'They are more like a young married couple now, going to bed early.'

'We were like that. Remember?'

Moses gave Douce his boyish grin.

'You do remember,' she said, taking another sip of wine.

'They are happier, but I've noticed Zev doesn't take much interest in Baruch.'

'Give him time. Men aren't very good with young children. They find them boring. When Baruch gets older, Zev will be a good father.'

'Do you think it has anything to do with the fact Baruch isn't his?'

'Maybe. You men are strange like that.'

'I wish he would help Arlette more. She's still not coping with Baruch. She just seems so tired all the time.'

'Don't forget, Moses, she's had a tough time. Be patient.'

Douce cherished these moments. Sitting by the fire with her husband. The children in bed. Zev and Arlette asleep. After three children, they were still very much in love but the passion of the first few years of their marriage was fading, replaced by companionship. They often stayed up late, talking about the children and about Moses' business and their plans for the future. The accusation against him for the murder of the young boy had not damaged business. In fact, Moses had never been busier. Aaron of Lincoln continued to send good business his way. Perhaps he felt guilty at turning down his niece.

'I think I'll go to bed, *chérie*. I'm feeling quite tired.'

'I'll be up in a moment. I just have to see to a couple of things in the kitchen.'

'I'll warm the bed for you,' he said, squeezing her hand.

Douce gathered up the wine goblets and walked into the kitchen at the back of the house. It looked out onto the courtyard. She was opening the back door to throw out some rubbish when she saw Brito sitting on the bench. His chin was lolling on his chest, and he was muttering to himself. Douce could tell he was drunk. Her contented mood swung to one of burning hatred. She thought about what she had said to Moses. Did she have the nerve to carry it out? Moses kept an old sword in his cellar. She hurried out of the kitchen and took a candle from one of the sconces in the fore hall. The cellar was pitch black at this time of night and Douce was never keen on going down there in the dark. Holding the candle in one hand she held on to the rope as she felt her way down the cold stone steps. There was an eerie feeling when she reached the bottom but fired by her desire to avenge Arlette, she carried on searching for the sword. It was propped in a corner behind a pile of hazel sticks. Douce reached over for it and grabbed at it. The weight of it surprised her. The blade was long and thin with a downward curving cross guard. The metal hilt was cold in her hand. She struggled back up the stairs, trying not to let the sword drag along the floor. She did not want Moses to hear the noise. Her heart was thumping, and she was out of breath when she reached the back door. Brito was still there, slumped on the bench. She walked over to him. He was snoring loudly. She nudged him with the tip of the sword. He woke with a start.

'I told you I'd kill you if you came back.'

Brito looked up at Douce with a bemused expression. 'Where's Arlette? I want her. I want to see my son.'

'You won't live to see your son grow up.'

Brito squinted at her; his eyes glazed. 'Why's that?'

'Because I'm going to make sure you don't, you black-hearted bastard,' she heard herself say, surprised at her boldness.

Brito groaned. Douce lifted the heavy sword above her head. Brito bolted from the bench and cried out, 'What are you doing, woman?'

Douce lunged at him with the sword. He dodged her, and the tip of the sword struck the ground with a dull clank leaving Douce unarmed and vulnerable.

'You're insane,' Brito shouted.

He was much taller than Douce and appeared to have sobered up. She was beginning to see the folly of her actions as she felt his menacing presence. She bent to pick up the sword, but Brito snatched it from her hand and pushed her to the ground. He stood over her, his derisive smirk belittling her, the point of the sword at her throat.

'I could so easily kill you.'

Douce lay on the ground. Thoughts of her children flashed through her mind, and she wondered whether she would ever see them again. Then she spotted Moses creeping up behind Brito, a metal pail held high above him. He brought it down with tremendous force on the back of Brito's head. Brito staggered and almost fell. The sword was still in his hand, but Moses acted quickly, taking advantage of Brito's dazed condition. He tore the sword from him, grabbed Douce's hand and pulled her from the floor.

'Leave my family alone. If you don't, I will deal with you myself.'

With that he stormed back into the house almost dragging Douce with him. Once inside, he locked the door and took her in his arms. 'Douce, what were you thinking? You could have been killed. Then what would become of me? You were lucky I came along when I did.'

Douce held on to Moses tight. She could feel her heart thudding against his warm chest. 'I hate him, Moses. I want him dead.'

'You don't really mean that.'

Moses had thought Douce had spoken in anger the other night about murdering Brito. Something said in the heat of the moment. He could tell this was not idle talk or wishful thinking. He had no idea his wife was actually considering murdering Brito.

'I do. I won't rest until he's suffered for what he's done to Arlette.'

'I can see I'll have to keep this locked up,' he said, propping the sword against the wall. 'Maybe you should drink less wine.'

Douce snorted with relief. Moses hoped his levity had brought her out of her murderous mood. He didn't recognise the woman she had become in the courtyard. They walked back into the hall and sat before the dying embers of the fire.

'Remember what Rabbi Solomon said about rising up against your neighbour?'

'No, when?' Moses said, helping himself to a cup of wine and sitting beside her in his chair.

'When we went to see him after Arlette was raped.'

'Ah yes, I remember.'

'Solomon said if the man forced himself upon Arlette, then he should be put to death.'

'Yes, but he didn't mean you to take matters into your own hands and kill him yourself.'

Douce had interpreted the rabbi's words and twisted them. What had become of her? Could this be the same woman he married? The mother of his children.

'I thought it would be easier. He was drunk.'

'I don't think the rabbi meant us to take that interpretation of the Torah literally.'

Douce took on a defiant tone. 'Why not?'

'You know why not. We can't go around murdering people. It's against the law.'

'He has to be punished. We have to do something.'

'So, what do you suggest now that your plan to kill him yourself has backfired?'

'I was foolish to think I could do it on my own,' Douce said.

'Are you suggesting we do it together? You can't really be asking that of me?'

'Not us personally.'

'Then what?'

'We are wealthy, Moses. Very wealthy. Why don't we use that money to protect our family?'

'I'm not sure I know what you mean.'

There was a long pause.

'We could pay someone to murder him.'

Moses almost choked at her words. His wife was a bigger schemer than her arch enemy Mirabelle. The words seemed to come from her lips with the ease of a murderous scoundrel.

'How long have you been thinking about paying someone to kill Brito?'

'Since just now. He's more of a match for either of us. I can see that now. You're a man, Moses, you have no idea what it's like to be violated. It's a woman's worst fear. It's not right that he has got away with it.'

Moses thought for a while before responding. 'You're right, as a man I can only imagine how it might feel. That doesn't change the fact that murder is a sin.'

'It is a sin to rape a woman.'

Moses needed time to think. Like Douce there had been times when he wanted to kill Brito. Not by his own hands. But could he bring himself to pay another to do it for him?

'An eye for an eye,' Moses said absent-mindedly.

'Exactly.'

'We can't, Douce, it's too risky.'

What she was suggesting was indeed a perilous undertaking. If anything should go wrong. He shuddered at the thought. They would surely be taken to the Tower of London, tortured and their heads stuck on a spike for the murder of a Christian.

'Not if we ask the Irishman.'

Dumbfounded by her suggestion, Moses sat back in his chair. 'I think I need another drink,' he said.

Douce refilled his cup, her hands as steady as a surgeon's. He looked at his own hands. They were shaking. Moses sipped at the wine and contemplated Douce's proposal.

'He'll need money for his campaign in Ireland. The king has cut off his source of funding,' Moses said, thinking aloud.

He knew Dairmait would be furious with the king for changing his mind. By issuing the letters patent the king had given his explicit permission to Dairmait. Dairmait had done nothing wrong, but the king was now against him. If he knew

Brito was behind his misfortune that would surely be a bone of contention. It might give him a reason to kill Brito. It could work.

'Do you think he would do it, if we paid him?' Douce asked, staring into the orange embers of the fire.

'You know what will happen to us if we're caught?'

'Yes. But we won't be. It won't harm to sound out the Irishman.'

'I wouldn't know where to find him.'

'Let's start in Bristol. Didn't Aaron say he was staying with Robert fitz Harding?'

'Surely, you're not serious?'

'I am. Let's just talk to him – see what he says. If when we get there, you don't want to go ahead, we won't.'

'Douce, we can't.'

'The Irishman already has blood on his hands. One more soul won't make any difference. He's still going straight to hell.'

'And where will we go, Douce? Have you thought of that?'

CHAPTER

SIXTY-TWO

On a cold January day, Douce and Moses travelled to Bristol hoping to find the Irishman. They left their children with Arlette saying they were going away on business. Arlette looked surprised when they told her because Douce never went on business with Moses, but she didn't question them further. Douce had noticed how much happier she was now. It made her even more determined to carry out her plan.

Moses knew of Robert fitz Harding, the only Christian moneylender. His home was in Baldwin Street near the harbour. They made enquiries at the nearby taverns and discovered Dairmait frequented the Sailor's Retreat near the fish market not far from Robert's house. Douce held on to her husband's hand as they pushed their way past wayfarers, vagabonds and women of ill repute, who were hanging around the entrance to the inn. Once inside Douce was surprised how busy the place was. A roaring fire blazed in the grate and tallow candles lit the dark corners. The smell of burning pork fat turned her stomach. Douce walked past women with their breasts unashamedly on display, sitting on the laps of leering men who looked like they needed a good wash. She could feel their eyes on her as she walked past them. She averted their glares, pulling her heavy woollen cloak across her shoulder and holding it firmly under her chin.

Moses pointed out Dairmait in the far corner of the tavern. He was sitting alone with a tankard of cider before him. His beard was unkempt and his face red from the heat of the room and the drink. He looked more frightening than the description Moses had given her. When they neared him, Douce noticed he gave Moses a look of recognition, mixed with suspicion.

'Well, who do we have here? Thought I'd seen the last of you and your kind,' Dairmait said, his voice gruff and booming.

'We've come on a matter of business,' Moses said. 'This is my wife, Douce.'

Dairmait gave Douce an appreciative smile, a glint in his green eyes. 'Sit down, why don't you?'

They sat down opposite him.

'You want to do business with me now, do you? You weren't so keen last time I saw you.'

'I understand you still require funding for your campaign in Ireland. I may be in a position to help you.'

Dairmait raised a straggly eyebrow and eyed Moses with greater suspicion.

'I have a problem that won't go away. I'd like you to deal with it and in return I'll pay you handsomely. This is not a loan. Call it a donation, whatever you will. I won't require you to pay me back.'

Dairmait's eyes widened, then narrowed. 'What is this problem?'

'We thought you'd like to know who told the king that Josce was funding you.'

There was a flash of unbridled fury in his eyes. They burned into Moses and Douce got her first taste of what he was capable of. She knew then she had chosen the right man.

'Who?' he growled.

'The knight they call Brito.'

Dairmait's brows drew close together as he tried to think if he recognised the name.

'Do you know him?' Moses asked.

'I don't recognise the name.'

'The king sent him to Gloucester to warn me not to lend you any money.'

'When was this?'

'Three years ago, last March.'

Dairmait interrupted. 'Three years ago?'

'Yes, why?'

'That traitorous bastard. He never wanted me to succeed from the beginning.' Dairmait slumped back against the wall. 'Crafty old dog.'

He didn't seem to mind he was using foul language in front of Douce, but then she could hear plenty of salacious conversations going on around her.

'That's why I couldn't lend you the money. He told me the king would be displeased if I did.'

'Did he indeed.'

Douce was becoming impatient. The smell of unwashed bodies, boiled pig and tallow candles was making her feel queasy.

'We have a proposition for you,' she said.

'Which is?'

'We want you to kill Brito.'

'She doesn't waste much time your wife. Straight to the point. I like that in a woman,' said Dairmait. 'Why should I kill him for you?'

'He raped my niece, Arlette.'

Dairmait had been with many women in his time. He had carried off *Derbforgaill* from that tyrant and enemy O'Rourke, but it had not been against her wish.

'We can pay you half now, the rest after,' Douce said, sensing hesitation in Dairmait.

She nudged Moses who produced a leather pouch and placed it on the table. The pouch landed with a thud. Dairmait pushed it back toward Moses. 'Don't flash that around in here. You're liable to lose more than your money.'

Moses tucked the heavy pouch back inside his cloak.

'That should help with your campaign,' Douce said.

'I haven't said I'll do it yet,' Dairmait said.

'Will you?' she asked.

Dairmait was a cruel man. He had slaughtered men in Ireland, made slaves of others. But his weakness had always been the opposite sex. Douce came across as an earnest, honest woman who needed his help. That alone would not have made him kill Brito, but if this fellow was the cause of his financial troubles preventing him from conquering Ireland – and from what Moses had said it seemed likely he was – then he needed to be punished.

'Where would I find this Brito fellow?'

'He frequents a whorehouse in Three Cocks Lane in Gloucester most nights. You'll find him there.'

'And what does he look like?'

'You can't mistake him. He has hair as black as a raven.'

'And the heart of a black beast,' added Douce.

'You don't care much for him, do you?' Dairmait said.

'I hate him,' Douce said, almost spitting her words.

'Follow me,' Dairmait said, swilling down the last of his cider.

They followed him outside into the cold, black night.

He held out his hand for the money. Moses pulled out the

leather pouch and gave it to him. Dairmait snatched it from his hand and tucked it under his cloak.

'When will you do it?' Douce asked.

'Soon.'

'I need to know when.'

'Why?' asked Dairmait.

'I want you to bring me proof of his death.'

Dairmait gave Douce an understanding smile. He studied her face, watching her breath turn to feathery white mist in the wintry night air. She fascinated him. On the surface she appeared to be an ordinary married woman. A law-abiding citizen, but there was something deep and unseen which surged within her veins to make her hate this man so much she wanted him dead.

'Very well,' he said, and walked off in the direction of Baldwin Street.

Moses stared after him until he disappeared into the darkness of the night.

'What have we done, Douce?'

'We've done the right thing for our family.'

Moses took her hand. 'This is between me, you and Hashem. No one can ever know. We must take this secret to our graves.'

CHAPTER
SIXTY-THREE

Earlier in the day, a light dusting of snow had covered the streets of Gloucester. It had turned to ice and snow was falling again. Large flakes hit Dairmait's face, landing on his beard and eyelashes. He struggled to stay upright, his leather boots losing their grip on the ice beneath. He cursed the weather as he made his way along West Gate Street although there was one thing to be thankful for. The streets were empty.

Since his meeting with Douce and her husband he had thought more about the king's treachery and the role this villain Brito had played.

Thanks to Moses and Douce's 'donation' he was able to continue his mission in Ireland. He had bought vital supplies for his men who were now gathering in secret on the west coast of Wales in readiness for a further invasion when the weather improved. Richard had proved himself useful and had used his connections to gather together an army of good men. He was committed and eager to marry his daughter and Aoife, surprisingly, was eager to marry Richard. He had been so close to launching his campaign when the king summoned him to the castle in Gloucester where the Jew Josce had been made an example of. He thought all was lost. He could not believe his luck when the truculent Jew Moses le Riche had walked into his local tavern. It was a sign. All he had to do now was fulfil his promise to Moses and his alluring wife and he would get the rest of the money to complete his mission. What's more, he was going to enjoy seeing this character Brito get his comeuppance.

When he reached Three Cocks Lane, he ducked into the shadows of a dark doorway and settled in for a long wait. His feet were turning to ice, and he was about to walk away and call it a day when he heard the bawdy laughter of women as the door to the whorehouse opened and out spilled a man, his hood covering his face, unsteady on his feet. The door to the whorehouse closed, the alley was plunged once again into darkness, and they were alone. Dairmait emerged from the shadows of his hiding place.

'Is your name Brito?'

'Who wants to know,' the man said, looking from underneath the hood of his cloak.

Dairmait lunged forward and flicked the man's hood from his head to reveal a shock of straggly black hair. He recognised him as the knight by King Henry's side when he had visited the king in France to ask for his help. He hadn't liked the look of him then. Dairmait felt for the sharp dagger at his belt. Brito was glaring at him and then his eyes widened in surprise when he saw Dairmait pull out the dagger.

'What the–'

Before Brito could finish his sentence, Dairmait plunged the dagger into his black heart. Brito looked down at the wound in his chest, then back at Dairmait with a startled look. They always did that, thought Dairmait, when they didn't see it coming.

'You bastard,' Brito said, blood gurgling at the back of his throat.

'And this is for betraying me,' Dairmait said, taking another dagger from his boot and plunging it into Brito's stomach. He gave it a determined thrust, twisting it until it was full hilt, then pulled it out. It made a squelching sound as it was freed from the soft flesh of Brito's innards. Blood gushed from the wound.

'And this is for the young woman you raped.'

He plunged the dagger into Brito's right eye. There was a popping noise as the blade pierced its delicate membrane. An agonised scream came from Brito. He fell to his knees, blood pouring from his wounds. Dairmait stood over him, the bloodied dagger still in his hand. He took a step back and pulled out his *estoc*.

'And this, you evil swine, is for Douce.'

With a mighty swing he severed Brito's head from his body. The head fell with a thunk onto the snowy ground. Still pumping blood, Dairmait gripped Brito's head by his lank hair and stuffed it into the sack. He hurried out of the lane leaving the remains of Brito sprawled on the icy ground, a blood-soaked circle where his head should have been.

He had told the lovely Douce that he would bring proof and he was nothing but true to his word. He hurried towards The Cross and on to Moses' house, darting into the alleyway that led to the courtyard.

Thud. Thud. Thud.

His fist knocking on the heavy wooden door resounded in the crisp, snowy night air. Moses answered it, Douce close behind him.

'You wanted proof. Here it is.'

There was an audible intake of breath when Douce saw Brito's head. Her legs gave way and she had to hold on to Moses for support. When she had gathered herself, she stared into

Brito's black, soulless eyes. His face had frozen into a startled expression. His blood dripped onto the virgin white snow. It reminded her of Arlette's virginal blood staining her linen shift that night.

Moses handed Dairmait a heavy leather pouch. Without saying another word, Dairmait tucked it under his cloak, put Brito's head back in the sack and walked away leaving a trail of red blood on the pristine snow.

CHAPTER
SIXTY-FOUR

The next morning Moses made his way to the dining hall where the stove was alight. Douce and Arlette had set out the table for breakfast and were already sitting down to eat. Douce was spooning warm milk into a bowl for Henne and Arlette was keeping a watchful eye on Baruch whose appetite was insatiable. His father Samuel was tearing apart a loaf of warm bread. He nodded when Moses entered the room.

'*Bonjour, mon petit choux,*' Moses said, bending to kiss Abraham on the head, calling him by his pet name 'my little cabbage'.

Abraham twisted in his chair to get down.

'Nu, nu, Abraham. You need to finish your breakfast,' Old Samuel said, stuffing more frumenty into his unwilling mouth.

Moses tore at the loaf of bread and dipped it into the pot of honey. He held it there to let the unctuous liquid drizzle back into the pot.

Zev, who had gone hunting with Baruch at the break of dawn burst into the room.

'Have you heard?'

'Heard what?' Arlette asked.

'About Brito.'

Douce dropped the bowl she held and Henne's warm milk spilt onto the table and dripped into her lap. She shot out of her chair, grabbing a cloth to wipe down her tunic. Henne squirmed in her seat, trying to reach the bowl.

'What about him?' Arlette said.

'He's dead.'

'Dead?' she repeated.

'Yes, he's dead,' Zev said again, a smile stretching across his face.

Arlette was full of questions.

'How? When?'

'Last night. Someone took his head clean off his shoulders.'

'Who?'

'Nobody knows. The sheriff is there now.'

'Have you seen him?' Arlette asked.

'Yes, his headless body is lying frozen to the ground in Three Cocks Lane for all to see.'

'How do you know it's him if the head is missing?'

'Whoever did it used a sharp sword, left bits of his hair still lying on the collar of his cloak. The sheriff thought he recognised him from that and the clothes he was wearing. It was right outside the whorehouse, so he went in there and asked some whore and she identified him. She said he left about midnight.'

'Didn't get very far,' said Old Samuel, dryly. 'I suppose someone like that has many enemies.'

Moses and Douce remained quiet, avoiding each other's gaze.

'Has the sheriff no clue as to the murderer or the motive?' Samuel asked.

'None so far. Just said he probably deserved it.'

'Probably did,' Douce said in a quiet voice.

'I can't say I'm unhappy to learn of his death. He won't bother Arlette anymore or come here at all hours of the night demanding to see...'

Zev stopped himself. He was about to say, 'his son'. It was an unacknowledged fact. Baruch was Brito's son. Both Moses and Douce knew of it since his drunken visit to the house but not a word had been said since that night.

'I won't mourn his passing,' said Douce.

She was refilling Henne's bowl with warm milk from a jug on the table. It seemed bizarre to Zev that they were talking about the brutal murder of a man; they might as well have been talking about the slaughter of a lamb, so mundane was the scene before him and so humdrum the reaction. Zev had been expecting shock, elation, perhaps even a few hurrahs. When he heard about the dead body in the alley, he had rushed over to see who it was, never dreaming the victim would be his adversary Brito. Many times, he had wished the man dead. Arlette would be safe now. Baruch would never know he was the product of a brutal rape or who his father was. Justice had been served. He sat down and poured himself a cup of milk and tore at the bread. He was hungry from his morning hunt.

Arlette looked at her son. He was too young to know what they were saying, that his father had been murdered. She felt only relief at the news Brito was dead. Baruch would know one father. Zev. She looked at her husband. He was teasing Abraham. She touched her belly. She was five months pregnant. Zev was elated when she told him she was expecting his child. A son of his own. She prayed the child would be a boy.

The troubling memories of that brutal night were fading,

less intense, the raw emotions dissipating with each year. When she thought of Brito, she no longer saw his face, smelt his breath. His death at the hands of an unknown assailant was the best news ever. It had brought her some consolation that justice had been finally served.

CHAPTER
SIXTY-FIVE

Arlette gave birth to a son exactly three years to the day of her rape by Brito. Douce didn't know if this small but significant fact had crossed Arlette's mind. She hadn't mentioned it. They named the child Rubin after Zev's father. Douce had never seen Zev happier. Their friends were in the great hall eating the food she had lovingly prepared and celebrating as they always did. Douce sat in the corner of the room to steal a quiet moment of reflection.

They had not seen the Irishman since that cold, wintry night but they had heard of him. Dairmait, it seemed, was still managing to be a thorn in the king's side. He had invaded Ireland, his daughter had married Richard de Clare and Dairmait had regained his title as King of Leinster. But it seemed King Henry was furious and was at this very moment mustering troops in Gloucester Castle to invade Ireland and reassert his authority over Dairmait and the rest of the Irish rebels. Douce wondered if the king would kill Dairmait. If he did, it would be justice for all the people Dairmait had killed and tortured. She had long resigned herself to her fate in the murder of Brito.

Brito's murder was investigated by the sheriff. No one had seen or heard a thing. No one came looking for Brito. No one missed him. She had never spoken of it to Moses, nor he to her. They probably never would. His headless body was buried in the grounds of St Peter's abbey in unconsecrated ground. Abbot Hameline and his sub prior were the only people in attendance. He was soon forgotten.

Douce was jolted out of her thoughts by Arlette's raised voice and the piercing scream of her son Rubin.

'Don't pinch.'

Baruch was at that age when he demanded more of his mother's attention. He was jealous of his baby brother and had developed a worrying habit of pinching Rubin. Arlette pushed Baruch's hand away from her baby son who lay cradled in her arms. Zev walked over and pulled Baruch away. Baruch struggled to free himself from his father's strong grip.

'Come and play nicely over here with Henne and Abraham. Don't pester your mother.'

Baruch grizzled but allowed his father to take him to the other children. They played nicely for a few minutes until Baruch pulled Henne's hair and made her cry.

Moses' father Samuel sat in his chair by the fire. His watery eyes stared vacantly at the flames. Douce didn't know how much longer he had and wondered how Moses would cope making that journey to the London cemetery again. Other than that, life carried on as normal. Moses was doing well in his business. Zev still worked for his father, but recently he and Arlette had started a small business making and selling gold and silver jewellery. Moses had lent them the money. It meant Zev could spend more time at home with Arlette and the children.

Douce often wondered what would have happened to Arlette if Zev hadn't married her. Chera had given up on Zev and settled for Baruch. They were married now and had a young son. She looked over at Arlette. Her young face was lined and etched with struggle. Being a mother had not come easy to her as it did for other mothers. At least her and Zev seemed more content and the late-night arguments had stopped.

'Are you feeling all right, *ma chérie*?'

Moses placed his hand on hers interrupting her thoughts.

'I'm fine. Just thought I'd take a few minutes to rest.'

'You looked deep in thought?'

'I was,' she said, dreamily. 'I was thinking about our lives. What we've been through. How we've all changed.'

'Don't be sad. Today is for rejoicing not for looking back. It's time to look to the future. The children's future. Come join me. I'm going to make a toast.'

Moses took Douce's hand and pulled her from the chair, handing her a cup of wine. He coughed loudly and tapped his gold ring against his cup to get everyone's attention. The room fell silent.

'I want to give thanks to Hashem for all that I have. My wonderful *isha*, Douce.' Moses looked at Douce, his eyes full of love, then turned to Arlette his eyes twinkling with pride. 'For my niece, her husband and their children.' Moses paused. His expression changed to one of sadness. 'These last few years have been hard for all of us, but I feel we are over the worst. Our businesses are thriving, our families are growing. What more can we ask of Hashem? May we go forth and prosper.'

As if a heavy weight had lifted from him, Moses' face cracked into a broad smile.

'*L'chaim.*'

THE END

ACKNOWLEDGEMENTS

I'd like to thank the team at Bloodhound Books for taking a punt on publishing this trilogy. I've always thought it was a period of history that needed to be illuminated and an important story to be told.

HISTORICAL NOTES

1. This is a work of fiction. The story is based on an entry in the *Historia Monasterii Sancti Petri Gloucestriae*, a history of the Abbey of St Peter written in the late fourteenth century by or for Abbot Froucester. This account was written some two hundred years after the event. Presumably, the original account has been lost. Prior to that in 1173 Thomas of Monmouth wrote about the blood libel accusation of Norwich in 1144:

'In the specific case of William of Norwich, the evidence, critically sifted leads one to believe that he actually existed and that his body was found after he had died a violent death. Everything beyond this, however, is in the realm of speculation.'

I think perhaps the same can be said of Harold. That he existed, that his body was found after he had died a violent death and that his body is buried in Gloucester Cathedral.

Subsequently the Catholic Church made him a martyred saint. Saint Harold. His saint day is 25 March. Everything beyond this, however, is in the realm of speculation.

2. Although the account in the *Historia Monasterii Sancti Petri Gloucestriae* states 1168 I have used the date of 1167 from Joe Hillaby's account in 'The ritual-child-murder accusation: its dissemination and Harold of Gloucester', *Jewish Historical Studies Volume 34.*

3. The letter Brito receives from the king is based loosely upon the papal bull (Laudabiliter) issued in 1155 by Pope Adrian the Fourth thought to have given King Henry II the right to possess Ireland.

4. The fine of 100 shillings was entered into the Pipe Rolls in 1170 with the words:

'Josce Jew of Gloucester owes 100 shillings for an amerciament for the moneys which he lent to those who against the king's prohibition went over to Ireland.'

Despite this, Dairmait and Richard de Clare continued their invasion of Ireland.

5. On the 23 August 1170, Richard de Clare landed in Ireland. By the 25 August he had captured Waterford. Dairmait made good his promise to Richard de Clare and gave his daughter Aoife's hand in marriage. Richard wed Aoife four days later at Christchurch Cathedral in Waterford on 29 August 1170.

6. Dairmait MacMurchada died in May 1171. He is most remembered as the man who invited the English into Ireland.

7. Throughout the Middle Ages and (sporadically) until the early 20th century, Jewish people were regularly accused of Blood Libel; a conspiracy theory that claimed the blood of Christians was used in Jewish religious rituals, and particularly in the preparation of Passover bread.

8. Dates have been calculated using HebCal, although some adjustment has been made to take into account the Gregorian calendar.

9. For descriptions of Jewish culture and religious services I have relied on Rabinowitz's book: The Social Life of the Jews of Northern France in the XII-XIV Centuries, L. Rabinowitz, M.A. 1938.

A NOTE FROM THE PUBLISHER

Thank you for reading this book. If you enjoyed it please do consider leaving a review on Amazon to help others find it too.

We hate typos. All of our books have been rigorously edited and proofread, but sometimes mistakes do slip through. If you have spotted a typo, please do let us know and we can get it amended within hours.

info@bloodhoundbooks.com

GLOSSARY

Aba: Father
Alaichem sholom: A greeting
Alta moid: A spinster
Amein: Amen
Ax: Brother
Ayin hara: The Evil Eye
Baruch Hashem: Thank God
Bashert: Fate, destiny. A match made in heaven
Bechor: Firstborn
Bet 'olam: Jewish cemetery
Bet tohorah: Cleansing house
Betulot: A virgin
B'ezrat Hashem: With God's help or God willing
Bimah: An elevated platform in synagogues, used for Torah reading during services
Birkhat HaGomel: A blessing for surviving illness or danger
Brit milah: Circumcision ceremony
B'samim: A specially decorated box containing the spices for Havdalah
Challah: Egg baked bread served on Shabbat
Chanukah: Eight-day, wintertime festival of lights
Chatan: Groom
Chevra kaddisha: A group of volunteers who help prepare the body for burial
Cholent: Slow cooked beef stew served on Shabbat
Chuppah: Wedding canopy
Cross Fleurée: A cross whose arms end in fleurs-de-lys
Cross Patée: A cross which has arms narrowing towards the centre, but with flat ends
Cross potent: This cross has a crossbar at the end of each of its arms
Dod: Uncle
Donum: Donation, gift
Erusin: Betrothal
Eschet chayil: Woman of worth
Gimel: The Hebrew letter meaning 'get all'

Gomke: A metal shield used in the circumcision ceremony

Halakhic: Of Jewish religious laws derived from the Written and Oral Torah.

Hamantashen: Filled triangular pastries. Literally means Haman's ear

Hasatan: Satan

Hashem: Literal translation: The Name. Used as name for God

Havdalah: Ritual to mark end of Shabbat

Hazzan: Reader, or prayer leader

He: The Hebrew letter meaning half

Ima: Mother

Isha: Wife

Izmail: A very sharp knife used in the circumcision ceremony

Kallah: Bride

Kamea: Amulet

Ketubbah: Marriage contract

Kiddush: A special prayer for Shabbat

Kesef: Money

Kosher: Food, sold, cooked, or eaten and satisfying the requirements of Jewish law

L'chaim: A toast

Mamzer: Bastard

Mazel tov: Congratulations

Metzitzah: The sucking of blood during the *brit milah*

Mezuzah: A parchment inscribed with religious texts and attached in a case to the doorpost of a Jewish house as a sign of faith and protection

Mikveh: Sunken bath for ritual cleansing

Minyan: A quorum of ten males

Ma chérie: French for my darling (to a female)

Mon chéri: French for my darling (to a male)

Ner tamid: Eternal flame

Niddah: A Hebrew term describing a woman during menstruation or bleeding after childbirth

Nu: No

Ones: Compelling a person to act against their will

Oy lanu: Woe is us

Pelotte: A ball game much like tennis

Pot de chambre: Chamber pot

Purim: A Jewish festival of feasting and rejoicing

Ra'ashan: A wooden rattle

Rosh Hashanah: Jewish New Year

Saltire: A diagonal cross, like the shape of the letter X

Seudat Mitzvah: Sacred meal after the brit milah

Seudat Purim: Festive meal on Purim

Shabbat: Jewish Sabbath

Shabbat shalom: A common Jewish greeting, particularly on Shabbat

Sheol: Hell. Used as an exclamation

Shetarot: Plural of shetar. A written credit agreement

Shin: The Hebrew letter meaning share

Shochet: Ritual slaughterer, butcher

Shokeling: The ritual swaying of worshippers during Jewish prayer

Sholom alaichem: To you be peace

Shomerim: A person who sits with the dead body out of respect, literally a guard

Siddur: Prayer book

Simchat bat: Celebration for a daughter or rejoicing in a daughter celebration

Sovinen: A wooden spinning top with four sides, each side featuring a different Hebrew letter

Syndekos: Greek Byzantine word for godfather

Tembel: Idiot

Tenaim: Part of the wedding ceremony announcing that two families had come to terms on a match between their children

Torah: A kind of Jewish bible, containing the five books of Moses

Yichud: The prohibition of seclusion in a private area of a man and a woman who are not married to each other